the
PINK
Balloon

Orna Taub

the
PiNK
BallOon

a novel

BInk
Bink Books
Bedazzled Ink Publishing Company • Fairfield, California

paperback 978-1-949290-71-4

Cover Design
by

Bink Books
a division of
Bedazzled Ink Publishing, LLC
Fairfield, California
http://www.bedazzledink.com

Once, when I was a child, my mother's yoga teacher took us for a ride in a pink balloon. I've been riding in it ever since.

I WAS BORN into crazy, a world tilting so strongly to its side, it almost stood on its head. They said I was born knowing. The knowing child. The child who knew. A sign. An omen. A symbol of the new, enlightened world they were aspiring to create. The child born out of their summer of love.

My mother swore that when they placed me on her belly, just as I slithered out of her womb, I propped myself up on my little elbows, picked my head up, my forehead creased like an ancient turtle's, and stared her straight in the eyes. Huge expanses of blue, like layered pools of infinite depth, looked out at her, out of a light olive-skinned face.

"My blue-eyed Arab," she'd say jokingly, every time she told me the story. "They say newborns can't see, but you sure could. You looked at me as though you could see straight through me, as if you could see everything, and even beyond. As if you could see it all."

Daddy says I was a quiet child, mostly keeping to myself. "Quite the observer," he liked to say, "listening quietly, putting things together, storing the pieces of the puzzle in your mind."

Mommy called me "the little thinker." "You think too much," she'd yank at my arm, pulling me away from myself. "Give your mind a break!"

Mommy said that in every culture, at all times, there were people who knew, people who were born knowing. But I had no idea what it was that I knew. In fact, the only thing I was sure about, even as a young child, was that things were not as they seemed, that there was always something wrong with the picture. As far back as I can remember, I'd had that nagging feeling that I wasn't quite getting it, that there was something else, something I was missing. But before I could figure out what it was that I was supposed to know, my whole world blew apart, taking everything I thought I knew with it. Without my realizing, and certainly without ever intending it, my life became a journey of discovery, sending me far and wide, to distant countries and cultures, on a quest for that illusive "knowing." It took me many years, almost half a lifetime, to find my way back home again.

LILY

THEY CALLED ME Lily, but even though I knew it was just my coconut name, I loved to hear them tell the story. Mommy's coconut name was Minna, but she called herself Madhavi, "a flower" or "the spring." She said it made her feel "fresh and blossoming." "A promise of a new beginning." Daddy's coconut name was David, but he went by Rajiv, "the beautiful lotus flower rising out of murky waters." They chose their new names when they left their old lives.

Mommy dropped out of college at the start of her senior year, and, together with some friends, joined a commune in Oregon. That's where they met.

"I'd just moved out of the 'temporary lodging,' the large tent I'd shared for several months with more than twenty girls, into my own A-shaped house, where I lived with my best friend Geeta. The house was tiny, two slates of roofing over a narrow living space that stood in a row of triangles, stacked between more rows of triangles, placed roughly on dry, splitting, yellowing red soil. It looked so awful, barren, and depressing."

Mommy wanted to fill the space with life, but she had never grown anything before. Her mother didn't like plants. She said they only brought dirt and insects.

"I want to plant something," she told the man at the nursery, "but I don't really know how."

"Don't worry, I'll show you exactly what to do." Rajiv had been so understanding. He told her he learned everything there is to know about plants growing up on a kibbutz.

"But now it's not the right season. You have to come back in the fall. Right at the start, yes?" he gently waved his finger at her. "Don't forget."

And Mommy didn't forget. She found herself waiting, and not just for fall. Rajiv's image kept popping into her mind. She caught herself thinking of his face. His voice. His smile. She looked for him on the way to work. She searched for his face at meetings and tried to spot him meditating in the Buddha Hall. At the first sign of rain, she ran to the nursery, afraid Rajiv wouldn't remember her.

"I'm so glad you came," he greeted, flashing a smile that immediately dissolved her fears.

"I got the most beautiful bulbs a few days ago, and I've kept some, especially for you."

"WHERE WOULD YOU like them?" he asked when he arrived at her doorstep after work that evening, just as he promised, holding the soon to be plants in a small white satchel in front of him. He said he'd plant the first few, so she could learn. She always says she fell in love with him that night, watching his strong slender fingers delicately parting the soil, putting each elongated bulb in its place. The way he patiently measured the distance between each one, spooning out the soil and then patting it down gingerly. Smiling at them, whispering little secrets in their ears, blowing life into each one.

"Come the beginning of summer," he promised before he left, "huge volumptuous pink and purple lilies will be growing just outside your door." That part always made me giggle, and Mommy would say apologetically, "His English wasn't so good, then. He still had a lot to learn."

THE FROSTS CAME early that year, and the lilies wouldn't flower. Mommy didn't mind, though. They were soon living together, in their own A-shaped house. Geeta and her boyfriend Gayndip lived right next door, the little stretch of land between them blooming with flowers of every color. And Mommy was in love.

The next year they made sure to plant the lilies even later, a few weeks before the freezing temperatures of winter, only for a virus to attack the little garden and wipe them all out. They didn't give up. The third year, they took every precaution, planting the lilies at three different times, some at the beginning of fall, some at the end, and the rest even later. This time all the conditions were perfect, but still, the lilies wouldn't bloom. Every day, from the beginning of summer, Mommy would run out of the house early in the morning, hoping to see the lilies, but June led into July and still they wouldn't blossom.

Many other things had stopped working by that time. The commune and its neighbors were not getting on and the entire area had become troubled and violent. The compound had been encircled by fences and barbed wire and armed guards watched all the entrances. Many members had left and everyone was discussing it. My mother was heavily pregnant, and the commune didn't like babies.

The night before they left, there was a big going away party. Others were leaving too. In the morning, they packed their belongings into two plump duffel bags, thanked the little A-shaped house for its hospitality and left. They couldn't believe what awaited them when they walked out the door. Elegant yellow bell-shaped lilies had shot up beneath their windows. Showy blooms of pink and purple trumpet shaped petals sitting atop tall erect stems towered above the sunflowers. Red and orange lilies dwarfed the pink and blue pansies huddling together closer to the ground. The entire front of the house had turned into a field of lilies. Every color. Every shape. That was the moment they knew. They looked at each other and both swore they said it at the same time, "If it's a girl, we'll call her Lily."

They had nowhere to go when they left the commune; they found themselves pregnant, jobless, and disowned by both their families. Like many of their friends, they were upset and disheartened by what had happened, but in no way disillusioned. The commune may have failed, but they still believed in what it preached. Now they had to figure it out, just the two of them. Drawn to Venice Beach by friends who had left before them, they pooled the little money that still remained with Geeta and Gyandip and rented a small, dilapidated house, just across from the famous California beach, to the left of the old fishing pier. The dilapidated wooden structure was covered by a light, cracked, and peeling pink paint, also so ancient, that the brown rotting wood beneath it kept peeping through, drawing dark uneven stripes of brownish black along the walls. They hung a big sign on the door that read "Venice Retreat," but it never caught on and everyone just called it "the pink house."

That's where I was born, about a month after they moved in. All my first memories are from that house, with its creaking floors and rattling windows. There was always something breaking down and people walking in and out, hauling things about, banging, painting. And Geeta and Gyandip, my surrogate parents. Their room was on the ground floor, just past the kitchen and living room. My parents and I had two small rooms on the second floor. The walls of my bedroom were a light yellowy pastel, the door and window frames a bright lemon. At night I would shut the checkered yellow and white drapes and sleep enclosed in my yellow tent, but during the day I would sit for hours at my desk, in front of the window, staring out at the vast, ever-changing blue. I loved the constant moving and churning of the ocean, whichever way I looked. It made me feel so calm. All the other houses in our row had another house right in front of them, blocking their view and hiding them from the ocean, but ours didn't. All we had in front of us was sun, sand, and sea and when I climbed up on the desk, I could even see part of the street and the path leading all the way up to the old boardwalk. I sat there for hours, my face squashed against the glass, watching the people go by. It was my favorite place in the world.

I don't remember all that much, but whenever I think back to those days, a warm wave of happiness flows through my body, filling it with a vague memory of openness and light, a knowing of another time. Mostly I remember the dazzling sunshine, hot white sands, and translucent, crystal clear, shimmering blue. And a sense of everlasting freedom. Time was slow and full and comforting. I didn't miss not having grandparents or uncles and aunts. I knew they existed somewhere and I was never lonely. I had a huge, colorful, constantly changing family, flitting like butterflies in and out of my life, like a perpetual rainbow.

There were always people hanging around, meditating silently in the living room or sprawling, deep in conversation on the front porch chairs. Groups of long-haired people, in colorful loose-fitting clothes were our guests at all hours, standing in circles, shaking, yelling, laughing. In the evenings there was an active meditation, which had to be held outside in summer, there were so many people in attendance. Some danced wildly, jumping up and down, flailing their limbs, and screaming feverishly, while others crawled around on the ground, muttering gibberish at each other.

The house smelled of sandalwood and incense, curry and ginger. Herbs grew in little pots that hung on the windowsills with fragrances like mint and basil, rosemary and thyme. Lavender leaves were dried and spread inside the cupboards and chamomile and lemon grass were used for teas and poultices. Fruits and vegetables grew in a little patch behind the house. Most of our meals were shared, people cramming into the little kitchen, washing and chopping vegetables, sorting rice and lentils, and there were always extra faces around the table.

The new world they were trying to create was magical, replete with superstition and ritual. Life was a celebration. We danced to the full moon, prayed and chanted to the rain gods. Each season was welcomed with special ceremonies and foods. There were housewarming celebrations and house purifications. In the evenings, guitar music filled the air and the sounds of singing and dancing carried on late into the night. People hugged when they came and hugged when they left, and also a few times in the middle.

In the evenings they gave "teachings," sharing their knowledge and practicing on each other. There were heavy, heated discussions on everything from Buddhist texts to channeling and numerology. They held séances and went on Shamanic journeys, taking special potions and vomiting all over the porch. I wondered in and out of their "sessions," joining when I felt like it, ignoring them when I didn't.

Geeta gave spiritual guidance. She put a big sign in front of the house offering "halo" readings and cures. She read the stars and palms and Tarot cards. Paying customers were guided into her room, where she had a small workspace set up, and the rest of the time she practiced on all of us. She would seat me on the little cushion and close the drape, as if I were just a regular client. Then she'd fold her hands in front of her face, recite a blessing, and ask me why I had come. She always knew what I was going to ask her; she prepared the questions for me in advance. But I already knew all the important things. I'd heard them a million times before. I'd live to be a hundred, be married twice, and have three children. My aura moved between amber and gold.

"The color of wisdom," she'd brag after each reading. "The color of a sage, of a wise and knowing being."

Gyandip had gone back to teaching maths, but in his spare time he studied Eastern medicine. He was a real caregiver, and whenever I was sick or hurt myself, he would pull me onto his lap, apply herb roots and poultices, and massage the pain away. Other times, he'd blow on his fingers and then rub his hands vigorously for a moment or two before placing them just above my body, moving his fingers slowly, up and down and in circles, creating invisible patterns in the air. He often collaborated with my father, who was studying aromatherapy and plant essences. They would throw everyone out of the kitchen, prepare the most exotic oils, and fragrances, and give them away in long narrow glass vials.

Plants and horticulture were Daddy's great loves, but he "had no profession" and "had to make a living." Since he had been a fighter in the Israeli Army, he managed to find a job doing shifts as a security guard. He kept a gun in the house, locked up in a green iron box, on the top shelf of the cupboard in their room. Mommy hated it and they were always arguing. "It's the last thing in the world I want to do," he was forever apologizing, "but it's the only job I can get."

My mother, the "almost college graduate," was "the practical one." She took care of the house and the finances, making sure "everything was paid up and in order," and worked shifts as a waitress in a diner on Washington Bld., just a few blocks from the house. She always said, "it was only temporary," and besides, she "liked the hours." In her spare time, Mommy made blankets and clothing, selling her "finer" pieces on the boardwalk, giving all the rest away "to the needy." A few of the stores even kept some of her pieces in their window, refusing to take a commission.

On the rare occasion no one was around to take care of me, I would spend the day at "Wonderland." Dara and Gaya, whom my parents had known briefly at the commune, ran a daycare of sorts from their home. Their house was tiny, but the fenced yard was huge, with grass and swings and a slide. The living room was covered with shelves, piled with books, games, and puzzles. There was a rundown plastic kitchen and a doctor's clinic. Cars and dolls and stuffed animals lay everywhere. The toys had all seen better days and the games and puzzles often had pieces missing, but that never bothered me.

"Wonderland" was the children's domain, and for me the main place to meet and make friends. There were no hours or rules in "Wonderland." Our parents dropped us off and picked us up at their leisure. Dara and Gaya made a point never to interfere unless it was absolutely necessary. That meant, basically, that they left us alone to do whatever we wanted, and we took full advantage of it, running and yelling like banshees, playing catch and hide-and-go-seek all over the field-like yard.

ON THE DAYS Mommy was home, we'd go out early in the morning to play in the sand. Before we left the house, we always took care to bless ourselves and each of our loved ones. Facing each other, we'd press our hands together, close our eyes and wish for a happy and peaceful day. Then Mommy would push open the old door, shouting "Open sesame!" and we would rush out into the sunlight. We had to be careful though, for it was not uncommon to find someone crouched in the doorway or fast asleep on the porch. Makeshift huts and shelters were popping up all around the boardwalk and Mommy always said we had to be extra kind to the "homeless," because "by the grace of God it could be us."

If someone was there, she would rush back into the house, prepare a cup of coffee and some sandwiches, and send them off with a blanket or package of clean clothing. Then she'd teach me some yoga exercises or we'd sit silently in the sand. When I got antsy, she'd place her finger across her lips and send me off with a twirl of her hand, without even opening her eyes. I'd wonder off, "never too far or near the water" and "never ever talking to strangers," combing the sand for shells or doing cartwheels up and down the shore, until I collapsed with exhaustion at her feet.

Some days we'd walk to the boardwalk, rummaging through the trash, searching for clothing or knickknacks the shopkeepers may have missed. They all knew us by name and would often call out, rushing to fetch the damaged treasures they kept for us.

"Everything is salvageable," Mommy would remind me, as we sorted through the piles.

Clothes that were too damaged to be worn were stored in the big cupboard in the entrance hall, to be used in one of Mommy's creations. But since most were only slightly impaired and could easily be mended, they were placed in the crate besides the sewing machine, to be fixed in her "spare time." Sometimes the problem was simply a misprint or a garment printed on the wrong side, upside down, or partial. These were washed and neatly folded, then organized by size and put away.

I don't remember any of the storekeepers names anymore, except for Rami and Swissa, who sold falafel and "homemade lemonade" from a little van on the boardwalk. They were Daddy's "special friends." They would always place a little bag of warm, spicy balls in my hands or give me a tall glass of icy lemonade. I remember the colorful stalls, though, filled with odd trinkets and souvenirs. The owners often spoiled me with little presents, letting me choose something from their stands or pointing at one of the display cases and saying, "Take a bracelet, Lily, or a necklace maybe?"

Everything was so beautiful, I could stand there forever, staring, trying to decide.

"Just choose, Lily." Mommy would finally get irritated. "You're over thinking, as usual."

When I really got on her nerves, she'd grab the two I seemed to like best, shuffle them behind her back and make me choose, "Left hand or right," and we were done.

Little signs and printed cardboard surfboards decorated the walls of my room and beaded bracelets and necklaces adorned my dolls and sandcastles. Tiny shot glasses that said "elcome to Venice," or "We love Denice" stood in a straight line on display on my windowsill, together with others portraying women in bathing suits without an arm or a leg. They were gifts the shopkeepers collected for me, my special prizes.

On the way back we'd play at "coconuts," squeezing our eyelids until they were almost shut and out of focus, and then looking out along the shore, at all the heads bobbing in the water, like coconuts. They all looked so similar. Some heads were slightly smaller, others larger, but other than that, they were exactly the same. No features, no age, no stories. They weren't even men or women or girls and boys anymore. Just coconuts!

DADDY CALLED ME Tiger Lily, and he was always my Peter Pan. He was the one who taught me how to fly. Mommy didn't like our game much, maybe because we always made her Wendy!

Daddy wasn't around a lot, working double shifts or studying, but on the days we were left on our own, he'd peel off his usual weary, serious face, tell me to think some happy thoughts, and off we'd go, climbing into our pink balloon, and flying high above the world. We travelled to foreign lands, visiting kings and queens and faraway tribes. Sometimes we'd stay in one place, looking at things the way they were, but also trying to see them differently. We'd go fishing or take long walks on the promenade, looking at things from above or from the sides. Sometimes, from the safety of our pink balloon, we'd zoom in on something, other times we'd zoom out. Occasionally, we'd bend all the way over and stick our heads between our legs, and watch the world turn upside down. But the best times were when we let the pink balloon decide where to take us. Closing our eyes, we'd rise, going where it wanted us to go. When I got tired Daddy'd pick me up and carry me home on his shoulders. When I was sad, we'd pounce about like Indians, dancing and shaking our limbs, howling at the moon.

My favorite time with Daddy was bedtime. He wasn't often around, but he took me up whenever he could, never letting me go to sleep angry or upset. "Relax." He'd sit down on the corner of my bed. "Smile, even if you don't want to. Send smiling energy throughout your body."

Then we'd both have to think of five things that made us happy that day, and another five that made us grateful. The trick was trying to find new ones every night. When I couldn't fall asleep, he'd switch off all the lights, then leave the door slightly ajar, so that it wasn't completely dark, lie down next to me, lower his voice to a whisper, and breathe with me.

"Close your eyes. Let your body become heavy. Breathe into your legs, all the way to your feet. Relax your toes . . ."

He'd go on and on, until my entire body was relaxed. Then we would go on our best trips.

"Keep your eyes deeply shut," he'd whisper gently. "Imagine a pink balloon. A big, round pink balloon."

"Pink Balloon," I'd whisper, summoning it, squeezing my eye lids tightly shut. "Pink balloon . . ." And soon it would appear, a small, round shimmering bubblegum that glided swiftly toward me, growing larger and brighter as it drew near, until it stopped right in front of me, a huge, round pink balloon, awaiting me like Cinderella's pumpkin.

"Imagine yourself entering it," Daddy would continue. "Sit down comfortably. Relax. Breathe."

I'd step inside, my body magically slipping through the light rubber-like material and sit down, cross-legged, right in the middle. If I was tired, I'd lean my head back, cradling my body in its curves. At this point he would always stop and ask if I was ready and I would nod my head. Pushing me gently aside, he'd squeeze in beside me.

"May we commence?" he'd ask in his most formal voice.

"Aye, aye," I'd answer, giggling.

"The pink balloon begins to rise slowly. It rises higher and higher, up above the cars and the trees and the houses . . ."

It always began the same, first drifting softly and then moving faster and even higher, until it soared so high above the boardwalk, the people walking below us looked like tiny, crawling insects.

"We fly above the marine, across the highway to . . ."

"To the zoo," I would scream, or wherever it was I felt like going that day.

"Hold tight, there's a bit of wind." Daddy would rock the bed. "Ah, look, Lily, we're flying right above the giraffes, can you see them?"

We climbed mountains and crossed the oceans. Every night was an adventure. We would fly on and on, visiting known and unknown places, often creating them as we flew.

WHEN BOTH MOMMY and Daddy had an entire day free, we'd set off early, not wasting any time. We'd bike down to the Santa Monica pier, me huffing and puffing on my little pink bike. When we got there, we stuffed our faces with burnt corn on the cob and sugared nuts. We made faces in at the corn dogs, but sometimes Mommy would "get off her high horse" and allow us to crunch up a bright red and sticky toffee apple or share a cotton candy. We'd grab huge clouds of the shivering pink blob and shove them into our mouths, crunching the burnt sugar with our teeth.

Sometimes we travelled even further, spending the day in Malibu visiting friends. I would ride with my father in my special little seat. We'd walk along the private beach, climbing the rocks, playing with the foaming surf that gathered in the little inlets, scrambling to get back before the rising tide. The adults would sit together talking, and I would be left to play on my own. No one disturbed me. I could do exactly what I wanted, and be whoever I wanted to be.

It was a primeval world of rocks and coves, seemingly untouched by man or time. I imagined I was stranded on a deserted island, all alone. But I was never really lonely. I sat in the sun, squeezing my eyes into slits, until the sun's rays connected to the sea and the sand and everything merged into one slim shimmering line. The entire world seemed to disappear as the sun and the sand and the sky and the ocean became one. And for a moment, as I sat there, I was part of it, just another shimmering light.

When I close my eyes and take myself there in my pink balloon, I can still feel it, that warm, pleasant feeling that I cannot name but will always recognize. The mild, clean scent of the ocean. The breeze stroking my body. Hot rays on my cheek. On the way home, I would fall asleep, snuggled against my father as he peddled back in the dark.

STRANGELY ENOUGH, MY first tangible childhood memories are from India, the summer I turned five, although most of them were pieced together many years later, from a box of old photographs my father kept for me. At the time, I was too young to understand why we went to

India, so for me everything was pure sunshine and fun. But the problems between my parents must have started long before; we had gone to India to try to salvage their marriage, to try to recapture their "summer of love."

Mostly I remember red. All my memories of that time are colored red. A deep, dark red.

"Maroon," Mommy called it, but I didn't like the color of the dresses she bought me one bit. I loved red, but these weren't red at all. They were much too dark and looked like dried blood.

"I want the lighter, brighter ones," I remember shouting. "What the hell color is this anyway?"

But Mommy wouldn't budge. "Don't swear, Lily, it's called maroon and it rhymes with balloon."

Everyone in India was wearing that color. Wherever I looked there were patches of red. Sitting above in my pink balloon, squinting like mad, all I could see were red coconuts. A sea of red coconuts, constantly bobbing about, singing, dancing. And the noise. Sometimes it felt like everything was moving, as if the whole world was in motion. Other times the red coconuts were quiet, sitting together, cross-legged and silent. Rows and rows of silent red coconuts.

I remember it rained all the time, and not like the rain in Venice. It poured for days, sheets of water thundering down from the sky in torrents, turning the alleys and streets into raging rivers. We spent whole days inside and whenever the rain stopped, I would stand at the door and beg to be taken outside. In these infrequent dry spells, I would run to help feed the animals. I have photos of myself leading the flocks of peacocks and will never forget the way they clucked and screeched. They were the most beautiful and noble animals I had ever seen, but they had the most hideous voices.

The red-haired German woman who was in charge of the animals would give me bags of dry bread and cut up vegetables and send me off to feed the ducks and the swans. When there wasn't any food left, she'd march off, me running behind her, swearing in her thick German accent.

"Fuck that shit," she'd storm into the restaurant, "I need fresh vegetables." I started to say, "fuck that shit" too, whenever something irritated me, but when Mommy threatened to "wash my mouth with soap," I stopped saying it out loud, but kept muttering it under my breath.

One day she arrived, red hair flying wildly around her face, a huge brown camel in her wake. It had a big orange seat on its back and wouldn't stop chewing. I had no idea where it had come from, but every time the rain slackened I would run to see if it was still there. When the rain finally stopped, she pulled the camel down and put me in its seat. The thick orange cushions were still wet, but I didn't care. I shrieked when it got up, though. It wobbled so much, I was sure I would topple over. But she just grabbed the rope and started walking. I remember my surprise when it left the compound gates, and I found myself riding my camel through the streets, like an Indian princess, all the cars behind us honking in my honor.

In the evenings the rain usually stopped and even though I was the only child there, they would take me with them to the big tent. It was the biggest tent I'd ever seen. When we were late, it was so packed, I couldn't see to its end. Many of the pictures in my father's box were taken in that tent, but the image of India that stayed in my mind didn't come from them. I can still see myself, rising up in my pink balloon, hovering beneath the tent top, looking down at all the white coconuts. At night, all the red coconuts turned white. There were so many coconuts, more than I had ever seen, sitting cross-legged in total silence, I thought, for sure, that that's what heaven looked like. For a while, I even thought the white-haired man with the long beard and talking eyes was God.

But Mommy just laughed and said, "Don't be silly, Lily, he's just a man. A very special, holy man, but just a man."

I asked her what made him so special. She thought about it for a while, and then said, "He's made of lightning." At least that's what I thought she said.

One evening, after I swore to sit quietly and not fidget, we plopped ourselves down in the front row, not far from the lightning man's feet. He saw me and motioned me to come closer. I immediately saw what she meant. His face seemed to be glowing and his eyes shone so brightly that when I looked straight into them, I had to quickly shift my gaze.

"So, what's your coconut name?" He held my hands in his.

His eyes were twinkling, as if he was sure I wouldn't understand, but I knew exactly what he meant and quickly answered, "Lily. They call me Lily."

The lightning man laughed. "Liiilyyy," he repeated slowly. "What a nice coconut name." He let go of my hands and held up a strand of my hair to the light.

"Look how red." He gently held it up for me to see. In the lamp light, the edges of my hair gleamed a burning red, as if they were on fire.

He sat there for a while, still holding my hair, seemingly in thought. "I think I'll call you Leela," he finally decided. "Lovely, playful Leela."

"Lily is who you are," I remember him saying, "Leela is what you can be."

I liked it so much, I decided to call myself Leela for a while.

"You're too young to change your name," Mommy protested. "You can call yourself whatever you want, but for me you'll always be Lily."

Whenever I encountered the lightning man after that, I would bring my hands together and bow my head, like I saw everyone else doing, but I don't remember him paying any special attention to me again.

WHEN WE RETURNED to Venice, although they kept it from me, my parents' relationship was even worse. Little did I know that the summer of love was about to turn into a long, cold winter of hate. For me the world was still made of magic and sunshine. I even got Charlie. I'd been begging forever, Daddy too, but Mommy always said, "No dogs in the house, Lily."

Dogs gave her the creeps. But when my parents arrived home one day, carrying a tiny white and orange puppy in a big cardboard box, I didn't ask any questions.

"He's not just a puppy," Daddy said, placing him in my arms. "He's the king of puppies."

He was a King Charles Spaniel, and he had long droopy ears and the cutest face I'd ever seen. I called him "Charlie," even though Mommy didn't like the name at all.

"Don't worry Mommy," I reassured her. "It's just his coconut name. He can change it when he grows older."

Mommy didn't go near him for a while, but gradually she, too, fell in love with Charlie. We took him everywhere. During the first weeks we'd carry him around in a cloth satchel Mommy made. Then, when he grew too big, we'd let him run along the promenade on a leash, pulling the two of us after him.

I THINK THE first time clouds entered my world was the summer before first grade, when I met Sergeant Bob. We almost fell over him. Mommy had thrown open the front door, crying her usual, "Open sesame!" and there he was, sprawled across the porch, completely blocking the way. I was a little scared at first, but Charlie didn't even bark, just jumped all over him, trying to lick his face. He was an immense black guy, wearing a long green army coat with three yellowish gold stripes on each shoulder. We must have woken him, because he jumped to his feet, his army boots making a crisp clicking sound, raised his arm in a salute and cried, "Sergeant Bob, at your service, ma'am."

"And who're you?" He turned toward me. He was so tall I could barely see his face, but when he bent down and stretched his hand out, I saw how gentle his smile was and how his eyes twinkled under his black woolen cap.

"Lily." I grabbed his hand.

"Ah." He pumped my hand up and down. "Most honored to meet you, Tiger Lily."

I immediately saw how smart he was. He got it right away.

MOMMY GAVE HIM some food and a clean shirt, like she always did, and "off he went." But he was there the next morning and then the next, very quickly becoming part of our lives. He always stayed outside though, refusing to come in, even when we invited him. Mommy tried to find odd jobs for him to do, but even then, he'd leave the moment he was done. We never saw him arrive, but he was always there in the morning, sprawled across the porch, wrapped in his old army coat. He never took it off. That and his black woolen cap and torn army boots. They were his uniform and that's who he was. Sergeant Bob. At least that's what everyone called him.

In the mornings, we'd have a breakfast picnic outside on the porch. Then he'd walk with us to the promenade carrying Mommy's big heavy baskets for her. He walked quickly, taking big bouncing steps.

"Come on." I'd pull at Charlie's leash, running to keep up with him. When Mommy took her time talking to the shop owners, I would wander outside and sit with Sergeant. Bob and Charlie, the sun in our eyes. Mostly we would sit together silently. Sergeant Bob knew how to be quiet. He didn't feel he had to talk to me all the time. When he did though, he had a million stories, and knew so many things. He didn't know how to fly though, but after I taught him, he'd take me with him to all the places he had been. But he never told me who he was or where he had come from.

One day, as we sat quietly together, I noticed he was staring at a little boy. He was around my age, tall and slim with tight black curls falling all over his face.

"Looks like Russ," I thought I heard him muttering. "Just like Russ."

"My son," he answered, shaking his head, when I asked who Russ was. "He'd be all grown up now."

I had heaps of questions, but Sergeant Bob refused to answer any of them.

A FEW MONTHS AFTER his arrival, we opened the front door to find him lying in a pool of blood.

"Sergeant Bob, are you OK?" Mommy ran to him and started to help him up.

His face and neck were swollen, red, and purple and streaked with blood. He looked awful. Some boys had attacked him as they were leaving a bar. They were drunk and had made fun of him. When he got mad, they had beaten him, hitting him over the head with a wooden stick and then kicking him when he fell. In his face. His chest. His back, arms, legs.

"Come on, Sergeant Bob, we have to get you inside." Mommy put her arm around his body, held him up, and pulled him into the house. "They've really done a number on you." She kept on shaking her head and clucking her tongue in irritation.

He didn't want to go in, but this time she insisted.

Mommy tried to persuade him to take off his black woolen cap. It was filthy and covered with blood. "I'll wash it and give it straight back."

I'd never seen Sergeant Bob without the hat. His head was completely bald and there was a long bleeding cut weaving all the way down his skull. But I barely saw it. My eyes were glued to what must have been an old wound. Part of his skull was caved in, as if something had pushed in half of his head.

"Shrapnel," was all he would say when he saw our look.

"No hospital." He became almost violent. "They won't let me out. When someone like me enters a hospital, they're never allowed to leave."

So Mommy "patched him up" as best she could.

He didn't want to talk about it, but I couldn't let it go. I kept seeing them beating him. Kicking him. I couldn't get the picture out of my head.

"Why did they do it?" I kept asking Mommy. "What did Sergeant Bob ever do to them?"

Sergeant Bob was such a good man. It just didn't make any sense. After that, on the mornings I didn't find him beside the door, I would worry. I'd search for him up and down the boardwalk and wait outside on the porch until dark.

"Don't worry, he'll be back," Mommy would try to reassure me, but I worried. I always worried. I knew nobody else would.

I think that's when it first occurred to me that there was evil in the world, that people could be bad, for no reason. Evil was something I had no idea what to do with, but the more I thought about it, the more I began to notice. I saw that people were afraid of Sergeant Bob and didn't treat him well. They were rude, sometimes cruel, and they even treated me differently when I was with him. Mothers walked quickly past us, pulling their kids away. Storekeepers shooed us from the fronts of their stores. Suddenly it wasn't Mommy saying, "Always be generous, Lily. Be kind. Put yourself in their shoes," or "that could be you." Now I could see it for myself.

That's also when I began to talk to God. I'd never really thought of him before, but Sergeant Bob talked to him all the time, asking his advice and thanking him for his help. "Praise the Lord," he'd say, or "the good Lord Jesus was looking out for us today." He blessed everyone he met in God's name and "Christ was always with us." I asked him where Christ was, but he just rolled up his eyes and said, "You gotta have faith, Tiger Lily!"

"How is it possible?" I kept asking God. "How could the good Lord Jesus have allowed any of this to happen?" Wherever I looked, I could see bad things happening to good people, and I couldn't understand it.

"THAT'S A TOUGH question. I really don't have an answer," Mommy said when I asked her. "And I don't know too much about Jesus, anyway."

"Sergeant Bob's god isn't ours," Daddy tried to explain. "We have a different god."

"The statue in the living room?" I was bowing in front of Lord Buddha as long as I could remember.

"No." Daddy shook his head patiently. "He was just a man. A man we have a lot to learn from."

"We all believe in different things," Mommy said. "I have one god, your father has another."

"But who am I supposed to believe in?" Now I was really getting confused.

"Ah," Mommy sighed, "that's a question you'll have to answer for yourself."

I COULDN'T WAIT for first grade to begin, but very quickly realized it was not at all what I had expected. I fought with Mommy every morning and would only go out to the honking school bus when Sergeant Bob came in to escort me.

"Good morning, Tiger Lilly." He bowed. "Your carriage awaits."

Mrs. Marlberger was a screamer. She was tall and skinny and at least a hundred years old. She would tower above us like a witch, her sparse red hair drooping over her wrinkled forehead, reminding us of "The Rules." And she had rules for everything. We didn't have any at home. I was used to doing exactly as I pleased. In Mrs. Marlberger's class I had to sit still for the "entire period," and couldn't even go out to pee.

"Only if It's an emergency," she said shrilly. "Raise your hand and wait for permission. And never more than one at a time."

I had never sat so long without moving and I hated it. And all that homework. "Practice makes perfect," was Mrs. Marlberger's favorite expression, which I soon learned, meant hours and hours of work. I got the letters right away, but writing them down proved an entirely different matter. Even holding the pencil with my fingers was difficult. I tried, I really tried, but my hands just did whatever they wanted. Just like when I tried to draw. I was always being sent away to paint someone a picture, but I could barely draw a line. I still can't. As if there's no connection between my brain and my hands.

"COUNT TO TEN before you answer," Mommy admonished, the first time she was called to school. "If you have nothing good to say, keep your mouth shut." But the teacher kept complaining. Suddenly I was "naughty" and "cheeky." "Doesn't wait her turn to speak." "Doesn't raise her hand." "Doesn't listen to anyone." And worst of all: "Doesn't do her homework."

"I hate Mrs. Marlberger," I cried. "She's mean and she yells at me and puts me in the corner, even when I haven't done anything."

"She must have a reason," Daddy always said. "Try to look at it from her point of view."

He was always telling me, "You're not the only child in that classroom" or "place yourself in Mrs. Marlberger's shoes."

"That's it," Mommy decided after being called to the school for the second time. "You leave me no choice. No more boardwalk until you've finished all your assignments."

Sergeant Bob took pity on me and tried to help, writing line after line of beautifully sculpted round letters for me to copy. I would sit on the porch agonizingly tracing them, seemingly incapable of writing them on my own. When I broke down and cried in frustration, he would decorate my crooked letters with tiny birds and flowers, and suddenly they didn't look so ugly anymore.

And then, one day, as I walked along the boardwalk, practicing my letters with Sergeant Bob, they magically began to come together and form words. He pointed to a purple t-shirt just above my head.

"V ... E ... N ... I ... C ... E ... B ... E ... A ... C ... H," I shouted out each letter without making any mistakes.

He pointed to a black sweatshirt with shiny gold letters on the other side of the room.

"V E ... N I C ... E B E ... A C H." I shouted out the letters again. "Find a different one, they're both the same." But there was something else familiar about the letters, something I recognized, as if I'd seen them before.

This time he pointed to a poster on the wall with a whole bunch of letters.

"W E ... L C O ... M E ... T O ... V E ... I know those letters," I told him crossly. "They're the same as before."

I stared at them, going over them in my mind, when they suddenly came together and started to make sense. "Venic . . . e . . . Venice bea . . .Venice Beach," I screamed at the top of my lungs. "It says Venice Beach."

When I looked back, the poster seemed to speak to me.

"Welcome to Venice beach," I roared, running through the store, calling out all the slogans and names that seemed to leap out at me from the walls.

I couldn't wait to get to school.

"I've never seen anything like it." Mrs. Marlberger was "most impressed" and I became her "star."

The other kids sometimes called me "teacher's pet," but I didn't care. She started tutoring me, pulling me aside each day to read with her and even stopped making a fuss about my handwriting. She brought me little booklets from the second grade and even a special beginner's edition of a book called *Little Women* she had found at the bookstore.

"I know it's a little early," she said when she gave it to me, "but I couldn't resist. It was the first book I read."

The book was a revelation, and even though I read painstakingly slow, I couldn't put it down. I sat on the porch with Sergeant Bob, reading each word out loud, sometimes several times, until I got it.

"In . . . flu . . . en . . . za," he'd say slowly, when I got stuck. "Flu." Or "sto . . . mac . . . ac. You gotta chop off the ending."

UNTIL ONE MORNING I woke up, and Sergeant Bob was gone.

"Don't worry," Mommy said, "I'm sure he'll be waiting for you when you get back from school."

But he wasn't there when I got back and we couldn't find him anywhere around the boardwalk. When he still hadn't returned three days later, I knew something was wrong. My worry quickly turned to panic. The night before he disappeared, we'd only managed a page or two when Daddy came to call me in.

"Please, Daddy, just a little longer," I'd begged. Jo had just met Laurie at the big party and we couldn't wait to find out what was about to happen.

"It's late Tiger Lily. Tomorrow's another day."

I tried to resist, but Daddy pulled me up.

"Daddy's right. We'll carry on tomorrow, right after school." Sergeant Bob blew me a goodnight kiss. "Sweet dreams."

"Something must have happened to him." I wouldn't leave the porch, even when it got dark. I knew he'd never abandon me in the middle of a chapter.

We searched for Sergeant Bob, walking all over Venice, all the way to Santa Monica, but no one had seen him. A few days later, as we approached the boardwalk, we saw some of the storekeepers standing together talking loudly. As we came nearer, we picked up slips of their conversation.

" . . . shot twice . . ."

" . . . no chance . . ."

Somehow, I knew they were talking about him. Before Mommy could stop me, I ran up to them, and by the time she caught up, I had heard all I needed to know. Sergeant Bob was dead.

IN THE BEGINNING, I didn't ask what had happened. I didn't want to know. I didn't want to talk about it. I didn't want to talk about anything. I just wanted to be left alone. But after a few weeks, I started to drive Mommy crazy, and although she asked around, there seemed to be very little to find out.

"Sergeant Robert Cleary . . ." The policeman glanced down at his notes.

"Sergeant Robert Cleary." I silently ran his name along my mouth. I'd never heard it before.

"Found him in Westwood . . ."

"It's down there," Mommy whispered to me, pointing away from the beach. "Far, far away."

"Shot in the street," the policeman continued reading, without even looking up at us. "Once in the head and once in the heart."

"But why . . . what happened?" Mommy asked, but the policeman just shrugged.

Then he shut his notebook and took off his glasses. "No one knows what he was doing there. Our only lead to who he was and where he came from was on all of his belongings, even his bag. It all said, 'Venice Beach.'"

"WHY DID IT happen?" I kept asking. "What did Sergeant Bob ever do to anyone?"

He was the smartest, kindest, nicest man I had ever known, and I couldn't understand what had happened.

"Sergeant Bob was a good, proud man." Mommy tried to comfort me. "He was wounded serving his country."

"He was a hero." Daddy hugged me. "He was in the wrong place at the wrong time."

But I couldn't let it go, my mind whirled endlessly, churning and seething with unanswered questions.

"How could something so bad happen to someone so good? Why would someone do something like that to someone else? What made people bad?" My mind went on and on. I paced around the house, talking faster and faster "getting myself into a state," until I could hardly breathe.

"Give your monkey mind a rest." Mommy would get angry.

"It's just a mind attack." Daddy held me tightly. "Take a deep breath," he'd count slowly to five, "and let the air out." Then he'd breath in and out with me, till my breathing slowed and I was feeling calmer.

"Smile." He would always say before he let me go. "Think happy thoughts."

But I had very few happy thoughts. Mommy and Daddy tried to help me as best they could, but they were fighting all the time. They thought I didn't notice, shutting up the moment I entered the room and acting as if everything was fine, but I heard them. And I saw. Less and less visitors came to the house, and Daddy was working more and more. And the nights he didn't work, he spent on the sofa in the living room. But worse than the arguments were the silences. I was used to silences but this was a different kind of silence. It was a silence I'd never met before and I could feel it all around me, dense and heavy, smell its bitter odor. It was a silence laden with anger and resentment and it filled the house, moving from room to room like an ill-boding spirit.

Mommy was mostly sad and quiet, and in the evenings there was less and less to be grateful for. Sometimes I was plain angry and couldn't "see it from her point of view," and certainly wouldn't "stand in her shoes."

Geeta and Gyandip tried to help, but only Charlie could comfort me. I held him in my arms as I sat, squinting out the window, talking and arguing with myself. My world was tilting, and I could make no sense of what was happening.

I tried talking to God about it, asking him why again and again. But God wouldn't answer. I spoke to Jesus, just like Sergeant Bob had done and then to Allah. I even tried my father's God, just to be on the safe side, but whatever I called him, he never answered.

"Are you there God? Can you hear me?" I'd ask, but nothing. God wasn't listening.

Then, finally, I got it. God didn't know either! And from that moment, I stopped asking, deciding that God didn't really matter. I didn't care if he existed or not, there was no way I would accept a God who allowed all these bad things to happen, while he looked the other way.

But just as I gave up on God, it seemed that he began to take an interest in me. For at that moment, my world swerved sharply, and I became a Muslim.

LILA

THE TAXI PULLED away from the curb. Lila was on her knees, tears pouring down her face, looking back at Geeta and Gyandip, who stood waving forlornly on the sidewalk, trying to hold on to Charlie, who was lunging after the car, barking like mad.

"We can't take Charlie with us," Minna had told her. "Your grandmother hates dogs. She says they're impure and won't allow them in the house."

Lila had no idea what "impure" meant, but was too upset to ask. Her mother sat slumped in the corner of her seat. Lila heard her loud uneven breathing and little snuffles, but refused to look in her direction. The car picked up speed, Geeta and Gyandip becoming mere shadows and her beloved house a pink blurry blob. She heard Charlie barking for a while, and then, that too, was gone.

"You've grown out of just about everything." Minna had marched her through Marshalls and J.C. Penny, throwing trousers and shirts into the shopping cart.

"I don't like this dress," Lila tried to object. "It's got fluffy, hideous sleeves and the skirt's too long."

"You need different clothes," Minna shook her head, "more appropriate ones. You're not a baby anymore."

"But I'll die from heat, and I want this one." Lila waved the short, sleeveless pink and white dress she liked so much in front of her mother's face, but everything Lila liked was "inappropriate" that day.

"Stop it." Minna frowned down at her. "I don't want to hear another word."

"These are all little girl things." Minna had made her leave almost everything behind. "We'll make you a brand-new big girl's room in our new house."

But Lila didn't want a brand-new big girl's room. She loved her yellow tent and wanted everything to stay as it had been. Minna allowed her to take some games and stuffed animals.

"And my favorite two Barbie dolls," Lila had insisted, even though one's eye was shut tight and the other had never recovered from her haircut. They were a birthday present from her father, and there was no way she was going to leave them behind.

David left the house the day before, packing all his belongings into two big duffel bags. "I'll phone you every day and come to visit all the time," he had promised, his voice breaking, as he hugged her. He hadn't been able to look at her when they told her he was leaving. Nor had Minna. And there was very little left to say.

THE CAR DROVE on, following the coast for a while. Lila fidgeted, moving uncomfortably in her new dress, ignoring all of Minna's attempts to talk to her. When she tried to caress her, she pushed her hands away roughly.

"Is it far?" Lila's curiosity finally got the better of her.

"Not too far. In between Los Angeles and San Diego, but more inland . . ."

Lila had no idea where San Diego was, and when Minna told her they wouldn't be living near the ocean, she wasn't really interested anymore. But Minna kept on talking. "I barely remember Laurel Valley. I only lived there for a few months. My mother moved there with my uncle and brothers after your grandfather died. It was just before I left for college."

Lila sat up and turned toward her mother. She was still mad at her and didn't want to talk to her, but this was the first time she had actually revealed anything about herself or her family.

Minna told her she was the only girl in her family, the youngest, after five boys.

"I have five uncles?" Lila couldn't believe her ears.

"Not all of them are here," Minna told her. "Two of my brothers moved to Abu Dabi to work in the oil industry. It's just about on the other side of the world, but you'll meet the others. They all live right next door to each other."

Minna told her that her parents came to America without anything. She told her about the war between the Palestinians and the Israelis, and how her grandparents had had to flee, taking their two young children, Machmud and Ali, with them. They spent a few years in a refugee camp and jumped at the chance to go to the US together with her uncle, her father's oldest brother. Her mother was pregnant at the time, and her third brother, Said, was born a month after they arrived in Los Angeles.

It was the first time Lila heard any of this. She knew her mother was from Palestine and her father from Israel, but had never thought anything of it. Suddenly it all began to come together, to make sense. Arguments she had overheard. Age old family feuds and hatreds.

"They opened a halal butchery in downtown Los Angeles, right next to China Town. That's what they did in Palestine before the war. Theirs was one of the first, and Muslims came from all over the city to buy their meat."

"After my brothers Khaled and Sameer were born, the doctors told my mother she wouldn't have any more children. She was devastated. She wanted a daughter more than anything. To everyone's surprise, hers mostly, I was born five years later. That's why they called me Minna." She smiled. "Thanking Allah for his gift."

As Minna talked, the landscape changed, turning into a dull, arid yellow. Dry, shriveled shrubs bowed their heads tiredly amid small clouds of dust. The car went up a hill, turned a bend, and there was the town, sprawled out in front of them, pouring out beyond the reaches of the valley.

"It's huge." Minna leaned forward, her mouth agape. "Not at all how I remembered it." She said that her stomach was knotted with fear, but also that she felt oddly excited. She had grown up with these people, seen them every day of her life. And now it had been ten years.

The cab entered the town, the streets becoming heavy with traffic. "I think we're getting nearer." Minna stuck her head out of the window, trying to figure out where they were. "Yes." She pointed out houses and buildings. "I recognize the area."

"Palm Street," the driver announced and turned to the left.

"Unbelievable," Minna gasped, looking down the long narrow street, filled with stores and stalls.

"What's that?" Lila asked, pointing to the big sign in foreign writing.

"Arabic." Minna laughed at Lila's dumbfounded look.

"Welcome to Little Ghaza." The driver chuckled. "You'd never believe how it's grown. It stretches all the way from Broadway to Lincoln now."

"When my family first moved here, the town hardly existed." Minna perched on the edge of her seat. "It was in the middle of nowhere. I couldn't wait to get away."

They drove past a large produce market and some grocery stores. The car slowed down. "My uncle Ibrahim's house." Minna pointed to an ugly brown two-story house, set back a little from the street. "And here's the butcher shop." She pointed excitedly to the store standing right beside it, only closer to the curb. "Your grandmother and one of your uncles live right above it."

"This must be Sameer's place." The neon sign was mostly in Arabic, but in the corner it said, 'Sami's Hooka Hall' in English, flashing in fluorescent pink. Lila thought she had misread the sign, but Minna told her she hadn't.

"You'll have to see for yourself, it's a bit difficult to explain. You'll like Sami, though, he was always my favorite, the one I missed the most." Sami was her youngest brother, and since he was still unmarried and "didn't show any signs," the family had decided that Minna and Lila would move in with him.

"He has a big, empty basement and I can go back to school to finish my degree." Minna pointed to a few more houses, rattling off names of uncles and cousins, but Lila wasn't listening anymore. All she could think about was how she'd just left everyone she'd ever known behind her and now almost the entire block, for as far away as she could see, was occupied by her mother's closest relatives.

Minna covered her head and shoulders with a black woolen shawl. "Remember to be on your best behavior," she told Lila, primping her dress and combing her hair with her fingers. "My mother's a religious woman, so think before you speak and if you . . ."

" . . . have nothing good to say, keep your mouth shut," Lila listlessly finished.

"And nothing about your father." Minna pushed Lila's chin up and looked into her eyes.

Lila stared back defiantly.

"And most important." She held on to Lila's chin. "Don't forget your new coconut name."

LILA OPENED THE taxi door and stepped into a disgusting puddle of filth. The pavement was covered with mud and grime and rotting vegetable peels and the air felt heavy, thick with a sweet and sour odor that seemed to wrap itself around her like a scarf.

"Watch where you step, you'll get all your new clothes dirty," Minna barked at her, pulling at her skirt.

"I've already . . ." Lila caught a glimpse of her mother's face. She almost didn't recognize her. Under the shawl her face looked long and bony, as if she had forgotten how to smile. For a moment, it seemed to Lila that the woman she had known all her life had disappeared and someone else had taken her place.

"Minna?" Two slim, well dressed young men came running out toward them. They closely resembled each other, only one was slightly taller and had the beginning of a moustache tracing his mouth.

"I'm Walid," the older one pulled out his hand, "Hussam's son. This is my brother, Fadi." He looked around sixteen and his brother a year or so younger.

"Wow." Minna shook her head in awe as she stretched up to kiss their cheeks. "You were just babies when I left and now you're both taller than me."

"Go, ahead, we'll bring your stuff." They waved them into the house. "Everyone's waiting for you."

As Minna and Lila walked up the path, a short, plump elderly woman came rushing out. She and Minna fell into each other's arms, talking excitedly. Lila couldn't understand a word they said, but she immediately knew who she was, the almond eyes gleaming under the golden spectacles and the slightly pointed pixie chin were so familiar.

"I'd like to introduce you to my daughter," Minna said to her mother, when they finally finished embracing.

"And this, Lila, is your grandmother, Taata Maryam."

Taata Maryam pulled Lila close, kissing her on both cheeks. Wisps of grey and black hair fell out of the white kerchief wrapped around her head, brushing across her forehead. Her skin was dark and wrinkled, and she smelled of lavender and cooking oil.

"You pretty," Taata Maryam kissed the tips of her fingers, "so pretty, al hamdulillah." She clucked her tongue, her smile sending flashes of gold through the air.

"Taata Maryam says you take after our family," Minna translated. "She says we all have the same eyes."

"Except the color." Minna didn't have to translate that part, she could tell exactly what her grandmother had meant when she pointed at her eyes and laughed.

"Yes," Minna chuckled, "they're a dead giveaway."

MACHMUD, MINNA'S ELDEST brother, stood in the doorway. He was plumper than she remembered, his forehead deeply lined, his hair gray and thinned out. Minna hardly recognized his wife Waffa, who stood beside him, she had grown so stout. But their two sons, Nabil and Nadar, both now in their early twenties, seemed to have remained exactly the same.

"I would recognize you anywhere." Minna kissed them on both cheeks.

The house was packed, people filling all the sofas and armchairs and most of the white plastic chairs scattered around the living room. Little tables overflowed with trays of dried fruit and nuts, and tea in tall narrow glasses, sparkling a rich reddish amber. An old man heaved himself out of a deep armchair in front of the door and moved toward them, leaning heavily on his cane.

"That's my uncle Ibrahim," Minna whispered to Lila, maneuvering her in his direction. "I can't believe how old he's become. I think he's almost eighty." A short, fat elderly woman with a bright red and blue scarf wrapped around her head, rushed to join him.

"Sallaam aleychum." Ibrahim spread his arms wide, waving his cane in the air.

"Aleichum hasalaam," Minna answered, kissing him and his wife Sara on both cheeks.

Their children and grandchildren all stood in a line to greet them. Minna was overwhelmed, reunited with all the people she had grown up with, but Lila was hot, irritated and bored. So many people. So many names. The room was stifling and everyone spoke a noisy mixture of English and Arabic which she couldn't understand. She barely noticed when Minna introduced her to her second brother Ali. She kissed his cheeks and those of his wife and two older daughters, turning her cheek automatically to kiss the next person waiting in line.

Auntie Fatima and Auntie Heeba pinched Lila's cheeks, clucking their tongues. Lila had no idea who they were, all she knew was that they were from "the old neighborhood," but since everyone was an auntie or an uncle or a cousin, once removed or twice, it didn't seem to matter and she wasn't sure they themselves remembered exactly how they were related anyway. They all kissed her cheeks and acted as if they were pleased to meet her, but Lila could see them staring, whispering, pointing at her eyes. She bit her lip and crunched her hands into fists, trying as hard as she could not to cry.

Suddenly she was flying through the air.

"Hi, I'm Sami." Strong arms placed her back on the ground. "I'm so glad to finally meet you." A tall, muscular man with short curly hair and a short mustache grinned down at her.

"You're Sameer, Mommy's youngest brother." Lila smiled back at him, liking him immediately.

"Sami." He pulled her by the arm. "C'mon, I have someone here who's dying to meet you."

"This is your cousin Jasmine." Sameer led her to the corner of the room, where a little girl was sitting, swinging her legs impatiently. "She's exactly your age, she's just turned seven."

Lila hung her head, feeling shy, but Jasmine jumped up eagerly when she saw her, grabbed her hand, and stood there shaking it, her entire face a huge, impish grin. Lila looked up. Two almond brown eyes, shaped exactly like hers, stared back at her. She had dark olive skin and straight, thick charcoal hair that reached her neck and surrounded her face like a helmet. She was slightly taller than Lila and even slimmer.

"C'mon, let's go outside," Jasmine took her by the hand and led her to the stairs. "I'm so glad you're finally here." She was so excited, she couldn't stop chattering. "I've been waiting and waiting for you."

Lila was at a loss for words. She had never even heard of her cousin, but it seemed she knew all about her.

"There's your house." Jasmine motioned to a staircase leading down. "I live over there." She pointed to an entrance right above it. "And that's Taata Maryam," she pointed to the building next door, "and Ali and Machmud. I'll show you around tomorrow, it'll be such fun."

Jasmine talked on and on, but Lila could barely hear her. Her head felt heavy, wrapped in cotton wool. And she kept thinking of Charlie. Charlie and her dad and Geeta and Gyandip. She missed them all so much already.

"JASMINE, LILA, COME eat." Taata Maaryam pushed open the screen door, beckoning the girls inside.

Lila gasped as she went back into the room, feeling sick to her stomach. Women carrying large silver platters overflowing with food were walking back and forth from the kitchen. Naked browned chickens and skewers with little shanks of flesh sat dripping fat onto mounds of yellow rice and vegetables. Sameer placed an enormous round dish in the middle of the long table. A huge, charred animal leg stared accusingly back at Lila.

"C'mon." Jasmine grabbed a plate and rushed to the table, but Lila wouldn't go near it. She'd never eaten meat in her life and the sight of it made her want to throw up. She could hardly breathe. The stench was so overpowering, she feared she would no longer be able to hold back her tears.

"Try, try." Taata Maryam shoved a plate of rice and meat into Lila's hands. "Mansaf. It good. I make specially for you."

"No thank you . . . no thank you, I don't . . ." Lila started to push the plate away as Minna miraculously popped up by her side.

"Maybe Lila'd just like some salads." Minna flashed her a warning look. "There's hummus and tahini . . ."

"But, Mommy . . ." Lila tried to object.

"Lila!" Minna scowled down at her.

"I'm not hungry, Taata, really."

"Too excited, eh." Taata Maryam laughed, removing the plate, her two gold teeth flashing.

AFTER EVERYONE FINISHED eating and the women cleared the empty plates away, they set out the sweets, filling the long table with plates of fruit and tiny round and square cakes. Huge platters crisscrossed with slices of shiny red watermelons, yellow succulent pineapples, and golden honey melons. White flowered bowls overflowed with ripe purple berries.

"Try something . . ." Minna tried to cajole Lila, who was sitting on the floor in the corner sulking. "They've made all my favorites."

But Lila shrugged her away. She was tired and irritated and didn't want to be there anymore. All she wanted was to be left alone. She shut her eyes and took three deep breaths, trying to steady her mind, climbing higher and higher in her pink balloon, until her head was touching the ceiling, and she could rise no higher. She grabbed hold of the ugly chandelier, squashed her eyes and squinted down, miraculously turning everyone below her into coconuts. But even that didn't make her feel better. From where she was looking, all the coconuts were black.

Jasmine sat on the floor besides her, pulling her back down. She silently placed a plate of little cakes between them, stuffed a little round one into her mouth and munched, her teeth making little chewing noises. Lila couldn't resist. She picked up a tiny brown rectangle and popped it into her mouth. The thin, crisp sheets crackled, sending bursts of crushed nuts and trickles of sweet, luscious syrup throughout her mouth. She had never tasted anything quite like it. She popped another one into her mouth and then another, sinking into the oblivion of comforting sweetness.

IT WAS STILL dark when she awoke and she couldn't see Charlie anywhere. She stuck her hand under the bed to feel for him, but he didn't come to lick it. "Charlie," she called softly, trying to find him in the shadows.

For a moment she had no idea where she was. "Laurel Valley." The memory flashed into her mind, and she sat up with a jolt. She didn't remember falling asleep or even how the evening had ended, and as she looked around her, her heart thumped rapidly in her chest. The room was pale and bare with no windows and the only light came in dimly through two narrow openings in the large front room. The bed was big and white and ugly, its four posters covered with ornate floral carvings that stretched across the desk and cupboard. Lila could see that everything was new, but it was all so blank and dreary, nothing at all like the yellow tent she was used to.

Her suitcase and the two boxes with her name written on them were standing in the far corner of the room. Lila tiptoed to the door and peeked out into the corridor. She saw a bathroom and then an open door which lead to another small room, where she could see her mother sleeping. On the other side of the corridor, there was a long, dark living room and then a kitchen, right at the end. There was a small table and some chairs and two oversized old black leather sofas. Everything was freshly painted, and the whole house reeked of it. From the corner of her eye, she caught something flashing from behind one of the sofas and decided to check it out. A new shiny pink bicycle was hiding there. It was a big girl's bike, with no learner wheels and a gleaming gold horn. Lila was elated. She had just learned how to ride, but her bike had been a "little girl's bike," so Minna had made her leave it behind. There was a big purple bow and a note on the handlebar.

"Welcome Lila," she read, "your uncle Sameer."

She climbed onto the bicycle and sat there for a while, imagining she was riding it. Suddenly she felt much better. She got off, went back to her room, and shut the door quietly behind her. Then she pulled all her clothes out of the suitcase and started to arrange them in the closet, like she had seen her mother do so many times before. Everything had its place. All the short shirts in one pile, the long ones in another. Socks and panties in separate drawers. There was even a special Venice drawer, for the few old shirts and dresses Minna had let her keep. When she was done, she pulled out her toys and games, climbed first onto the chair and then onto the desk to place them on the shelves high above, before finally tucking her dolls into her bed, exactly as she had done at home. It didn't take long, her mother hadn't allowed her to bring much, but she had been "quiet as a mouse," and Minna hadn't heard a thing.

Lila climbed into the bed, hugging her dolls, but she couldn't quite find herself. The room wasn't as strange anymore, but she still felt lonely and all closed in, as if she were in a box.

"A box within a box, buried underground," she whispered to herself forlornly.

Images of the night before filled her thoughts. The people and the smells and the noise. More and more faces popped into her mind, but she couldn't remember who most of them were. She thought of her father and everyone else she had left behind and her mind twirled and weaved, until everything got confused and scary and her breath caught.

"It's just a mind attack." She heard her father's voice. "Take a deep long breath." She breathed in counting to five and then slowly let the air out. "Your head is becoming heavy and your eyes are sinking deep into your skull."

"Breath in deeply," Lila told herself quietly. "Blow the air out into your right leg. Blow it all the way down to your feet, to the tips of your toes. Relax your legs, until you don't feel them anymore."

At first, her mind tried to distract her, throwing out disturbing thoughts and images, but Lila kept resisting. She took a deep breath and blew the air through her left leg. "Relax your foot. Your toes." She blew air into her arms and her chest and her tummy, until her entire body seemed to disappear and she was left floating in the air. She took a few more deep breaths and let the pink balloon carry her away. She didn't tell it where to go, but she knew exactly where it was going. It let her down gently, right on the sand in her favorite spot, just before the water. She kept her eyes closed and allowed the hot sun to stroke her face.

"ARE YOU UP?" Minna poked her head into Lila's room, pulling her out of herself. "Wow!" She walked in. "Your room looks great. You've made it so nice."

"I hate it." Lila jumped out of bed. "I hate this apartment. It's underground and I can't see anything, and . . ."

"Stop it, Lila," Minna said crossly. "Look how good they've been to us, taking us in . . ."

"But why do we have to live here, it's ugly and I want to go home." Lila started to wail.

"Give it a chance." Minna tried to stroke her face, but Lila pushed her hand away.

"We have so much to be grateful for." Minna sat down on Lila's bed, folding her hands in front of her face, but Lila would have nothing of it. She didn't feel grateful for anything. Except, maybe, the new shiny pink bike.

She went to the cupboard and pulled her favorite dress out of her "Venice" drawer.

"That's too small." Minna shook her head. "Wear something else."

"But I want to wear this one," Lila objected, pulling the dress over her head.

"Take it off and put on something else," Minna insisted, her voice rising in irritation. She took a pair of jeans shorts and a pile of short-sleeved shirts out of the cupboard. "Choose one. Any one."

"Why can't I wear my own clothes, I hate the new ones," Lila shouted.

"Enough, Lily!" Minna raised her voice. "Their house, their rules. Just get dressed. I don't want to hear another word." She marched out of the room.

Lila didn't say another word. She knew there was no point. Her mother never spoke to her like that before and they'd never really had a fight.

"She doesn't care what I feel," Lila said, tempted to tell her to "place herself in her shoes" or "try to look at it from her point of view."

"Only now, there's only one point of view." She sniffled crossly. "Her point of view."

She picked up the first shirt in the pile and pulled it on. It was the blue one. Suddenly she stopped and snorted out loud. She'd made her mom so mad, she'd forgotten herself and called her Lily.

JASMINE ARRIVED BEFORE they had time to think about breakfast.

"Don't worry." She rang her bicycle bell madly. "We'll eat on the way."

They burst out laughing when they saw each other. They were dressed exactly the same, only Jasmine's shirt was red. Lila couldn't get over it. They could have been sisters, except that Jasmine looked even more like Minna than she did.

"You can't go out by yourselves," Minna started to protest, but Jasmine dismissed her with a wave of her hand.

"Don't worry, there's a bunch of kids waiting for us. We always go out together. Auntie Nissrine's daughter Dalia will be there and she's ten, and Riad and Rami are twelve."

Minna carried Lila's new bicycle up the stairs.

"You can keep it here, next to mine." Jasmine pointed to a little shed on the side of the building.

"Be careful, and don't leave the sidewalk," Lila heard her mother calling as she pedaled away, but she didn't bother looking back.

JASMINE LED HER up a hidden path behind their house to the neighbor's garden.

"Can we go through?" Lila stopped her bike, afraid to carry on, but Jasmine kept on pedaling.

"It's Auntie Nissrine's," she shouted back. "C'mon, they won't wait forever."

The kids were sprawled on the front lawn. Cousin Dalia was Ibrahim's great granddaughter, and, it seemed, in charge of Jasmine and Lila.

"C'mon, you're late." She immediately started bossing them around.

Rami and Riad were twins, but they didn't look like each other at all. They were also Lila's "cousins," although how exactly they were related,

Lila didn't quite know. They jumped on their bikes and sped away, without even giving them a second glance. Dalia rode after them, followed by Jasmine and Lila, pedaling like mad. People waved at them as they cycled by, shouting, "Salach alchyr," and the kids screamed it back in a chorus. Lila wasn't sure exactly what it meant, but after a while she started shouting it too.

Elm Street was the total opposite of Palm. It was a residential street, with no shops or businesses, which made it quiet and slow paced, with very little traffic or pedestrians. They slowed down at the end of every block, waiting for Dalia to wave them across. Children of all ages came out to join them, some racing ahead, others stopping to introduce themselves to Lila. At first she felt self-conscious and hung back, smiling shyly, but soon she realized, that they really didn't care. For them she was just another cousin, and they accepted her naturally as one of the gang.

They rode on and on, the street seeming to go on forever. Small groups of children broke away from the large group, disappearing for a while, only to join up with the rest a little later.

"That's the masjid." Jasmine pointed to a low, one-story building, set slightly aside from the street, with a large square in front of it. The building looked old and deserted, but Jasmine told her that it filled up in the evenings, when the men came to pray.

"Taata Maryam says the masjid's not a place for women. They should stay at home and pray. But I love coming with my father, he doesn't miss a prayer."

During the day, it was where the children would gather.

"We're not allowed to go beyond the masjid," Jasmine warned Lila, "except when we go to school. It's two blocks down, on Pine." She pointed in the general direction. "Laurel Valley Elementary."

There was very little shade in front of the mosque, but they played there for a time, the boys exchanging baseball cards or kicking a ball around, the girls playing hopscotch and jumping rope.

"Yallah, scram, I'm the catcher," someone yelled from somewhere beyond Lila, and all the kids stopped what they were doing and ran, shrieking through the square. Lila barely made it away in time. They played hide and seek between the houses, cutting through the streets and backyards, moving between the chaos of Palm to the quiet of Elm in an intricate set of paths that linked the yards together, creating a labyrinth, only the kids could decipher.

But what had first seemed completely chaotic to Lila, quickly took form, as the unwritten rules of the children's domain and its borders became clear. They could roam freely between Palm and Elm, all the way from Lincoln, the road just before their house, and the mosque, but they weren't allowed to cross Broadway.

"That's a different neighborhood, and we don't mix with the people there," Dalia told Lila, as they took a right on Broadway and headed back toward Palm.

As they approached the street, the sound of traffic grew deafening. It was midday and the sidewalks were jammed with people. Cars filled the road in both directions, standing bumper to bumper, their drivers sticking their red faces out of their windows, swearing and honking. The entire street was covered with shops and little businesses, flashing their wares in Arabic on huge neon signs, and spilling over onto the sidewalk in booths and stalls that sold anything from fruit and produce to bath rugs and brassieres. The busy street was filthy and smelled of cooking and dirty water and the sidewalk was so constricted, the girls had to get off their bikes and walk most of the way.

They waved back at the barber and the women working in the grocery store. Dr. Al-Masri was standing outside his practice, talking to Mr. Hariri, the chemist.

"Dalia, Jasmine," he called them over. "And who may this be?" The two elderly men had known the girls all their lives. Dr. Al-Masri was even responsible for bringing them into this world.

"Lila. She's my cousin, my auntie Minna's daughter," Jasmine introduced.

"Very pleased to meet you." Dr. Al-Masri shook her hand vigorously.

"Minna? Maaryam's daughter?" Mr. Hariri rushed over and grabbed her hand.

"Ya habibti." He clapped his hands and rolled his eyes. "I remember your mother from the old neighborhood. I knew her when she was so small." He bent and placed his hand just below his knee.

"I had a tiny store, right next to theirs. Maryam would send her in for something nearly every day." Mr. Hariri chuckled in delight beneath his long mustache, looking Lila up and down. "You look just like her."

"Except the eyes." Lila waited for him to say, but he didn't. He went running off excitedly, calling, "Farha, Aisha, Mervat, bint Minna . . . bint Minna."

Women gathered from the stores and stalls around, crying, "salaam aleichum," their sweaty faces creased in smile. "So pretty." They clucked their tongues, calling her "habibti" and "bint," as they patted her hair and face and pinched her cheeks. But they weren't as well-mannered as Mr. Hariri. They didn't say anything to her, but she could see the way they looked at her and then glanced sideways at each other, exchanging whispers in Arabic behind her back. Auntie Jenna even pointed at her eyes and cackled out loud.

The girls stopped at almost every store and stall to introduce her, and they never left empty handed. Auntie Sabha, from the bakery, gave them a little bag filled with long narrow pastries. They looked like little sticks and were crunchy and covered with a thick sticky syrup. Auntie Nafisa gave them rolled balls of dried fruit and nuts she called "malban." When Lila unraveled them, they looked like leather, and tasted sweet and sour on her tongue. She ate a whole bag of tiny drops of fried dough, dipping each one in honey and popping it in her mouth, and stuffed her face with fruit and sweets. Before they left, Auntie Mirvat filled her arms with little packages of treats, nuts and dried dates, wrapped in cellophane and tied with colorful ribbons to take home to her mother.

Sami's Hooka Hall was closed, but they peeked through the windows. It was dark inside, so Lila could only make out some low tables and chairs and a bar with lots and lots of tall colorful glass vases.

"That's a hooka." Jasmine couldn't stop laughing. "They don't put flowers in it, they smoke it." Lila had no idea what she was talking about, so Jasmine promised to take her when the hall opened.

Taata Maryam was waiting for them outside the butcher shop. "You late," she scolded, ushering them in. "Your lunch get cold."

Dalia and Jasmine went running in, cutting through the store and out the back way, but Lila refused to enter, preferring to take the long way around. The sight and smell of all the pieces of meat hanging in the window made her nauseous. Ali, Jasmine's father, waved at her, beckoning here in, his arms and apron covered with blood. Lila waved back and rushed away. She rested on the landing for a moment, trying not to retch. When she came in, Taata Maryam was already filling the girls' plates, pouring a mixture of meat and vegetables over heaps of yellow rice.

"Nothing for me." Lila pushed away her plate. Luckily she wasn't hungry, she had eaten too much on the way.

Late in the afternoon, when the heat abated, Lana and Manar called them out again. They were Jasmine's best friends and would all be in the same class. At sundown, Jasmine took Lila to help Sami prepare the Hooka Hall.

"Sometimes we can hear the music, late at night," Jasmine told her, as they spread brightly colored cushions onto the low chairs and benches while Sami swept the floor of the large hall. Once customers arrived, they were supposed to leave, but Jasmine had a hideout next to the kitchen at the back of the hall.

"Under here." She pulled Lila down under a long table and handed her a cushion. "We can stay here for a while and watch. Nobody can see us."

"I'LL COME VISIT as soon as I can, Tiger Lily," David promised when he called in the evening. Lila was so excited and had so much to tell him, she forgot, for a moment, how much she missed him. But when Minna came to tuck her in, she wouldn't even let her enter the room.

"I'm a big girl now, I can sleep on my own." She closed the door in her mother's face. She was exhausted, but it took her a long time to fall asleep. Her head was so full of thoughts, try as she might, she couldn't make them go away. Still, she wouldn't forgive her mother. "It's all her fault." She was mad at her for taking her away and there was no way she was going to let her in.

AS THE SUMMER flew by, Lila learned to traverse the labyrinth of paths like a Laurel Valley native, knowing every house and street and even most of the people who lived there. Thursdays were Sami's "day off" and he always planned something special for his nieces. He took them to the zoo and Sea World and Mission Park, where they rented tricycles and boats or just paddled about in the water. Sometimes he would convince Minna to take a "time out" and join them. "Time out" was his favorite expression. When she agreed, they'd go to the mall or a movie, pigging out on popcorn and pizza.

On Fridays all the shops closed early and, by late afternoon, Palm Street was deserted. Most men attended the special midday prayer, while the women closed up before hurrying home to prepare the evening meal.

"Friday, the best day," Taata Maryam would say, awakening early, cleaning, cooking, baking.

Around six o'clock, the family gathered, coming together each time at someone else's house. Each woman brought her special dish. At first Minna would make sure to bring something without meat, especially for Lila, but after a while some of the other women caught on and would bring dishes Lila could eat too.

At first, David came to visit every other Saturday, although never to the house. Lila begged him to come see her room, but he always said, "Not today, Tiger Lily, maybe next time."

Minna got mad every time he called her that, but David didn't pay her any attention. The Saturday before the first day of school he took her and Jasmine to Disneyland. He met them on the corner of Palm and Lincoln, but wouldn't turn onto their street even to see the house from the outside.

"We don't have time, ladies." He pushed his foot down hard on the gas and sped off in the opposite direction.

WHEN SCHOOL STARTED, the girls were allowed to cross the border to walk two streets up on Broadway to Pine. This was unchartered territory for Lila, who had never moved beyond Elm. The houses on this side of the road were bigger and prettier and she liked to walk by slowly, peeking into the well-kept gardens that were perpetually in bloom, searching for hidden gnomes and water fountains.

The school itself was larger than her old one, but it had a tiny yard and the fresh coat of white paint that covered it gave it a solemn, almost hostile look, like a hospital or a prison. Lila and Jasmine were in classroom 2b, on the first floor and their desk was right behind Lana and Manar's, who had arrived early on the first day and saved a place for them. Lila was the only new kid in class, but she wasn't really worried. She knew most of the kids already. Walid and Ismail, who sat behind them were already her friends. Walid lived two houses down from them and Ismail a little further down the block. There were two black kids whose names Lila didn't know yet who weren't from the neighborhood but came to the mosque with their father, and a Chinese girl, Lee, who was sitting all by herself. Her parents ran a dumpling shop on the corner of Broadway and Lincoln, but on the side Lila and her friends avoided.

The other kids, it seemed, didn't matter. Very quickly Lila learned it was "us" against "them." There was no real animosity, but the children from "Little Ghaza" stuck together and kept to themselves. Each neighborhood had its own "gang" and they never mixed. They even had their own territory. The moment the bell rang, kids of all ages poured out and rushed to their designated areas.

"Our place is the best." Jasmine led Lila out to the back of the school. The entire back yard was theirs and Lila immediately felt at home, recognizing most of the kids gathered there.

At first Lila found Miss Davis a little frightening. She was a tall, rakish woman, who had been teaching "for over thirty years" and liked to remind them of it. The kids thought she was too strict and not as fun as Mrs. Ayar, who taught 2a and was "from the neighborhood." But all their parents adored Miss Davis because she was "old school" and gave lots of homework. Miss Davis had been the class's first grade teacher and since Lila was the only addition, she had immediately called her up to test her reading skills. Miss Davis was so impressed, it took her a while to figure out she couldn't write.

"C'mon." She marched Lila off to the library, the very first recess. "I don't have much time today, so I'll just show you around and leave you to choose something for yourself."

The library was immense, spread out over two floors. The first floor was more of a reading center, with a large open space and loads of books and activities for the first grades.

"You can look through here later, we're headed for the second floor." Miss Davis bossed her up the stairs. The books on the second floor were for older readers and there were so many stands and shelves filled with them, that Lila simply ran after Miss Davis, gaping in awe.

"I've got an idea," Miss Davis said when she noticed how flustered Lila was becoming. "All the kids love these ... B ... B ... B ..." she muttered, turning toward the shelves on the far wall. "Got to run." She pulled out a book from the second shelf, handed it to Lila, and rushed off.

"*The Secret Seven*," Lila read out loud, settling down on the floor to leaf through the book. It had plenty of pictures, but it looked like a grown-up book with words covering most of the pages. She looked at the cover again and checked how long it was. Then she started to read and it was love from the first page. She could barely tear herself away when the bell rang. Apart from the back yard, the library became her favorite place at school. She was there every day changing books or helping put them away. She meticulously read every single book in the series, one after the other, and always in the right order. From time to time, she even had to wait a few days for the next in line, but she never skipped a book, waiting impatiently until the one she was waiting for was finally returned.

THE THIRD TIME Miss Davis asked her to come by, Minna was really irritated.

"There was never any problem with you at your old school. I don't have time for this." Minna shook her head, exasperated. "I've just gone back to school myself and I've still got two full years before I can even start my law degree," she told Lila for what seemed the hundredth time. "Can't you please, please, do what your teacher asks?"

But this time Miss Davis had a new idea. She had tried everything she could think of to make Lila write, but Lila still wouldn't. She tried the merit system, offering her prizes, and then the demerit system, taking them back again. She tried to make her write lines and then copy sentences, but whatever she told her to do, Lila just shook her head and said, "I can't!"

"She's such a delightful child," Miss Davis told Minna the last time she called her in. "And so bright. She reads books way above her level. I just can't understand why she refuses to write."

"This is for you, Lila." Miss Davis placed a thick purple notebook on the desk in front of her. "Go ahead, open it."

On the first page, right in the center, she had written in big bold letters:

LILA'S JOURNAL

"One entry, every day," Miss Davis insisted. "Two to three sentences, about anything you want. That's your homework."

Still, Lila wouldn't do the journal assignment, resisting all of Minna's commands and pleas.

"This can't continue," Minna told David on the phone one night, admitting defeat, when she thought Lila was asleep. "The child just won't listen to me."

"Just try, Tiger Lily," David pleaded on his next visit. He placed the purple notebook in front of Lila. "C,mon, let's do the first entry together."

At first, she labored over each letter, only to change her mind, erase her efforts, and start all over again. It was a slow and frustrating process, for although the words came easily, her main battle was with the letters. She wrote short, tiny sentences, condensing everything she wanted to say into as few words as possible. Each day she pulled out her journal and painstakingly traced out the letters, pausing after each word to make sure to leave a space before attempting to write the next. Every word was a hurdle, a new height to leap over. She learned to prepare her sentences beforehand, going over each word again and again in her head, until she was sure it was accurate and there would be no crossing out. Sometimes rebellious words changed themselves in mid-sentence, so she had no choice but to erase them, but usually, when she was finally ready to put pen to paper, every word was in its place and each sentence perfectly formed, exactly as she wanted it to be.

Now she became bolder, her sentences longer and more elaborate. She graduated from snips of information to longer descriptions, slowly adding tones and colors and emotions. Her handwriting didn't improve much, the letters remaining twisted and awkward, but even Miss Davis stopped nagging her.

"Don't worry about it," she told Lila every time she apologetically handed in her journal. "What matters is that you write, not what it looks like."

In fact, she was so thrilled by Lila's progress, she told her to choose one of her entries at the end of the week and read it in front of the class.

At first, Lila was hesitant, embarrassed to share her writing. She chose short, light entries, describing her home and her life, reading them out loud, her head held low, her words hesitant and her voice shaky. She was sure the other kids would hate her writing and make fun of her, but they seemed to be interested, commenting and even asking questions. She started to plan what she would read to them, jotting down all her ideas. Every week she'd sit, sometimes for hours, trying to decide what she should write about. Sometimes it was easy. A holiday. A surprise. A strange or unexpected event. Often, it was the kids themselves who told her what they wanted to hear, coming up to her in the breaks with their suggestions. Other times were more difficult and she couldn't decide what to choose, what to write, what to say.

She began making deals with Miss Davis, trading her daily entries for lengthier weekly ones. "The Hooka Hall's worth at least three entries," Lila bargained. Miss Davis was delighted. The student who had refused to write was beginning to consider herself a writer.

LILA WROTE ALMOST an entire page, she had so much to say, but she wasn't sure all the other kids would know what a hooka pipe was. She grinned to herself, remembering how she had no idea before moving to Palm Street. Now that Minna worked for Sami, she went there all the time. She and Jasmine would sneak in every evening before the crowds to hide behind the kitchen bar. Minna and Sami always knew they were there and let them stay for a while before making a big fuss of discovering them and sending them off to bed.

"What should I write?" Lila kept asking herself. It was taking much longer than she had expected and was much more difficult. Even explaining what a hooka was, wasn't as simple as she had thought. She described it fine, even thought to take one with her, just like in "show and tell," but when she tried to explain how it was used, she realized she didn't really know. More importantly, she couldn't figure out why people smoked them in the first place, even though she watched them night after night, filling their lungs and blowing out billowing fragrant white clouds of smoke.

"Put the nozzle in your mouth and take a deep breath." Sami placed the water pipe in front of her.

"Fill your mouth slowly, don't let it . . ." he started to warn her, but it was too late. The hot air filled Lila's lungs till she felt she was going to explode as bursts of smothering smoke sent her body into a coughing spasm and tears rolled down her face.

"Try again?" He held the mouthpiece up to her, when she finally stopped coughing and caught her breath.

"Don't breathe into your lungs, just fill your mouth with air, and slowly let it out." This time Sami held the nozzle and pulled it away from Lila's mouth just as the smoke filling the jar rose to the tip.

"It tastes like Fanta." Lila laughed, her mouth filling with a sweet, fizzy orange tang that tickled her throat. She waited a while, but nothing else happened. "That's it? I don't get it."

"It reminds them of the old country." Sami took a deep puff. "Where we come from people have been smoking hookas for centuries. It's a way of relaxation, of bringing people together. They can sit and talk for hours, passing the pipe from one to the other ..."

"Like a peace pipe?" Lila asked.

"Exactly." Sami took another puff and offered her the pipe again.

"No thank you." Lila pushed it away, grimacing. "I'm never going to smoke again." But she was glad she had tried. Now she knew exactly what to write.

In the first sentence she introduced her uncle Sameer. Then she painstakingly explained what a hooka was and how it was used, going into the smallest detail. She described the hall with its low cushioned tables and soft yellow lights and wrote about the people who went there. Only those who went there at night, though. She didn't say anything about the men she saw entering the hall during the day. They would sit there with her uncle Sami for many hours, their voices rising and clashing like an angry sea, spilling through the walls in salty, incomprehensible bursts.

"They fight for the old country," Taata Maryam told Lila, waving her fist.

"They just meet and talk." Minna tried to keep her daughter as far as possible from anything political, out of respect for David.

Lila sat for days, working out exactly which words to use, but when she finished, she wasn't quite satisfied. She went over it again and again, adding or changing a word now and then. She still felt something was missing, but couldn't make out what it was.

"It's your journal," Miss Davis said, after giving it some thought, "but where are you? Maybe you should add something about yourself, make it more personal. I'm sure the other kids would love that."

Lila thought about Miss Davis' advice and decided she was right. But it changed everything. For the first time, she had to write about herself, and this, she quickly discovered, was even more difficult. She kept starting and stopping, crossing everything out and starting again. Eventually she decided to leave it the way it was, apart from a new beginning:

> The hooka hall is one of my favorite places in the neighborhood
> I go there nearly every day with my cousin jasmine
> She's my best friend and we do everything together
> We live just behind the hooka hall
> At night when we can't sleep we like to listen to the music and the voices coming through the walls

She read through everything again and again, feeling very pleased with herself. Before she put it away, she decided to add a few words about her mother. She barely saw her now, and that suited her just fine, but she did work at the Hooka Hall, so she felt she had to at least mention her.

This time, when she read her entry to the class, she couldn't keep the excitement out of her voice. After she answered an endless stream of questions, all her classmates came up to the front and lined up to touch the hooka pipe. Her friends all knew what it was, of course, but the others had never seen anything like it before. Lila was really proud of herself.

"Quite the little journalist," Miss Davis said, beaming.

SOME OF THE other kids decided they wanted to write a journal too. Soon everyone was journaling. Miss Davis even gave them time to write in class and every week ended with their presentations. Lila always had something ready. She worked on it all week, trying to write a proper paragraph, like Miss Davis had shown them.

Lila wrote her next long entry just after Mawlid al nabi. Miss Davis traded her a whole week's entries for it. Mawlid al nabi required days of preparation, making lanterns and colored paper chains and hanging lights all over the house and the Hooka Hall. Since it was the biggest hall in the neighborhood, it also doubled as the community center and all holidays and festivals were celebrated there. The butcher shop had remained open until late at night the entire week before and even Taata Maryam spent most of her time helping out. Minna and Lila still refused to enter, so they were kept busy running all the other errands.

On the day of the holiday the children were invited to the masjid for a special meeting with the Imam. It was Lila's first time inside the holy place, although she often peeked in to watch her uncles pray.

Imam Zaccaria, their cousin from Auntie Waffa's side, patted her head as she took off her shoes to leave on the rack outside.

"Hi, Lila, glad to see you joining us." He smiled down at her, the skin around his eyes wrinkling as the sides of his mouth disappeared into his beard.

She saw him almost every day, but today he seemed even taller than usual, his voice deeper and more severe. Lila looked around, her bare feet sinking into the thick green carpet. The walls of the mosque were covered with woven tapestries all the way up to the ceiling where colorful strands of lights flashed in a rainbow.

"Welcome children," Zaccaria called out loudly, gesturing for them to sit around him. "Does everyone know what day this is?"

"Mohammad's birthday," Lila shouted confidently, together with all the other kids.

"Anyone know a story about the prophet?" Zaccaria let a few children speak and then he began to talk.

Lila was relieved. She had been dreading the point where she would have to pray. Despite Taata Maryam's persistent efforts, she still didn't know how. Minna had interrupted Taata Maryam's last lesson, almost shrieking in horror at the sight of her daughter kneeling on a prayer mat, her forehead pressed to the ground in a full bow—one of the few postures she managed to learn before her mother came from school that afternoon.

"Leave her alone." Minna yanked Lila up from the floor, her knuckles whitening as she gripped her by the elbow.

"I just show him, he already seven," Taata Maryam stuttered. When she was upset, her English was even worse than usual. "He gotta know how pray."

"Just leave the child alone," Minna repeated, wagging a long finger in front of Taata Maryam's face.

LILA WANTED TO start her entry with one of Imam Zaccaria's stories, but she had to choose which one first. After some deliberation, she decided to write about how Mohammad had left his home to live in a cave, where he stayed for many years all alone, until the angel Gabriel told him about Allah. She remembered that part vividly, because it had made her think of herself. Sometimes, she felt that she too lived in a cave under the ground, but she didn't write about that.

"But the really exciting part came after the special prayer," Lila continued. "All the men came, even Uncle Sami. My uncles Machmud and Ali go to the masjid every day, but Sami says he prefers to pray at home, although I never see him."

She described the chanting from the mosque growing louder, competing with the noise in the square outside, as more and more people congregated, waving flags and banging on musical instruments. Women gathered on all sides, the younger ones adorned in their most festive dresses, their hair and bosoms covered with multicolored scarves. The older women were wrapped in the traditional hijab, their heavily made-up faces framed by their tightly wrapped head dresses.

When the prayer ended, the men leaving the mosque embraced those around them. They formed a procession, beating their hands on enormous clay drums and shaking tambourines. The men at the front held flags the size of blankets. Lila noticed all the flags had stripes connected by a red triangle on one end, just like the smaller one on the Hooka Hall wall.

"What's going on?" Lila asked Jasmine.

"Yalla!" Jasmine answered, pulling her into the procession.

Someone handed her a rattle and Jasmine grabbed a small wooden drum. Cymbals clashed. Tambourines clanked. The drums began with a tap that became a roar, and the parade surged forward. The women on the sidelines bombarded the procession with fistfuls of sour balls and candy, as they passed, sending Lila and Jasmine high up in the air, jumping and screeching with all the other kids, trying to catch the sweets as they were thrown. Then, they threw themselves down, crawling and scrambling on all fours in a crazed hunt for fallen sweets. The snake of people grew longer as it traveled, winding and weaving through the streets, until Lila could no longer see its beginning or its end.

It was the loudest noise Lila had ever heard. Trumpets flared above the thunder of drums and Lila waved her rattle frantically in the air as the procession turned onto Palm. The street and sidewalks had been swept and washed clean and all the little ramshackle stalls removed. Stars and crescents sparkled from every tree and storefront where neon signs flashed red, blue, and green, dousing the entire street in a fairytale air. To Lila, the scene was nothing short of her own little wonderland.

"Like Easter and Christmas combined," Lila ended her entry.

LILA WROTE IN her journal every day now. When she rediscovered the tattered notebook years later, she was grateful to herself for recording every detail of that first year. Everything was new and strange, but apart from Jasmine, she felt she had no one to talk to, and writing it down, somehow, made it easier. More importantly, even though Miss Davis had assigned it, she wasn't writing for her anymore. Now she was writing for herself. It had truly become her journal.

"YOU'RE SO TALENTED," Miss Davis told her. "You have your own special way of looking at things."

All the kids had written about Halloween, describing their costumes and the candy they got, but Lila's entry was completely different.

"Taata Maryam hates Halloween," she began. "She tried to stop us from going out." She wrote about her grandmother and all the fears and superstitions she had brought with her from "the old country." She believed in witches and sorcery and was sure they all came out on Halloween. "We go movies and pizza." She tried to bribe the girls and when they wouldn't budge, sent them out with blue glass beaded bracelets, to ward off the evil eye. She wouldn't even let them go out with both of their mothers tagging along and only let them leave the house when Sami promised to go with them.

"Spit three times," she warned them again, as they were leaving, pointing behind her left shoulder, "if someone put spell on you."

Lila felt pangs of homesickness for Venice as Thanksgiving approached. She remembered the cloud of tranquility and contentment that settled over the entire beach at November's end. Hundreds of people would sit in the sand around a huge, crackling bonfire, passing around colorful plates of fire-roasted vegetables. After the meal, there was always a special meditation, though Lila, tucked in bed with a full belly, was never awake for it.

In Little Ghaza it was also a communal event, celebrated in the Hooka Hall with gigantic bronzed turkeys, stuffed with rice and pine nuts.

"We make different." Taata Maryam waved a plate in front of Lila's face, trying to entice her to take a bite. "Try. Palestinian turkey."

The familiar aromas of anise and cumin filled the air, but Lila, who had never eaten turkey before, had no intention of starting. Besides, the sight of her great uncle rolling up his sleeves, wiping his brow and then carving up bird after bird, stacking up the slabs of white meat in towers and passing them around, was making her sick. The kids couldn't stop giggling when Lila read out her entry, describing the huge dead birds sitting on trays so big, each one had to be carried by two men.

ALTHOUGH ITS RESIDENTS didn't celebrate Christmas, Palm Street wore its glittering lights and the stores were packed with customers stocking up on coveted seasonal treats. Throughout the break the girls were treated to sugared candies and chocolate Santas every time they ventured out.

"Too much sweet, you come see me soon." Dr. Al-Masri waved his finger at Lila and Jasmine every time they biked by, stuffing their faces.

On New Year's Eve they stayed up late, wrapping yellow sour balls and white almond coated sugar drops in small, rectangles of white cheesecloth, each tied like a tiny sack, with a little light blue bow.

"We have our New Year and they have theirs." Taata Maryam refused to join the celebration.

"It's everyone's New Year." Minna had taken a "time-out" and was busy cutting fabric and ribbon, trying to match the kids' demand. Just before midnight the children lined the roads and streets around Little Ghaza, handing tiny sweet packages through car windows. At midnight, honks erupted from all the cars and people hugged and kissed, feverishly screaming, "Happy New Year!"

"IT'S NOT EVEN a matter of belief," Minna explained to her daughter when Ramadan arrived, "it's out of respect."

"A whole month?" Lila didn't think it was possible.

"It's all about family and tradition," Sami added.

"I fast every year, from I your age," Taata Maryam told the girls.

Lila and Jasmine decided to fast too, skipping breakfast the first day.

"Maybe just something small." Jasmine grabbed an apple from the fridge a few hours later.

"It's only eleven," Lila ridiculed her. She lasted till lunchtime.

"You don't need fast," Taata Maryam consoled her. "You still young. Plenty time."

Every day during Ramadan they did their homework as quickly as they could, before rushing to help Taata Maryam. First they prepared the tamarindi juice, pulling swollen gobs of disgusting blackish brown tamarins out of the foul water Taata was soaking them in, then tearing them into small pieces. They crushed and strained the mixture again and again until Taata was satisfied.

"Khallas," she finally clapped her hands, "it ready."

The girls carefully measured in ten cups of sugar and then squeeze a few lemons, letting the juice sift through their fingers, catching the little pips before they fell in. Taata cooked the juice and left it to cool. Before she poured it into bottles, she added a few drops of rose water and the whole kitchen smelled like a garden in bloom.

Then they prepared qatayef, filling little pancakes with walnuts and cinnamon, for Taata to fry. They would be smothered in honey and served right at the start of the Iftar dinner. The entire family broke the fast together, gathering each night at a different house. In the late afternoons, they accompanied Jasmine's father and all their uncles to the masjid.

"Assalaam Alaikum," (peace be upon you), the Imam welcomed them.

"Wa alaikum assalaam," (and upon you be peace), they'd shout back in unison, and run straight back out the door. Several women attended the prayers, but none from Lila's immediate family. They entered discreetly from a separate entrance at the back and prayed in a tiny curtained off area behind the men, with a buffer of children separating them. Lila liked to watch the men through the open door, as they stood in rows, bowing and prostrating themselves, sitting on the floor or standing up in unison, following the leadership of the Imam, their voices rising and falling in prayer.

As the sun set, the girls ran home ahead of the men to help the women prepare trays of little glasses filled with iced water and tamarindi juice. When the sun went down, Lila and Jasmine carried the trays around the room, serving juice and little cakes, helping the grown-ups break their fast.

On Fridays during Ramadan, the entire neighborhood came together, and Iftar dinners were held in the Hooka Hall. Everyone brought a special dish or treat.

"That what Iftar about." Taata beamed at Lila, sending her off to one of the neighbors with a heaped plate of freshly fried qatayef. "We send food to friend, to family and he send back."

"Wait till come last night, Eid el Fitr," Taata told Lila, "you see what feast we make."

Lila knew each woman's special dish by heart. Great Auntie Sara and her daughter Selma, who had moved out of the neighborhood but returned for holidays, made maqluba, turning the huge pots upside down just before it was time to serve. They spent the entire day preparing the meat and vegetables for the dish, cutting onions and carrots and browning the cauliflower and eggplant. Auntie Nadia and Auntie Waffa were in charge of the mansaf. They would place whole legs of lamb on flatbread, freshly baked in the taboon, cover them with jameel yogurt and a sprinkling of fried nuts and almonds. Their husbands kept the best cuts for them and they were the central dishes of every communal meal. Auntie Heeba made the best kube, stuffing them with freshly ground lamb and pine nuts mixed with cardamom and cinnamon and Minna cooked her special baba ganoush, sprinkling pomegranate seeds on top as garnishing.

She tried to recruit Lila's help. "C'mon, Lila, we'll have such fun cooking together."

But Lila refused. She wanted to spend as little time as possible with her mother. Instead, she and Jasmine would make muhalabiyeh with Taata Maryam.

"You young people, no know make anymore," Taata complained, every time they made it. She shook her head sadly as she stirred the rice, slowly adding milk and sugar and tiny drops of rose water. When the pudding was ready, the girls carefully ladled it out, covering each serving with a sprinkling of pistachios and cinnamon.

Auntie Heeba baked manakish, a flat bread topped with z'aatar and olive oil and Auntie Fatima stuffed vegetable "mahshi" or waraq dawali, filling grape leaves with a tangy, lemon flavored rice that was one of Lila's favorite dishes. She knew who made the best lentil stew and who made the best freeka or bamia. She knew who'd make the tahini or the taboula and who was the hummus queen. Auntie Lubna and Auntie Aysha, who ran the Nablus Bakery, at the other end of Palm, always prepared special sweets.

"The best baklawa from Nablus," Taata liked to reminisce. "I remember, when I child, some time we get special sweets from Nablus. For wedding or holiday. It different from Jaffa sweets. More soft. Melt in mouth."

Lila couldn't wait for Eid el Fitr to arrive. There was no school, and all the stores on Palm were closed. The girls spent the day baking and running errands. Toward late afternoon everyone showered and put on their most festive dress. Taata Maryam bought Lila and Jasmine new clothes, convincing Uncle Sami to take them all to the mall. The girls chose the same dress, only Lila's was pink and Jasmine's blue.

"You could be sisters." Taata couldn't get over the resemblance.

"Except for the eyes," Lila and Jasmine finished, laughing.

TWO LONG TABLES covered with snowy white linen ran along separate halves of the hall.

"This side men." Taata pointed to the front of the room. "Women there, close to kitchen." She gave the girls little floral decorations and bowls filled with watermelon and sunflower seeds, or a mix of pistachios and cashews, dried fruit and dates, and they ran about placing them on the tables, feeling so important.

"Ahalan wasahalan." Lila welcomed the guests, as was the custom.

"Kayf haalak?" she asked Uncle Riad how he was doing, and answered, "Al hamdullila," proudly, when he asked her back. To her surprise, he kissed her on both cheeks and then placed a crisp dollar bill in her hand. Ali and Machmud each gave her five dollars and Uncle Sami gave her "a whole tenner." Auntie Nafisa gave her a blue beaded bracelet and Auntie Amal a small box of nectarine chocolates she had made especially for the occasion. At the end of the evening, Lila had a whole pile of jewelry and little gifts, and thirty-seven dollars in cash.

"It's the most money I've ever had," she wrote in her journal. "And two more than Jasmine got."

She thought a lot about what was perhaps the most important thing that had happened to her on the night of Eid el fitr, but finally decided not to share it with her class. "I don't have to tell them everything," she told herself.

The truth was she was still a little embarrassed. And she hadn't really meant to, it was an honest mistake. She thought the samosas were filled with goat's cheese, like Auntie Sabha always made them. How was she to know auntie had suddenly decided to do something different? It was only after a few bites that she realized what had happened, but by then the rich smoky unknown flavor had spread throughout her mouth and throat and although at first she didn't want to admit it, it didn't make her feel sick at all. In fact, it was quite delicious. She took another small bite and then finished the entire little pie. She still wouldn't touch the shanks of flesh, but she dipped some kube in tahini and even tried a few bites of makluba.

"Mabrouk habeebti." Taata Maryam clapped her hands every time Lila took a bite, smiling so widely her eyes almost disappeared behind her spectacles.

DAVID CAME TO pick Lila up the day school ended. She hadn't seen him for over a month. Now that he had moved to Vegas, she saw him less and less. He worked as a security guard for one of the new casinos and had promised to take Lila there on her vacation.

"You won't believe how big it is," he bragged. "It's the biggest hotel in the world. It has everything you could ever dream of right inside it."

He didn't have much time to spend with her, though. He had to go back to Israel to visit his mother.

"She's really sick. My sister says she barely recognizes anyone anymore, so I thought I should go for a visit before it's too late."

"You have a sister?" Lila knew her grandfather died when her father was very young, but she had never heard of an aunt. "And anyway, I thought you didn't talk to your family?"

"I got back in touch with them last year." He told her that when he married Minna, they had stopped talking to him.

"Mostly my mother. She became more and more religious and when she heard I was marrying a Muslim, she said it was the worst possible sin. She wouldn't even let my sister stay in touch with me."

He told her that his sister, Hanna, who was almost six years his senior, had been married for a short while, but had returned home when she divorced. Lila asked if he missed them. "My mother was never the hugging type." David grimaced.

He told her he had been born on a kibbutz and raised in the children's house, away from his parents. "It's not that they didn't love me, that's how they raised kids at the time. I hated it and cried every night. Some nights, I'd call out for my mother, but she never came. My sister would take pity on me and sneak in to comfort me, but only till she was caught. After she was punished, I lay awake for weeks crying out her name, but she never came again."

"IT LOOKS JUST like a magical castle." Lila's eyes glazed over when the colored towers came into view.

"It is a castle," David declared. "King Arthur's Castle."

"It's even better than Disneyland," Lila decided. There were bridges and moats and secret passageways.

"Look." She stood on the tips of her toes and pointed to the highest tower. "There's Merlin, looking down at us."

He took her all over the casino, a proud smile plastered on his face as he introduced her.

"Pleased to meet you," Lila would say, stretching out her hand. After the second or third time, she knew exactly what they were going to say:

"Your eyes, you have exactly the same color as your Dad's," or as his roommate Peter put it: "Can't miss those eyes, bro."

On the last night of her trip, he took her to a special show. It was sold out weeks in advance, but David had somehow managed to get tickets. At first Lila was so overwhelmed by the noise and seeming chaos, she grabbed for her father's hand, clutching his fingers tightly. The basement of the casino had turned into a giant arena, full of wrestling knights and fair large bosomed maidens, and even horses trotting back and forth, to add to the confusion. The heavily armored men held long sticks and seemed to be trying to knock each other off their horses.

"They're jousting," David explained, as he led Lila to their stand.

"Why're we red?" Lila noticed that each section of the audience had a different color.

"It's a competition. Each color is a different team."

"And we're the red team." Lila finally got it, drumming her feet and hands, as the red king bowed down in front of her.

Pages blew their trumpets and barefoot wenches served the banquet, plonking their heavy trays onto the narrow tables in front of the spectators.

"How are we supposed to eat?" Lila looked all over but didn't see any knives and forks.

"Like this." David picked the tiny browned chicken off his tray with both his hands, tore off a leg, and took a huge bite. "You eat meat now, don't you?"

"A whole chicken?" Lila picked up her chicken incredulously, pulling her lips back in disgust. "With our hands?"

"We're in the Middle Ages, after all." David tore off one of the wings, grease dripping from the tips of his fingers.

Lila brought the chicken closer to her face. It had a pleasant smell. She bit into the savory meat and pulled a tiny morsel of the bone with her teeth. She took another bite, this time pulling off a bigger piece.

"You don't have to eat the whole thing," David teased, but Lila's focus was elsewhere. She cast the wing aside to clap her hands and stomp her feet, as the red rider finally knocked the yellow one off his horse, prompting a swell of applause from everyone in their section.

WHEN LILA ENTERED Mrs. Martinez class on the first day of third grade, she was expecting her new teacher to resemble Miss Davis, who she missed a great deal. She was surprised to see a petite blonde woman who didn't look much older than her teenaged cousins, sitting behind the teacher's desk. She wore light-wash blue jeans and a floral blouse that hung loosely on her narrow shoulders. Lila immediately decided to dislike Mrs. Martinez, out of loyalty to Miss Davis, but her resolve was no match for her new teacher's charm.

"I've heard all about you." She smiled at Lila when she read out her name. "This year we'll be working on a special writing project, and I expect you to be my star." Mrs. Martinez excitement was infectious, and Lila found herself smiling back at her and nodding vigorously to show her enthusiasm.

"This year," Mrs. Martinez announced, "we'll be taking part in the annual writing competition. It's the first time our school will be starting from the third grade, and it's only because of all the wonderful work you all did with Miss Davis last year."

"We've never written a whole essay before," someone whined from the back row, after Mrs. Martinez explained the contest rules.

Several children nodded in agreement and exchanged worried looks.

"Don't worry. We have all year to work on our essays. You'll have loads of free time during class," she promised.

Lila couldn't wait to start the "special project" and her excitement only intensified when she realized elementary schools all over the country would be taking part.

"The best essay in every district will go on to the national level," Mrs. Martinez explained, "and the winner will be published in one of the national newspapers."

"The topic this year is something that has lately become very close to my heart." She turned and wrote on the board, each letter capitalized and stretched so the whole class could read it:

MY COMMUNITY

THE FIRST FEW months were spent figuring out what exactly a community was, and more importantly, what made it a community. Mrs. Martinez started them off simply, talking about her own experiences.

"I was born and raised in San Diego, part of the same community all my life. Recently I married a Mexican engineer, and now, suddenly, I find myself part of an entirely different community." She talked about the similarities and differences and sent them off to find out as much as they could about their own community. "Hopefully, by the end of the year we will have created a map of all the different communities in our area."

Lila had no trouble describing her community. The challenging part was explaining what made them a community. The entire class seemed as perplexed as Lila, so Mrs. Martinez sent them outside the classroom to find the answer.

That was when Lila heard the word "refugee" for the first time. Every person she asked said the same thing.

"We Palestinian refugees," great uncle Ibrahim answered her, "waiting go back our homeland."

"We are a community of refugees," Dr. Al-Masri told her. "Freeing Palestine is our life's mission. A group of us, including your uncles meet every week to discuss the situation. We go to demonstrations and are willing and waiting to fight for our homeland."

She even asked the Imam. "When we came here, our mosque was called Masjid Ali." He pointed to the sign above the entrance. "We changed it to Masjid Alkoutz, to remember Jerusalem every day of our lives."

"One day we all go back Palestine, Inshallah." Taata Maryam raised her eyes to the heavens. "I live in Jaffa in big house, right next the sea. Baba was fisherman. We have quiet, happy life. I marry cousin Muhammad, my uncle Said son. I know him from when we kids. He family have big store. Biggest butcher store in Jaffa. Have houses, shops. First Machmud born. After Ali. Suddenly war come and the Jews throw us out. We leave everything. We go Nablus for a time and then Amman. After two years we come here, in America. But we refugees here. All our lives we wait. We wait and we pray Allah take us home."

"We're all refugees," Sami shouted, banging his fist on the table, sending a piece of pita flying off his plate and onto the floor. "You're a refugee too!"

Lila had never thought of herself that way. She had been born in America and had never considered herself to be anything else. She asked more and more questions, realizing how little she knew. Great uncle Ibrahim told her how their family had been dispersed. He and his brother Muhammad, Lila's grandfather, managed to get their families into America, but their parents were left behind, living in Nablus in poverty until they died. Ibrahim and Muhammad never saw them again. Their brother Yussef died in Syria, while two other brothers found their way to Jordan and another to Saudia Arabia.

"My son Hamude and two of your uncles Khaled and Said also go there. We no see them near ten years."

"I barely remember Palestine, I was too young," Uncle Machmud told her, "but I remember the refugee camp near Nablus and then later in Amman. There were so many people and so much noise. I remember it was always either too hot or too cold. The clothes they gave us didn't fit, and I was hungry all the time."

Machmud sighed, thinking back. "Truth is," he smiled sadly, "mostly I remember running through the streets with a million other kids and coming home after dark."

It wasn't the first time Lila heard their stories, but it was the first time she realized they were a part of her own. Minna had tried to keep her away from the conflict, but now there was nothing she could do. Lila even tried to ask David, but he didn't want to talk about it.

"It's complicated," was all he would say. "You shouldn't worry your pretty little head about it."

He said he didn't want to waste the little time they had together. She saw him less often now, sometimes once a month, sometimes even less. When he did show up, he and Minna exchanged barely a word, and wouldn't even look at each other.

"IMAGINE," MRS. MARTINEZ told the class, "you're given a camera and have to take three pictures of places that are important to you and your community. You'll have to describe each place and why you chose it."

Lila and Jasmine set out on their bikes, Sami's old Nikon tucked safely in its padded carrying case in Jasmine's basket. They had decided to actually take the pictures, but couldn't stop arguing what to choose. The only place they agreed on was the masjid. To Lila, the masjid was an obvious choice, as was her uncle's Hooka Hall. These were the two main gathering places for the community. The masjid was, of course, its spiritual center and the Hooka Hall was the community's political center.

"The butcher shop's much more important and it's been here forever," Jasmine disagreed.

But it was her third choice that really irritated Lila.

"You can't choose your mother's beauty salon, it has to be important to the community." Lila dismissed the idea scornfully, but Jasmine insisted.

"I think it's the most important place for women. They don't go to the masjid like the men. The salon is where they can meet and talk between themselves."

Lila had never thought of it that way, but she still wasn't going to choose it.

"And anyway, she said it should be personal." Jasmine winked at her. "So I choose my mother."

The girls rode up and down Palm Street, but Lila still couldn't decide on her third photograph. "I think I want to take a picture of the whole street," she joked, but Jasmine wasn't amused.

"Choose already," she snapped, irritated by Lila's indecision. "It's not so important, you already have two, just choose one more."

Lila considered the butcher shop, but decided against it. She considered each storefront, feeling none the right choice. They were both tired and she was losing her resolve. She was about to choose at random, when her third choice finally revealed itself.

"That's it!" she shouted excitedly, jumping off her bike in front of Nablus Sweets and grabbing for the camera.

"Nablus Sweets?" Jasmine rolled her eyes, but Lila was already running through the store.

"Come, Lila, have some knafe, fresh from oven," Auntie Lubna beckoned, handing her a plate of steaming filo flakes stuffed with sweet goat's cheese, before she could respond.

"See," Lila told Jasmine in between bites, "this is why I chose them."

Auntie Lubna and Auntie Aysha were sisters whose family once owned a sweet shop in Nablus, famous for its knafe.

Sami brought a dish every Friday afternoon, and all the brothers would come and reminisce, talking of the "homeland." Lila would place the warm syrupy heaven on her tongue, her nose filling up with the delicate fragrances of orange blossom and rosewater, her mind conjuring up pictures of the Palestine they were describing.

"One day, one day, you go," Taata would say, as if she could see the images in Lila's mind. "You see!" She'd grab Lila's face, her soft crooked fingers squeezing into the child's cheekbones before leaning over to plant a kiss on her mouth.

CHOOSING THE PICTURES, Lila's class quickly realized, was the easiest part of the assignment. Now the hard work began. They spent weeks on each picture, learning how to write openings and closings. Mrs. Martinez assigned a whole page on each one, but most of the kids found it too difficult. Filling three whole pages with writing—one for each photo—seemed like an insurmountable task. Not for Lila though. She was asking and interviewing anyone who was willing, laboriously recording their words in her notebook. Every evening, she reviewed the new material, putting a star next to the very best things.

Friday was Lila's favorite day of the week. School ended earlier and all they had to do was write and share. Lila loved hearing the other kids.

She knew Little Ghaza was just one community, but she had no idea how many communities could exist in one place. She asked lots of questions, eager to learn as much as she could about their lives and customs. The best presentations had the pictures printed out so they could be passed around the room. Lila and Jasmine's were too large to pass around, thanks to Palm Street Printer's.

"Even the kids in back will see every detail," Cousin Akram assured the girls. "All you need to do is hang them on the board."

THE FINAL ESSAY had to be turned in at the end of March, just before Easter, which coincided that year with the end of Ramadan. Jasmine finished hers quickly; she was ready to put the whole project behind her.

"I'm not going to win anyway." She shrugged at Lila. "Not with you as my competition."

Lila wrote relentlessly, toiling over every word. Throughout the month of Ramadan she came up for air only when Taata needed her help in the kitchen, only to rush back to her notebook as soon as she was no longer needed.

"What you writing all time?" Taata chided her, although both knew she was her biggest fan. She'd silence everyone in the vicinity whenever Lila read aloud, listening to every word, tears filling the creases around her smiling lips and disappearing at the edges of her hijab.

Lila wrote and rewrote her essay, but no matter how many drafts she completed, she still wasn't satisfied. "It's not exactly how it should be," a voice in her head kept insisting.

"Maybe you should make it more personal. It's your community after all. Try putting yourself into the essay," Mrs. Martinez suggested.

"No problem," Lila decided. "I'll write another sentence or two for each photo, something personal about each place, to explain why I chose them."

She described going to the mosque with her uncles and playing outside while they prayed. The Hooka Hall section already mentioned her Uncle Sami, so she had nothing much to add. Nablus Sweets proved more difficult. She couldn't think what else to say.

"Their knafe," she finally wrote, "is my personal favorite, made just like it was in the homeland."

"I really didn't think you could do better," Mrs. Martinez gushed, beside herself. "Now all it needs is a title."

EVERYONE BUT LILA was thrilled when "My Refugee Community" won second-in-district. She was so disappointed it wouldn't move on to the national level after she'd worked so hard, she didn't even want to go to the ceremony.

"I promise, you'll never regret claiming your prize in person." Mrs. Martinez tried to change her mind, but it was Taata Maryam's mortified look that finally convinced her.

The whole family came, the night of the ceremony, filling the entire second row of the auditorium. Mrs. Martinez was so proud, she strutted around like a peacock.

"Congratulations." The principal shook her hand vigorously before giving her a notebook with "JOURNAL" engraved on the leather-bound cover.

"May you write wisely and beautifully." He shook her hand again and moved on to announce first place.

By the time the ceremony ended, Lila was already imagining the next year's contest. "A sixth grader might have come in first this year, but next year it will be a fourth grader." She smiled to herself.

She realized she was the last person still seated on stage when a dark-haired man with thick glasses tapped her on the shoulder, shaking her from her fantasy. He was "a journalist from the most popular newspaper in San Diego," and he wanted her second place essay to be published in the Sunday paper. Her heart wrenching story of the Palestinian refugee community trying to keep up with their traditions, while dreaming of their homeland, told from the eye of a young refugee girl, had caught his heart.

"I'll have to speak to your parents, but we want your name and picture in there too."

THE FOLLOWING SUNDAY she was sitting restlessly on the Hooka Hall stairs, waiting for the paperboy, listening for the whirring of his bike and the thud, thud of the papers hitting the concrete. He saw her and aimed the paper straight at her. Lila jumped up and caught it in mid-air. She ran inside, threw herself on the floor, and leafed through it quickly.

"It's not here," she told Taata miserably. "I don't think they're going to publish my essay after all."

"Must patient." Taata tried to console her. "I sure it come next week."

On the last Sunday of May, two days before Eid el Adha, the "Feast of the Sacrifice," Sami came running into Taata's kitchen, holding an armload of papers, yelling, "It's here, its here."

Lila and Jasmine were in the kitchen, rolling dough with Taata.

"Look, Lila, page two." Sami opened one of the papers and waved it at her.

For a moment, she didn't recognize her own face inside the frame. Small, rebellious wisps of sandy brown hair had escaped the confines of the black fabric covering her head, fanning her tanned temples and accentuating the deep blue of her eyes.

The journalist suggested she wear something "authentic" for the photograph, and, in a matter of hours, all the aunties had brought their old embroidered dresses for her to choose from. Lila tried on several, but felt more and more uncomfortable.

"It's too much," she complained miserably to Taata. "I don't feel authentic in these at all."

"Maybe just something to cover her head?" Minna suggested.

"Come with me." Taata took Lila to her bedroom. "I have idea."

She climbed on a chair and pulled down a box hidden in the back of a high shelf in her cupboard.

"It my favorite."

The shawl was wrapped inside layers of soft paper, so Lila knew it was precious.

"My Taata make for me when I child. He sew everything with hand." Taata placed it around Lila's neck, showing her how to wrap it around her head and shoulders. The traditional black fabric had taken on a dark greyish hew, but the embroidered flowers remained unchanged, still saturated in color and shining brightly, their threads a semi metallic red, yellow, and blue.

Lila's ode to Little Ghaza was all anyone talked about. When Taata sent her out on an errand, she was greeted with cries of "mabrouk!" and "al hamdoulillah!" Some of the store owners had even pinned copies of the article to their store windows, and they called out to her when she went by, showing her off to their customers. At lunch time, Sami arrived with the Imam.

"I want Lila to read her essay out loud for the whole community," he announced, inviting Lila to be one of the speakers at the Eid Al-Adha feast.

"Only men speak at the Hooka Hall." Jasmine couldn't get over it. "For women it's haram. And children?"

"We've never had a child give a speech before." The Imam nodded.

Lila felt so honored.

AT FOUR, SHE stood on the curb, almost hopping from foot to foot with anticipation. David was coming for an "unscheduled visit."

"It'll be a short one," he had told her over the phone. "I really need to talk to you." He wouldn't tell her anything more and nor would Minna.

"Daddy has something important to tell you," was all she would say.

"Who's going first?" David asked after they ordered. He had taken her to the new ice cream parlor on Riverside Street, right at the other side of Laurel Valley.

"Me, me!" Lila yelled, pulling out the folded newspaper from her bag and placing the article in front of her father. David took his time reading, pausing to look at his daughter for a few seconds before turning back to the article.

"Ah . . . Tiger Lily." He sighed when he finished reading. He took off his glasses and folded the paper neatly, then sat silently for a while. Lila was silent too. This was not at all the reaction she had expected. When he began to talk, his voice was low and he looked so sad, the saddest Lila had ever seen him.

"I have to go back to Israel." He took her hand. He told her that his mother was dying, and he didn't know when he'd be back.

"When will I see you again?" Lila began to cry, but David just shrugged unhappily.

"How can you go back there?" She waved the article in his face.

"Things are never the way they seem, Tiger Lily," he shook his head, "and there are always two sides to every story, you know that. Maybe I made a mistake by not telling you our side, but I wanted to protect you. I thought you were too young. I still do, but it seems I'll have to tell you some of it, at least. I owe you that. We don't have to go into all the gory details."

Lila had no idea what he was talking about, but she didn't say a thing, just sat there quietly, listening as his terrible story unfolded. David told her about the Second World War and a man called Hitler and something called "the final solution." Then he told her about her grandparents and the death camps. He didn't tell her everything, but he told her enough.

"My mother was fourteen when she was taken to the camps and separated from her family. She was the second oldest of eight children and she never saw any of them again. Her little sister, Haya, was one year old when she last saw her, clinging to their mother at the train station. None of them survived. When she returned to her little village in Transylvania, there was a Romanian family living in their house."

David paused for a moment, sighing deeply.

"My father came from Germany and he too lost all of his family. It took him two years to get over the tuberculosis he had brought back from the camps and he never really recovered. That's why the state of Israel exists, Tiger Lily. It was established after the war as a refuge for the Jews who had nowhere else to go. No one wanted us. We were always hated and persecuted everywhere else."

Lila didn't understand everything he said, but she was so shocked by what she did, she didn't even ask him any questions, just stared at her untouched sundae, watching as the ice cream slowly melted, becoming a puddle of dirty brown and white.

He told her his parents had met on a kibbutz in the North of Israel. His father was always sickly and died when David was eight. That's when they moved to a small apartment in Tel Aviv. That's also when his mother's mental health began to deteriorate.

"She became more and more religious and more and more paranoid, afraid to let us out of her sight. There was no one to help us, so my sister had to take charge. She was only six years older than me, but she had to become our mother's mother, as well as mine."

"They still live together in that ancient apartment on the fourth floor, without an elevator." David smiled at Lila, hoping for one in return.

"But why do you have to stay there? Why can't you just go for a visit like last time? What if you never come back?" Lila panicked, her heart beating loudly in her ears, the muscles around her chest tightening.

"My sister's been taking care of her all of her life. It's too much for her on her own now. I have to go help. I'll call all the time and come back as soon as I can," David promised.

LILA GOT UP early on the morning of Eid el Adha and spent the day helping Taata make Ma'amul. She rolled the pastry into little balls, filled them with smaller balls of crushed dates, and carefully closed them, crafting them into little crescents and decorating them with the tip of her fork. Usually when she and Jasmine helped Taata, they competed with each other, each creating different, complex and elaborate shapes, but this time Lila's thoughts were elsewhere. She barely noticed what she, herself was doing, and her oddly sized, misshapen cookies were far from pretty.

"Why long face?" Taata tried to lift Lila's spirits. "Today greatest holiday of all."

But Lila was in no mood for celebration. She couldn't stop thinking of what David had told her. She was a little angry at him for not telling her sooner, but also understood what he had meant when he said it was complicated. Every time she thought of him, she saw his face before he left. They had both cried when they said goodbye.

"Something happen?" Taata kept asking her why she was so quiet, but Lila felt she couldn't talk to her about it. Minna tried to get her to open up, but Lila was angrier than ever.

"She's the last person in the world I want to talk to." She blamed her mother for everything. She didn't feel like going to the masjid with Jasmine and her uncles, like she always did, but it was the only way she could avoid her mother and Taata. They just wouldn't leave her alone, questioning her relentlessly, driving her inward more and more.

At the mosque she was treated like a celebrity, the men lining up to shake her hand, their children kissing both her cheeks. Lila was overwhelmed, but try as she might to move aside, they just wouldn't let her. Slowly, everyone found their way inside.

"Allahu akbar, Allahu akbar," the men chanted.

"La ilaha illa Allah," (there is no god but Allah) Lila chanted silently in her head.

"Wallahu akbar, Allahu akbar," the voices repeated.

"Walillahi l-hamdu" (and to Allah goes all praise).

As the prayers began, the kids gathered outside, in the far side of the square. Lila started to follow them, her mind still repeating the takbir. "Allahu akbar," it shouted silently, as the round of dodge ball began. She dodged the first ball, but the voices were getting louder and she couldn't concentrate.

"Move, move," she heard Jasmine shout, just as the ball hit her squarely in the chest.

"I'm fine," she wheezed, holding back her tears. It really hurt, but it was the perfect excuse to go back home. As the masjid filled, she had felt more and more uncomfortable. Everyone, she realized, would be at the Hooka Hall later, listening to her. Her stomach churned at the thought of her essay, reminding her of her father's face when he read it. But the voices were gone. Everything was gone. Her mind was an empty room.

"It's just stage fright." Minna tried to calm her down. "It'll pass once you start speaking."

"I'll stand in the first row, right in front of you," Sami promised. "Don't look at the audience, look at me and talk to me as if I'm the only one there."

But it was more than stage fright, Lila realized the moment she entered the Hooka Hall and saw her enlarged image looking down at her from the wall, Palestinian flags hanging at its sides. Her article had also been enlarged and put in a gold frame and she felt more and more uncomfortable, almost as though she wanted to crawl out of her own skin. The more she looked at it, the more she knew there was something wrong with the picture, although she had no idea what it was. Her head pounded and her stomach churned.

After the food was cleared away, the Imam got up to speak. This was usually the signal for the children to make themselves scarce, but this time none of them moved from their seats. They were all waiting to hear Lila.

The Imam took his time blessing the community and updating them with all the news. He reminded them why they were there, telling the story of the prophet Ibrahim and his son, Ishmael. The Imam told the story in great detail, but also so simply and dramatically, that even the children were enthralled, even though they'd heard him tell it many times before.

Just as her urge to escape started to subside, the pink balloon appeared beside her. Lila couldn't resist climbing in and soon floated off, rising higher than even the Imam's voice could travel. She looked down at all the coconuts, each one exactly the same as its neighbor. Lila squinted, her eyes searching the sea for even the tiniest ripple. She recognized herself right away. She was the only blue-eyed coconut in a sea of black-eyed ones.

"Theirs is a story of great sacrifice," the Imam's voice thundered. "A father willing to sacrifice his son."

Lila thought about her father and the balloon came crashing down. He had only left two days before, but she missed him already. She felt awful about the way they had parted. She kept seeing his face as he read the article. He hadn't said a thing, but she had felt so guilty. Suddenly she knew what had been bothering her.

"In our story," she started to cry silently, "it was the other way around. It was the child who sacrificed her father."

"Lila . . . Lila." The Imam's voice broke her reverie. Everyone was looking at her, smiling and applauding. Lila rubbed her eyes as she walked slowly toward the podium, pulling Taata's scarf tightly over her head and shoulders, wishing the pink balloon would come to take her. Her hands were shaking and she had never felt so self-conscious in all her life.

"A round of applause for Lila," the Imam shouted. "You've brought so much pride to our community." He turned to her and leaned to kiss both her cheeks.

Lila looked for Sami in the audience, but the stage light blocked her view. Blurry faces danced at the light's edges and she could barely make out the letters on her page. Worst of all, her mind was blank.

"MY REFUGEE . . . COMMUNITY," Lila started, her voice shaking.

"Louder," someone shouted from the back.

"My refugee community," Lila repeated, trying to control her voice.

"Pssst," someone was calling her from the crowd, but she couldn't see who it was.

"It's me, Sami." He was standing right in front of her, just as he had promised.

Lila pulled her shoulders back and stared straight at his blur until she could make out his features.

"Dear uncle Sami," she whispered under her breath. "My refugee community." She summoned up all her strength. "I am a Palestinian refugee, part of a community of refugees, living in Laurel Valley, California.

A refugee is someone who had to leave everything behind to survive. Refugees can find new homes across the world, but they are always waiting to go back to where they came from."

Lila took a breath as applause filled the hall. She tried to focus on her Uncle Sami, but her father's face stared back at her wherever she looked. She forced herself to carry on, her stomach churning and her skin on fire. The audience laughed when she mentioned "Little Ghaza" and erupted in cheers when she ended her essay with her version of Taata's famous saying: "One day, Inshallah, we will return to our homeland."

Lila slipped away before the next speaker reached the podium, afraid the dam holding back her tears would break before she reached her room. For once, she was glad it was hidden in the basement. No one, she was sure, would be going down there. As she locked the door behind her, just in case, she caught her image in the mirror and froze, looking at herself as if she were a stranger. The girl in the scarf looked exactly like her, but was also completely different. She moved closer to the mirror, staring at herself. Lila looked back at her. Now she definitely knew there was something wrong with the picture. She had worked so hard, writing and rewriting, trying to be as accurate as she could, only to end up creating someone she wasn't. Lila began to cry. She realized she had been so focused on fitting in, on impressing everyone and being a part of the community, that she had betrayed her father and totally forgotten herself. She grabbed the leather-bound journal she had been so proud of and shoved it under the bed, vowing never to write again.

"WOULD YOU DO me the honor of accompanying me to the father-daughter picnic this coming Sunday?" Sami knelt on one knee in front of Lila, trying to lift her spirits.

"You're not my father." Lila shook her head. It was the first time she would be spending father's day without David.

"They always made such a big deal out of it," Minna told her brother, who was happy to be her substitute. Lila was, after all, the closest he had to a daughter and he would jump through fire to put a smile on her face.

"And you're not technically my daughter," Sami took her hands in his, "but you're the only daughter I got."

Lila hugged Sami, but still, she refused to go.

"Would you like someone else to take you?" Minna offered, after Sami left, but Lila just shook her head.

"You can go with Jasmine and Uncle Ali." Minna wouldn't let it go. "I'm sure they'd love to take you."

"I'm not going to the stupid picnic," Lila finally yelled at her. "It's none of your business anyway. Just leave me alone."

That became her mantra, whenever Minna tried to talk to her. Minna noticed other changes, too. Lila seemed quieter, keeping more to herself. She didn't go out as much as she used to, sometimes spending entire days on her own, reading in the basement. She wouldn't go to the mosque with her uncles anymore, making excuse after excuse, until Minna stopped asking.

"It's just a phase," Nadia tried to reassure her.

"She'll grow out of it. Jasmine's also going through something. She's been driving me crazy. I wish this summer would end," she groaned. "At least Lila spends her time reading, which is much more than I can say about my daughter."

"Leave the child alone," Taata told her. "She good girl. She be fine."

So Minna left her alone. She didn't really have the time to worry about her, she was so pre-occupied, studying and working intermittently. Once she finished these courses, she could finally graduate and start law school come fall, but summer was the busiest time in the Hooka Hall and she was exhausted. During summer the Hooka Hall became the men's refuge, the place they escaped to when their homes filled with disgruntled wives and noisy children. Sami always joked about it.

"Wife give you a time-out?" was Uncle Sami's favorite greeting, and when someone left early he'd mockingly ask, "Time-out over?"

"We need more help," Minna kept telling Sami, even though her cousin Selma, Uncle Ibrahim's youngest daughter, worked with them every night.

"You're right," Sami agreed with her each time, but "more help" never arrived.

"THERE'LL BE NO competitions this year, so we're going to go back to journaling," Mrs. Martinez announced at the beginning of fourth grade.

"Do we have to?" Lila whined, prompting a furrowed brow from Mrs. Martinez. "We did it already. I really don't feel like doing it again."

Mrs. Martinez was so disappointed. "It's merely a phase," she said to herself, doing whatever she could think of to revive Lila's enthusiasm. But whatever she tried, she just couldn't seem to get the spark back in Lila's eye. She simply wasn't interested. When her disappointment turned into frustration, she called for Minna.

"It's not that she's falling behind." Mrs. Martinez tried to reassure a worried Minna. "She's one of my brightest students. It's something more general. If it were one of the other kids, I probably wouldn't have noticed. She doesn't act out and she does what she's supposed to, but it's as if she's going through the motions, as if nothing interests her anymore. She used to be so full of excitement, of enthusiasm. I haven't seen that side of Lila this year. Especially her writing." She shook her head. "That's a real problem. She's such a gifted writer, but she refuses to do any writing at all."

Mrs. Martinez paused, drawing in a deep breath. "I guess I'm calling to ask if something happened?"

Minna took a deep breath. "Her father left the country a few months ago and she's taken it very badly. The truth is, I can't get through to her, either."

"Perhaps she just needs some time to adjust," Mrs. Martinez suggested. "I can cut her some slack. But writing's a school requirement. If she doesn't start journaling again, she might be kept back."

"YOU SAID YOU were keeping your promise and everything was fine at school." Minna raised her voice, finally losing her patience with Lila, when Mrs. Martinez asked to meet with her a few weeks later.

"I've been doing everything she assigns," Lila yelled back. "I do all my homework. I write a paragraph in my journal every single day. I don't know what the hell she wants from me."

"Don't swear," Minna told her crossly. She had been sure that Lila had calmed down and that everything was back to normal at the school.

"She is writing something every day," Mrs. Martinez told Minna, "but it's not real writing, if you know what I mean, at least not the kind I expect from Lila."

Minna didn't really know what she meant, so Mrs. Martinez read out some examples. Each entry was made up of four or five short sentences and although they were always well written and grammatically correct, they were factual and boring, nothing at all like Lila's writing in the past.

"But that's not really the worrying part." Mrs. Martinez placed Lila's open journal between them on the desk. "See for yourself."

"It doesn't even look like English." Minna turned the page. The next entry was equally alarming.

"Like a five year old," she muttered to herself. "And a backward one at that." It pained her to see the crooked, agonized letters appearing once again.

"She's clearly regressing." Mrs. Martinez cut into her thoughts crisply. "I think we've given her enough time."

LILA THOUGHT MRS. Dawson was nice enough. She was young and wore short sleeveless shirts and tight jeans and sat on the floor next to her. They had an appointment every Tuesday at ten.

"At least it's instead of writing class," Lila told Jasmine. "Anything's better than that!"

She couldn't see the point of it, though, getting more and more frustrated. Stupid word games. Pick-up-sticks. Painting. There was nothing Lila hated more than that. She couldn't draw a line to save her life, but Mrs. Dawson didn't care. Lila could either go back to class and write, or she could keep up the arts and crafts, one morning a week. Lila chose the latter, finding herself, week after week, applying charcoal to paper or creating misshapen voodoo dolls from the scrap chest's bottomless selection of twigs and recycled plastic, that try as she might, never really took form or came to life.

"Why do I have to go?" Lila usually started her weekly protest on Monday evening.

"Mrs. Dawson is only there to help you," Minna always replied, knowing that no response would satisfy Lila.

"There's nothing wrong with me." Lila would get mad. "She keeps trying to make me tell her things, but I have nothing to say."

Mrs. Dawson didn't seem to be making any headway, and Lila was angrier and more detached than ever. At school, she kept to herself, preferring to read at her desk instead of playing outside with her friends. She stayed away from the masjid, refusing to pray or take part in anything that even smelled faintly of religion.

"He no go out enough," Taata complained. "And he cheeky. Suddenly he no understand what I say. I talk and he say: What? No Arabic. I no understand."

As the outside world became more difficult for Lila to negotiate, she found herself going back to her old world, finding solace in all the practices she learned to love in Venice.

"Take a deep breath," she coached herself through a body scan meditation. "Relax your arms. Relax your feet, down, down to your toes . . ."

When she finished, the pink balloon would be waiting at her side.

"Take me away, pink balloon," she'd say as she climbed in, and the pink balloon would rise gently, drifting higher and higher, above the treetops, floating silently over the streets and highways.

"There," she would tell it, pointing to a spot on the beach, just before the promenade. She loved the sound of the waves, the sand squishing beneath her toes. She'd do cartwheels on the hot sand, splash about in the shallows, or roam through the stores, stuffing herself with tacos and falafel, reading all the familiar signs. Sometimes she insisted the balloon take her to the old house, even though she knew she wouldn't find the home she missed so much. Even in the pink balloon, the house remained silent and empty, her father, Geeta and Gyandip and all the other friends that had passed through it, just a fading, lifeless memory.

And then, one night, the pink balloon took on a life of its own, carrying Lila away, further than ever before, bypassing Venice and even Malibu, flying over dense forests and mountains before setting her down gently on the most beautiful beach she had ever seen. There was no one around for miles, just blue waves breaking gently over sand so white, it could be mistaken for sugar. She didn't know where she was, yet the beach felt familiar and comforting. The murmur of the waves. The faint tangy odor. The ocean spray coating the breeze. Lila lay down and closed her eyes, feeling her body sink into the sand, its fine grains enveloping her in their warmth, like a cocoon, until she was ready to fly again.

The next night the pink balloon let her down a little further, besides a little half moon bay. High, white cliffs sheltered it from the wind, leaving its calm waters gleaming and almost motionless. She walked along the entire shore, collecting seashells and skipping in the foam at the bay's edge. It was love at first flight, and she came back in the pink balloon again and again, until she had explored it's every nook and cranny.

"My place," she'd tell the balloon whenever she was upset or needed a time-out, and it would rise up and take her there, away from the anger and confusion that often brewed inside her.

"I'M NOT GOING to see Mrs. Dawson anymore," Lila told her mother. "I don't need her."

"It's almost the end of the year, Lila, let's wait and see what she says." Minna dreaded the thought of another argument with her daughter. Lately, it seemed to Minna like they were living in different worlds, and she couldn't enter Lila's without throwing her into a rage.

"If I keep going there, I really will go crazy." Lila couldn't take it anymore. "If I have to draw another stupid . . ." She clenched her teeth, remembering Mrs. Dawson's last drawing assignment.

"OK, OK, I'll speak to Mrs. Dawson." Minna finally reached her breaking point, preferring to give in than engage with her daughter in yet another shouting match. "Before Tuesday, I promise."

RAMADAN WAS EARLY the next year, beginning in the middle of winter. "It good first time fast." Taata Maryam encouraged the girls, explaining that the cold weather made it much easier. They had both turned ten the previous summer and were expected to begin to pray and worship like the adults. Jasmine even went to a special class at the mosque, but Lila refused to participate.

"Leave her be," the Imam told Minna. "She's a good girl. She'll come around."

On the second Friday of the holy month, Lila and Jasmine rose early to help Minna and Taata roll tray after tray of ma'amuls. As Minna stood up to pull the first tray out of the oven, her vision became blurry and her head felt like it was in a washing machine. Her legs went numb, and she collapsed back into her chair.

"Drink," Taata poured her a glass of cold water.

"It's nothing." Minna tried to push her hand away. "I just need to sit a second."

"Drink," Taata insisted, "maybe better eat something. It not first time I see you feel bad."

Minna drank the water but declined to eat. Taata forced her to break her fast a few hours later.

"Eat, Mashs'Alla," she said as she placed a plate of food in front of her daughter. Minna didn't have much of an appetite, but felt too weak to argue.

"Maybe go see doctor," Taata suggested when Minna's color didn't return, but Minna was sure she was just a little weak from the fast.

"Take her straight to the hospital," Dr. Al-Masri told Sami, in the early hours of the morning of Eid el Fitr. He had come rushing over when Minna hadn't been able to get out of bed, his hair all disheveled and his moustache standing on end. "To the new one, the one in Chula Vista. I know it's far, but it's brand new. All the best doctors. I know some people there. I'll give them a call, they'll be expecting you."

"YOUR MOM'S AWAKE and doing real well," Sami told Lila when he returned from the hospital. "The doctors say she'll be fine and Taata Maryam's staying with her just in case."

"We'll go visit her tomorrow," Auntie Nadia promised, sending Lila back to Jasmine's room.

"Surgery went well," he told Nadia, once Lila was out of earshot. "The growth was larger than expected, but they said they got it all out."

Lila was relieved, but still she tossed and turned, unable to fall asleep. Sami hadn't told her much, but she had heard them whispering. The more they didn't say the more worried she became. She'd heard the words "breast cancer" and "violent strain" but every time she asked they waved her away.

"He be fine, inshallah," was all Taata would say.

"It's just a small operation," Minna had told her, "nothing to worry about."

But even the pink balloon couldn't calm her mind, which went on buzzing, bombarding her with a million thoughts a minute. She kept seeing her mother's face, just before they wheeled her away, thin and frail, her skin so white it was almost transparent, her large brown eyes sunken and lifeless. They had barely had time together, the entire family had come to visit, to give her their blessing.

LILA STOOD OUTSIDE her mother's room, too scared to go in. She didn't know what to expect, it had all happened so fast. One moment Minna had been fine and the next she was in the hospital.

"Lila?" she heard her mother call out.

She took a deep breath and marched in. The room was cold and the bright fluorescent lights turned everyone's skin ghost white.

"Careful, sweetie, can't hug. Come give me a kiss." Minna held out her hand, smiling at Lila.

She looked almost herself, her hair plaited behind her back, her lips shaded a light pink. Lila smiled back, grabbing hold of her mother's hand. When she leaned over to kiss her, Minna flinched, and Lila backed away, her face twisted with guilt.

"I'm fine, it's just a little sore." Minna smiled weakly, but Lila could see that every little movement was laborious and caused her pain.

"YOUR MOM'S DOING so well, they've decided to release her early," Sami told Lila.

She was coming home the very next day, two days before they were expecting her. Lila was overjoyed, suddenly filled with energy by the good news. She and Jasmine cleaned the house, did the laundry, and made Minna's bed with fresh linens. Then they took some of Lila's holiday money to buy the pink and white flowers that were Minna's favorites and some baklava at Nablus Sweets.

"Take for Mommy." Auntie Aysha gave her a small box of chocolate halva she had just prepared.

"I come later, when knafe ready," Auntie Lubna promised. "Fresh knafe bring back your mama's appetite, you see."

Lila wasn't the same girl when Minna returned. Each day, as soon as school ended, she would come running home. She tried to spend as much time as she could with her mother, doing whatever she could for her. It wasn't only that she was sorry for her, mainly it was because she felt so guilty. She had treated her mother so badly, blaming her for everything.

Once a week, when Minna went to the hospital for treatment, Lila stayed with her aunt Nadia. Before they went to sleep, Nadia and Jasmine invited her to pray with them.

"We don't pray like in the masjid." Nadia laughed, noticing Lila's resistance. "Allah also hears our hearts. We talk to him every night. We tell him what troubles us and we ask for his help."

"I've never prayed before," Lila admitted sheepishly, but Nadia told her that Allah didn't mind. "I'm sure he'll listen to your prayer anyway."

So Lila began to pray, at first only with her aunt and cousin, but later also on her own. She wasn't sure exactly who she was praying to or if it would help, but it gave her something to do and it was comforting. As time passed, she found herself talking to Allah, begging and bargaining, ready to promise him anything.

"Please Allah," she'd plead, "if you're really there. I'll do whatever you want me to do. Just make my mother better."

And Allah seemed to be listening. Minna was recuperating, gradually getting stronger and everyone said she looked so much better. She regained her appetite and started taking long walks with Lila. Often, when they were still out at sunset, Minna would lead them toward the mosque. They didn't go in, just sat outside in the square, listening to the men pray.

ON THE DAY before Minna's second surgery the entire family went to evening prayers, even the women. The Imam had announced a special healing Du'a. Lila watched as the masjid filled with people, overwhelmed by the thought that they were all there for her mother. She had never seen so many people at the masjid, even for the holy days. There were even people praying in the square outside the packed prayer hall. Taata took Lila by the hand and pulled her through the crowd. The little section in back was crowded, but the women immediately made a place for them.

"Allahu akbar." The Imam's call brought everyone to their feet. The prayer began and Lila found herself going through the motions, sitting, standing, bowing, kneeling, and prostrating herself, pulled along by the crowd. For the first time in days she felt her mind quiet down, lulled by the singsong voices.

"Allahu Akbar." The congregation rose to their knees.

"Allahu Akbar," Lila called out again, before placing her forehead on the floor, listening as "Subhannarabb'iy-al-A'la" resounded three times throughout the mosque.

She waited until everyone had left before approaching the Imam.

"We pray for your mother, she will be fine, Inshallah." He bent down to kiss her cheeks, but stopped when he noticed how disturbed she looked. "What's wrong, Lila?"

"I need you to convert me," she told him.

"What are you talking about?" The Imam looked at her in surprise. "Your mother's a Muslim. You were born a Muslim."

"But I haven't been a good Muslim," Lila began to cry. "I don't pray like I'm supposed to and I've lied to everyone, pretending to be something I'm not. Please, please let me take the oath."

The Imam looked at her questioningly, not sure exactly what she wanted from him.

"Like Fadi's wife and child, remember, you converted them."

"You don't need to pledge the Shahada." The Iman looked down at her kindly. "That's only for people who were born a different religion."

"But what if it's all my fault? What if Allah is punishing me for doubting him?"

"Ah, Habibti." He sighed. "You have nothing to worry about. Allahu Akbar. He knows everything. He sees into our hearts. He's looked into yours."

"But there has to be something I can do," Lila insisted, her voice cracking, as the tears gushed from her eyes. "I have to do something."

"Pray to Allah, Lila." The Imam ruffled her hair. "Pray and do good deeds. Allah is merciful, you'll see."

SAMI BROUGHT MINNA home the day before Eid el Adha. He carried her down the stairs and showed Lila how to fold the wheelchair and stack it besides her bicycle.

"It's just for outside," he told Lila when he saw her face. "Till she gets back on her feet."

He offered to stay and help, but Lila would have none of it. She would take care of all her mother's needs. She had been "on her best behavior" the whole time Minna was gone, helping Taata and her aunts or volunteering at the masjid and at the Hooka hall. The day before she had even gone from door to door with her uncles Machmud and Ali, handing out meat parcels to the needy, something she'd never agreed to do before.

Minna was quieter than usual, but she smiled a lot and didn't seem in pain. Taata and all the aunties stopped their preparations and came by to see how she was doing, bringing piles of ma'amul and baklava. Lila and Jasmine stuffed themselves, and even Minna couldn't resist a few bites when Auntie Lubna came in with a steaming hot tray of her special holiday knafe.

"Eat, eat." Taata shook her head and clucked her teeth. "Look her," she kept repeating. "Thin like leaf."

After her nap, Sami carried Minna upstairs and Lila wheeled her to the mosque.

"Don't need go masjid." Taata tried to convince her, but Minna insisted.

"You're the one who taught me it's the holiest eid." Minna smiled at Taata, making her blush.

Lila put the chair in the corner, right against the wall, and sat down beside it. They were the only women in attendance, but a row of children sheltered them from the men. When the prayer began, Minna rested her head back and closed her eyes.

"Stay with me?" She offered her hand to Lila.

Lila took her mother's hand and recited the prayer silently. Slowly the world outside of her disappeared until all that remained was a distant chanting and the swishing and thudding of the men's bodies as they kneeled and prostrated. Gentle veils, like cloud strands enveloped her, cradling her body, creating a deep sense of quiet. She felt as if she were floating, becoming herself a part of the prayer. "Just like in the pink balloon," Lila realized, when she thought about it later.

THE NEXT MORNING, Sami took Minna to the hospital while Lila was still asleep.

"Nothing happened." Sami tried to calm Lila, who was waiting for him outside when he came back.

"She was supposed to go back. She just came home for the holiday."

"What are you talking about?" Lila yelled at her uncle. "She's so much better. You said so yourself."

"She's still really sick," he took Lila's hands in his, "you can see that. She had to go back."

Lila wasn't allowed to see her mother for the first few days.

"Why won't you take me? Why can you and Taata go and I can't?" She knew they weren't telling her everything.

"The doctors said you can visit on Sunday," Sami promised. "For Mother's Day."

LILA PLACED THE flowers on the side table. Auntie Heeba had cut the long green stems and tied the yellow roses into a small bouquet, just as she had asked, but Minna barely glanced at them.

"She's taken a turn for the worst," Sami tried to warn her, but nothing could have prepared her for what she found. Minna was so white and frail, she almost disappeared into the sheet. A small plastic tube pumped oxygen into her nose, and her chest seemed to tremble with effort for every breath. Lila tiptoed in, trying not to disturb her.

Minna shifted her head in her direction and moved her hand slightly, beckoning her to come closer. Lila sat down on the bed and took her mother's hand in hers. She was so scared, her knees were shaking. She tried to talk to her, but Minna didn't answer. She pressed her hand from time to time and tried to smile at her, but Lila could see that every movement caused her pain. After a while she slipped out of consciousness, moaning and groaning in her sleep. Lila waited desperately for her to wake up, pleading and bargaining with Allah as the hours passed, but Minna remained asleep.

"We have to go, it's getting late," Sami eventually said, struggling to keep his tears from falling in front of her.

"Just a little longer," Lila begged, sure her mother would open her eyes any moment. Finally she had no choice. Visiting hours had long been over and the nurse asked them to leave for the third time. She had to give Minna her nightly medication. Lila kissed her mother's cheek, but it wasn't Minna who was lying there. She barely recognized the emaciated form beneath the blanket, and the chill of her cheek seemed to stay on Lila's lips long after she left the room.

"CAN YOU LET me off at the masjid?" Lila asked Sami once they left the hospital. "I have to talk to the Imam."

"I think it'll be too late by the time we get home," Sami answered, but promised to stop there, when he saw how determined she was. Lila was desperate. She had tried everything she could think of, but still Allah wouldn't listen. When they got there, the square was empty and the mosque stood dark and deserted. Lila asked Sami to stop while she ran to check, just in case, but even though she banged and banged at the door, nobody answered.

When they got home, Taata Maryam was waiting outside.

"I'm really tired. I think I'll go straight up to Auntie Nadia," Lila said.

She kissed them goodnight and waited for the door to shut behind them, before quickly slipping down the stairs and into the basement, bolting the door behind her. She went into her room, pulled out the prayer mat Taata had bought her, and rolled it out next to her bed. She covered her head and shoulders with Taata's embroidered shawl, stood in the middle of the mat, and raised her hands to her ears.

"Wrong direction," she realized with frustration and stopped in her tracks, trying to figure out where Mecca was, just like the Imam in the mosque. But the mosque was in the opposite direction, and that confused her even more. Lila moved the mat around the room, crying as her desperation grew until she was finally sure she had it right.

"It has to be perfect," she told herself, "or it won't count."

"Allahu akbar," Lila called out, raising her hands to her head. Her voice rang out loudly in her ears, resounding through the basement. She bowed deeply, and then knelt down, placing her head, knees and hands on the floor, remaining like that for some time.

"Please Allah," she arose, remaining on her knees, "please, please help my mother." She promised to be good. She promised to pray and do good deeds, just like the Imam had told her. She promised to be a good Muslim. Suddenly she knew what she had to do.

"I testify," she cried out loudly. "La ilaha illa Allah, Muhammad rasoolu Allah."

"I testify," she called out again. "There is no true God but Allah, and Muhammad is his messenger."

Tears covered her cheeks as she pulled the scarf tighter around her head.

"La ilaha illa Allah, Muhammad rasoolu Allah," she screamed again and again, a torrent of tears pouring down her face.

BUT ALLAH WASN'T listening, or maybe he was. For just as Lila took the oath, finally committing herself to Islam, her world took a sudden jolt, twisting completely over onto its side. And she became a Jew.

LIA

THE TAXI PULLED away from the curb.

"Is it far?" Lia asked.

"Not really," David answered. "Less than an hour."

Lia leaned back trying to take in as much as she could, but all she could see was a highway and cars. She closed her eyes and took a deep breath, hugging her journal to her body, images of Little Ghaza still running through her mind, competing for her attention.

"Mashs'Alla, God has willed it," Taata Maryam kept muttering, wringing her hands, and shaking her head uncontrollably. She dabbed her handkerchief under her steamed up glasses, sighed and sniffled and muttered. Jasmine and Sameer just hugged her and cried.

Sami threw a going away party at the Hooka hall, with food and cakes and speeches. Everyone tried to be cheerful and Auntie Heeba even put on a recording of Ul Kul Tum and tried to get everyone to belly dance, but no one was really in the mood, and by ten the hall was empty.

"Take, take." Taata stuffed a cardboard box into her hand. "I make for you, special last night."

Whiffs of rosewater and orange blossom filled the air.

"Allah yu sallmak. May God protect you." Taata kissed her one last time.

HE WAS STANDING on the curb, next to the taxi, dressed in a shiny black suit and hat. At first, she wasn't even sure it was him, he looked so much older than she remembered, slimmer and slightly stooped, his brown hair streaked with grey and a long beard covering his face. When he moved toward her, two long curls bobbed beneath his ears. It had only been two years, but she hardly recognized him. Even his smell was strange to her.

She was glad when they were finally on the plane. David had become restless and agitated, worried about leaving the settlement for too long. It had only been established a few months before and there were still very few families living there. He had bought her new clothes and new shoes, now that her old ones had become inappropriate again. She even had a new coconut name.

"I like my name," she had tried to argue, but David ignored her.

"Now you're Lia, to me God," he explained, bringing his fingers to his chest and then spreading his hands out dramatically. "A good, Jewish name."

"Alla Yirachmu," Lia whispered under her breath, realizing the extent of her father's newfound religiosity. She could see how clearly he believed it. A little twist, a mixing up of the letters, and a new person was born.

THE CAR BEGAN to pick up speed. Lia opened her eyes and looked around her. They were travelling through hilly, tree-covered terrain. The air conditioner was on, but she felt hot and sweaty.

"No trousers," David had said, when she had held up a pair of cut-off blue jeans for his approval.

"What do you mean no trousers, are you talking about shorts?" Lia wrinkled her nose in dismay.

"No trousers at all." David wagged his finger at her. "Except your pj's."

Lia couldn't believe her ears. She was used to dressing modestly, but now he was telling her she could only wear skirts or dresses, and even those had to be so long, they almost swept the floor.

"What's this? I can't wear this. I'll trip over it," she argued, trying to convince David to allow her to shorten the skirt she was trying.

"Long sleeves only," he told the saleslady who was trying to find a matching shirt. He even made her wear stockings.

"It's so hot, I'm suffocating," Lia complained loudly as they walked out of the store. "I hate these clothes."

"I HATE THIS dress." Lia pulled at the dark blue skirt that was sticking to her calves. She kept pushing her sleeves up, and David kept telling her to pull them down. Her hands were sweaty, but she wouldn't let go of the leather-bound journal. She hadn't planned to take it with her, but Taata had insisted, shoving it into her bag just before she left. Lia leafed quickly through it, surprised by how much she had written. David had fallen asleep the moment the plane had taken off, but Lia had started to think about Taata Maryam and Jasmine, wondering if she would ever see them again.

"Nothing will ever be the same again," she thought sadly, thinking of all the people she had left behind. She could barely remember Geeta and Gandyip. Or Sergeant Bob. She thought of her mother, hot, salty tears flowing down her cheeks. Her eyes became misty and her mother's image faded. For a moment, she couldn't imagine her face.

"What if I forget them all?" She panicked, her thoughts becoming jumbled and her breath short. She tried to call out to her sleeping father, but her throat was so constricted that hardly any sound came out.

"It's just a mind attack." Lia forced herself to take a deep breath. She raised her hands above her head and brought them down slowly, bending from her waist to touch her toes. Her head hit something hard. She noticed the journal poking out of her bag and was flooded with relief, realizing what she had to do.

She wrote VENICE in capital letters on the first page and LAUREL VALLEY on the second, and then began to list. Every person. Every place. Everything she could remember. She wouldn't stop even after David woke up.

"Have to get it all down," she muttered, when he tried to get her to take a break. "If it's written, I won't forget."

AS THE CAR drove on, the dense pines dwindled and small groves of olive trees took their place. The land itself seemed to change, becoming rockier and harsher. Steep slopes the color of dust arose on both sides of the road, with only a few sickly pale shrubs clinging to their sides. An armored vehicle waved them down. Men in uniforms, with helmets and big black revolvers peeked through the car windows.

"What's going on?" Lia asked, terrified, remembering all her Uncle Sami's stories of the occupation.

"It's just the army, silly." David laughed and waved at the soldiers. "They're here for our protection. The settlement's just past the blockade."

But the big black guns were all Lia could think about.

"There." David pointed toward one of the tallest hills, but Lia could only see a few small structures at its peak. The car took a sharp left and climbed slowly up a narrow, freshly paved road. They stopped outside a tall iron gate behind which a pack of barking dogs greeted them with bared teeth and wild eyes.

"Where the hell are we?" Lia couldn't hold her fear in any longer. She looked around her. Everything looked the same, yellow, sparse, and monotonous. There was nothing around for miles, except some black and brown goats, idly grazing on the slopes.

"It's not as isolated as it seems." David tried to placate her.

"Nabi Musa's just over there, behind the bend. It's a peaceful Arab village, and we're on very good terms. There's an Israeli town just a few kilometers away and a couple of small Israeli settlements just over that ridge." David pointed to a high cliff over to their side.

"You'll love it once you get used to it. It's so peaceful and quiet. Like going back to nature."

He opened the gate and the dogs came bounding out, suddenly friendly and desperate for a pat. A huge, ugly brownish black mongrel nearly knocked Lia down.

"Artsa Chuka," David shouted, but Chuka just placed her paws on Lia's shoulders, sniffling and licking at her face. Lia stroked her long nose and scratched behind her ears.

"I see you found yourself a friend," David said when he looked back to see Chuka following Lia loyally.

The settlement was tiny, just a few concrete buildings surrounded by sand colored caravans, all enclosed by a heavy barbed wire fence. Bare electric wires ran crisscrossed between the buildings, connected crudely with ugly knots and peeling pegs and clips. Lia couldn't imagine anywhere as uninviting as her dad's new home. Her new home.

"Where is everyone?" Lia asked. The distant barking of dogs joined the humming and whirring of the old, broken down air-conditioners that were kept running day and night.

"Too hot." David closed the gate behind them. "It'll start cooling off in a few hours, and everything will come back to life."

"Worse even than Laurel Valley," Lia thought, the dry air scratching her lungs.

He showed her the goat pen and some workshops that were still under construction. They walked past the day care center and a small thrift shop.

"That's our synagogue." He pointed proudly toward a large elongated building. "Not as fancy as the one we went to in Los Angeles, but it's the center of our community and people come here to pray from all the surrounding settlements."

"What's that?" Lia pointed to a second square building just to the right of the synagogue. The two buildings were the largest structures and the entire settlement seemed to have been built around them.

"That's our school." David beamed as he showed her around.

"We're the lucky ones. Before we took over, this place used to be an army post, so we have running water and even electricity."

Some hens crossed their path chattering furiously, on route to join a larger group huddling in the shade of a young olive tree.

"Here we are." David led her to a caravan right next to the tree. "Welcome home." He smiled at her and opened the door.

Whiffs of vanilla and chocolate filled the air. Esther placed the last batch of cookies on the cooling tray and rushed to embrace Lia. She was short and rather plump, with a pale, freckled face and pretty blue eyes. Lia didn't really know what to do, so she hugged her back. That's when she noticed she was pregnant. David hadn't said anything about a baby when he told her about his new wife.

Esther was raised Protestant in New York City, but was drawn to Judaism from a young age. She converted in her late twenties and moved to Israel. Her old coconut name was Eva, which could have easily become Eve, but Esther had picked her name herself. "Just like the queen."

They had been married for almost two years.

"I'm so glad you're finally here," Esther gushed when she released her. When she smiled, wisps of reddish blond hair escaped the austere black crochet that covered her head, giving her face a softness that made her even prettier.

"Not as pretty as my mother, though," Lia couldn't help thinking, but before she could start feeling sorry for herself, Esther grabbed her hand and took her on the "grand tour."

The whole place was ridiculous, not even half the size of their basement in Laurel Valley, but its saving grace was the large wooden deck attached to the tiny kitchenette and living room, scattered with colorful mats and cushions.

"This is where we spend most of our time. Not now, of course," Esther laughed, "but in the morning and late afternoon, it's beautiful."

There was a tiny bathroom and two more rooms. David and Esther's bedroom was so small their mattress filled all the space from one side of the room to the other.

"I saved your room for last. We have a special surprise for you." She flung open the last door.

Suddenly, Lia was crying. The walls were pale lemon yellow and the doors and windows a ferocious egg yolk. All the lamps and fixtures were different shades of yellow. It was smaller and a lot less elaborate, but there it was, unmistakably, her yellow room all over again. Her eyes were so blurred by her tears, she didn't even notice the yellow crib until it shivered and shook and howled.

"Good morning Rachel." Esther pulled a little creature out of the crib. "Come say hello to your big sister."

Rachel crinkled her nose and stretched her arms toward Lia, who stared at her in disbelief. She had her mother's round face and snow white skin, but her mouth was a little too large and full, just like Lia's, and her eyes were unmistakable. Smaller and rounder than hers, they were the exact same shade. Only her father had that deep blue green. "Like looking into the ocean," everyone always said. It was love at first sight.

The yellow room and infant roommate weren't the only surprises her father had in store for her.

"I left this for you." He pointed to a shoebox lying on the bed. "All the old pictures."

Lia sat on the bed and opened the box. It was brimming with old photographs, thrown together in disarray. She flipped through them eagerly. Pictures from Venice mixed together with those of her parents' old commune. A young, heavily pregnant Minna smiling up at the camera. Old baby pictures. India. Behind each picture was a date and title, written in Minna's delicate rounded letters.

"The camel," Lia gasped, staring at the picture of herself riding through the streets of India in the rain. She hadn't seen it for so long, she had begun to think she had made it up. She hugged the lost photograph to her chest, her tears welling up again before she closed the box and shoved it under her bed.

AS THE SUN'S rays shortened in the west and the air cooled, the little settlement came alive. Esther opened all the caravan doors, ushering them out to the veranda. A slight breeze tickled Lia's face. The setting sun's dazzling glare was gone and the entire landscape was brushed a slightly tainted orange. Children ran outside yelling and laughing loudly, barking dogs at their heels. A long-nosed mongrel leapt onto the deck and snuggled next to Lia's feet.

"I see you've found a friend." Esther laughed.

"Chuka adopted her from the first moment." David scratched the back of the dog's neck.

A woman wearing a long skirt and sleeves, her hair wrapped in a red kerchief, passed by and waved at them. Someone opened the neighboring caravan door and a female voice yelled, "Jonathan, come quick, Lia's here."

Jonathan was thirteen, two years her senior, but they were quickly inseparable. Like Lia, he was originally from LA, and although he had spent most of his life in Israel, his English was perfect. He and his family had been at the settlement since it was first established a few months earlier.

"I nearly died when we first got here," he told Lia. "I thought it was the end of the world, but it's not so bad now. You'll get used to it, you'll see."

He was over a head taller than her, and he wore a grey knitted circle attached to the crown of his head and some knotted strings that fell over the sides of his blue jeans. Lia noticed that all the men in the settlement wore them.

"Religious men are compelled to wear them," David explained to Lia later. "As well as these." He pointed to his long curling sideburns.

"We were a completely normal family," Jonathan told her, "until my parents became religious."

They moved to Israel when he was five, just after his brother Matan was born. "His name was Mark then, but a few years ago they changed it. The younger one, Yissaschar used to be Dean." He laughed at her expression. Luckily for him, he had always been Jonathan. His mother Rebecca's coconut name was Sharon and his father Michael was still Mikey. Lia didn't say anything at first, she had promised David, but finally she couldn't help herself.

"Lia's already my third name," she whispered and swore him to secrecy.

TOWARD EVENING, EVERYONE congregated outside the synagogue. The settlement population was even smaller than Lia had expected. The two Russian families spoke no English, but the men smiled and nodded vigorously in greeting, while their wives clapped their hands eagerly and kissed her on both cheeks. She'd met their kids earlier in the afternoon, but since they were all younger and had no way of communicating with her, they had quickly lost interest.

"They live the farthest, on the other side of the settlement," Esther whispered in her ear.

Nadav and Atara lived in the caravan to their right. They were heavily pregnant, expecting their first child.

"Hope you like animals." Atara lost no time trying to recruit Lia's help. "Jonathan works with us all the time."

They were in charge of the goats and chickens. "They're our number one baby," she joked, promising to teach Lia how to make goat cheese and yogurt.

Lila thought the couple in the next caravan looked too young for it, but they were newly married, and both were studying to be teachers.

"I help out all the time," Jonathan explained. "There are so few of us, and I'm the oldest child. But everyone helps out, you'll see. It's actually fun."

The young men, who shared the large caravan at the entrance to the settlement, attempted to joke around in broken English. Small children ran around barefoot, playing happily.

"Any kids our age?" Lia asked Jonathan.

"They're mostly into babies here," Jonathan snickered. "The more the better. But some other kids come to school, so it's really not so bad. And anyway, my dad says not to worry, we're just the start."

"The start?" Lia had no idea what he was talking about.

"We're just the first ones to come," he explained. "There'll be more and more families joining us. They say there's a waiting list."

Lia looked around her, shaking her head in disbelief. Bare asphalt, a few concrete structures and a handful of caravans perched on the top of a hill, in the middle of nowhere. The sun disappeared, and the men entered the synagogue, leaving the women and children outside.

"We need you," David called out to Jonathan. "We're short one."

"For the minyan," Esther explained to Lia. "They need ten men to pray."

"Beezrat Hashem, Jonathan's just been bar-miztva'd," Rebecca told Lia proudly.

"Bar what?" Lia asked.

"It means that since he turned thirteen, he's considered a man," Esther explained.

"And Hashem?" Lia had heard her say the name several times that day, looking up at the heavens every time, but had been too embarrassed to ask. "Is that the name of your God?"

"Oh no." Esther chuckled, covering her mouth with her hand. "We just call him Hashem. It means 'the name.'"

"The name?" Lia didn't really get it. "What name?"

"That's exactly it," Esther tried to explain. "We're not allowed to say the name of our God, so we say 'Hashem' instead."

The men's chanting voices rose and seeped out of the concrete block. Lia sat down on the asphalt, leaning her head on the synagogue wall, trying to make sense of it all.

"God's god." David had dismissed her question with a wave of his hand. "It's always the same god, Lia, we all just call him by a different name."

"A God with no name," Lia said to herself. Instead of a coconut name, this god had no name at all.

Lia closed her eyes, listening to the men's voices rise. She didn't understand a word, but there was something comforting in the guttural sounds they were making and some of the words seemed vaguely familiar. As the chanting died down another sound reverberated through the hilltops.

"Allahuuu akbaaar." The familiar Muslim call to prayer bounced off the hillside and echoed through the valley, weaving its way into the men's prayer.

Lia opened her eyes in surprise.

"It's just the muezzin from the neighboring village," Esther whispered to her.

"Allahu akbar," Lia mouthed, smiling to herself, as the second call echoed through the hills.

The men's sing-song voices rose again in unison.

"Ashhadu an la ilaha illa Allah." The muezzin's voice cut through the air, swirling through the chant.

"I bear witness that there is no god except the One God," Lia repeated to herself.

The men's voices rose and turned into song, overwhelming the muezzin. They sang and danced, stomping their feet and clapping their hands feverishly.

"Haya 'ala-s-Salah, hurry to prayer." The muezzin's voice took over again.

The voices rose and fell, echoing through the empty valley. Sometimes Allah had the upper hand, and sometimes it was Hashem.

"Two gods perched on a hill, competing to fill the silence," Lia thought.

But as Allah and Hashem, the god with no name, mixed and intermingled, they seemed to stop fighting and began, instead, to talk to one another, each voice rising and falling in its turn. There were even moments when they seemed to forget themselves and sing together, their voices creating such a perfect harmony that she could no longer even tell them apart.

THE SOUNDS OF a baby crying woke Lia up. Before she could even begin to figure out where she was, Rachel was banging on the wooden bars and whimpering. Lia picked her up, and Rachel nestled into her body, rested her head on her shoulder, and went back to sleep. The sun had begun to rise in the horizon, its first rays turning the room a dull, shadowy lime. Dogs barked in the background. Every time Lia tried to return Rachel to her crib, she whimpered and Esther and David showed no signs of waking up.

"C'mon." Lia placed the baby on her bed next to the wall and lay down beside her.

"Hashem be praised." Esther's cry woke them. "I'm so sorry, Lia, you should have called us."

She offered to put the baby's crib in their room, but Lia wouldn't hear of it, even though Rachel ended up in her bed nearly every night. As she grew older the bond between them strengthened. "Li," was her first word, and when later, more and more babies arrived in their household, Rachel remained her favorite.

THE LITTLE DAYCARE center was Esther's kingdom. She was a trained nursery school teacher and this had always been her dream. David had prepared a sandbox and put up a colorful slide and some swings, and although the concrete playground didn't look the most inviting, Lia soon learned that even the older kids spent most of their free time there.

"Any help will be deeply appreciated." Esther pointed at her bulging stomach. "There're only a few kids now, so your father helps out, but once I have the baby, we'll open the younger class and two other mothers will work here permanently. We're having a baby boom." She laughed. "In the coming months, just here and in the few neighboring settlements, we have over ten babies due."

Just before eight, Jonathan called her out. "C'mon, Lia, the school bus is here."

A group of toddlers and older children came up the path toward them. Jonathan introduced her to the two girls she would be studying with, Tamar and Arava. They were both twelve and didn't speak much English, but with Jonathan translating, they managed to exchange a few words. The girls lived in a neighboring settlement and were best friends, still, they tried to include her, holding her hand and leading her from place to place, pointing and gesticulating. By the time school ended, they understood each other perfectly.

"Welcome, Lia." Rebecca called her in. "You'll sit with the older children."

She had been a high school maths teacher before Jonathan was born and was now in charge of the school. She explained that there were two classrooms and the kids were divided according to age, but much of the work was individual and often both groups would work together.

"Especially when we're short a teacher, like today." She grimaced. "Never mind, you'll be spending most of your time working on your Hebrew, anyway. Don't worry. You'll pick it up in no time."

Lia wasn't sure, but very quickly realized she was right. She didn't even need most of the books and worksheets Rebecca had so painstakingly amassed for the purpose. The other kids took it as their personal assignment, pointing out every place, person, or object, making her say the words, again and again, until she got them right. Once she got used to the sound, it didn't even sound so strange, especially since they used a lot of the words Taata Maryam had used. When David was upset, he swore exactly like her uncle Sami, and just like him, always apologized when he saw she had heard.

Pretty soon her conversations were seasoned with Hebrew words. She had to be careful though, as every time she opened her mouth, the words tried to pop out in Arabic. She loved listening to the Arab peddlers offering their wares by the gate and to the kids leading donkeys or goats and sheep near the settlement.

"What's so funny?" Jonathan asked her one day, when she suddenly burst out laughing. They were helping David with the vegetable patch when two little boys appeared. They were no more than six or seven, and they were trying to drag an exceptionally stubborn donkey, braying and baring its teeth as it held its ground.

"Brrr," they were shouting at it, one little boy pulling it from its bit, the other pushing its behind. "Yallah, hooissa ahmar."

"Now!" the boy in front screamed. "Push!"

They pulled and heaved, hitting it across the back with long sticks, yelling and swearing, until it reluctantly shifted its feet and moved forward.

"Yallah, brrr," they both yelled, smiling excitedly. The donkey took a few small steps and stopped in its tracks. Lia was giggling uncontrollably.

"You understand them don't you?" It wasn't the first time Jonathan had noticed, but Lia just nodded, smiling sheepishly, and kept her mouth shut.

SHE WAS READING in no time, the letters coming together miraculously to form new words for her to learn, but when she tried writing them down, they proved even more difficult than English, curling and curving unexpectedly in ways she found impossible to copy.

"Don't worry about it," Rebecca encouraged. "Practice makes perfect."

But Lia knew differently. She sat diligently for hours copying lines of letters, but no matter how much she tried, they still came out crooked, hesitant, and illegible.

After school, there was plenty to do around the house. As Esther's pregnancy advanced, David and Lia took on more and more of her chores, but somehow the tiny caravan was always a mess, even after they had tidied up.

"Just do the best you can." Esther had to put up her feet after she came home from work.

There was a load of washing most days and they were forever hanging clothes on the line out back, then sorting, folding, and stuffing things away.

Esther was a terrible cook, so after a few days of burnt schnitzel, sweet Bolognese sauce made with ketchup, and overcooked pasta, Lia decided to take over. That's when she first noticed how different her new world was from Palm Street. Suddenly, there were all kinds of complex rules and regulations. Instead of halal, there was now a new word governing anything she put in her mouth.

"It's not enough for something to be stamped kosher," David explained. "It has to say 'glatt' or 'lemehadrin.' Strictly kosher."

Lia didn't even know what regular kosher meant, but she learned soon enough.

"That's why we have two sinks, even though it's such a small kitchen," Esther explained patiently. "The sink with the red sponges is meat, the blue, milk."

"We never ever mix meat with milk, it is forbidden." David told her they had to wait seven or eight hours after eating meat before having a dairy product.

Lia thought it all a load of nonsense, but she tried as best as she could to respect their wishes. At first, Esther watched her like a hawk, ensuring she never mixed the wrong ingredients and always used the correct dishes.

"Wrong bowl," she'd say to Lia. "That's the meat cupboard."

"Margarine, not butter, it has to be parve."

Parve meant neither meat nor dairy, and as Lia swiftly learned, was synonymous with boring. Without Taata's butter and yogurt, her cooking came out bland and tasteless. But it didn't take her long to find her way about the kitchen, experimenting and substituting oils and spices for the ingredients she could no longer use. When Lia started baking Taata's baklava and maamul, the aroma rising from the little caravan was so intoxicating, the entire settlement stood in line for a taste.

It was still too hot to leave the caravan before late afternoon. They spent most of their time on the shaded veranda, the young children and babies splashing in large plastic tubs or spreading smudges of colorful paint on large sheets of paper with their fingers.

"Close the net," David would remind them, whenever they went out.

The caravan was never locked, and the only intruders they were afraid of were insects. Furry brown spiders the size of golf balls were always trying to get inside and try as they might, there was always something buzzing about in the night and they would inevitably wake up with a new swelter or two.

"I told you to close the nets," David never tired of repeating.

Toward evening, just before prayers, Lia and Jonathan did their chores. They helped David, preening the vegetable patches and watering the flowerbeds and took turns manning the thrift store, but as often as they could, they helped out with the goats. They loved leading them out to pasture with Nadav. He'd bring a shepherd's flute and show them how to play, guiding the animals with the music. If all was quiet and there were no threats or alarms, they would go down all the way to the valley, often meeting Arab boys shepherding their flocks. They would always exchange greetings and sometimes even sit and talk together for a while. Other times they had to stay close to the fence or weren't allowed out at all.

After a while Nadav taught them how to milk the goats, squeezing their udders slowly but firmly, feeling the warm sweet smelling white liquid run through their fingers, dripping down their upper arms. Atara was so heavily pregnant, they had to do almost everything for her, but they didn't mind. Nadav would pour the fresh milk into the big pasteurizing vats, leaving them to mix it, measuring the temperature with a long glass thermometer.

"Not more than seventy degrees," he would call out from time to time, in case they forgot. They would ladle the milk into long glass bottles, mix the yogurt, and prepare the cheeses, stacking everything away in the fridges like seasoned milkmen.

"Pour all the water out through the cloth." Atara would boss Lia around. "Careful, mind the salt."

She taught her how to make soft, smooth feta and a salty grainy white cheese, but Lia's favorite was the fresh, creamy Ricotta. It was Rachel's favorite food, so whenever they made it, she would bring home a large container and the two of them would sit outside on the porch, finishing the fluffy sweet cheese with one spoon between them.

Lia's favorite time was sunset. Whenever she finished her duties early enough, she and Chuka would climb up to her quiet spot, an old rusty bench, right at the top of the settlement, where they would sit silently, watching the sun begin its descent, its lowering rays painting the sky a vivid purple and pink. She could sit there forever, losing time and space, starring out into the vast beyond, watching the circling cranes or a flock of bickering ravens. She watched as the last of the pecking sparrows took its leave and the sky lost its colors, till only a blackish blue remained.

The most important day of the week was the Sabbath, beginning at Friday sundown and ending, as David liked to say, "when three stars twinkle in the sky." But since "there was no time to be lost," the preparations for "the Sabbath Queen" began early Friday morning.

By early afternoon, the settlement was packed with friends and relatives, and there was always a couple, sometimes an entire family, spending the night in their living room. Once the Sabbath set in, there would be no moving in or out of the settlement and since they were deeply religious, no work of any kind was allowed. This turned out to mean much more than Lia had anticipated. They didn't drive or cook, or even turn on the lights. No work, she found out, seemed to cover almost every possible activity, except for praying and reading the Tora.

That also meant that everything had to be prepared in advance. The house cleaned, the washing dried and put away, the food cooked and the cakes baked. A huge pot would be placed in the oven to slow cook overnight, while other dishes were kept warm on a hot plate that stayed on all the time. Esther always tried to finish before their guests arrived. They made sure to start with the house, cleaning and sprucing it up as best they could, but inevitably, when their friends walked through the door, they would still be spooning batter into dishes, braiding the challa bread, or preparing the ingredients for the overnight chulnt, the house smelling of fried onions and cinnamon.

The ceremonies began just before dusk. The women would congregate in the kitchen, freshly bathed and dressed in long skirts and blouses, their legs in stockings. Even in the heat, their heads were tightly wrapped in colorful turbans. They'd cover their eyes, swaying from side to side as they recited the Sabbath prayer and lit candles.

"Do you want to join us?" Esther always offered, but Lia politely declined. She watched as they all gathered outside the synagogue for "Kabalat Shabat," singing and passing around sweet grape juice and wine. There was guitar playing and drumming. The first time she participated, there was a vague memory, a feeling of déjà vu. David laughed when she told him.

"When you were small I'd sometimes take you to Rami and Swissa. They held a Kabalat Shabat every Friday evening."

But Lia knew it was much more than just Rami and Swissa. It was why, she realized, she had immediately felt at home, even though she hadn't wanted to. Inside the barbed wire, on top of the hill, in the middle of nowhere, it was just like Venice all over again.

"Only Venice with God," she thought, immediately correcting herself. "Venice and Hashem."

Just before the high holidays, two more families joined the settlement. Workers from the neighboring village straightened the land with a tractor, and huge cranes placed two shiny caravans on the newly dried concrete squares.

"You see," Esther was delighted, "another two kids for the daycare."

"Even though they're all younger than me," Lia thought. "At least, I won't be the new kid on the block anymore."

As the Jewish New Year approached, the settlement seemed to be bursting at its seams, as more and more visitors arrived for the festivities. They had to spread mats and mattresses on the school and daycare floors to accommodate the families that had nowhere else to stay. The sound of a lamb's horn blowing in tandem with the singsong chant of prayer filled the air from early morning and was often heard throughout the night.

"In Hebrew we call these the terrible days," David explained to Lia. "The days before Hashem's judgment."

As the holiday set in, the settlement turned white. The men went down to the synagogue dressed in soft white trousers and freshly ironed shirts, their beards and side locks primped and preened and the women floated around in flowing white dresses and robes. Esther looked like a bride, the billowing white lace hiding her bulging stomach, her head covered with gleaming blonde curls that reached all the way to her shoulders.

"What the hell?" Lia blurted out the first time she saw Esther put on her hair. "That's supposed to be modest?"

She reminded her of the dancing girls they had seen in Vegas. David told her that married women had to cover their hair, so that no man other than their husbands could see it.

"As long as my real hair is covered." Esther whirled around the room. "And anyway, I only wear it for a 'simcha' or a special occasion. Feel, it's real." She pushed her head into Lia's face.

Lia ran her fingers through the hair. It was thick and smooth, much more like her own than Esther's thin uneven strands.

"WELL," ESTHER PULLED the wig lower around her face and straightened the bangs, "how do I look?"

"Pretty," Lia managed to blurt, before the words got stuck in her throat.

Suddenly it wasn't Esther standing in the room beside her. Images of her mother during the last weeks of her life filled her mind.

"Pretty," was what she said whenever Minna pulled on the short black wig Sami had bought her to cover her balding skull. "You look so pretty."

THE VACATION FELT endless to Lila as one holiday led into another. There was no school and all work and construction in the settlement ceased, but Lia found herself busier than ever, helping a heavily pregnant Esther clean, cook, and bake.

"It's a mitzve to have people over during the holidays," Esther told her, whenever she complained. "Hashem himself decreed it."

Before Yom Kippur, they worked from morning to night.

"Only one day?" Lia was contemptuous, remembering the month long Ramadan in Laurel Valley.

"For us Jews, it's the holiest day of the year," David answered her seriously. "But don't worry. You don't have to fast yet."

"Only next year, after your bat-mitzva," Esther added, promising her a big party for her twelfth birthday.

Early in the morning, they packed picnic baskets with freshly baked challa bread and honey cakes, grabbed a crate of sweet wine for "kiddush" and set off to visit the army post.

"Maybe I should stay here?" Lia didn't want to go. The soldiers she had seen through heavily armored cars, flashing their rifles behind helmeted faces, still frightened her.

"Don't be silly." David wouldn't hear of it. "They're our friends. Without the army, we wouldn't even be here."

"In Israel everyone goes to the army," Esther told her. "It's an army of the people." She smiled at David. "Your father's still an officer on reserve duty."

Lia looked at him, amazed, but David smiled back and nodded. "I go to 'miluim' a few times a year to train and practice. But not for too long now." He ruffled her hair. "I'm getting far too old!"

AT THE POST, the soldiers clapped each other's shoulders and bear hugged, gruffly cat calling and jibing each other. Without their helmets, their eyes gleaming in the hot sun, the soldiers looked like smiling, friendly kids, eager for some treats and affection. Although they were mostly secular, they wrapped the black leather strands of the 'Tfilin" around their foreheads and wrists, repeating the words of the prayer, their bodies swaying slightly, just as they were shown. David poured sweet wine into thimble-sized cups and they all wished each other a happy new year.

"TU TU TU tu tu tu tu . . ." the ram's horn blew on and on for the last time and the worshippers began to leave the synagogue. Lia looked up. Three stars twinkled back at her brightly.

"Please." She held her tray high in the air, offering sweet iced tamharindi juice to break the fast.

"Sounds perfect." Esther had approved when Lia suggested it, sending David off to buy everything she needed.

Lia worked hard, cooking and cooling, pouring and measuring, preparing the ice days in advance and stacking the cubes in their neighbors' iceboxes. She wasn't sure why, but the moment she heard that they were going to fast, all she could think of was Taata Maryam's tamharindi juice.

They had barely broken their fast, when the sound of hammers filled the settlement, metallic bangs that seemed to echo across the valley.

"Sukkot." David jumped to his feet, forgetting how tired and weak he had felt a moment earlier. His entire demeanor changed as he straightened his hunched back and marched out the door, calling a perplexed Lia to follow.

Mikey and Jonathan were already outside, hammering nails into long planks, while Matan and Yissaschar ran about, feeling important, carrying tools and pieces of wood. The entire settlement was in an uproar, everyone banging and yelling, putting up the little huts that would be their homes for an entire week. David and Mikey were even more ambitious than most. They had decided to work together, building a shack big enough to house both of their families, as well as all their guests.

"Just like the people of Israel in the desert." David put the last pieces of the frame together.

"Hold tight," David told Lia, as he pulled the white fabric across the frame, wrapping it around the first wooden pillar.

"Come see our sukka, it's the biggest." Matan and Yissaschar ran around taunting all the other children, until Mikey threatened to send them inside.

It was after midnight when they finished spreading the branches and leaves that created the roof.

"Can you see anything?" David, who was still perched high up on the ladder, yelled down.

Jonathan lay down on the floor.

"It's perfect," he shouted. "Come see." He motioned to Lia to join him.

Lia lay down next to him and looked up. The moon and the stars were looking right at her, shining brightly through the leafy canopy.

EVERY FREE MOMENT was spent making decorations. The women set up a long table outside the synagogue, where everyone came to work together, cutting and painting and gluing, preparing pictures and cutouts and papier-mâché balls that would be strung up in all the huts. The excitement was contagious, the air itself filled with anticipation. Lia spent most of her time stringing together strips of colored paper, recreating the simple chains she had learned to make in Laurel Valley. But whereas there she had been limited to black, white, red, and green, she could now use any color she desired. She decided to experiment, weaving together strands of purple and mauve, with little golden baubles embedded like shining stars in the middle for the ceiling and spirals of soft pink and lilac for the walls. For the entrance she chose strings of flowers, strung painstakingly on long colored threads. They were all simple enough, but so ambitious, they took her days to complete.

"It's just a campout." Jonathan ridiculed her at first, but when he saw how seriously she was taking it, he decided to join in.

"We've never had anything quite so festive." Esther clapped her hands, when Lia finally let her in. "It's a scene straight from Scheherazada."

The campout turned into a week long time-out, in which inside and out intertwined. The hut stood just outside their doorway, but everything seemed different, lighter and impermanent. Even the air felt different, each breath somehow fuller and richer. Time slowed down, becoming longer and flatter, stretching itself out in all directions. But it was good time, mysterious and magical, filled with singing and dancing and goodwill. The days began early, as the first morning rays reached stealthily through the gaps in the canopy, shining into their eyes and waking them, until late at night, when the last person in the hut finally fell asleep.

Inside the confines of the barbed wire, the kids roamed freely, running barefoot from hut to hut or chasing the animals through the vegetable patches. For the adults, too, the return to the earth was a celebration. A celebration of their God. Everything they did that week was in his honor, every breath devoted to his glory. The God with no name was everywhere, in their song and in their prayer, almost in every word.

In the evenings, after the remnants of the communal meal had been cleared away, the adults spread blankets and cushions on the concrete square outside the synagogue in preparation for their evening lesson. As they all congregated, Lia and Jonathan could slip away, usually climbing up to Lia's bench, where the sounds from down below barely carried. It was the most free time they had had, since she arrived, but as there were no TVs or computers, and all the books were in Hebrew or talked about God, they had to find other ways to amuse themselves.

The first evening they started talking and joking around like they usually did, telling each other of books and movies and places they'd been, but as the hours advanced and the silent darkness deepened, they found themselves suddenly sharing their deepest, darkest truths.

"I really need to tell you something," Jonathan said, "but I don't know how you'll react."

"There's been something I've wanted to tell you for a long time, too," Lia answered, "something you can't tell anyone else, either."

"I keep having this dream." Jonathan averted his eyes, looking down at the ground as he spoke. "It's a sexual dream, of me, making love to someone."

"So?" Lia asked, when he didn't continue.

"But that someone is always a boy," he whispered in her ear. "I feel so different from everyone else here." He shook his head. "And I'm so scared someone will find me out. I've never told anyone. Just the thought of saying the word 'homosexual' out loud here makes me want to puke. There's no way they'll accept it."

"I don't really fit in here either," Lia told him, trying to work out how much she should say. But once she started talking, she couldn't stop. She told him everything, about Venice and Laurel Valley and her mother and Taata, feeling lighter and lighter as she spoke, as if a great burden had been lifted off her shoulders. The weight of the secret had sat heavily on her, but finally there was someone she could be herself with, instead of passing herself off as someone she wasn't.

"I don't know what to do." Jonathan was desperate. "There's no one I can talk to about it."

"You can always talk to me," Lia offered, trying to think how she could help.

"Sometimes I feel that I'm suffocating, that it's just too small around here," he continued. "I feel like I'm stuck, with no place to go. Sometimes I wish I could just get away. Not even forever, just for a while."

"That I can help you with." Lia smiled to herself. She couldn't physically take him away, but she could teach him to fly. "Rest your head back and close your eyes."

"Just as long as you're not starting all the meditation crap." Jonathan stretched out his legs and laid his head back.

"Trust me," Lia said quietly. "Take a deep breath. Imagine a pink balloon. A big round pink balloon. Climb inside the pink balloon. Sit yourself down as comfortably as you can . . ."

The pink balloon took to Jonathan right away, carrying him high up into the sky. It knew he needed a getaway, a time-out, a place far away from his parents and the settlement. Jonathan took to it too, floating and gliding happily in the wind. He quickly became an excellent flier.

"OH!" AUNT HANNA couldn't stop gushing. "You eyes, she got you eyes."

Hanna's eyes were also blue, but they were small and shrunken in her prematurely wrinkled face and their pale greyish hue wasn't even reminiscent of David's. Still, the resemblance between them was obvious to Lia. They had the same slim, lank body and long, pale face with the slight jutting chin and they shared the small but slightly hawkish nose. Hanna's had a thin, silver framed pair of spectacles perched right above it, slightly obscuring her eyes, and making them appear even smaller. She

wasn't at all what Lia had expected, dressed in jean shorts and a light blue
tank top, her rakish arms and legs sun-tanned and exposed. Lia looked at
her father and aunt, thinking how similar they looked, yet how different.

"Come in, come in." Hanna ushered them in, planting a kiss on Lia's
cheek and grabbing hold of Rachel who screamed in delight.

It was the first day of the intermediate days of the holiday.

"We invited Hanna to join us," David told Lia on the drive over, "but
she wouldn't come. She refuses to visit us here."

David told her his sister opposed the Jewish settlements in Samaria and
wouldn't set foot beyond the green line."

"Since your grandmother's death, she's become extremely anti-religious.
She and Esther don't usually see eye to eye." He winked at Lia. "I try
to take Rachel to see her every couple of months, though, she's the only
family we have left."

"The only family you have left," Lia thought.

"Hanna," she said, the first time Lia approached her. "Just Hanna, no
auntie." She waved her finger at her, the skin crinkling around her beady
eyes.

NEARING THE BIG city, traffic had slowed down to a crawl as the
roads got narrower. The streets surrounding the old, dilapidated building
were filled with small, crumbling structures that were similarly in disrepair.
The elaborate engravings on Hanna's building might have been beautiful
once, but now they were covered with filth and grime. The ancient iron
balconies were rusted, their ornaments worn off or almost totally decayed.
The apartment was surprisingly large and airy inside, with high ceilings
and lots of windows. It was on the fourth floor and the climb up had been
slow and agonizing. David sighed and wheezed carrying Rachel up all the
flights of stairs, but Lia, although she was holding everything else, didn't
complain.

"Where's the sea?" Lia rushed to the balcony, but to her disappointment,
she could only see other gray and equally decrepit buildings wherever she
looked.

"It's just over there." David pointed in the opposite direction. "We cross
through the market and it's a few blocks away."

"Come, Lia," Hanna called her in.

The apartment was spotless, but filled overbearingly with old and frayed oversized furniture. Lia picked Rachel up and sat down in a large ruby colored armchair. From close up, Lia could see how stained it was and smell its unpleasant musky odor. Hanna covered the table with a tablecloth and then pulled a lengthy strip of transparent plastic over it.

"I want make." She shrugged as she placed paper plates and cups, a large coca cola bottle, and a box of store bought cookies on the plastic. "But I no enough kosher."

"Can we go, Daddy?" Lia grabbed a cookie, interrupting her father and aunt's conversation for the third time. She couldn't follow what they were saying and she was losing her patience.

"C'mon, Daddy, please, you promised. Rachel wants to go too, don't you?"

"Woo, woo." Rachel nodded happily.

"Where you want go?" Hanna asked.

"To the beach," Lia said excitedly. "I haven't been there yet. It's my favorite place in the world."

"Me also." Hanna grinned at her, pointing to her tan.

"We can't." David shook his head. "We don't go to the regular beach."

He explained that they went to a special beach where men and women swum separately.

"The girls no swim." Hanna joined forces with Lia. "We just take walk on promenade."

"Half an hour," David finally relented. "But only when the heat goes down."

"THAT'S WHERE I work." Hanna pointed to a large red building, a short while after they had set out.

"It's the central post office, the largest branch in all Tel Aviv," David added. "And Hanna's the general manager." Lia could hear the pride in his voice.

When they had left the kibbutz, their mother had sold stamps and envelopes to support them, running a small office from their apartment and walking from door to door, offering her wares. The monthly stipend she received from the government as a holocaust survivor wasn't enough and all three of them had to work. David and Hanna had helped her from an early age, delivering letters and packages all over South Tel Aviv.

"I had a delivery route from when I was twelve," David recalled, maneuvering expertly through the winding alleys. "I know these streets like the back of my hand."

After her army service, Hanna started working at the post office as a junior clerk, advancing rapidly to chief supervisor. After her divorce, the old apartment and post office job welcomed her back as though she had been on vacation.

"WE'RE ALMOST THERE." David pointed, just beyond those buildings.

Lia stretched forward, craning her neck, but couldn't see a thing. Suddenly she glimpsed it, shimmering bluely between the buildings. As they walked on, the buildings became sparser and the road widened, revealing a huge expanse of blue stretching across the horizon wherever her eyes could see.

"The ocean, the ocean!" Lia shrieked, walking even faster. It was a hot day and the water glimmered flatly, seemingly motionless. The beaches were dotted with people, swimming in the shallows or basking in the sun. Lia thought it was the most beautiful sight in the world.

"PLEASE, DADDY, PLEASE." Lia begged David to go down to the beach, but he shook his head stubbornly.

"We said only on the promenade."

"I take the girls." Hanna tried to convince him, rattling off her arguments in such rapid Hebrew, Lia couldn't follow.

"Just to the edge," David finally conceded, sighing unhappily.

"Take off shoes," Hanna whispered to Lia when they reached the sand. "This, also." She pointed at Lia's stockings. "Quick, Abba no look."

Hanna pulled off Rachel's clothes, leaving her standing in the sand in just her diaper. Lia glanced at David. He was sitting in the shade on the promenade, facing away from them. She pulled off her stockings and rushed toward the ocean, the sun-soaked white sand soft and warm beneath her feet. She yanked her skirt up and waded into the almost motionless water. It was as warm as Rachel's bath.

"This feels so good." She bounced Rachel in the water. "So much warmer than Venice. I wish I could swim."

"Eeee ..." Rachel screamed, smacking the water and sending it flying in the air. Hanna and Lia splashed back, roaring with laughter.

Before they left the apartment, Lia wasn't impressed by her aunt. Hanna hardly spoke any English and didn't seem like the most interesting or affectionate person, but now, playing and chattering wildly as if she, too, were a little girl, Lia felt an immense fondness for her. They sat down in the sand, their toes in the water, digging a tunnel with Rachel.

"I come every day," Hanna told her, as she pulled mounds of wet sand out of the hole.

"We used to live right on the beach." Lia found herself telling her aunt about Venice, miming and gesticulating whenever she didn't understand.

She told her about Minna and Taata Maryam, and Hanna—garnishing her broken English with Hebrew words and phrases—told her about her other grandmother. Oddly enough, they understood each other perfectly.

"Hanna! Lia!" David's cries finally reached them. "Time to go. It's getting late."

RACHEL FELL ASLEEP as soon as they started driving.

"I want to talk to you about something. Esther and I have been discussing it, and your aunt has such strong feelings, that I thought, maybe now would be a good time to bring it up."

Lia noticed her father and his sister conversing with uninterrupted seriousness on the way back, but she only understood bits and pieces.

"We think maybe we should get you some help, that perhaps you need someone to talk to."

"Someone to talk to?" Lia wasn't sure what he was suggesting.

"Esther thinks you're unhappy, that maybe all the moves and your mother—"

"A psychologist?" Lia remembered the voodoo doll she'd made of him the last time she was sent to "talk to someone" about her problems.

"Just for a while, to help you adjust," David answered.

"No thank you!" Lia didn't wait for him to say more.

David ignored her. "We've even talked to a lovely lady. She comes highly recommended and lives near us. She's really excited to meet you."

"I think it's a little early for that." Lia changed her strategy. "And it's not that I'm unhappy, Daddy, I think I just need a little more time to get used to everything."

"Maybe we could just go once, so you can meet her." David tried to convince her, but Lia was more stubborn than him.

"You're the reason I have to go to therapy in the first place," was on the tip of her tongue, but she managed to hold it back.

"Well, maybe you're right, let's wait and see how you're doing," David gave in. "But if you feel you need help, of any kind, don't hesitate. You know you can always talk to me."

Lia snuggled into her seat beside her sleeping sister. She closed her eyes and thought about the day and her father's words. It was true that she wasn't happy, but she wasn't necessarily unhappy either. She missed the hustle and bustle of Palm Street and all her friends and family, but even though she visited them in her pink balloon nearly every night, she never went down, preferring to watch them from above.

Life in the settlement was much quieter, with no books or TV and almost no contact with the outside world, but there was always something to do or someone to help out. She liked the school and her friends, especially Jonathan. It was clear to her from the day she arrived, that although they spoke another language and worshipped a different God, they were good people, no different from those she had left behind. Like her mother's family, the settlement took her in with open arms, never asking any questions. Still, she knew, she would never truly be one of them. Here too, she had a secret. Here too, they thought she was someone else.

But this time, she was smarter. This time, she knew what was expected of her. They wanted her to adjust, to be Lia, and Lia was what they were going to get. She didn't want to talk to anyone, because she knew exactly what she had to do. She would be good and polite, do everything she was asked, and everyone would be happy and leave her alone.

"I'll never show a thing," she vowed to herself. "But they mustn't be able to tell. Not even Esther or David."

Instead of talking, she wrote now, filling the pages of her journal with all her thoughts and feelings. Writing things down, she had discovered, immediately gave them some kind of sense, or at least order, making it easier to figure them out. Her writing was different, she noticed, freer and more open. It looked worse than ever, but she didn't care. No one would see it anyway. This time she was writing just for herself. At night, before she went to sleep, she slid her notebook under her mattress, just in case. She wasn't really worried, though. No one, she knew, would be able to decipher her handwriting. She barely could.

WINTER ON THE top of the hill was brutal. The young trees did nothing to break the wind and the little caravan shook and swayed, raindrops falling like pellets on the tin roof. David tied ugly pieces of nylon around all the doors and windows, but there was always a draft or some water leaking from one of the openings. Still, it was pleasant inside, warm and even a little stuffy, like a well-worn sweater. There was always something on the stove or baking in the oven, filling the tiny space with the thick aroma of chicken soup or the sweetness of chocolate chips. But there was also a lightness, a feeling of impermanence she found exhilarating. Something about the tight proximity in the tiny cramped caravan created a closeness, a sense of intimacy, a togetherness.

Esther never tried to take Minna's place, but they got on well from the start, and every new child brought them closer. Hodi arrived on one of the coldest days of the year, only two days after Rebecca gave birth to a baby girl. Hod and Hodaya were never apart, and everyone treated them like twins. Lia fell in love with him the moment Esther placed him in her arms. He was so small and fragile, she was afraid to move. He had his mother's round face, a light brown fluff on his head, and eyes the color of the sea. Not quite theirs, but similar enough. Still, having a new baby in that small, confined space was challenging, especially now, when they hardly ever left the compound, and not only because of the weather.

As the situation between the Palestinians and the Israelis heated up, the world around them shook. For the first time Lia realized she was living in a war zone. Buses exploded, people were knifed in the streets, and cars were ambushed. One morning the minibus bringing the children to school was stoned. Luckily no one was injured, but suddenly they had an armed escort, and no one was allowed to leave the settlement on their own. The gate was double locked and the men patrolled the compound throughout the night. The dogs were tense and alert, barking at every errant noise, like they smelled everyone's fear.

"I knew this would happen." David was furious. It was just what he had anticipated, dreading the moment the Palestinian Authority took over.

"They can't be trusted," Esther agreed. "There'll never be peace."

Lia remembered Taata Maryam and Uncle Sami arguing about the peace treaty. They were watching a news broadcast, clips of Yassar Arafat and Yizhak Rabin shaking hands in Washington D.C.

"You see." Taata pinched her cheeks. "I tell you one day come peace."

"Peace? This isn't peace." Sami snarled and waved his arms in irritation, dismissing everything she'd said. "Do you think there'll be a red carpet leading up to your old house in Jaffa, laid out by the Jews who stole it from you? There'll never be peace. They can't be trusted. Just an old woman talking," He nearly spat at her.

Lia had never heard him talk to Taata that way.

LIFE IN THE settlement continued, but everyone was on edge. The radio broadcaster's baritone voice could be heard constantly, emerging out of every caravan. Every hour on the hour David and Esther would hush everyone and huddle together to listen to the news. David was the army liaison officer for the settlement, so all the alerts and messages passed through him. The walkie-talkie clipped to his belt sputtered loudly at all times of the day and night, sending him running off to gather the settlement's tiny combat unit, shouting out orders to passers-by. Some days they barely left the caravan, confined to its tiny space the moment it got dark. Army patrols came by regularly, much more often than before, and all the men carried guns.

"There's nothing to worry about." David held up his revolver. "No one can get through me."

Still, Lia worried, lying awake at night listening to the nearby barking of the dogs and the sounds of jackals howling in the distance. This was a new kind of fear, one she had never felt before. Lia had never been afraid for her life, but now she was constantly on the lookout. Watching. Waiting. Jumping at every sound. But the icy cold emptiness at the tip of her tummy was no stranger, whirring and churning endlessly, with the same awful helplessness she remembered from her mother's illness.

Some nights, she was so scared, the pink balloon wouldn't rise, remaining anchored to the floor, as if held down by an enormous weight. When it did take off, Lia would rise above the settlement, letting the balloon take her wherever it willed. Usually it took her far away, to different times and places, but sometimes it remained nearby, hovering gently above the neighboring villages and settlements. She had never even visited the adjacent village, just driven by a few times with her father, but from the pink balloon she could see it all. The little stone houses. The olive trees. The grazing goats and donkeys. She liked to go down and fly really low, nearly touching the people as she went by. But wherever the pink balloon took her, over Arab villages or Jewish settlements, when she rose up high and squinted down, they all looked exactly the same. No matter how hard she tried to differentiate between them, all she saw were a bunch of living, breathing coconuts.

"BRING THE GIRLS to Tel Aviv, I want to buy them their costumes," Hanna suggested to her brother. With everything that was going on, they hadn't come to Tel Aviv for ages and she really missed them.

LIA WAS THRILLED to get out of the settlement. It had begun to feel like a prison, being cooped up for so long.

"Purim," Jonathan explained to her, "is the Jewish Halloween."

It was all the kids could talk about. Everyone was excited, even the adults.

"We'll have an extra special holiday this time," David promised. "Beezrat Hashem, nothing will spoil our festivities."

"That's where I got my name," Esther said, concluding her story of the Jewish queen who saved her nation.

"I don't feel like dressing up," Lia told them. When she had gone trick or treating with Jasmine, they had always worn the same costumes, fighting and arguing over them for months. The year before she left, they were both Cinderellas and the year before that Alices in Wonderland.

"You have to," David snapped. "It's a mitzvah, an edict, a decree."

"It's the best holiday ever." Jonathan tried to convince her. "Everyone gets drunk and goes crazy." Lila only changed her mind when he suggested they dress up together.

HANNA WAS WAITING at the entrance to Dizengoff Center, tapping her fingers impatiently.

"Pleased to meet you." She shook Jonathan's hand and bent down to kiss the girls.

"I like your hair, it suits you," she said to Lia, running her fingers over her head. Irena was the settlement's hair dresser and she had cut Lia's hair to just above her shoulders, like she used to wear it when she was a small child. Lia loved the way it framed her face, making her eyes look larger and longer, just like her mother's.

"And your Hebrew." Hanna beamed at her. "It's unbelievable how quickly you picked it up.

"She has no accent at all," David said proudly. "Sounds like a true tsabar. Someone who was born in Israel," he explained to Lia. "Just like the cactus, rough and prickly on the outside, soft and sweet inside."

"Let's go to the other side, the best store's just after the bridge," Jonathan suggested.

Lia could hardly hear anything above the din of squawking children and irritated parents, shopping for last minute costumes and accessories. Loudspeakers blared silly Purim songs and clowns handed out balloons and "ozen hamman," a triangle of dough filled with chocolate or poppy seeds.

"Right here, at five o'clock, exactly." David admonished them with his finger. "Don't be late. I don't want to have to go looking for you in this crowd. Maybe you could find something biblical," he suggested to Jonathan.

"Sure," Jonathan nodded. "No way in hell," he whispered in Lia's ear.

"Leave the children alone." Hanna handed Lia two crisp hundred shekel bills. "Let them be whatever they want."

"That's way too much." David shook his head at her and sighed.

"It's Purim." Hanna grinned. "Go on, get whatever you want."

THEY TRIED ON wigs and masks, pulling on disguise after disguise but couldn't find anything they liked. They didn't want to be king and queen or witch and wizard. Lia didn't like the prisoner costume and the skeletons gave Jonathan the creeps.

"Most of the good disguises are gone." Jonathan was beginning to despair, when the saleslady had a sudden thought.

"I have two costumes I was keeping for someone, but they never showed up. I think they'd fit you." She returned a moment later with Peter Pan and Wendy.

"Yeesss!" Jonathan shrieked, grabbing his disguise.

"Noooo!" Lia pouted as she pushed hers away.

"I love Peter Pan." Jonathan held the costume close to his body while he peered at himself in the mirror.

"Well I hate Wendy." Lia picked up the long blue dress, shaking her head. "I was always Tiger Lily. But Daddy doesn't call me that anymore," she added sadly.

"No Tiger Lily," the saleslady told them, overhearing their conversation.

"Maybe you could be an Indian?" Jonathan suggested. "We'll make you our own Tiger Lily."

"All out." The saleslady shook her head. "No Indian."

"I don't want to be Tiger Lily anyway. I may as well try Wendy on," she decided, seeing how much Jonathan wanted to be Peter.

"At least I'll be modest enough." She laughed when she stood before the mirror. The light blue dress went down all the way to her ankles and the puffed sleeves covered her arms till her elbows.

"Positively kosher," Jonathan couldn't help adding.

AT FIVE O'CLOCK they were waiting under the bridge. Hanna and David arrived a few moments later, a little elephant strutting in between them. Rachel wouldn't take off her disguise. It was soft and grey, with a big white belly, and it covered her from head to toe, her feet perfect little paws. Only her little smiling face could be seen, sticking out under the long grey trunk that came out of the top of her head.

Lia scooped her up in her arms and threw her in the air. "What does an elephant do?"

"Hooo . . . hooo . . ." Rachel answered, sounding more like an owl.

"Wooooo . . ." they all trumpeted together, roaring with laughter.

David showed her what he had bought. A long blue cape for him and a red one for Esther, with matching crowns.

"Since the first Purim we spent together, we always wear the same disguise. I'm King Achashverosh and she's . . ."

"Queen Esther," they all shouted out together.

Lia hadn't felt so free since the last time they came to Tel Aviv.

"Just a little longer," she kept begging, each time David said they should start heading back.

"C'mon, there's a lovely ice cream parlor just outside the center." Hanna saw David was beginning to get irritated. "My treat."

BUT THERE WAS no real Purim that year. The eve of the holiday, while the adults were fasting and the children busy decorating the synagogue for the reading of the Megilla, the Purim scroll, all hell broke loose. Screams erupted from all the caravans. Lia dropped the clown she was holding up for Jonathan to hang and they ran out to see what was happening. Esther came running down the path, her red kerchief awry, Rebecca at her heels.

"They bombed the center," she was screaming hysterically. "They bombed the center."

People came running out of the caravans, disheveled, their clothes in disarray. Everyone was screaming and crying.

"It was just outside the center," David told them, tears running down his cheeks. "On the crossing. Just where we were standing, yesterday, eating our ice creams."

Lia's arms and legs shook as the images of the day before filled her mind. The street had been packed with merry, boisterous faces, many already wearing their disguises, all filled with anticipation.

"There were a million people there," she started to say, but the words stuck in her throat. David wiped her cheeks and held her close. Lia hadn't even noticed she was crying.

"WE HAVE TO pull ourselves together and go to the reading," David said, as the sun began to descend. The children had spent days filling plastic containers with rice and beans, preparing the rattles they would shake every time the name of Hamman "the evil" was mentioned. He was the Jews' arch enemy, and the Purim festival was a celebration of his defeat.

"I don't feel like going." Lia couldn't stop crying, her mind filled with images of children in fancy dress, being blown to smithereens. Suddenly there was terror all around her. It had even followed her to Tel Aviv. She felt like she would never be safe again. "And I'm sure not going to put on my stupid costume."

"You have to." Esther finally stood up, gathering herself together. "C'mon, we all have to. Purim is a celebration of Hashem, and we have to be merry. It is commanded."

But what was usually a noisy and cheerful affair was quiet and guarded that year. Lia and Jonathan found a place together, right at the end of the synagogue, slipping out the moment they could. They went straight up to their bench where they just sat quietly, dismally listening to the sounds of praying and singing, that went on until late into the night, a sad and solemn Peter Pan and Wendy, their feet so heavily grounded, they couldn't even fly.

BY SUMMER, THINGS had calmed down somewhat, and Esther and David began to plan her Bat Mitzva. Lia didn't want a big party, but they insisted.

"You're only twelve once." David laughed.

"You're becoming a woman." Esther took her hands in hers and looked her straight in the eye. "That's something we have to celebrate."

"But before we can do anything," David told Lia, "there's a little matter we have to take care of."

He had already made all the arrangements. The day before the party, she was to immerse herself in the "mikve," the Jewish ritual bath, to cleanse and purify herself.

"Daddy said it's because my mother wasn't Jewish," she explained to Jonathan.

"And going to the mikve will make you one?" Jonathan had no idea it was done that way.

"That's what he says." Lia shrugged. "Who cares anyway?"

DAVID TOOK HER to a "mikve" in Tel Aviv, far away from anyone they knew. Esther put on her finest holiday clothes and left the babies with Rebecca for the first time. Lia hated the long white dress that her father bought her for the occasion. It was uncomfortable and scratchy, especially the little white flowers embroidered around the neck and its sleeves were so long, they almost covered her hands. The night before Esther had made sure she bathed, carefully trimming her hair and nails, even the ones on her toes. She knew exactly what had to be done. Like every religious Jewish woman, she went to the "mikve" every month, bathing and purifying herself after each menstruation.

"We'll comb your hair again tomorrow," Esther told Lia before she went to sleep. "And leave your ring and bracelets at home. There must be nothing between you and the water. No knots or jewelry. Not even dirt."

"It's a beautiful experience," she added, when she saw Lia's face. "For me, every time I dunk myself in the water, it's a confirmation. I feel like I become a Jew again for the first time."

Lia didn't want to go to the mikve. She didn't really want to be a Jew either, but no one asked her opinion. Hanna was waiting outside the door. Lia almost didn't recognize her in the long, black dress. She and Esther would be accompanying her throughout the ritual.

The attendant was an old, bent Yemenite woman and Lia could hardly understand what she was saying. She took her hands in hers, checked her nails, and then turned them over. She held her hair up, her nose pressed so closely to her face and neck, Lia could feel her breath, smell its slight sourness. The attendant examined her naked body carefully before nodding her approval, then motioned for her to get into the water.

Lia felt awful. No one had ever looked at her that way before. She had even made her open her mouth and stared at her teeth, as though she were an animal or a piece of meat. The attendant said something to her, but Lia was so overwhelmed, she didn't understand. She looked up at Esther.

"Dip in the water, Lia." Esther came down to stand by the bath. "Immerse yourself. The water has to cover you completely to wash away the past."

"I don't want to wash away my past," Lia thought, as she obediently ducked her head beneath the water, staying there for a while. The water was warm and pleasant and Lia allowed herself to float, to be carried away, lulled into numbness. For a moment, she saw herself from the outside, looking down at herself, as if she were a stranger, idly wandering who the naked girl holding her breath under the water was, but before the thought could take her over, she heard the attendant's voice calling her name.

AS SHE RELUCTANTLY pushed her head out of the water, the attendant waved her out, pushing an ugly beige robe at her. Lia lunged at the robe and quickly wrapped it around her body. It felt coarse and scratchy.

"Not as bad as I thought it would be," she said to herself, thinking she was done.

"In." The attendant motioned her back into the water. Lia looked at Esther and then at Hanna, thinking maybe she had misunderstood, but both women waved their hands motioning her to go back down. Lia began to take off the robe.

"No, No," Esther called out to her. "Keep the robe on!"

Lia stared at her, dumbfounded. Then she climbed down into the water, the robe fluttering around her body, till it grew heavy and clung to her legs. The attendant motioned for her to immerse herself in the water again. As Lia blocked her nose with her fingers and descended, the door opened and some men stuck their noses through the doorway. They were staring right at her, as her head disappeared. Lia had never been so humiliated in all her life. She stayed under the water as long as she could, coming up gasping, to find only the women in the room again.

"Mazel tov, mazel tov," Hanna and Esther congratulated as she stepped out of the water, pelting her with sweets, while the sour faced attendant splayed her tongue, letting out long winding ululations. "Koo loo loo . . . koo. Loo loo . . ."

"She's almost as good as Taata Maryam," Lia thought, just as Esther and Hanna wrapped their arms around her in an unexpected group hug.

"Mazal tov, my daughter," David greeted her proudly when they finally came out. "Now you're officially a Jew."

TIME WAS SLOW in the settlement, but full. There was always something to do and Lia worked hard, appeased with the knowledge she was needed. Just like a roller coaster, the conflict slowed after a terrifying plunge and a relative quiet resumed. The army went back down the hill, and the emergency squad that had been patrolling at night was disbanded.

The entrance gate was rarely locked during the day, and Arabs reappeared, selling their wares or looking for work. Kids roamed freely throughout the settlement and Lia and Jonathan were once again allowed to take the goats out to pasture.

"Don't stray too far from the fence," Mikey warned them whenever they went out. "And always keep sight of the settlement."

"Yes sir," they promised, eager to get going. This was their favorite time of day, strolling down the hill and meandering through the valley on their own with only the herd of goats for company. Keeping to their word, they never went farther than the first valley, where they would find a good spot for the goats to graze. Some days the goats seem jittery, darting unpredictably from place to place, keeping them on their toes, but usually they were peaceful and calm, content to stay in one spot, and Lia and Jonathan hardly had to pay them any attention. Then, they'd lie back under a ridge, close their eyes, and summon the pink balloon.

They flew differently together, more daring and adventurous, the pink balloon taking them beyond the confines of the settlement, to all the forbidden territories surrounding them. They were no longer allowed to enter any of the Palestinian cities, and even neighboring villages were often out of bounds, but in the pink Balloon Jonathan could invoke them all. At least those he'd been to. The rest they just made up.

Lia liked taking them to Nablus, eager to visit the family Taata Maryam had told her so much about.

"Schem's over there, in the far hills." David had shown her the general direction, using the ancient biblical name. "Maybe twenty minutes away."

In the balloon, it was even faster. She didn't remember everything Taata had told her, but she tried to imagine her family, to think of their lives, so near, yet so far away.

With Jonathan she was bolder, no longer content to view things from above. "Down," she'd tell the pink balloon, hovering just above people's heads.

"Who's that?" Jonathan would ask.

"Meet my Auntie Fatma." Lia's would begin her story. "She's married . . ."

"To the side." They'd fly around, eager to see what else they would discover.

"Behind her. To the floor."

But no matter what they saw up close, the moment they rose up again, the differences between them disappeared and all that remained was a group of ordinary coconuts, working hard and doing the best they could. Jonathan saw them too. The only thing they disagreed about was the color. For, often, while Lia saw white coconuts, Jonathan just saw black ones. And vice versa.

THE SETTLEMENT GREW quickly with new faces appearing almost each week. Every few months, in the dead of night, the men would gather for their "special operations," opening the fence and moving it backward, enlarging the settlement and preparing space for the new families' caravans. They no longer had to worry about not having a minyan of ten to pray, and very soon the synagogue itself had to be enlarged. The women got their own, private section, overlooking the men's, and had all taken turns embroidering the curtains that divided the two sections.

The square in front of the synagogue was paved and reinforced with new concrete structures. This was now the commercial center. There was a bakery, a cheese factory, and a grocery store that opened for several hours every day. The thrift shop was full, almost busting at its seams, rewarding Lia with countless hours of happy rummaging and several delightful treasures. Most often she would find a toy or stuffed animal for her little siblings, but sometimes she even found a shirt or a bag for herself. Her best find, undeniably, was the antique mirror she brought home, wrapping it carefully in her arms, so as not to harm its delicate carvings. David hung it at the entrance to the caravan and everyone was always admiring it. Years later, when they finally moved to their permanent house, it was one of the only things that moved with them.

Further from the new center, more businesses were opening. Shabtai and Yaacov finally opened their car workshop, and were employing half a dozen other men. Irena, the hairdresser, opened a beauty salon in a caravan attached to their home, and women from all the surrounding settlements came to wax their legs or color their hair. There were always women sitting around gossiping, and Lia could never enter without thinking of her Auntie Nadia. The daycare was so full, Esther had to turn kids from other settlements away and the waiting list was so long, she refused to add more names to it. The school had five classrooms, with two more under construction.

When Jonathan was sent off to study at a yeshiva high school, almost an hour's drive away, Lia felt abandoned, even though there were now quite a few kids around her age in the settlement. She knew that she was likeable enough because she was constantly surrounded, still, she couldn't get rid of the feeling that she was an outsider, an impostor who would never really fit in. Every day, come five o'clock, she stood nervously by the gate, waiting for Jonathan's return.

But as the weeks went by, she started enjoying the time she had to herself. Soon she looked out for those times, those precious minutes, sometimes even hours of solitude, when she could sneak away, free to be whoever she wanted to be, and do exactly what she wished to do. Any time there was a sudden free period or her chores were over early, she would find a way to ditch her friends. Her favorite place to hide was the synagogue. No one ever disturbed her there. Quite the opposite. And Esther and David were so impressed.

"Lia seems to be finally settling in," she overheard her father telling Esther one night. "I've noticed her slipping into the synagogue quite a few times."

"I've been told she goes every day," Esther happily concurred. "Every spare moment she can find."

Lia didn't mean to deceive them, but she loved the deep, resonating silence of the empty building. It immediately calmed her down.

"It's just a mind attack," she told herself the first time she sought refuge there. "Take a deep breath, and slowly let all the air out." Somehow, her breathing stabilized and her mind slowed down.

"Follow your breath." She suddenly heard Minna's voice instructing her, just as she had so many years before. "Watch your belly go up and down . . ."

She found herself going back to all the old practices, pulling them out of distant, almost forgotten nooks and crannies of her brain, sometimes following her breath to clear her mind, other times, just the opposite. She always brought her notebook with her, writing down her thoughts or whatever it was she wanted to work out, in capital letters, on top of a blank page, then closing her eyes and letting her mind wander. Whatever came up, she made sure to jot down. Writing was her solace, the only way she could cope with all her fears and uncertainties. It wasn't like the pink balloon. Quite the opposite. Writing gave her a tether to the world around her, rather than taking her away from it.

Other times, she went to her bench, still high above the burgeoning settlement. Lia couldn't believe how much it had grown, stretching and swelling in all directions until she could no longer encompass it all in just one glance. She learned to sit quietly, settling her mind, breathing in and out gently, or simply following the sounds.

Sometimes, as she sat there quietly, the Moezzin's drawling prayer would begin, echoing through the valley, carrying her away from herself, away from time and place, away from knowledge and thought, far away into a moment where nothing existed, but a sense of endless calm and beauty. She became the sound of the water. The yellow haze over the hills. The wind whispering through the valley.

EMMANUEL ARRIVED JUST after Lia's fourteenth birthday. Hodi was in the midst of his terrible twos and constantly had to be stopped from trying to kill his baby brother. He would pull Emanuel's little blanket over his face, hoping it would make him disappear and Lia would have to rush over and save him. It was a stressful time but also one of great excitement. The first permanent homes were finally under construction and they were to be one of the first families to move in. Lia couldn't wait. She would still be sharing a room with Rachel, but only because she wanted to. Still, they had decided on a more grownup room, at least Lia's part. She went to check on the house every day, marveling at the way the naked wooden structure took on a life of its own. She walked through the large empty space that would be their living room and up the stairs, entering each one of the bedrooms, imagining what they would look like when they were finished. Best of all, Jonathan and his family would still be their neighbors. Lia couldn't wait to meet the new kids moving in on the other side.

"They're a lovely family," David reported eagerly, "with twin girls, exactly your age."

Yael and Tamar were the oldest of seven siblings, including another pair of twin boys who were the loudest, wildest little boys Lia had ever come across, wilder even than her own littler brothers. Lia ran out to meet them the moment she heard their car arrive. The girls looked exactly the same and even had the same voice, but Lia learned to tell them apart very quickly. Tamar was the no frills tomboy, who hated girl talk and was always on the lookout for some action, while Yaeli was happy to sit around knitting or braiding ribbons for her hair. They were cute and compact, shorter even than Lia, who was now slightly below average height. But, like her, they were tough and determined. As a first order of duty, the twins together with Lia and Jonathan collected leftover building materials, and enlisting their fathers' help, built a hut at the edge of the common ground between the houses. It had one ramshackle room, but they furnished it with all the tattered mats and worn cushions from the old caravans. Rebecca gave them a rickety, broken-down table and some chairs. They worked for days, hammering nails, sanding and polishing until they looked "good as new." The four of them spent all their spare time in their hideaway, but it didn't stay secret for long.

That's where Lia first heard about the school the twins were going to the following year. She heard about it constantly. They couldn't shut up about it, and their excitement was infectious.

"It's in Tel Aviv," Lia told her father. "Please, please let me go."

She knew she would go to high school outside the settlement, but hadn't really given it much thought. Esther and David had tried discussing it with her a few times, mentioning a few options that were all rather close by, but the thought of going to school in Tel Aviv had never even crossed her mind. Now, it was all she could think of.

"Tel Aviv? Are you crazy?" David didn't want to hear it. "It's much too far."

"But I won't be the only one. There are other girls going, too. Yaeli says there are another four girls already registered. They're organizing a minivan and everything."

"Too far away and far too dangerous." David tried to dismiss her. "There are some very good schools right here and you'll go to one of them."

"But there's nothing like this school, Daddy. It has teacher training from the beginning, and if I stay the extra two years, I'll have a profession."

Lia was pulling out all the stops to get her father to agree. She knew it was something he worried about. He was forever talking to Esther about "preparing Lia for the future," or "finding her an occupation."

"I think you'd make a great English teacher," Rebecca often told her. She had been helping out at the school, teaching English to small groups of kids. They adored her, running after her during breaks and fighting over who would sit next to her in class.

"I'm a really good teacher. I'm patient and all the kids like me. Ask Rebecca," she added for good measure, sure she, at least, would take her side.

Lia had never really considered teaching as a vocation, but she knew it would appeal to her father, and she had to find a way to get to Tel Aviv. It was a dream she hadn't even allowed herself to consider, though she fell in love with the city from the first trip. She loved the endless blue water and the crowded beaches and the friendly, laid-back atmosphere. There were also markets and noise and hustle and bustle. More than anything else, she loved the way the city made her feel. Even the air was different. It had a lightness, a sense of freedom, even abandonment, perhaps. Whatever it was, it made her feel like a child again. And there was so much she still wanted to explore, she had seen so little.

"Please, Daddy," she begged each time they came to the city, "just a little further."

"I'm sorry, Lia, we have to get back, it's getting late," David would inevitably answer. "Maybe next time."

"Please, Daddy," she begged him again and again. "Please let me go to school in Tel Aviv."

"I'll talk it over with Esther," he shook his head, "but no promises. I don't like the idea at all."

"She's much too delicate," Lia overheard Esther saying. "They'll be leaving early in the morning and returning late at night. I think it will be too much for her."

"I'm more worried about how it'll affect her, going to Tel Aviv every day." David thought there were too many bad influences in the big city. "I wouldn't want to tempt her, she's lived differently, after all."

Lia wouldn't let it go. She nagged and pleaded, cried and cajoled, but nothing she did would change their mind. Help arrived from a most unexpected place. A week before the school registration closed, in the early evening, after David returned from the synagogue, there was a knock on their door.

"Hanna!" Lia cried, pleasantly surprised to find her aunt standing outside.

"Is everything alright?" David came running to the door. It was the first time Hanna had come to the settlement. She hadn't even come to Lia's Bat Mitzve or the boys' britot.

"I've come to discuss Lia's education," she announced as she walked in. Lia was dumbfounded. She didn't see her aunt very often, and had no idea she even knew about the school. But Hanna was a woman on a mission. She didn't know Lia very well, but she felt it was her duty to make sure she had every opportunity. She had been denied so much as a girl, she wanted to make sure that it didn't happen to Lia.

"She's been cooped up in the settlement for so long," she told them. "Let her see something else, how other people live."

"That's exactly what we're afraid of," David was quick to answer. "She's settled in so well."

"But she's not from here," Hanna insisted. "What if she wants something else? Hasn't she the right to choose her own future? She has to have a way to support herself."

"She's perfectly happy with—" David started to say.

"Actually," Esther said, "I quite agree."

I would like her to have a profession, something to fall back on. And teaching is something she can always use." Esther paused for a second.

Lia's heart skipped a beat, she was sure she was finally coming around.

"But it's much too far away." Esther shook her head. "What if something happens?"

"It's far too dangerous," David agreed. "And much too much responsibility for such a young girl."

"Then I'll take the responsibility," Hanna announced.

"What?" David was white as a sheet, his mouth agape. Lia and Esther were also staring at her, waiting for an explanation.

"You know where the school is, right? On the corner of the market? Well, that's exactly three blocks from my house." She turned to Lia. "You remember where I work? It's straight down that road."

Lia began to feel excited as she realized what her aunt was about to say.

"I promise to take full responsibility for Lia. If anything happens, if there's any problem, I'll be there in a minute. If there's any kind of tension or curfew and you're worried about her getting through, she can always stay with me. I'll watch her like a hawk, I promise."

David and Esther exchanged a long look.

"What about food? How will she manage?" Esther furrowed her brow and placed a hand on her hip.

"I'll keep special food and utensils for her," Hanna promised, grinning at them.

"I don't know." David scratched his beard.

"What do you think?" he asked Esther.

"Please, please . . ." Lia begged.

"Well," Esther shrugged, "I guess we can give it a try."

Hanna was so pleased, she agreed to sleep over. The next morning, it was decided, they would go into the city together to register Lia for high school. Lia couldn't believe it. She was going to school in Tel Aviv.

EVERY MORNING WHEN Lia stepped out of the minivan, she'd marvel at the sight awaiting her, as hundreds of girls in long grey skirts and blouses, crowded together before the gate, turning the sidewalk into a dark, chattering river. Cars slowed down to stare and pedestrians smiled at the sudden, slightly alien apparition. It always amused her, although she did feel somewhat uncomfortable, feeling so many eyes on her. It wasn't a big school, but she had never seen so many overdressed girls in the same place.

The building was hideous, a grey square three-story structure that looked like an old government establishment. The inside wasn't much better, but at least it was clean and freshly painted. The girls from the settlements were all in the same class, the one in the corner, on the third floor. There were tons of steps, but the class had huge windows, and it was so high up, that when Lia looked out, the ocean was all she could see, nothing obstructing her view. She chose the second-to-last desk directly in front of the window.

School hours were long, but the work proved not too demanding. Lia liked the girls and tried to get on as well as she could with all her teachers, making sure to always smile attentively and hand in her assignments on time. She even attended all bible and religion classes, bowing her head in prayer, fervently reciting all the psalms and verses she had memorized. Every now and then, she'd raise her eyes and stare out at the huge expanse of blue right in front of her, quieting her mind and surrendering to the immense sense of freedom and possibility that seemed to fill her entire being.

Just for a moment though. Whatever happened, she couldn't be caught daydreaming. She knew what was expected of her, and that was exactly what she intended to do. If she had to, she was willing, at least outwardly, to play the dutiful, devout Jew everyone wanted her to be. She was finally in Tel Aviv, and there was no way she was going to give that up.

But inwardly, everything was slowly changing, fluctuating, opening up. For the first few weeks, she seldom left the school grounds, and then only taking brief excursions, exploring the colorful market just footsteps away. But the first time they were given a free period, Lia convinced her friends to walk down to the beach promenade. They bought lemon popsicles and sat licking them on the little wall just before the sand. Lia was jealous of all the people sunbathing half naked in the sun or splashing in the water. Most of all, she envied the cyclists, the female ones especially, riding by so carefree and happy, their hair flapping wildly in the wind. In Laurel Valley she had practically lived on her bike, but in the settlement it was forbidden.

"Hashem yishmor," David admonished her. "Girls can't ride bikes. It's not modest."

THE NEXT FREE period, the girls embarked on a journey of discovery, led by one of their classmates who lived just a few streets away. Tehila took them through the open market and into a pedestrian mall filled with stands and stalls selling arts and crafts and handmade jewelry. Almost all the girls in their class had tagged along, and the large group pushed their way noisily through the sea of people. Every few minutes, Tehila stopped to wait for all the girls to gather. Lia strained her head, eagerly taking in all the splendid old buildings, still poshly holding up their tarnished necks, oblivious to their dingy, filth ridden, surroundings. It felt as if by merely crossing the street she had travelled back in time to an old European city. Tehila pointed to a kosher bakery, and the girls gorged themselves on burekas, a warm filo dough pastry packed with cheese and vegetables.

As the girls turned up the winding road, the city noises grew louder and the thick air carried unidentifiable smells, not all of them pleasant.

"Allenby." Tehila crinkled her nose in disgust. "It's just junk. Let's go back."

"Can't we walk down to the promenade from here? There's plenty of time." Tamara didn't want to go back yet.

All the girls nodded their agreement, begging her to go on.

"Okay." Tehila turned toward the ocean. "But we'd better hurry."

The girls joined arms and started following her again, chattering and pointing as they went. The street was lined with shops selling shoes and clothing, bars, cafes, and restaurants. Every now and then a bunch of girls would stop, press their faces into a store window and then argue and giggle about what they had seen.

Lia was walking with the twins, one on each side, trying to referee as usual.

"Why do we always have to wear the same clothes?" Tamara yelled at her sister. "We're not three years old."

"We can wear different colors," Yaeli pleaded. "It'll be so cute. Everyone says . . ."

But Lia didn't hear what "everyone says." Lia wasn't listening anymore, mesmerized by a small sign with an arrow pointing left that said, "Used Books, English and Hebrew, 10 shekels."

She slowed down, trying to see as much as she could without actually stopping. The store was narrow and long, and from where she was standing, it seemed to go on forever. Lia looked around the street, mentally taking note of her exact location.

"I have to get back here," she promised herself. "The very first chance I get."

Lia missed reading more than anything. Learning how to read had been a revelation for her and she had devoured almost every book in the Laurel Valley School library. The walls of her home in the settlement were covered with books, but they were all about scripture and God and ethics. Desperately trying to find something to read, she had even tried *The Way of Hashem* in Hebrew, slowly voicing each word out loud, almost reaching the middle and a couple of books on *The Ways of the Righteous* before giving up and approaching Esther's English contributions. The *Kuzari* and the *Zohar* proved completely incomprehensible, even in English, and all the books describing the Jewish family, holidays, or dietary laws were slammed shut before the end of the opening chapter. The only book she had read from start to finish was Anne Frank's diary, a book that lay by her bed for months, while she devoured every entry again and again, until she almost knew it all by heart.

A FEW WEEKS past until the girls finally had a few hours off. Lia waited for all her friends to leave the school before slipping out and was careful to take the long way, walking swiftly through the streets and alleys whose names she hadn't yet learnt. A bell rang loudly as she walked through the door of the bookstore, but it seemed deserted. Lia wandered idly from room to room, browsing the headings. The store was bigger than it seemed, its narrow entryway leading to more hidden rooms, packed with books, each one meticulously labeled and catalogued. The first room had mostly Hebrew titles, devoted to Judaism and Israeli history, so she didn't even stop. But the next room was full of science fiction and mystery novels, all in English.

"Can I help you?" a man called out.

Lia looked around her but saw no one. She walked into the next room. A stocky, elderly man was standing high up on a ladder, placing a pile of books on the very top shelf.

"Just came in this morning," he muttered. "A full set of Dickens, from the very start of the century. Quite a coup. Would you mind?" He pointed to a stack of books on the floor beneath the ladder.

"*Oliver Twist, Great Expectations, David Copperfield,*" she read as she handed him the crimson bound books. He put each novel in its place and then climbed down, sighing with effort as he wiped his brow with a crumpled handkerchief.

"Gideon." He held out his hand, but then started to pull it back as he noticed her clothes.

"Lia," she said, quickly grabbing his receding palm and giving it a shake.

"Sorry, I thought . . ." he began to say. "Never mind, what can I do for you?"

"I don't really know myself." Lia felt overwhelmed. "I don't even know where to start."

"What kind of books do you like to read?"

"Wow," Lia guffawed. "I haven't read for so long, I have no idea. Perhaps you could recommend something. In English, though, my Hebrew's great, but I still read so slowly."

"I think I know where we should start," Gideon declared, after she told him a little more about herself.

"Follow me." He shuffled slowly into the next room, pulling his feet after him. Bad knees." He smiled, switching on the light. "Here we are. Young adult fiction. Take your time. I'll check up on you in a while."

Lia walked from stand to stand, feasting her eyes. She was so excited, she pulled books out at random, reading their covers and then returning them to their place. There were so many books, just waiting for her, she couldn't make up her mind. She pulled out some of her old favorites, overjoyed to meet them again. *Little Women, The Wind in the Willows, The Wizard of Oz.*

"Maybe you should start with the classics," Gideon suggested, "or some turn of the century women's novels." He pointed to the back wall.

"I can't make up my mind," Lia said. She wanted to read every book in the store.

"Take a few," Gideon offered. "You can pay next time, if you don't have enough."

"I can only take one," Lia told him, realizing she would have to hide it. No one could know and her father wasn't the only problem. Reading unauthorized secular books was strictly forbidden by her school and if she were caught, she would be severely punished, probably expelled.

"Well." Gideon scratched his brow. "We must certainly make it count."

"I'm running out of time." Lia glanced at her watch. It was already after one thirty and her next class was beginning in twenty minutes. "I really have to get back."

"Let me think, let me think." Gideon surveyed the room. Then, he snapped his fingers, walked up to the last rack, and retrieved a book from the bottom shelf.

"Tolkien," he chortled has he handed it to her.

"*The Hobbit,*" Lia read and began to cry. "I was just about to read it when my mother died. I forgot all about it. I . . . I . . . I'll take it," she stuttered, pressing 10 shekels into Gideon's hand and pushing the book into the depth of her backpack.

"Return it when you're finished and you pay half on the next one," Gideon called after her as she rushed out.

LIA MADE SURE to take her backpack with her wherever she went. Hidden inside it, between the pages of a large prayer book, sat *The Hobbit*, waiting for those precious moments she was left on her own. She spent hours in the toilet, complaining of stomachaches, or straining her eyes with a flashlight under the covers, once she was sure Rachel was asleep. But her favorite place to read was the synagogue, where she would sit over her prayer book, like a dutiful Jewish daughter, with *The Hobbit* skillfully disguised between its pages.

Oh, what a time she had following Bilbo Baggins and Gandalf and Smaug deep into the undergrounds, through hidden cave dwellings and passageways, searching for hidden kingdoms and treasure. Lia had never read anything remotely like it, and she immediately fell in love with the magical land of dwarfs and elves and goblins. At night, before she fell asleep, she flew her pink balloon high above the misty mountains and down through the secret door into the underground. She flew above man-eating trolls and boulder throwing giants, dodging evil wargs and gigantic speaking spiders. She didn't have much time to read, but she didn't mind. She didn't want the book to end.

"I'D ALMOST GIVEN up on you," Gideon called, waving frantically at her from where he was perched, high up on the last rung of the ladder. "I was beginning to think you wouldn't come back. So, how did you like the book?" He started to climb down, panting heavily.

"Oh, Gideon." Lia waved the book at him. "It's the best thing I've ever read. Do you have anything else by Tolkien?"

"Ah, yes." Gideon nodded. "There's nothing quite like Tolkien. I've been keeping something aside, in case you did return."

He motioned her over to his desk, pushing aside a mound of books waiting to be catalogued, then bent down and pulled a large box out of the bottom drawer.

"Someone brought this just last week." He placed it on the desk. "*Lord of the Rings*, the entire trilogy."

Lia felt she was in heaven.

"But I won't be able to take it all." She immediately began to worry.

"Of course not," Gideon reassured her. "They'll be waiting here for you. You can take one at a time."

MUCH TO HER delight, Gideon took it upon himself to complete Lia's literary education. Whenever she arrived, there was a book waiting for her. He began with the classics, leaving special editions and rare copies in her drawer. She loved the old books with their thick, crisp pages and soft musky smell, happily carrying them around, even when she couldn't read them. She made sure to go out to the market and the pedestrian mall with the other girls, whenever they had a break, but whenever she could, she made up an excuse and beelined to the bookstore.

Often when she came in, Gideon was arguing with his customers, scolding them, in some cases even kicking them out. But he was always pleased to see Lia.

"Shouldn't I be paying more for some of these books?" she asked him once, after she noticed that other customers were charged more.

"No one reads anymore." he shook his head, blowing dust off a pile of books. "Certainly not kids. And anyway, you're a regular."

She spent as much of her spare time as she could helping him around the store, tidying, dusting, cataloguing, and putting books away. There was always a lot to be done. Sometimes, as they were working, Gideon would come across a book he thought might interest her, and he'd call her over to share. He gave her introductory philosophy books and pamphlets, introducing her to Socrates, Aristotle, and Plato. Before the summer vacation he gave her a copy of Edith Hamilton's *Timeless Tales of Gods and Heroes*.

He refused to take payment. "It's a present."

Lia loved it so much, it remained hidden for years under her bed.

IT WAS A quiet year, the political situation stable, and the area peaceful most of the time. She met her Aunt Hanna a few times, but she never had to stay over. School was easy and there was little homework. David and Esther, together with most of the adults in the settlement, were kept busy, moving from place to place in the occupied territories. Every day brought another demonstration against the government evacuation of illegal settlements. They would come home late at night, exhausted and agitated, sometimes bruised and bleeding. David was arrested on more than one occasion when the demonstrations turned violent, but that only bound him more tightly to his cause, asserting Jewish sovereignty over all of biblical Israel.

"What about the Palestinians?" she'd dared to ask him the first time he was wounded. "Don't they have any rights? What about Mommy's family? What about their land?" Before she could stop herself, all the questions that had been troubling her came tumbling out.

"This is the Jewish homeland." David shook his cast at her. "The land of our forefathers. It is our birthright and we can't give it away. Any of it. Don't you understand?"

Lia didn't understand. She knew there was another side. A side she knew and loved. But she also knew it was no use, nothing she said would change his mind. And besides, she quickly realized, the more pre-occupied he was, the freer she became. She started visiting the bookstore every week.

"Thursday at twelve, like clockwork." Gideon would hold up his watch every time she came in, pointing to the stack of books he'd put aside. Every now and then she'd take something for Jonathan. He was in his last year of high school and had very little time, but he treasured the books she brought him, hiding them away to read when no one was around.

ALL HELL BROKE loose just before the high holidays, at the start of Lia's second year of school, as the roller coaster took a downward lurch. The anger and frustration that had been seething for so many years finally ruptured, spewing violence and hatred in its wake. Terror returned to the settlements as cars were stoned or shot at, and the entire surrounding area turned into a gurgling mass of uprisings, riots, and mayhem. But it was not only the occupied territories that were under attack. In the big cities malls, busses, and coffee shops were targeted, suicide bombers blowing themselves up, leaving a trail of blood and anguish behind them. Suddenly, no one was safe.

Still, Lia couldn't wait for the New Year holidays. Esther was about to give birth, another girl, this time, and Jonathan would be back from the army, his first visit home since he had enlisted.

"I'm not sure I'm going to be very popular," he half-joked, when he phoned to tell her.

"Don't be an idiot," she scoffed. "Everyone will be happy to see you."

All the boys from the settlements around them went to a Hesder Yeshiva after high school, a combination of advanced Talmudic studies and military service, but Jonathan had refused and nothing his parents did could change his mind.

"I want to go to the regular army," he told them, "with regular people from all over the country. I've been sheltered all my life. Just this once, I want to do what everyone else does."

"That's just what I'm afraid of," Rebecca complained to Esther. "All the temptations."

"The thought of spending another five years in the yeshiva is enough to make me sick," he told Lia. "Always hiding, afraid to be found out. I can't wait to get out of here."

"I've never thought of you as a fighter." Lia had been incredulous when he had decided to join a combat unit. "You don't have to prove yourself to anyone."

"I have to prove myself to myself," Jonathan insisted. He had no intention of returning to the settlement after his release.

"After the army," he told Lia, "I'll finally be free."

But it was a dismal new year, all the festivities were cancelled and none of the guests arrived. Instead, the men rolled out fresh reels of barbed wire, encircling the settlement with yet another line of defense. At night they resumed guarding in turns, manning the entrance or patrolling the grounds. The army post moved closer, settling just below them and armored vehicles could be seen moving up and down the little hill at all hours. Soldiers and settlers shared the holiday meals, praying and singing together, trying to revive the holiday spirit, but everyone was tense and on edge, worried about what the coming days would bring.

Lia hardly had a chance to see Jonathan before he was called back the very next day. The riots were spreading throughout the territories, and the military was enforcing a strict curfew. The day before the Succot holidays, Esther's water broke and she was rushed to hospital. Lia stayed behind to watch the kids and help them decorate their makeshift hut. She put them to sleep and waited for David, even though he'd told her not to.

"Everything's fine," David had said when he called. "Esther's feeling good and Naomi's just beautiful. She reminds me of you when you were first born."

"Something's wrong." Lia felt it the moment David returned. "Did something happen to the baby, to Esther?"

"No, no," he reassured her, but he couldn't hold back his tears. "It's not them, it's . . . something terrible happened . . ."

He told her that two reserve soldiers had lost their way and inadvertently entered a Palestinian city. They were attacked by a mob and beaten to death, their corpses badly mutilated.

"There was a TV in the waiting room. It all unfolded in front of our eyes. The men were lynched, their bodies thrown out of a window, just because they were Jews," David seethed.

Lia was appalled. She had always tried to see both sides, but this was not something she could accept. "Nothing can justify that kind of behavior," she told herself, afraid to think of what would happen next. She hugged her father tightly, her stomach a nauseous knot.

The lynching was all everyone could talk about for the rest of the holidays, blaming "Oslo" and talking of "Arafat's War." The situation escalated rapidly and they found themselves shut in, enclosed behind barbed wire, as if they themselves were in prison. After Nadav's car was ambushed and stoned, very few people came or left the settlement, and when they did, they travelled in an armed convoy. His baby had been with him and was luckily unharmed, but his forehead needed twenty stitches.

The settlers held frantic meetings, trying to decide how best to defend themselves. One of the main issues was what to do with the kids, with many of the older ones commuting large distances. Some of the parents from Lia's school decided to pull their daughters out.

"There's no way you're going to Tel Aviv every day," David agreed. "The Ulpana in Ets Efraim isn't too far away and they've offered to place all the girls from your school together."

"Right now, even that's too dangerous." Esther shook her head. "I've spoken to Rebecca. We'll set up a class for the girls right here and they'll join the school when things settle down. Anyway," she smiled at Lia, "I'd love for you to be closer to home at the moment, I could really use the help."

Lia was happy to help, but going to school in Tel Aviv was the best thing to happen to her since she could remember. "Tamara and Yael are still going and so are Libby and Yifat."

"They all lived in Tel Aviv and have families to take care of them there." David was adamant. "You barely even know the city and the only person you have there is Aunt Hanna."

But Hanna, it turned out, was the only one she needed.

"She can stay with me the moment there's any sign of trouble," she promised.

David wasn't quick to agree. "I don't want her wandering around Tel Aviv on her own either."

"I'll walk her to school on the way to work, and wait for her when she finishes," Hanna swore. "On the days I work late, she'll come straight to the post office. It's exactly two minutes away."

David still didn't like it, but finally agreed that if the girls remained in the settlement until things quietened down, he was prepared to give it a try.

"But no more running around like before." He shook his finger at her. "You go to school and then you come home or straight to your aunt."

Lia promised.

NEARLY A MONTH passed before the girls were allowed to go back to Tel Aviv. Only five of them were still enrolled, so the fathers took turns driving them back and forth in an armored vehicle. David drove them the first day, and Lia sat on the edge of the front seat the entire way, waiting for her first glance of the ocean. As promised, Hanna was waiting at the school entrance to take the bag Esther had packed.

"Just in case," Esther told Lia before she left. She shoved a purse with some spending money into the bag. "Let's hope you won't need it, but you never know."

"I'm still not happy about this," David told his sister as he handed her Lia's bag.

"Don't worry." Hanna waved him off.

"If there's any problem, I'll be waiting for you when school ends." Hanna held Lia's hands in hers. "Hopefully everything will be OK, but if not," she looked into her eyes, "I'm really looking forward to spending more time with you."

THE FIRST DAYS were relatively quiet and the girls got to school and back without mishap. No one was allowed to leave the school grounds without special authorization and during the breaks, the girls gathered around the radio that had been set up in the front courtyard, apprehensively listening to the news. Wednesday was the girls' "long day," but by the time it ended, the "sporadic skirmishes" reported throughout the day had turned into "violent clashes all over the West Bank."

"There'll be no transportation to the settlements," Principal Luria announced. "If you don't have anywhere to go, come to me. I have a list of families that have volunteered to take you in."

Hanna was waiting for her outside the gate. She put her arm through Lia's and they walked home briskly.

"I've prepared the spare room for you." Hanna couldn't wait to show her what she had done. She had removed all her mother's old furniture and replaced it with a new sofa bed and nightstand. The walls were painted a soft pastel blue and everything looked fresh and inviting.

"You didn't have to do all of this for me." Lia was touched and a little embarrassed.

"Nonsense." Hanna waved her off. "I should have done it a long time ago. C'mon, I'll show you how to use the computer."

Lia had never had one at her disposal before. The girls studied computer literacy at school, but everything they did was supervised. There could be no independent searching of the web, and any girl caught looking where she shouldn't was strictly punished. Tamara had already lost a month's worth of privileges. As she was about to sit down at her aunt's desk a screen flickering in the background caught her eye, filling her with a sudden longing.

"TV." Lia rushed towards it. "Please Hanna. Please, can we watch?" It had been so long since she had seen TV or gone to the movies.

"I'm not sure I'm supposed to let you." Hanna was torn. "On the other hand," she swiftly made up her mind, "no one specifically mentioned it."

Hanna walked her to school the next morning and was waiting for her at school's end.

"You're going to stay with me for the entire weekend," she informed her happily. They walked through the market, picking up some extra clothes for Lia, including a pair of loose trousers for her to wear around the house.

"You don't really have to get special food for me," Lia said, but Hanna felt she had to keep her word.

"I promised your father and anyway, I've made a decision. I bought some extra dishes and from now on everything that enters the house will be glatt kosher. Even your father will be able to eat at my house."

LATE FRIDAY AFTERNOON, just before the Sabbath, there was a knock on the door.

"I wonder who that could be?" Hanna opened the door to find Jonathan standing outside, a green duffel bag and a long, black rifle slung over one shoulder.

"I've got the weekend off, but it's too late to get home." He smiled sheepishly. "I think I'm kind of stuck."

"Come in, come in, put your things down," Hanna welcomed. "I'm sorry you'll miss seeing your family, but we're thrilled to have you."

"I'm not sorry at all," Jonathan told her, much to her surprise. "I'd much rather spend my weekend here, with you guys."

He told them that going back to the settlement was becoming harder for him. "My whole life there is a lie. I have to be careful, watch what I say. I don't belong there anymore."

"He can sleep on the couch," Hanna told a distraught Rebecca over the phone. "It's absolutely no bother."

THEY DIDN'T EVEN do much that first weekend, content to sit on the balcony playing cards and board games, or simply watch people passing down below. The entire country was seething with unrest, but Tel Aviv refused to live in fear and everyone was trying to get on with their lives as best they could.

When the sun began to set, bringing the Sabbath to its end, Hanna could take it no longer.

"C'mon." She jumped to her feet with a sudden burst of energy. "Let's go for a walk. We can't hide inside forever or they get exactly what they want."

The streets surrounding them were almost deserted, but the promenade was alive with families and couples. A group of teenagers on roller blades made their way through the crowds and cyclists waved to each other as they rode by.

"To the water?" Hanna laughingly asked Lia, although she knew the answer. Lia held her skirt and waded in up to her knees. They walked down the beach until they reached Jaffa's old city, its walls towering above them. The sun had just set and as the city lights took over, the old fortress stood out, tall and imposing in the indigo glow, overlooking the entire city.

"Let's start back," Jonathan worried. "Jaffa's too dangerous."

"Nonsense," Hanna scoffed, waving him off. "Jaffa's perfectly safe. I've been walking these streets since I was a child. No one will harm us."

She led them through the old port and up winding stairs and narrow alleyways, past hanging balconies and gardens, till they reached the cliff. The streets were nearly deserted, but the people they passed by were friendly, and they quickly forgot their apprehensions.

In the weeks and months to come, they would keep coming back, wandering through Jaffa's streets, exploring the old mansions and markets.

"You know, Hanna, despite the circumstances, I can't remember when I last had such a wonderful time," Lia told her aunt as she hugged her goodbye the following morning. David had phoned to say he would be fetching the girls after school.

"Me too." Hanna planted a kiss on her cheek. "I like having you around. Come and stay whenever you feel like it. I mean it."

Hanna and Lia had finally discovered each other, and they each had their own reasons to be grateful. They used any pretext available to keep Lia in Tel Aviv. At the first sign of unrest, and there were plenty, Hanna would call her brother for a "consult," and no matter how bad the news, Lia's face lit up when she walked out of school to find Hanna waiting for her.

At school, the girls were monitored closely, but the guard at the gate had become lax and could sometimes be cajoled into letting one or two out for a quick run to the market. They all took turns, setting out with a list of all their friends' requests. Lia was the first to volunteer, but it was a few weeks before she walked through the gate and into the city. She quickly bought all the items on her list and then headed straight to the bookstore.

Gideon was working at his desk, most of him hidden by an enormous pile of books. He glanced up when he heard the bell and smiled as he shuffled in Lia's direction.

"I've been so worried." Gideon greeted her like an old friend. "I thought something happened. It's not like you to disappear for so long. But I was sure you'd be back. I've got so many books ready for you."

Lia pulled out her drawer using both hands it was so heavy, full to the brim with turn of the century novels of manners, romances, and historical fiction.

"Books every young girl should read." Gideon chuckled when he saw her expression. "At least they'll be a great distraction from everything that's happening."

And they were. Between horrific images of wounded children and exploding buildings, Lia read *Jane Eyre* and *Wuthering Heights*. She went through Dickens and Austin, Shelley and Oscar Wilde. At first she tried to hide her books from her aunt, but when Hanna inadvertently walked in on her, she realized she didn't have to. In fact, Hanna was thrilled when she saw what she was reading.

"*A Room of One's Own*, Virginia Woolf, wow." Her eyes widened in surprise.

"You won't tell my father, will you?" Lia asked, dreading his reaction.

"Don't worry, my lips are sealed." Hanna always took her side. "Not allowing children to read books. I've never heard of anything so stupid. You can read whatever you want. You can leave your books here. I'll make some room for you in the bookcase."

THE COUNTRY WAS on fire, and there was no time to grieve and nowhere to go. Shootings and bombings occurred on a daily basis, leaving Lia with plenty of time to spend with her aunt. True to her beliefs that "you can't give in to terror" and "life must go on," Hanna dragged Lia out of the house whenever she could, through the streets of south Tel Aviv, until Lia could navigate them almost as well as her. Jonathan seldom had time off, but whenever he could, he joined them, and the three of them would wander the streets until late at night, licking popsicles and ice cream and stuffing their faces with piping hot falafel and knafe.

Some days, the situation was so bad, they didn't leave the house, preferring to lay about the living room or hunch in front of the screen, eyes glued to the glimmering images, unable to comprehend the atrocities that seemed to be coming from both sides. In the settlement, there was only one point of view, but at Hanna's, Lia could see the other side clearly, and she didn't like what was happening there either.

Other times they'd shut the TV, play a game, search the web or silently read together. Sometimes they stayed inside for days, but Lia didn't mind. Strangely, however bad it became outside, inside her aunt's apartment she felt alive, freer than ever before. It was the only place she didn't have to be Lia. She could be Lila or Lily, or someone else entirely.

SCHOOL CAME TO an abrupt end that year after a suicide bomber exploded into a crowd of teenagers waiting outside a nightclub on the promenade, a block away from the school. Twenty-one kids were killed and hundreds wounded. Except for some windows, the school building remained undamaged, but the girls, like everyone else around the country, were deeply shocked, and their parents, together with the principle and school board, decided to cut the year short and let them recuperate at home. Lia couldn't get the images out of her mind. She had walked past the club grounds every day on the way to school and couldn't help but take the attack personally, feeling as though she herself had been targeted.

It was a long and cruel summer, the air lay heavy and stagnant and time was slow and unrelenting. Jonathan had finished his basic training and was doing a paramedic's course, so he barely made it home, and the entire country was now under attack as busses, malls, and restaurants were bombed in the towns and cities and violence in the occupied territories erupted on a daily basis. A few families left the settlement, including the twins, and their houses stood empty and abandoned, a constant reminder of the difficult times.

"Any other time, families would be fighting to get their houses." David was furious, but had no intention of leaving, no matter what happened.

Lia felt she was suffocating, unable to breath within the confines of the settlement, but nothing she said changed her father's mind. He wouldn't even let her visit Tel Aviv when Tamara and Yaeli invited her. Hanna called her nearly every day, still, she missed her aunt terribly and couldn't wait for the summer to be over.

"I don't want you travelling on the roads for hours every day," David told Lia just before the beginning of the new school year. "We've decided you'll stay with Hanna during the week, returning for weekends and holidays."

Esther didn't like the idea at all, but Lia was delighted.

"I'll be back for Shabbat," she promised a mournful Esther and Rachel as they waved goodbye.

AT FIRST LIA'S life in Tel Aviv was limited to the few streets between the school and Hanna's apartment, so when Hanna finally relented and enlarged Lia's territory to include the two blocks leading up to Gideon's store, Lia was elated. When she began showing up there nearly every afternoon, Gideon offered her a job.

"It's getting too difficult for me, climbing up and down the ladders, straining my eyes on the little print," he complained.

"You don't have to pay me." Lia was happy to work for free, but Gideon insisted. "And all the books you can read."

Apart from school and the store, Lia spent her remaining time with Hanna. On one of their evening walks they discovered a new Buddhist center, right at the entrance to the pedestrian mall. The doors were locked, so Lia tried to peek in through the windows.

"Don't even think of it." Hanna pulled her away. "That's what got your father started."

"What do you mean?" Lia had no idea what he had "started" on.

"He went to India and got involved with all that Osho crap. From there it's easy to see how he became a newly religious Jew. Personally, I don't see any difference between them. They're all completely crazy."

But Lia was intrigued. She passed by the center every day on her way to the store, and one evening, after she had stayed late to help Gideon, the lights were on and the door was open.

"Would you like to come in?' a young woman called out from inside. "The meditation's begun, but you're welcome to join. Go straight in." She pointed to the closed door behind her, then brought her finger to her lips. "Just don't disturb them."

Lia slowly opened the door, trying to be as quiet as she could. There were a handful of people sitting cross-legged in a circle, and most didn't even look up. A young man, who later introduced himself as Tomer, pointed toward an empty cushion. Lia sat down, closed her eyes, and took a deep breath. Someone lit a stick of incense, and the long forgotten odor of sandalwood filled her nostrils, immediately transporting her to another time and place. It was so long ago, she hardly remembered a thing, yet it felt so pleasant, so familiar.

The chiming bell pulled her out of her reverie. Lia opened her eyes and looked around. Everyone smiled and nodded, seemingly not noticing the "haredit," the obviously deeply religious girl who had suddenly appeared there, sitting silently beside them.

"We have workshops and daily meditations." Tomer shoved a pamphlet into Lia's hands. "Feel free to join us whenever you want to."

HAPPY AS SHE was in Tel Aviv, unlike Jonathan, Lia couldn't wait to return to the settlement, counting the days to the weekend. She missed her family, especially all her little brothers and sisters. Mostly, she missed Rachel, who still climbed into her bed every night. Her face was the first thing she saw in the morning and the last before she fell asleep at night.

"Wake up, sleepy head," Rachel would say in the mornings, while Lia pretended she was still asleep.

"Wakey wake." She'd tickle Lia, who held her breath as long as she could before turning over and tickling her back. They would play and giggle, disregarding Esther's calls until she really began to get angry.

"C'mon, girls," she'd say exasperated, "we're going to be late."

Jumping out of bed, Rachel would put on her serious face, bossing her little brothers around, trying to get them ready, while Esther took care of the baby. Rachel wasn't even seven yet, but she had taken on many of Lia's duties, always ready to help out around the house or take care of the little ones. Smart and persistent, she could read in an instant, just like Lia, but unlike her, sat for hours practicing her penmanship, diligently copying words and sentences, curving her letters and measuring the spaces between them. When Lia was around, Rachel was always in her wake, following her and shadowing her friends. Lia didn't mind. She loved her little sister more than anything in the world.

Hodi was only five when Rebecca placed him in first grade, together with her daughter Hodaya. The two were inseparable, always up to mischief, and then placing the blame on little Emanuel, who although two years younger, was forever tagging behind them, trying to do whatever it was they were doing. He was constantly falling off trees and hedges and had already broken his front baby teeth and been stitched up several times, but nothing deterred him. Hodi and Hodaya tried to scare him off, but he wouldn't budge, even when they threatened to beat him. Every morning Lia would watch Rachel run after her brothers, trying to pin the little yarmulke on their heads. They would dash about the house, their long, curling sideburns flying around their faces, leading her up and down the stairs, dodging her grasp till the last moment.

Naomi was just beginning to walk. She would stand herself up, wobbling, take a few steps and then stumble and fall, wailing before she even hit the ground. A moment later, she would pick herself up and start again. Every now and then she'd get really frustrated and stay down, kicking and screaming, until Esther or David scooped her consolingly into their arms.

"Bekarov exlech." Esther would bless Lia, every time she picked up the baby to comfort her. "Soon it will be you."

"Bekarov exlech," became the new mantra, pressed on her at every engagement, wedding and circumcision. It had also become a major point of contention between David and Lia.

"You have to start to think about it," David badgered her. "You're already seventeen."

"So there's still a whole year." Lia tried to laugh it off, though all her friends could talk about was getting married. Getting married and having kids. As many kids as possible. "Be fruitful and multiply," was the most important commandment and they were determined to follow it. Lia was disgusted by the thought.

"Yaeli already has a serious suitor and even Tamara has met with a few young men." Esther was quick to join the conversation. The twins may have returned to Tel Aviv, but everything they did was still reported back to the settlement.

"Most of the girls are already meeting young men," she added, emphasizing the "most."

Lia managed to put them off for a few months, but when the twins got engaged at the same time, Esther and David were beside themselves with envy. Without Lia's knowledge, they spoke to the local matchmaker, sending her off to make enquiries for a suitable suitor. The first young man was invited to meet Lia during the Passover vacation.

"What do you mean, he's coming to meet me?" Lia tried to protest. "I told you, I'm not ready."

"You can't put it off any longer." Esther knew she had to be tough. "All the other girls have been meeting young men. There'll be no one left for you by the time you're ready."

"If you're not married or at least engaged," David threatened, "you won't be able to carry on studying."

"We can't allow you to keep gallivanting around Tel Aviv," Esther added. "We have your reputation to protect."

"WHAT DO YOU mean, you agreed to meet a suitor?" Hanna was horrified. "You're much too young to even be thinking of marriage."

"They won't leave me alone," Lia complained. "They've been driving me crazy, trying to make me meet some of these boys."

"Can't you try to put them off, buy some time?"

"I've been trying, but now they've started to talk to people and set up meetings and there's nothing I can do anymore." Lia exhaled loudly, a plan hatching in her mind. "I'll do what they want to buy time, but don't worry, I'll find a way out. I have no intention of getting married."

AVISHAY WAS THEIR first choice. He was twenty-two and had a year left at the Yeshivat Hesder.

"He's third generation orthodox," David said, raising his eyebrows. "Already his grandparents returned to Hashem. They've built quite a tradition. It's an honor he's agreed to meet you."

"He's studying to be a rabbi," Esther told her proudly, as if it were the most attractive thing in the world.

"That's all I need," Lia thought, hanging her head to hide her twitching lips.

"I know the family," Esther added. "I met his mother, Yochi, a year or two ago. She's a really nice lady. She runs the daycare in Emanuel. I went to their house." She rattled on and on, but Lia had long stopped listening.

When he arrived, two days before the Passover Seder, preparations for the holiday were in full force and sounds of sweeping and banging could be heard all over the settlement. Long lines straggled before huge vats filled with boiling water, as people waited to immerse their dishes and utensils, purifying them and making sure they were kosher for Passover. The houses as well as the entire settlement had to be cleansed, rid of any "hametz," leavened or fermented food, just like their ancient ancestors fleeing Egypt. The night before the holiday, David lit a candle and led the entire family around the house, checking every corner and cavity for any last crumb they may have overlooked. The children took turns, happily giving the "all clear," until the entire house was declared hametz-free.

"COME IN, COME in." Esther led him inside, her cheeks red and eyes flustered.

He nodded in Lia's direction, quickly pulling his head down when their eyes momentarily met. He was so embarrassed and overwhelmed, he could hardly say his name, just stood there mumbling, nervously crushing the edges of his black hat with his fingers.

"Breathe," Lia said to herself, battling to keep a smile on her frozen face. It was even worse than she had expected. He wore a cheap black suit and tie, and sweat was pouring down his cheeks, intermingling with his long black curls that swayed from side to side whenever he moved his head. She made herself busy, helping Esther serve tea and freshly baked honey cake, and then "the couple" was sent outside to get to know each other.

He waited until she sat down then sat on the opposite side, making sure to keep the width of the table between them.

"Have you been here before?" Lia finally broke the silence.

Avishai shook his head and mumbled something, his eyes bashfully glued to the floor.

"You live close by, don't you?" Lia desperately tried to keep the conversation alive, although she could hardly make out a thing he was saying.

"Can you speak a little louder?" she finally suggested.

Avishai cleared his throat and managed to say a few semi audible sentences before they were interrupted and called in.

"ARE YOU CRAZY?" Lia shrieked the moment he was out the door. "He's the most religious person I've ever seen. Did you see his clothes?"

"You have to give him a chance," Esther said, calmly stacking the dirty dishes onto a tray. "He's just shy. You can't know anything from just one meeting."

"Shy?" Lia huffed. "I could barely understand him. I never want to see him again."

"Never mind." David patted her head. "He's just the first. I'm sure you'll like the next one better."

THE NEXT SUITOR was scheduled to come on the third day of the holiday, but finding Lia a husband had to be postponed. The events of that Passover were so horrific all thought of marriage was delayed indefinitely. The emergency phone started to ring a moment after the end of prayers, as the men were ceremoniously washing their hands. Everyone stopped in their tracks, a sudden tension gripping the entire room. No one spoke or moved. They just stared at the phone. It had been one of the worst months in Israeli history and everyone knew that this desecration of the sacred holiday could only mean further disaster. David was in charge of the combat unit. He wiped his hands and answered.

"What?" His entire body started to shake. He felt everyone's eyes on him and struggled to regain his composure.

"I see," he said slowly, and then, "How many? Yes of course. We're on call every night. Yes, yes. We'll pay special attention."

"Get the kids out," was all he managed to say, his hands waving frantically in the air.

There had been a terrorist attack at a major hotel during the holiday feast. Thirty people, many of whom were children, had been slain and many were wounded. Two days later, on the first day of the "intermediate days" of the holiday, Yaakov and his family were ambushed five kilometers from the settlement. Svetlana and Elad were only slightly wounded, but Yaacov and their two-year-old daughter, Lital, were killed.

The news of their murder, coming straight after the Passover massacre, hit them hard and the entire community went into mourning. Yaacov was a founding member of the settlement and was always around, fixing, helping out, or arguing passionately. He and Svetlana tried to have another child for years before Lital was finally born and the whole settlement had rejoiced with them. She was sweet and mischievous, with ash blond pigtails and enormous light blue eyes. Lia helped out at the daycare whenever she was home and Lital had been one of her favorites. She even babysat for them a few times.

The funeral was awful, the tiny body being lowered into the ground beside her father. Lia stood silently beside Esther as she tried to comfort the remaining mother and son. She didn't know what to say. She couldn't even look at them. Traditionally, only blood relatives were obligated to keep the seven day mourning period, but the entire settlement seemed to be sitting "shiva." Even the children felt it, talking in whispers and keeping themselves out of the way at the far side of the compound. But when the week ended, the settlement pulled itself together, more determined than ever, its underlying beliefs even stronger than before.

"How can everyone just carry on?" Lia asked her father.

"They can't break us." David looked into her eyes. "What doesn't kill us makes us stronger, Beezrat Hashem. Hashem will never give us more than we can bear."

Lia wasn't sure she agreed.

"Maybe it's me that's finally broken," she thought. Throughout the years, she'd tried to see both sides, but nothing could explain all the blind hatred surrounding her, or excuse its terrible results.

"They'll never give up," she thought. "Either side."

"THE MATCHMAKER CALLED me again today," Esther told Lia. It had been about two months since the first suitor and although she had tried to leave Lia alone, she felt she couldn't delay any longer. "She doesn't even want to work with us anymore."

Realizing she had no choice, Lia agreed to meet a few more of the chosen ones. Elai was so short, his eyes reached her throat and Hillel had to stick his thick lenses right into her face in order to see her. Lia didn't even bother trying to get to know them.

"Not interested," she told her father, thinking she could go on like that forever.

"You're being too picky," Esther scolded. "And you won't even meet any of them for a second time."

"I don't know what she thinks is out there," David told Esther, shaking his head. "It's hard enough to find a good match for her as it is, with her background."

"What do you mean?" Lia had no idea what he was talking about. "Do you mean my mother?"

"Well, there's that," Esther tried to mitigate what he had said, "but in general, the orthodox Jews don't like their sons to marry hozrim betchuva."

Lia couldn't believe her ears. Now, it seemed, she wasn't even a good enough Jew.

"Enough." David stamped his foot and laid down his final ultimatum. "You have the entire summer ahead of you. If you're not engaged at its end, you won't be allowed to go back to school."

"I DON'T KNOW what to do," Lia told Jonathan. "I don't want to get married, but if I don't, they won't let me graduate. I wish I could just run away."

"I know the feeling." Jonathan shook his head. "I'm dying to get out of here." He had a new boyfriend in Tel Aviv, but no one except Lia knew anything about him.

"Where can we go?" Lia asked and they laughingly called out all the exotic places they could think of.

"India," Jonathan called out.

"Seriously." Lia stopped laughing. "I've been thinking about it more and more lately. Of running away. And it's funny, but lately, when I can't fall asleep, that's where the pink balloon keeps taking me. To India, to a place I visited as a child. Maybe it's telling me that's where I should go."

"But India?" Jonathan repeated, not laughing any more.

"Yes India." The moment she said the words out loud, they became real to her. "In a way, I think that's where it all began. My story, I mean."

She told him about the meditation center she had started frequenting. "I can't explain it, but I feel so welcome there, so comfortable."

"But going on your own?" Jonathan wasn't sure what to say. "You're just a kid. You've never been anywhere on your own. Do you even have a passport?"

"I have an American passport," Lia answered after a moment, remembering that she had gone to renew it with her father the year before. Her plan was starting to grow wings. "But I have to wait till I'm eighteen. And I don't have enough money." She began to worry. "Although I do have the money from the bookstore."

"I have some money too," Jonathan offered. "You know, if you really decide to do it, I'll help you. I may even join you once I've finished my service." He grinned.

"But I still have to find a way to go back to school, once the summer's over, or I'll be stuck in the settlement and never be able to get out." Lia hid her face in her hands. "What the hell am I going to do?"

They sat silently for a while before Jonathan had an idea. "I know what you have to do. It's not enough to meet some suitors. You have to get engaged."

"Are you crazy?" Lia looked at him dumbfounded.

"No." Jonathan shook his head. "It's the only way you'll be able to buy yourself time and still stay free. You have no other choice."

URIEL ARRIVED IN an army jeep, wearing a combat uniform and boots, a rifle like Jonathan's hanging over his shoulder. He smiled bashfully when they were introduced, but looked Lia straight in the eye, the cutest dimples appearing through his reddish golden beard.

"I've been looking forward to meeting you." He smiled down at her. His voice was strong and masculine, but he spoke softly and deliberately and Lia felt a delicateness under his seemingly militant exterior. She had to raise her chin to meet his gaze, he was so much taller than her, and she felt a strange excitement building up at the tip of her tummy.

"Calm down," she reminded herself. "You're not really looking for a husband."

"Strange we've never met before," Uriel said when they were finally alone. He came from a settlement not too far away and his family was politically active, never missing a demonstration.

"Maybe we have." Lia smiled up at him.

"I would have remembered." He smiled back, his eyes sparkling. His Hebrew had a strong Anglo inflection, but when they switched to English, she couldn't place his accent.

"South Africa. I came here when I was seventeen." He told her he had just turned twenty- two and had a few months left in the army.

"And then another year at the yeshiva." But he had grand plans. He intended to study to be an engineer and even though he had no intention of leaving the occupied territories when he got married, he was looking forward to a career in high tech.

"I'd like my wife to work and have a career, too." Uriel told her his mother was a dietitian with a large clinic, right under their house. "But her children always come first. That's kind of how I see my wife."

"I DON'T THINK I'll be able to do it," Lia wailed to Jonathan, when he finally came home. "I really like Uriel."

"Would you rather do it with someone you don't like?" Jonathan thought she was being silly. "You'll have to meet whoever it is several times and spend time with him. I'd go with someone I actually like."

"But I'll end up deceiving him." Lia didn't know if she had the stomach for it. "What if he really likes me? He'll be terribly hurt."

THE SECOND TIME he arrived, Lia led him straight down the path to the old clubhouse, still standing triumphantly at the edge of the garden. Jonathan was on leave and waiting to meet him, together with all the older kids. The boys slapped each other's shoulders, spouting army jargon and the girls looked him over carefully. They all sat together, talking until the middle of the night and Uriel crashed in Jonathan's parents' living room. He left early in the morning, before Lia was even up.

"Everyone loved him," Jonathan reported to Lia. "I had to keep reminding myself what was actually going on, that we weren't really going to be friends."

"It was true," Lia thought. "He had blended in perfectly, immediately becoming one of the crew."

"I'll be happy to meet your family," she agreed reluctantly, when Uriel brought it up, the third time they met. She didn't want to hurt him, but she felt she had no choice. David had made it very clear. If she wanted to continue her studies, she had to be engaged. And she was running out of time.

THEY ARRIVED AT the end of the Sabbath, just before the start of the school year.

"Lovely to meet you." Muriel hugged her. "You're even prettier than Uriel said."

She had a plump, kind face and when she smiled, Lia could see where her son's dimples came from. She introduced her daughters, and each hugged her in their turn.

Esther and Muriel hit it off immediately and chattered non-stop, while the girls sat around, trying to stick in a word every now and then. Lia kept herself busy, serving coffee and iced tea to the adults and lemonade to all the kids.

"Lia is the chef in our house," Esther boasted proudly. "She taught me most of what I know."

"Mmm . . . delicious." Muriel bit into a ma'amul Lia had baked just before they arrived. "Melts in your mouth like butter."

They discussed where the "kids" would live, both sides wanting them to stay close by.

"I can't wait for them to have children." Esther was beaming. "Lia's helped raise her brothers and sisters since they were born. She'll make such a good mom."

"Uriel can't wait to have kids." Muriel waved her arms at them enthusiastically. "Look at them. They'll have such beautiful children."

Lia heard everything they were saying, but was too on edge to utter a word. She kept on smiling and nodding, trying desperately to get through the evening without committing herself.

"Just a little longer," she tried to calm herself, "and they'll be gone."

She couldn't wait for the evening to be over, but before it ended and she had realized what was happening, she found herself engaged.

"Mazal Tov," Esther called out happily. "Baruch Hashem."

"Hashem yevurach," Muriel blessed back.

"Lehaim." David filled everyone's glasses to their brim.

HANNA WAS SO furious, she didn't even want to talk to Lia.

"Please," Lia begged. "I have to see you."

"I can't even look at you right now," Hanna refused. "You barely know him and you're still so young. You said you were just buying time. You promised."

"It's not what you think," Lia was desperate. "Please, I really need your help."

LIA ARRIVED AT school on the first day of class to find Hanna waiting outside the gate.

"I can't help you with that." Hanna shook her head forlornly, when Lia told her of her plan. "I'd do anything in the world for you, but I can't deceive my brother like that. He'll never forgive me."

"I have no choice," Lia tried to explain. "I can't stay in the settlement, and I have nowhere else to go."

"You know you're always welcome here." Hanna had grown used to having her niece around. "You can come live with me. I'll be lonely without you."

"They'll never allow it." Lia shook her head sadly. "And they'll never leave me alone. But it's not only that. I need to get away from it all, to get as far away as I can. I can't take it anymore, all the hatred and the violence, the constant battle between Allah and Hashem. I don't care who's right and who's wrong anymore. It'll never end. I've had enough. I need some quiet, some peace, somewhere I can be on my own, to figure things out for myself."

"What kind of things?" Hanna tried to understand.

"I don't really know. I feel so lost, as if I don't even know who I am anymore."

"What do you mean?" Hanna had never tried to ask herself any of those questions.

"I look in the mirror and don't recognize myself. I know it's me," she paused, not even sure how to explain it to herself, "but it's also not. As if the girl in the mirror is just a part of me. *But* what about the rest? Sometimes I feel torn in two, or even three. There's Lia, the Jew and Lila the Palestinian refugee, and then there's Lily. Or there was Lily. I barely remember her anymore. I don't want to be Lia. I don't want to live like this for the rest of my life. There has to be more. I owe it to myself to find out, to figure out who I really am."

"But why so far away? Why India?"

"Because it's so far away." Lia laughed. "I need to get as far away as I can. From everything and everyone."

"But where will you go?" Hanna crushed her fingers nervously. "Do you know anyone?"

"That's the whole point." Lia leaned over and placed her hand on Hanna's. "To go somewhere new and unknown, where I know nobody and nobody knows me. It's a journey of discovery. No maps. No plan."

"Where will you begin?" Hanna was skeptical, but she could tell Lia had made up her mind.

"That's easy." Lia told her everything she remembered about the place she had visited as a child. "You see," she smiled at her aunt, "it's not so strange and unknown after all."

Hanna took a deep breath. "I get it. I understand why you have to go. But I still can't help you. My brother is my only family. He and you kids are the only thing I have. I can't lose that."

"I won't tell your father," she promised, after giving it some thought. "But please, don't tell me anymore. The less I know the better."

THE NEXT MORNING, the minivan was late and the girls arrived at school just as the bell rang. To Lia's surprise, Hanna was once again waiting for her just outside the gate.

"Sorry Hanna," Lia apologized, "I have to go in. Is everything all right?"

"Everything's fine." Hanna motioned her over. "It'll only take a moment. I hope you can forgive me." She took a surprised Lia's hands in hers. "I need you to forget everything I said yesterday. I was just being a coward, like I always am. I didn't sleep all night. I kept thinking how different my life would have been if I had had the courage to leave, to run away. I've decided not to sit on the sidelines this time. Of course I'll help you. We'll work it all out together."

It was Hanna who went with her to the Indian Embassy, and Hanna who waited impatiently for her visa to arrive. She bought her a bag and some clothes and even found her a place to stay in Pune. "Just for a week or two, at the beginning. Until you get organized."

"You don't have to leave right away." Hanna tried to convince her to stay a little longer, but Lia insisted she had to go.

"I don't want to stick around for the official engagement party. Whatever I do, Uriel will be badly hurt. If I leave before we set the date for the wedding, he'll be spared a lot of the humiliation. It's the least I can do."

They booked her ticket for the week after the high holidays.

THE DAY BEFORE Lia was to leave, a suicide bomber blew himself up at the gas station at the entrance to Ariel and the entire surrounding area erupted, with both settlers and Palestinians running rampage, rioting and protesting violently. Just before sundown, the army enforced a curfew. Still Lia could hear shots and explosions ringing out throughout the night, some soft and vague, as if they came from far away, but others so loud, they seemed to be coming from right beyond the doorway.

Lia didn't sleep a wink, worried she would miss her flight. Rachel moved restlessly in her bed as Lia kept rifling through her bag, pulling out the few items she would be taking with her and exchanging them for others. Her only important possessions were a handful of photographs and her journals. She knew she couldn't take them all, there was quite a stack under her bed, but trying to decide which ones to take was driving her crazy. They all seemed indispensable.

"Only two," she finally decided. "The first and the last. That way at least I'll have a bit of all the different stations of my life."

"I think you should stay at home this week." David was afraid to let her go, even though the curfew had been lifted.

"You never have a problem catching up on your school work," Esther added, "and you know how much I love it when you're here. I could certainly use your help." She pulled out her last card, looking around the living room and grimacing at the mess.

"I really have to go today." Lia had prepared for just such an eventuality. "It's my first day as a teaching assistant. I've been assigned a class and everything. I've been preparing for this for years."

She said goodbye as calmly as she could, but as if they could sense it, all the kids came running after her, following her all the way to the minivan.

"Don't go," Rachel said, as Lia was about to get in. "I have a bad feeling."

Naomi jumped into her arms, hugging her neck and Hodi and Emanuel clung to her legs. They'd never done it before. "Maybe they really do feel it, sensing something with their kid sensors," she thought, beginning to doubt herself.

"Maybe I'm making a mistake." She didn't know how she would survive without them.

"Maybe I shouldn't leave after all," she thought, just as Naomi started crying and the boys joined her in a chorus of wailing, reminding Lia of what her life would be like if she stayed. She hugged the baby one last time, handed her back to Rachel, and peeled the boys off her knees.

"See you later," Rachel called as she stepped into the minivan.

"Later," Lia called back, fighting off her tears.

JONATHAN GOT THE morning off and was waiting at Hanna's apartment. He would be taking her to the airport. Hanna didn't want to go. She said she preferred a quick goodbye.

"I'll miss you so much." Hanna stroked Lia's face and hair, tears running down her face. "I've grown to love you like a daughter and I want you to know you can always come back. You'll always have a home here, with me."

She gave Lia the travelling bag she had prepared for her and placed a thick envelope in her hands.

"Are you crazy?" Lia cried out, astonished. There were a thousand dollars, in crisp fresh bills inside it. "I can't take this. You've given me so much already."

"Please." Hanna waved her hands away. "It's just a little extra pocket money. Put it away. Put it away."

THEY HELD THEMSELVES together all the way to the departure gate.

"I'm so scared." Lia finally allowed herself to crumble, bursting into tears.

"I know." Jonathan hugged her closely, his tears mingling with hers.

"You've got to go." He finally pushed her away. "They're calling your flight."

"But what will I do there?" Lia panicked, realizing the enormity of her next step. "I'll be all on my own."

"You'll be fine," Jonathan tried to reassure her. "I'll join you as soon as I can. The moment I'm released."

"That's almost a whole year," Lia said, her face still buried in his chest.

"It'll pass before you notice," he promised, wiping her eyes and placing her bag in her hand. "Go on." He gave her a little nudge. "I'll see you in a year!"

"See you in a year." She gave him one last hug and walked through the gate.

LEELA

"FIRST NAME?" THE attendant asked again, emphasizing her words, but she still didn't answer.

She had no idea what to say. She looked around her at the elegant marble welcome center, overlooking a bamboo pond with a statue of Buddha at its center. A huge, life sized portrait of Osho stared at her from the wall. He looked straight into her eyes and suddenly she seemed to hear his voice.

"Lily is who you are," she heard him say, as he had so many years ago, "Leela is what you can be."

"Leela," she answered, watching the attendant write it down. "My name is Leela."

SHE HAD BEEN in India for a few weeks, and although she had walked around the compound nearly every day, it was the first time she had entered, and that was only because her newfound friends had forced her.

She barely remembered the flight, just hours of moving about uncomfortably, her mind flying a thousand thoughts a minute, bombarding her with sights and sounds and memories, and then the strange quiet that descended on her as she stepped out of the airport in Mumbai and into the waiting cab. There was a faint, unpleasant odor that she couldn't place and everything seemed to be moving and honking as the car made its way through the busy streets. She laid her head back, staring as though through a fog, her brain turned into mush. Skyscrapers and slums, cars, bikes, and pedestrians flowed by, like in a movie, but nothing seemed to register. The city gave way to long stretches of green and the landscape changed dramatically as the car climbed a steep mountain and traversed perilously over a river and then a gaping gorge. She pushed herself deeper into the seat and shut her eyes.

"PEEP, PEEP" ... "HAW, haw" ... "Beep."

The noise and the heat had become unbearable.

"Still far?" she asked the taxi driver for the tenth time.

"Two minutes away," he answered, "just as soon as we can get off the main road."

North main road, as he called it, was a narrow, two lane road, filled with stores and restaurants and congested with cars, rickshaws, and cows. They had been standing in the same place for at least fifteen minutes, waiting for the cowgirl to move her herd from the middle of the street.

"Shoo, shoo," she shouted at them, nostrils flaring, the bracelets on her arms clinking madly as she waved her flaming pink sari at them.

"Hoo, hoo," they answered, shaking their tails and weaving their way between the traffic.

"Hot . . ." she said, fanning herself.

"You better get used to it." the driver moved his head up and down and then to the sides. "Monsoon season over. Now it go from hot to even more hot."

"Lane four," the driver announced, turning into a side street.

They drove past a few small grey buildings and a little shopping complex. The driver pulled up next to a fruit stand.

"Straight down." the vendor waved his hand at him, trying to move as little as possible. "Just before South main road."

As they drove on, the road became narrower and the sidewalks were lined with tall, green trees. The houses became larger and more and more elegant, many enclosed by tall stone or wooden fences.

"There." She pointed, seeing the sign on the second building before the last. Hanna had chosen the room and made all the arrangements.

"It's not the nicest or the fanciest of places," she told her niece, "but it's cheap and clean and most importantly, it's run by a Westerner."

Hanna felt it was up to her to do everything she could to ensure her niece's safety. She had communicated directly with Anna, a Swedish woman, who ran "A+V" together with her Indian boyfriend, Vipul, and had even received letters of recommendation from them.

Anna came out to greet her and showed her around quickly. She was a tall, slim woman in her late thirties or early forties and had been living in Pune for many years. She and Vipul had an apartment on the first floor and the other two floors had been divided into rooms, with a communal bathroom at each end.

"The roof's the main gathering place." Anna led her to the top of the building.

There was a large, covered kitchen and dining area, leading out to an oddly attractive veranda covered by a jumble of plants and shabby chairs.

"No one's here now." Anna smiled. "They're all at the Ashram, but I'm sure someone will be back soon. There's nearly always someone around."

"I take only people from the Ashram," she had promised Hanna in her letter, "I check everyone, and we've never had a problem."

"By the way," Anna led her back down to her room on the second floor, "there's another Israeli girl staying here. Her name's Hadas. I told her all about you. She said she'd come by later and show you around."

The house was old and grey and the rooms were tiny. There were six in all, each called after a different flower. Hers was The Rose Room, its walls tinted a faded salmon, a large rose print hanging behind the large, meshed bed. There was a small, stained red armchair and a little dresser. It wasn't the most beautiful room she had ever seen, but behind the huge screen doors, hid her own private terrace, with her own little table and her own little chair. Suddenly the weight of all that had happened during the last few days pulled her down. Her head pounded and her limbs felt heavy and listless. The moment the door closed behind Anna, she threw herself on the bed, her thoughts flying at her from all directions, pictures, sounds, and smells bombarding her.

"Mind attack," she whispered to herself, trying to catch her breath. "It's just a mind attack." But nothing she did calmed her or slowed the unrelenting stream.

"WOW, YOU LOOK like a kid, how old are you?" Hadas bounced into her room a few hours later, full of energy and good will.

"I was so scared when I found myself here, all alone," she told her, noticing her puffy red eyes. "But lucky for you, you have me. Come on." She towered above her, over a head taller, her long sandy curls almost obscuring her face. "Let's get you out of here."

HADAS HAD ARRIVED in Pune two months before Leela and felt quite the veteran. She had come to India with her boyfriend, after finishing her army service, but they had broken up when she had decided to stay at the Ashram.

"The truth is, he was really starting to get on my nerves," Hadas frowned, "acting all controlling, as if he was my father."

They strolled lazily through the quiet back streets that were almost deserted in the early afternoon heat. Huge, elegant mansions stood side by side with tiny makeshift shacks, and the only sound was the faint "tss, tss," of the sprinklers, splashing water over green luscious lawns. As they neared the ashram, the streets became busier, filled with people in maroon dresses and robes.

"Do you want to go in?" Hadas stopped before the heavily armed gate.

Leela tried to peak in, but couldn't see anything behind the tall wall. Now that she was finally here, she was suddenly hesitant.

"Not today," she decided. "I'll go tomorrow."

But tomorrow dragged on and on, and she couldn't quite force herself to go in. She walked passed the ashram every day, but still something was stopping her. Old forgotten memories kept popping up, of David and Minna, things she hadn't thought of in years. For the first time in her life, she was free. No school. No chores. No parents to tell her what to do. But she wasn't really enjoying it. Instead, she felt angry and disoriented, her mind constantly active and her thoughts spiraling. She couldn't sleep or meditate and even the pink balloon declined to take off, remaining heavily on the ground.

"Rise, pink balloon," she'd beg restlessly every night. "Take me away." But the pink balloon just stayed on the ground, refusing to budge.

In the evenings, the tenants would gather on the roof, cooking dinner together or just hanging out. There were two other young girls in the house, Zoe and Ellie, both Australian, and like Hadas, they soon became friends. Twenty-five-year-old Alfonzo hit on her the moment they met and Helmut, the eldest of the group, immediately placed himself between them. Helmut had been coming to Pune for years and was a good friend of the owners, having lived together with Anna in the ashram many years before. Often, after dinner, they'd all return to the ashram.

"There are pubs and bistros and wineries," the girls tried to convince her. They told her there was live music and dancing and although they always came back late and boisterous, she preferred to stay behind.

During the days, when they all left for the ashram, she'd wander through the streets, trying to gain the courage to enter. She quickly learned to avoid North Main Road, hating the chaotic traffic and unending cacophony of honking rickshaws and cars.

"It's suicide crossing the street," Helmut joked every time he found himself there, though he was forever going to Annand's on the far corner, bringing back freshly fried potato dossa and savory tiny chickpea samosas. She'd only go up as far as Raja's stall, a few blocks away. Most people just called him the "momo man." Helmut had introduced her.

"Never buy anything from any of the street merchants," he warned, waving his finger in front of her face. "The only place that's clean is the momo man."

Raja always sat on the same corner, steaming his momos over a small gas flame. They were light parcels of dough filled with tiny morsels of heaven. His wife made them freshly every day, stuffing them with whatever she had at hand. Onions, yams, potatoes or spinach, smothered with cumin, fennel seed, and other exotic spices. Raj would arrive sometime in the early afternoon, moving crookedly on his bad legs as he set up has little stall. He'd pull a thick rug into place next to the fruit stand, placing a little burner in the middle. Then he would stack bamboo trays filled with uncooked momos one atop of the other in a tower, open his raggedy "Pepsi" umbrella and lower himself into his plastic chair. It took almost an hour until the first ones were ready and Leela often had to wait. Sometimes a long line of people would form, waiting patiently until the first batch was ready. They'd joke and exchange greetings, but Raj never joined in, remaining hunched quietly on his broken plastic chair, lifting the bamboo cover from time to time to check on the momos. When they were ready, he'd place the little plate in Leela's hands, count out the change and place his hands together silently, before moving on to the next customer. One never knew when he would arrive, but he was there every day, staying until the last momo was devoured.

She'd stand outside the school grounds, munching her momos, watching the kids playing cricket, a game she'd never seen before. When they weren't playing, they were all dressed up in their formal uniforms, the girls in their little blue skirts, the boys wearing blazers and a tie, even in the unbearable heat. A group of old ladies were always sitting around watching. They would call her over, and she would sit on the hot sidewalk by their side. Often she would find one or two of the oldest lying on the ground asleep, their faces covered by their brightly colored sari, and have to walk around. She went down to the railway and then all the way to the squatter's encampment, exchanging greetings with the young goat girls who were always milling around. In the afternoons she'd sit quietly in Osho Park, just a few blocks from the house. It was the most beautiful place she'd ever seen, covered with luscious green vegetation and serene sparkling streams and ponds. She liked to traverse the narrow pathways, searching out the little hideaways, where she could be alone, sitting beside the pink and white water lilies, watching the birds peacefully soaring above, as she tried to settle her mind.

"Quiet," she'd tell it when it wouldn't stop, "shut the fuck up!" But it just went "yackety yack," pinging and ponging, refusing to be controlled. Other times, she'd sit there silently, her mind in a fog so thick, no thought could penetrate the heavy blanket.

One day, as she walked a little farther down South Main Road, she saw a rusty broken gate, hanging half open on its hinges, a bunch of old, dilapidated graves hidden behind it. When she got nearer, a Star of David and some Hebrew letters caught her eye. She pushed the gate aside and found herself in an old Jewish cemetery. She made her way through the grey brown headstones and broken caskets, climbing through the outgrowth of weeds and thorny plants, a carpet of brown leaves crackling beneath her feet, as she tried to decipher the old engravings, comforted by the familiar letters and words. The cemetery was much larger than she had first thought, going down all the way until the railroad, where the old crooked elliptical headstones, probably the earliest, had fallen down, much, she thought, like a row of forlorn looking dominoes.

She climbed over half open stone caskets, toward a bunch of what looked like tiny miniature houses, with walls and a roof and all, covered with barely legible English, Hebrew, and even Indian writing. They were badly damaged, cracked, and broken. Much to her surprise, just behind them, right next to the eastern wall, stood a group of recent tombstones, also filthy and unkempt.

"Gabriel, David Sampson, 1998," she read out loud. "Aida Isaac Levi, 1994."

Toward the end, shrouded by a group of tall eucalyptus trees, lay a group of caskets, covered with large marble slabs. They seemed to be the oldest graves, as the writing on them was so ancient, she could hardly make anything out. Leela pushed the dirt and leaves away, rubbing the stones with her hands. Some were so old, the writing had almost disappeared and just an engraved Star of David still stood out, while on others, the names slowly became legible. "Elisheva, Alber, Raymond, Yaacov. Leah, Sassoon, Readon, Noagon," she read out loud. Some retained their entire message.

In loving memory of our beloved mother, Aziz Segulla Bay, daughter of Hanna, 1945

In loving memory of Hoel Uziel Elijah Walwatkar, who left for his heavenly abode on 23 June, 1948

The heat was stifling and the hot light rain offered no relief, making her even hotter and stickier. Still she remained, finding solace in the familiar sights, even if they were just letters and words engraved on a tombstone. She visited them almost every day, rummaging through the stones and caskets, searching for the oldest ones, running their long lists of names over her tongue, until finally settling herself in her favorite spot, above master Samson (Sunny) Aaron Rodecker, 3rd June 1948, age eighteen years, just opposite from the casket of Leah Neah, daughter of Cainey, 1938.

LEELA LOOKED AROUND her. It was nothing like she remembered. She still wasn't ready, but she didn't really have a choice. Not after the night before. They were all waiting for her, when she went up to the roof, even the owners, Anna and Vipul, who rarely made an appearance.

"Enough is enough," Hadas said. "You're wasting your time and money and not doing anything."

"We're all worried." Anna patted her arm. "You're so quiet and your friends tell me you hardly eat. I promised your aunt I'd take of you."

"The ashram is exactly what you need," Ellie told her, Zoe nodding vigorously in agreement, while both Helmut and Alphonso offered to escort her and remain by her side.

"OK," she finally agreed, knowing she was defeated. "I'll go tomorrow. I swear."

"Bright and early," Hadas insisted. "Shall I call you?"

"Bright and early," Leela promised. "But I think I'd like to go alone."

LEELA FELT UNCOMFORTABLE in her new maroon dress and flip-flops, her long robe and bag heavy on her arm. Everywhere she looked she could see only other maroon coconuts, flitting silently across large expanses of marble before disappearing into shaded green paths. Leela stood transfixed, trying to take in the huge black pyramid that seemed to rise out of the water, surrounded by landscaped gardens, towering trees, and bamboo groves. Swans and peacocks roamed the grounds, dipping their necks in ponds and under waterfalls.

"Disneyland," she chuckled to herself, "but for adults."

"C'mon, Leela," the attendant ushered her on, "we're all waiting for you."

Leela hurried to join the group. The attendant led them through mysterious paths, covered with shrubs and vegetation, all the way to the other side of the resort. They passed a small group of women silently practicing Tai Chi in the Buddha Grove, almost hidden from sight by tall bamboo trees and a few people sitting on a platform made of boulders, meditating cross-legged in front of a tall, bluish grey, serene looking Buddha. Nearly everyone she passed was Western, although there were a few Indians and a sprinkling of Asians. They visited the huge kitchen facility and then the immense, pond like pool and gymnasium. There was even a Jacuzzi, a sauna, and tennis courts. Leela couldn't believe her eyes. The quaint, rustic ashram she remembered, with the help of her father's old photographs, had disappeared and a lush, green luxurious resort had taken its place.

LEELA LAGGED BEHIND, deep in thought. Suddenly she found herself on a bridge, walking across water. She raised her head. The gigantic black pyramid loomed above her.

"We opened the pyramid hall last week," the attendant was saying breathlessly. "You'll be one of the first to use it."

The room seemed endless, its marble floor so shiny, the dazzle almost blinded her. The attendant told them it was large enough to hold five thousand people.

"Much bigger than the old Buddha hall," she continued proudly.

"The Buddha Hall." Leela gasped as images of the enormous white tent flashed through her mind. She had forgotten all about it. She couldn't believe it was gone and that the immense glittery pyramid had taken its place.

She followed the group into a matted room and chose a cushion in back. A tall, slim bearded man introduced himself as Sati. He seemed in his mid-forties and spoke with a heavy Italian accent, gesticulating and waving his arms energetically. He welcomed them, wishing them success on their journey, and then went on to discuss life in the ashram. As his voice droned on and on, Leela felt her concentration phase out. After some time she realized he had gone on to discuss Osho's philosophy, flipping charts with pictures of people of various ages and different ethnicities. He said something about the new human being they were trying to create, but Leela had lost him.

"Concentrate," she told herself, straightening her body. "Concentrate."

"We are taught to follow basic rules and to behave in certain ways." Sati's eye's caught hers for a moment. Leela smiled at him and nodded.

"We become emotional, expressive Italians, like me,"—everyone laughed—"polite British or obedient Japanese. We become Christians, Jews, Muslims."

Leela laughed silently to herself.

"Our goal here is to deprogram you," he finally came to the end of his talk, "to allow you to develop a new path. A path of your own."

Before letting them go, Sati opened his arms widely as if to embrace them all and cried, "This is just a big laboratory. Talk to each other. Talk to strangers. Experiment. Express yourself."

Everyone smiled, looking at one another and nodding. Leela felt a little lost, but she smiled and nodded too.

"Hug!" Sati shouted frantically. "Everybody hug!"

Now she felt even more uncomfortable.

"What the hell am I doing here?" she asked herself.

Breaking out of a huge man's hairy embrace, she was the first out the door.

"WELL." HADAS WAS waiting for her anxiously when she came in. "How was it? What are you going to take? Did you sign up for any courses?" She bombarded Leela with questions, too excited to wait for her to answer.

"Slow down." Leela tried to calm her. "I just went for the orientation. I have no idea where to start."

"Leave it to me." Hadas knew exactly what Leela should do. "Don't worry about it. But go to sleep early, we have to be up at five."

"Five? It's still dark," Leela tried to argue, but Hadas just kissed her on the cheek and bustled away.

TO HER SURPRISE, it wasn't only Hadas who was waiting for her in the morning. Just before six, they were all gathered outside.

"What's happening?" Leela asked.

"We decided we should all go with you." Helmut beamed at her.

"Are you crazy?" she asked.

"Zoe and I both wanted to be with you the first time you go," Ellie explained. "And the boys said they'd come too."

"So here we are." Alphonso put his arm through hers, and they all set off briskly.

"JUST SIT OR lie down quietly." Hadas led her into the room. Leela couldn't believe how many people were there at that time of the morning.

"I must be dreaming," she thought, not sure she was really awake. She sat down and looked around her. She had no idea what to expect, as none of them would tell her.

"Don't worry," was all Hadas said. "Just follow along."

A MAN WEARING a black robe spoke into a microphone, welcoming them. He told them to stand with their feet shoulder width apart, knees relaxed, and slightly bent. He had a heavy German accent and Leela had difficulty understanding him. Suddenly the music began, a chaotic percussion to which the crowd gasped and panted, all the while shaking their bodies and flapping their arms. Leela looked around her, trying to figure out what to do.

"Stay where you are, breath through your nose and wave your hands and body," Hadas whispered in her ear.

Leela felt a little stupid, but since everyone around her was doing it, she decided to do it too. She raised her arms and shook her body.

"That's it." Hadas smiled encouragingly. "Just do what everyone else does."

AFTER SOME TIME a gong sounded and the music shifted into big digital beats.

"Let everything out!" the leader cried out. "Live your emotions, totally. Scream them. I want to see your entire body moving."

Now everyone really went crazy. The entire room seemed to burst out of its seams as people jumped around, jerking their bodies, screaming and roaring at the top of their lungs. Ellie disappeared from sight, laughing and gesticulating like mad, Alphonso following right behind her. They all dispersed around the room, but Hadas made sure to remain beside her.

"Follow your body," the leader shouted into the microphone. "Give your body total freedom. Explode! Go totally mad!"

Leela wanted to, but didn't know how. It reminded her of her parents and the things they used to do when she was a child. She tried to let herself go, but was totally self-conscious, her feet a ton of bricks. She felt herself screaming, but realized after a moment, she hadn't uttered a sound.

After a while, the music shifted again taking on a stable, march like rhythm, and everyone stood in their place, raised their arms, and jumped up and down, crying, "hoo, hoo," at the top of their lungs.

"Totally idiotic," Leela thought, as she jumped up and down.

"Hoo, hoo," Hadas hooed at her.

"Hoo, hoo," she hooed back.

The rhythm accelerated. Leela felt her feet hammering the ground and heard herself hooing madly. For a moment she forgot where she was, everything disappeared, and her entire world became a mass of storming, hoo hooing humanity.

"Stop!" the leader shrieked, and the crowd froze, remaining still and quiet as statues.

"Shut your eyes, but remain aware," he instructed.

Later, Hadas told her that it was only fifteen minutes, but it seemed to have lasted forever. Stuck with bent knees, arms up in the air, Leela could feel everything that was happening in her body. Her breath was short and shallow, and much too fast and her heart was pounding. Her entire body seemed filled with energy, an inner heat that sent sweat rolling down her back and thighs. She was dying to move, to scratch under her arms.

"Don't," she kept telling herself. "Stay still!"

"Last part," Hadas whispered, as a melodic flute took over and the crowd danced gently, celebrating the coming day.

"WHAT DO YOU want to do now?" Hadas was fully energized and bursting with plans.

"I think I'll go home." Leela felt she'd had enough for one day. But as she walked, taking the long way back, she had to admit, if only to herself, she felt different, better than she had in a long time.

"Lighter," she wrote later in her notebook. "Almost as if I had been turned upside down and shaken."

"At least go to some of the meetings, or a workshop or two." Hadas tried to convince her, when Leela refused to register for any of the courses. Leela resisted, but promised to join her for the early morning meditation.

"I feel like an idiot," she complained to Hadas after a few days. "Everyone seems so in to it, but I'm just going through the motions." She felt as though she was looking at them all from the outside, as if, as usual, she didn't belong. "I feel like everyone's looking at me, like I'm doing it all wrong."

"There's no wrong or right." Hadas smiled patiently. "Just do your thing. No one cares what you do. It'll change, you'll see. Simply carry on. One day something will open up in you and everything will be different."

IT TOOK SOME time, but eventually Leela began to enjoy it, waiting for the moments in which her mind would finally let go, allowing all thought to disappear as she became one with the music and the movement. At first these were only short intervals of peacefulness, of a sudden quiet calm, until something caught her attention again, and the room with all its sights and sounds came flooding back. But as she allowed herself to let go, throwing herself into the meditation wholeheartedly, shaking and screaming and really letting everything out, the moments lengthened, until she could go through almost the entire meditation without a thought, feeling a unity with everyone in the room, as though they had all melted into each other and become one.

"I finally don't feel like an observer," she told Hadas. "I think I'm ready to start getting serious."

FOR LEELA GETTING serious meant taking every course and workshop the ashram had to offer. She practiced with an urgency, as if her life depended on it, spending days crawling on the floor speaking gibberish or splashing color on huge white canvases, sucking her thumb and playing like she had as a child. She laughed for an entire week, shouting "yaa-hoo" every time she forgot, pulling faces, tickling and being tickled. Then she spent a week, screaming "yaa-boo" and crying. At first the tears refused to come, but when the group wept, a huge sadness arose in her, as long forgotten images of her mother and all the people and places she had left behind flooded through her mind. Burning hot waves cursed through her body like torrents, releasing all the untouched pockets of pain that had remained dormant for so long. She had never really mourned her mother's death, everything had happened so quickly. Suddenly she felt convulsed by an immense anger, all the words that she had kept buried inside bursting out of the tip of her tummy, bubbling out like a poisoned gas that had remained hidden, festering silently.

"Why?" her mind screamed at Minna, finally able to release the questions she had held inside for so long. "Why did you die? Why did you leave me? How could you?"

"Why?" she shouted at David. "Why did you leave us? Why did you and mommy get married in the first place? What were you thinking?"

"What did you think would happen?" she asked them both, tears rolling down her face.

And once she began to cry, she felt she'd never be able to stop. She cried for Minna and for David and for Venice. She cried for Taata Maryam and for Jasmine and all her aunts and uncles. She cried for her little brothers and sisters and for Esther and even for her jilted fiancé. She cried for her friends and for Jonathan and the entire settlement. She cried and cried until she had no tears left. And when all the tears were gone, there remained a huge emptiness. And with that emptiness came a sense of clarity, as if the fog had finally lifted and she could see. Now she could quiet her mind, to lengthen the brief intervals of silence in which she could simply sit, look, and listen.

"Just be," her counselors were forever telling her. "Become the watcher on the hill."

She studied Tantra and Zen and Sufism and practiced yoga and Chi Gong and even Japanese kabuki, learning the traditional steps and painting her face white. She learned all the different meditation and breathing techniques, often lying on her back for hours, huffing and puffing herself into rebirth. She was taught how to open her chakras and use essential flowers and oils. She went to tarot readings and lectures on astrology and numerology. Once she even agreed to see a therapist and had her heart opened up like a zipper and then filled with love and compassion. Her day started at six with Osho's dynamic meditation, and ended with Kundaleni at sunset, shaking her body madly and then prancing about as if there were no tomorrow.

Now she joined her friends, returning to the ashram in the evenings, allowing herself to simply hang out and have fun. At night the pyramid turned into a huge disco with live bands and loud music. Indians, Italians, Germans, Japanese, Korean, Israelis. People from all countries and nationalities came together to party and celebrate. There were pubs and bars and alcohol ran freely. She wasn't used to drinking, so a beer or a glass of wine was enough to make her quite tipsy, but since she was never alone, she allowed herself to try new things, to experiment. She learned to relax, to allow her body to move freely, to go with the music. She danced with abandon, tossing her body about, feeling a sense of freedom she'd never known existed. She felt young and alive, and for the first time in her life even sexy.

"You have a really nice body," Ellie complimented when she joined them on the roof to sunbathe, wearing shorts and a tank top.

"You're always wearing loose fitting, big clothes," Zoe agreed with her. "They totally hide your body. You're really hot, girlfriend."

Later, she locked the bathroom door and undressed slowly in front of the full-length mirror. She was used to averting her look whenever she took her clothes off. Vanity was a sin in the settlement, and looking at your own nudity unheard of. There were no life-sized mirrors in their house, so whenever they got dressed up for a holiday or special occasion, she and Esther would hold up a mirror for each other, moving it about to reflect different sections of their body, but they were never really able to see the whole picture. The mirror above the bathroom sink was wide but so short, she could barely see beyond her neck.

Now she really looked at herself. She looked at her hair, marveling at its light mocha color. It turned lighter the longer it grew, and now reached below her shoulders. Esther had always chopped it off long before it reached them. She looked at her impish, light olive face and thought how much she looked like her mother. Staring into her father's green blue eyes, it felt as though he were standing right beside her, staring right back. She looked at her neck and her arms and her breasts, and down to her stomach and legs, then turned to look at her backside.

"I really am hot." She chuckled, twisting her arms and legs and dancing gently. She thought she could have been taller, but she liked her body.

"Nice tits and ass." She shook them in front of the mirror.

She began to dress differently, flaunting her body, celebrating her newfound womanhood. She walked slowly barefoot in the ashram, letting her feet feel the warm earth and the cold marble, the crinkling of a tiny pebble or a sliver of grass sending light shimmering tremors up her ankles and the top of her shins. She even took on a few lovers, spending a short while with each, before sending them on their way. Her first was Alphonso, who told her he'd wanted her from the moment they met. He was forever asking her out and he never gave up, buying her chocolates and flowers, until she finally relented, a few weeks before he was to return home.

"Ay ay, kara mia, why didn't you tell me." Poor Alphonso wrung his hands wretchedly, about to burst into tears, when he realized she had been a virgin.

"I'm fine," she tried to reassure him. "It didn't hurt at all."

It was true. She'd barely felt a thing. In fact, it had been a big disappointment. But once Alphonso realized what had happened, he took it upon himself to be her mentor. He was such a romantic, cooking for her and buying little gifts. For those few weeks, he wouldn't let her out of his sight and when he left, weeping and swearing his undying love, she was actually quite relieved.

Gitamo came next. His coconut name was Claudius, but everyone just called him Git. He had rented Alphonso's old room for a week, but ended up sleeping in Leela's. He came and went, and that was just the way Leela wanted it. Deepak lived in London, but came to the ashram every year. His family was originally from Mumbai, so he visited his relatives at the same time. He lasted for three days. Like the men before him, he really liked her and wanted more, but Leela wasn't interested. She liked them all, but they were just part of her experiment, something she felt she had to try. But now that she had, she decided to put it on hold. It was too big of a distraction, and not really worth the effort. She had never believed in love and romance and not only because of the way her parents had ended. David and Esther's marriage had always seemed more of an arrangement, and anyway, she had much more important things to discover.

SHE STARTED TO work at Ken's coffee shop, on the corner of Lane Two and South Main Street. It was their favorite place and Hadas had already been working there for a while. The pay was lousy, but the tips were good. There were still many months until Jonathan's arrival and since they planned to travel, Leela thought it would be a good idea to make some extra money. Twice a week the girls volunteered at the squatter's encampment, giving much needed English lessons to the women. The place was huge, running all the way from North Main Road to the railroad. The conditions were appalling and the girls always brought biscuits and snacks to hand out. Entire families squashed into tiny one room stone huts, devoid of furniture, sleeping on the floor, bunched together on torn mats, with only a straw awning in place of a roof. Still, they were the lucky ones. Torn colored tarpaulins hung over rugged wooden frames were where most people slept, crowded together to form some kind of protection. Goats wandered freely, grazing on whatever they could find, and snot nosed children ran around, supervised only by their slightly older siblings.

Her days were so full, when she got into bed at night she usually collapsed, falling into a dreamless sleep. Sometimes she'd call on the pink balloon, but more often than not was asleep before it took off. It didn't really matter, though. It wouldn't take her far. On the rare occasions she tried to fly, the balloon rose only as high as the rooftops, hovering in circles above Koregaon Park, refusing to go any further.

Remaining between the confines of North and South Main Roads, Leela felt completely at home, spending her time with like-minded people, who, she felt, spoke her language. Just like her, they were all on a quest, everybody looking for something. Still, her mind wouldn't stop, remaining constantly active, tormenting her, seldom allowing for more than a brief moment of silence.

Every free moment, she'd sit herself down and try to meditate, first following her breath and then trying to slow down her thoughts. She found it difficult to concentrate, her mind constantly attacking her, throwing memories and old stories at her, triggering a flood of painful emotions she found hard to control.

"Don't run away from your feelings," Sambavya had taught them. "Stay with them. If there is anger, let there be anger. If there is fear, let there be fear. Look at it. Where does it rise?"

Anger and pain, she found, rose at the bottom of her stomach, right beneath her bellybutton. And the more she looked at it, the redder it became, and hotter, until it actually burned. But she learned to stay with it, looking, feeling, suppressing all thought, until it began to dissipate and disappear.

"Mindfully observe your monkey mind. Even if you can't control your thoughts, follow them, watch them as they come and go."

So Leela watched her monkey mind, following her weaving thoughts, seeing the chains and the loops it created. She learned to witness, to look at herself from the outside, watching everything go by like a movie. Gradually the moments of silence between her thoughts grew longer and she found she could sit quietly and meditate.

Still she couldn't control the mornings, her mind attacking her when she was most vulnerable, throwing its most powerful stories at her the second she woke up, reeling her in.

"It's just a story," she'd tell herself, but her mind wouldn't shut up, repeating its worn tales like an old vinyl record.

"Go away," she'd tell it. "I've heard it all before."

But it just pushed out its chest and banged its fists on the table, churning away relentlessly, almost as if the story was attached to her and not her to the story.

"Quiet!" She would force herself out of bed, banishing all thought, ending the battle for as long as she could.

WHEN THE MONSOON arrived, she had more time for herself. On the days the rain refused to stop, coming down in sheets, hammering unremittingly on the windows and roof, there was less work at the coffee shop, so she stayed home, meditating and practicing on her own. She gave herself assignments, carefully jotting them down in her notebook. One week she worked on her emotions, breathing out all her anger and pain. The next week she moved to her thoughts, banishing anything negative.

"No more bad thoughts, brain, if you have something bad to say, I don't want to hear it."

For a while she was love and compassion. She wasn't sure quite what that meant, but she practiced fervently all the same, giving thanks to whatever she could think of and trying to live the moment.

"Choose to feel good every moment and moment," Sambavya had said, before releasing them on the final day of the course.

"Choose to be happy."

"The only thing I know for sure is the past," Leela told her.

Her present was dubious, and her future even more so, still for an entire week she focused only on what was happening to her, dismissing all other thoughts and memories, carefully jotting down all her infractions.

"Stay in the now," she'd tell herself, every time she found herself carried away by her thoughts. "See things as they really are, no more stories," or "Stop! Who are you talking to? You're having an imaginary conversation with your mind again."

"Who's in?" she'd stop from time to time to ask herself, constantly trying to grapple with the questions that had brought her to the ashram in the first place. "Who's thinking? Who am I?" "No me" was the main buzz word and entire courses were devoted to finding it.

"Look down down, deep, under all the masks," her councilors advised her, but the more she looked, the more confused she became.

"I don't get it," she'd tell the girls. "Wherever I look, there's always somebody."

Mostly she would sit and meditate. She found she could now sit quietly for long periods of time, and the more she sat, the more she fell in love. The only enterprise she never missed was her work with the women. Every Monday and Thursday, no matter the weather, Leela made her way to the encampment, knowing they'd be waiting. As time passed by she felt she was actually making a difference. Koregoan Park was a wealthy, upbeat area, yet there was poverty all over, makeshift huts on every corner and little hovels covered in rags and torn awnings, harboring entire families, sheltered in the nooks and crannies of the grandest houses. But the sheer magnitude of the squatter's encampment turned it into something quite different, a bleak and harsh world within a world, with its own rules and understandings, that both and fascinated and repelled her.

The settlement was made up of about a hundred small concrete structures, built in two long lanes on either side of an uneven pot holed earth path, but most people lived in back of them, in tiny makeshift structures, made of wood and rags. During the monsoon, large families huddled together, cramped inside their tiny dwellings, almost buried in a sea of mud. Rivers of sewage flowed through the encampment and everything reeked of urine and feces. The girls would leap from stone to stone, making their way to the center, where the men had built a wooden platform, covered with awnings and long sheets of plastic. The tent was used mostly for gatherings and religious festivals, but twice a week it turned into a classroom, just for the women. No matter the heat or the rain, they always arrived early, and sat about chatting, eagerly awaiting the girls. Even the women who worked outside on the roads, hauling stones and cement for construction were never late. The girls had divided them into groups and each met with the same seven or eight women in their particular section of the tent.

Leela's group had the back right side, a small cozy enclosure that kept quite dry, even in the heaviest rains, with only a few small leaks and a drizzle now and then. They practiced talking for the first hour, learning new words through pictures and games and songs, while the second hour was devoted to reading and writing. She had to start from the very beginning, teaching them the alphabet and helping them trace rows and rows of crooked letters in the notebooks she herself provided. The girls bought pencils and crayons and finger paints and the women valued every second, often pleading with them to stay longer. Leela loved her women and took pride in their progress. They had learned all the letters and while most could only read short sentences, some were already reading entire paragraphs. They insisted on calling her "Miss Leela," and always awaited her happily, diligently applying themselves to every task, grateful for her attention. In return, they invited her to all their festivities. Ignoring the filth and poverty, no matter the conditions in the encampment, they never complained, remaining smiling and joyful, every occasion a reason to celebrate.

The ashram had its own festivals, but Leela preferred the authentic, local celebrations. Deafening Indian music blared from huge speakers on Krishna's birthday and the skies burst into flame in a brilliant display of fireworks as the girls danced ecstatically for hours, almost crushed by the crowd. When spring arrived, the women painted the girls' faces and invited them to join them, singing and dancing in the streets. As they stepped out of the encampment, they were turned on and bombarded with colored powders, till Leela's eyes stung and she could hardly breathe. For a moment everything turned red, and then blue and yellow.

"Buran a maano Holi hai!" the women yelled merrily, singing and dancing feverishly, as all the colors began to intermingle.

"Buran a maano Holi hai." One of Leela's women placed a plastic gun in her hands. It had a huge container filled with water. Leela tried to ask her what they were all saying, but she just laughed and repeated, "Buran a maano Holi hai." Green and orange powder filled the air. Someone shot water into the crowd. Everyone was screaming.

"Buran a maano Holi hai!" Leela shouted out, aimed her revolver straight in front of her, and pressed the trigger as the entire road broke into a free for all.

No one was safe. Passersby were attacked, splayed with powders and water, forced to join the festivities. Drums sounded and a band played, trying to create some kind of order, but everyone ignored them. Wherever Leela looked, she saw only a mass of writhing bodies, covered in runny colored paint, frolicking and squirmishing, screaming with glee.

When autumn arrived, she helped the women distribute oil lamps and candles for Diwali, commemorating the victory of light over darkness. On Ganesh Chaturthi, a few of the women invited her to their homes to see their idols. Leela was a little reluctant, until she realized how important it was to them.

"Take sweets for offerings," Vipul had instructed, and the man at the sweet store suggested tiny round white sugar pearls.

"They're Ganesh's favorite." He placed a big bag in her hand. "Make sure to place a large handful in front him."

"Don't you have a smaller bag?' She could barely lift it.

"You'll need it." The seller grinned. "Hand out the rest to the children."

INSIDE THE HOUSES were even worse, each sleeping as many as ten or twelve people. The first one she entered was Naaz's. She was a quiet, gentle woman who worked as a cleaner in one of the industrial buildings. She had three small children and a sickly husband who was usually to be found sitting on the ground outside their house or walking the goat. His parents lived with them.

"They do nothing all day," Naaz would joke. "Only fight and complain."

"Please," she welcomed Leela, bowing to her in reverence.

Leela took off her shoes. A bunch of mattresses lay piled against the wall, large plastic bags bursting with clothing and linen stacked above them. The remaining space was stark and uninviting, except for a pedestal around which the room now seemed to center, upon which stood an almost man sized statue of Ganesh, the elephant god, his four arms elaborately carved and his neck and upper body covered with little round pink and yellow flower garlands. Naaz lit little bushels of incense, and the room quickly filled with the fragrant smoke. She poured oil into a copper lamp, lit the wick, and moved it above her head in circles, muttering a prayer. When she was done, she offered it to Leela. Leela placed her hands together, bowed slightly, and circled her head with the burning lamp. Following Naaz's lead, she placed a large handful of sweets on Ganesh's tray.

"Put your hands together," she told the children before she left, filling their palms with the tiny sugary drops.

Bahaar's house was much the same, shared not only with her two children, but also with her brother and sister and their families. They were all standing outside in a row when she arrived, eager to shake her hand, and since it had begun to drizzle, they all crowded in after her. Their idol was a lot smaller but bulkier, and even more elaborately decorated than Naaz's. This was a seated Ganesh, made out of clay, a gigantic golden turban covering most of his forehead.

Kumari's Ganesh was the largest and most impressive, sitting in its wheeled cart, complete with carved columns and a jeweled headdress. Leela shook her head, amazed. These people had virtually nothing, yet they were spending so much on the idols, competing against each other, for no reason she could comprehend. Their living conditions were appalling. There was no electricity or running water. They cooked outside, sharing fires and utensils, but had to carry their pots and dishes to the stream on the far side of the encampment. They washed their clothes in the river, across the main road, carrying shirts and trousers and saris on their heads, in wide wicker baskets. Some showers and toilets had been set up on the outskirts, but asides from being filthy, there just weren't enough, leaving people to find their own, creative solutions.

"I can't understand it," she said to the girls, when they met on the roof in the evening.

"They believe Ganesh will bring them good fortune." Hadas smiled.

"So they spend a fortune to make a fortune?" Ellie rolled her eyes.

"Well," Zoe chuckled, "India has its own logic. They believe the more they spend, the more good fortune they'll get."

ON THE ELEVENTH day of Ganesh Chaturthi, the women invited them to join the main procession. They were to meet them on Fifth Road at the entrance to the park. When they arrived the street was crowded, people standing in a long line, stretching all the way down the block. Entire families stood together, carrying or pushing a Ganesh figure. Naaz was waiting impatiently, wearing her finest sari, pink with gold edges and her face was heavily painted.

"C'mon." She grabbed Leela's hand, and the girls pushed after her into the crowd.

Naaz's entire family was grouped together halfway down the road, their standing Ganesh on a child's trolley, tens of fresh flowered garlands around his neck. Women called out to them from up and down the line. They were all wearing their finest, their families pushing and pulling their elaborately figured idol.

"Leela, Leela," someone called out to her as she was admiring the statues.

"Raj?" At first, she didn't even recognize him, and not only because he looked so different, all dressed up in a white suit with gold trim and buttons, with a ruby red turban and sash. But what made Leela doubt that it was him, was the agility with which he moved. The bad-legged momo man was jumping up and down the line, pushing and pulling people into place, shouting out orders, telling everyone what to do. His entire demeanor had changed and he seemed almost ferocious.

"Come, come." He pulled the girls out of the line and marched them forward to the beginning of the procession.

In front stood a gigantic Ganesh figure, surrounded by gloved men holding ropes, whose job it was to move him around. Girls in colorful saris danced before him and leading the procession were rows and rows of men, dressed in white, with loud orange turbans and a matching sash. They held huge drums and were now trying them out, hammering on them in disarray.

"Here," he cried excitedly, moving some people back and pushing the girls into the second row. "Good spot." He continued talking, but they couldn't hear him above the ruckus. Raj left them, running back up the aisle, bossing everyone around.

"Great place." Hadas clapped her hands happily.

"Right behind Ganesh's backside," Ellie complained.

"Sshhh . . ." The girls shut her up, giggling.

Just then Raj came rushing by.

"We're starting, we're starting," he cried out.

"Where's he going?" Leela watched in disbelief as he walked right up to the top the procession.

"The momo man's the master of the parade." Zoe couldn't stop laughing as Raj lifted his arms, signed something in the air, and the drums beat a lively march.

The dancers swiveled and contorted their bodies as Raj leaped nimbly in the air, turned, and moved forward. Slowly the entire parade moved, sliding like a snake through the crowded streets, growing longer and longer as more and more people joined in. Everyone was singing and shouting boisterously, the dancers shaking and moving their bodies in a frenzy, the drums thundering, while Raj, leaping and gesticulating, lead the parade with great honor.

"WHERE ARE WE going?" Leela asked the girls.

The parade had passed through South Main Road and was now making its way through North Main Road, but in the opposite direction. The girls all shook their heads.

"Down to the river," a man standing next to Leela informed them.

"Maybe we should call it a day," Ellie suggested. The light drizzle was turning into a downpour and the girls were getting drenched.

"You can't leave now." The man waved his finger at them. "We're nearly there. The river's the most important part."

He laughed when he saw their inquisitive faces, but wouldn't tell them why.

"You have to see it to believe it," was all he would say.

The sight at the river was truly incredible. The men pulling the statue didn't stop when they reached its bank. They carried on walking, pulling the enormous Ganesh into the river, together with them.

"What are they doing?" an amazed Leela asked the man.

"Immersing Ganesh in the water!" he exclaimed to the dumbfounded girls, who sat themselves down on the bank in the pouring rain, watching as dozens of families climbed into the streaming water, pulling their idols in with them. They said a prayer and threw flowers and rice and sweets in the wake of their Ganesh as the idols floated slowly down the river.

SOMETIMES IT RAINED for days without end, but whenever she could, Leela made her way to Osho Park to meditate. When the weather allowed it, she'd take the long way, stopping off to visit her old friends, making sure to take a moment to call on Master Sunny and another to see how Leah Neah was doing. They had been good to her when she had first arrived and she always took care to clean them off. When the sun came out, she'd settle herself right on top of Sunny and practice disappearing into the light.

"Feel the warmth of the sun," she'd tell herself. "Feel each and every ray entering your body. Feel the warmth becoming deeper, moving to each and every cell. Feel it move into your arms . . ."

Her favorite place was Osho Park. She could stay there as long as she wanted without being disturbed. She had begun to find comfort in silence, trying to lengthen the spaces, the little gaps in which she was able to keep her mind still.

"Let it go," she told herself, when any thought arose. "Be present, aware, pay attention to the moment. Watch your thoughts and feelings as they rise and then disappear."

As she watched her thoughts, the quiet between them grew and she felt a certain spaciousness, a quiet, ever-present awareness behind her thoughts.

"Imagine you are grounded and peaceful. You are an ocean of serenity." She'd lie down on the grass besides the stream, close her eyes, and imagine she was floating.

"Listen to the sound of the water. Feel it touching your body, so cool and refreshing. Feel it enter you, course through your body."

As she lay there, floating on the water, the world around her disappeared and her body became light and warm, until it no longer felt solid or real. For a moment she became the river, flowing peacefully through the garden. Other times she was the light or the wind or the rain. Sometimes it was the garden that disappeared, and she would find herself sitting cross-legged in outer space, hovering lightly among the stars, utterly quiet and tranquil in face of the vast emptiness.

A MONTH BEFORE Jonathan was supposed to arrive, he phoned to tell her he was postponing his trip.

"A year!" Leela shrieked in his ear.

"I'm doing it for us." He tried to placate her. "We'll have enough money to do whatever we want."

He had been worrying about expenses, and now that the army had asked him to stay on for an extra year, he decided to do it.

"I'll come the second I'm released," he promised, "and save every shekel."

"Now that I've calmed down, I'm not as upset as I expected," she told the girls later, realizing that although she really missed him and had been counting the days till he arrived, she was quite happy on her own where she was. Jonathan wanted to travel, to see the world, but she had only begun to settle down and build a life for herself.

"I wouldn't mind spending some extra time at the ashram, but I can't stay here, and what will I do all on my own for another year?" she groaned.

They had all given their notice at A+V's and their rooms had already been rented. Knowing that Leela was leaving, the other girls had volunteered to work on one of the organic farms that supplied the ashram. They were all supposed to leave the house on the same day.

"Come with us," Hadas suggested, and the others enthusiastically nodded their agreement.

"We get food and board and only have to work a few hours a day." Ellie tried to convince her. "And we even get free entrance to the ashram."

"It's just out of town, less than half an hour's walk," Zoe added, "and only 80 rupees by rickshaw."

"Do you think there'll be place for me?" Leela liked the idea of staying with her friends.

"Ellie and Zoe are sharing a room, so you'll share with me," Hadas decided.

SANJAY CAME TO fetch them, driving his biggest van.

"Where's the rest of your stuff?" He glared at them, irritated, his long black hair and thick moustache overshadowing most of his face. He was around forty, tall and slightly on the heavy side, and was sweating profusely, a constant stream rolling down his face and onto his checkered shirt.

"I told you to have everything out on the curb. I don't have time for this." He mopped at his face. "I don't usually pick up the volunteers. They're supposed to come on their own."

"That's it." The girls laughed, picking up their rucksacks and climbing in. "That's all we have." They had so few belongings none of them needed more than just one bag.

The van drove slowly through South Main Road, past the encampment, and across the bridge to Kahalani Nagar. Just before the main road, Sanjay took a sharp right onto a dirt road and followed the river. Houses and buildings quickly disappeared, leaving open fields and a handful of farms and small squatters encampments. He drove for a few minutes longer and then stopped outside a closed gate.

The sign said: "Earthly Enterprises Organic Farm," in big red letters, and underneath, in green: "no pesticides or insecticides allowed!"

A slightly slimmer version of Sanjay came hurrying toward them, waving his hands.

"Sandip," he introduced himself. "C'mon, I show you around."

The brothers ran "Earthly Enterprises," and although there was a year between them, they looked so much alike, they could have been twins. Leela could hardly tell them apart, but while Sandip was always cheerful and boisterous and Sanjay sullen and quiet, it didn't take her long to see that both had their hearts in the right place.

"They were both lawyers," Hadas told her later. "They left Mumbai and returned to farm their family's land."

Sanjay and Sandip lived with their families in the main house, an old, grey, crumbling two-story stone building, just by the entrance. The workers' compound, a group of rough looking huts, was right on the other side, just by the river.

"The barn our pride and joy." He pointed to a large, straw roofed concrete structure. "Most important place in farm."

The pride and joy of Earthly Enterprises was its herd of thirty Gir cows. They were the weirdest cows Leela had ever seen, reddish brown with a humped spine and bulging forehead and their ears hung down like long, folded leaves, while thick horns shot up from the back of their skulls, pointing out and up, but backward. Black hooded eyes stared at her out of long, tender faces, making them seem almost human. Some milled around the house and nearby fields, grazing and relaxing in the shade, while others roamed all the way down to the river.

"You do milk in morning," Sandip told them. "You know milk?"

Leela was the only one of them with any experience. "But only with goats," she apologized.

"No problem." Sandip shook his head to the sides and up and down at the same time. "You learn quick, quick."

The cows were hand milked twice a day and most of the produce went to the ashram. Whatever was left was sold in the little store they opened, adjacent to the main house.

"The fridge always open and you welcome to take what you want." Sandip poured them some milk.

Leela took a long sip. It was smooth and creamy and delicious.

"We make our very own ghee butter and panir cheese," he boasted. "And the most delicious dahi. All gone now, but I make some tomorrow, special for you."

There were also a few orchids growing pomegranate, papaya, and lime and a few rows of seasonal vegetables.

"What's that smell?" Leela blocked her nose as a terrible stench reached her nostrils.

"Everything completely organic." Sandip proudly showed them the immense compost barrels where cow dung and urine were combined to make the obnoxious slush that covered the soil. Leela moved away quickly, trying not to retch.

A number of Indian men and a few westerners were sitting outside the workers' huts. One of them was playing a guitar and a few were drumming little sticks on the ground in accompaniment. They waved and nodded when the girls passed and exchanged some banter with Sandip, but didn't stop what they were doing.

Leela liked the large kitchen and dining hall, set right in the middle of the ring of bamboo huts, but when she walked into the hut she would be sharing with Hadas, she shook her head in dismay.

"Are you crazy?" She looked around her.

Besides two small mattresses lying on a thin mat on the floor, the room was totally empty. There was no electricity and the few showers and compost toilets down by the river, were shared by all the workers.

"Why didn't you tell me?" Leela sat down in the doorway, holding her head. This was not at all what she had expected.

"It's just for a month." Hadas dismissed her with a wave of her hand. "Here," she pulled out a flashlight, "I bought you a present."

IT WAS A simple life and Leela soon learned to enjoy it. Living in nature, her day began before sunrise and ended after sun set. Unlike the other girls, she took to the cows right away, often bringing them treats and letting them nuzzle from her hands. They were the most even-tempered and gentle creatures and she loved to place her face against their smooth, hairy skin as she was milking. The brothers refused to name them, hanging numbers on their collars instead, so everyone just called them "humpy one, humpy two, humpy three . . ." Leela was in charge of humpies twenty-three to thirty but she often helped the other girls out, they milked so slowly.

Once the girls poured the fresh milk into huge round shiny metal vats where it was cooled and then pasteurized, they were done, but Leela often stayed behind to help Chandra and Tanirika, the brother's wives, scraping off layers of cream and churning it into ghee or straining curds through a light cheesecloth, to create the finest, most delicate paneer. While she was working, she would fill her mouth with little chunks of the soft warm cheese, moving it around with her tongue before chewing slowly, savoring its fresh milky taste. It always made her think of Rachel. She missed her sister so much.

On days the cows were especially generous with their milk, they made "dahi," a traditional yogurt that was kept strictly for the farm. On those days the workers were served fried vegetable pakoras with fresh, creamy sour dahi, curd rice, and honey sweetened lassi. Dinner was served after the evening milking and whenever Leela had the time, she would go to help the women. The main house had a huge cooker and oven, but more often than none, the women liked to cook outside, chattering and laughing together over the open fire. Usually it was "tali," served out of huge pots of white rice and yellow dahl, made with black and red lentils, and one or two vegetables. They taught her to make chapatti bread and naan and how to mix her own spices. She learned to prepare different rice dishes and curries, using fruit and vegetables and nuts. Sometimes she'd cook for them, trying to conjure up one of Taata Maryam's beloved dishes as she stuffed vegetables with rice and dried fruit or browned onions for her savory lentil stew.

"Excellent." The women always complimented her. "But maybe a little more spicy?"

"Same day delivery" was the brother's slogan. They prided themselves on delivering their goods within four hours of milking, which also meant the girls had a free ride to the ashram several times a day. But other than Saturday, which was her day off, Leela hardly went to the ashram now, preferring instead to meditate quietly when everyone else left.

When the month ended, the brothers asked the girls to stay on, promising a small fee. They agreed on three months, but ended up staying the entire year. They each took on some more duties, helping to plant and weed and sow.

"I expect everything to be spick and span," Sanjay instructed Hadas, putting her in charge of the volunteers.

Hadas had no idea what that meant, but the job suited her perfectly. She had been an officer in the army and she loved bossing everyone around. She created work schedules and daily rotations, checking up on everyone and making sure everything was "spick and span." The other girls were in charge of the little store, but since it was only open for three hours a day, and just one of them had to be there, it didn't really add much to their workload. They held daily yoga and meditation sessions, attended by most of the volunteers and often by the brothers and their wives and in the evenings there was always someone strumming a sitar or a guitar.

When the new year arrived, the farm held its traditional spring festival, Baisakhi, bringing hordes of friends and relatives to their gate. Just before the celebrations were to begin, Chandra, Sanjay's wife, invited the girls to the main house, where the women were getting ready, painting each other's faces and exchanging chains and bangles. The women braided their hair and placed a tikka on their forehead, then dressed them in colorful saris.

"I make red for all the girls, but for you I make different." Chandra presented Leela with a shimmering sky blue sari. "Special for eyes."

Leela walked through the grounds, handing out the little bags of toffee and sweets the girls had prepared the day before. Everyone was having fun, dancing and singing loudly. The men were grouped together in circles, executing vigorous leaps and kicks to the rhythmic beats of a double headed drum and the women stood around Tanirika clapping rhythmically. Every now and then she would shout out something in Hindu and all the women would repeat it in unison, roaring at her exuberantly.

"You should go professional," everyone was always telling Sandip's wife and although she would shake her head modestly, she made sure to place herself at the center of all the women's gatherings.

SPRING WAS HOT and humid and the months following almost unbearable. Nights in the bamboo hut were sticky and suffocating and often the girls would lay a mat on the ground and sleep outside. Leela couldn't wait for the summer to be over, but the monsoon was late and the intense heat seemed to go on forever. When the skies finally opened, they danced in the fields, quickly getting drenched, as the ground around them turned into churning piles of red mud and slosh.

Leela was happy on the farm. She tried to live consciously, to be aware of everything around her, paying attention to any sound or movement, watching as life unfolded before her, moment by moment. Her mind was mostly quiet now, her family a distant memory that only rarely came back to haunt her. She learned to appreciate the small things. A kind smile. A good meal. Dancing in the rain. All her spare time was devoted to meditation. She would sit for hours, following her breath or silently watching, listening, waiting patiently for those magical moments, those little pockets of time when everything disappeared and there was no Leela and no world, just a quiet, calm clarity, a little moment of grace.

It was a good, peaceful time, but the pink balloon was getting restless, taking her away every night now, even when she didn't want to go. When they first started flying again, it had only taken her on brief trips, visiting nearby temples, a hill station or lake, but gradually it dared more and more, taking her farther and farther away. Lately, it seemed out of control, flying all night over open fields and rice paddies, through thick forests and jungles, taking her all the way to the ocean, to remote little seaside towns and villages.

"Move," it seemed to be telling her, when she didn't want to go, shaking and bouncing her around, as if trying to wake her from a deep sleep. She tried to ignore it, but she knew what it was trying to tell her. It was time to go. There was nothing left for her here. She had taken what she could.

"Patience, pink balloon." She tried to slow it down. "We have to wait for Jonathan. We'll leave the moment he arrives."

"And won't he be surprised." She chuckled to herself, looking down in wonder. For although the coconuts she saw beneath her remained the same, they were now different too. Shining and shimmering in the sun, alluring and mysterious in the rain, the coconuts now dazzled brightly in all the different colors of the rainbow, moving across the distant ground in brilliant hues, of green and yellow, red and orange, purple and pink and blue.

"I BARELY RECOGNIZED you." Jonathan finally released her from his bear hug. "You look so different, so grown up. Your hair's so long too." He caressed her head and hugged her again.

"You look like shit." Leela couldn't stop crying. He seemed so different, tired and gaunt, his skin pale and lifeless, his forehead creasing worriedly when he spoke, as if he was carrying the weight of the world on his shoulders. He looked so much older than she remembered. Even his smile seemed strained and somewhat contrived. She hadn't realized how much she had missed him.

"It's been a tough two years." He smiled dryly.

Leela knew he had been having difficulties, but now realized he had actually told her very little.

When his parents had started pressuring him to get married, he had finally sat them down and told them the truth. He had been trying for years, but they hadn't wanted to know. They still didn't.

"My mother said it was just something I was going through." Jonathan shook his head. "She said I was confused, that she'd go to the rabbi, ask him to speak to me. My father nearly jumped out of his skin. He didn't want to hear about it. 'Not a word,' he kept shouting at me, trying to shut me up. 'Not a word!' No one was to know about 'this nonsense.' In fact, no one was to talk of it again."

"Somehow I always thought they knew." Leela couldn't believe that Jonathan's kind and loving father could have behaved the way he had, but Jonathan told her it got so bad, he had to leave.

"He practically threw me out, telling me I was a disgrace, bringing shame on his house."

He rarely went back after that, spending holidays and vacations at friends' houses, until he managed to rent a little room in the city.

"It was just a tiny place, with a lot of other boys, but I could finally close the door and be whatever I wanted to be."

His parents had sent rabbis and emissaries to try to "talk some sense into him," but after the first few, Jonathan refused to meet them.

"These last months were the worst. I've been counting the days. I was only released yesterday. I caught the first flight."

Leela had taken a room in the Colaba district, right off the big bazaar. The girls had shared a taxi to Mumbai, but only Leela was staying. Hadas, Ellie, and Zoe were all returning home. The night before they left, "Earthly Enterprises" held a going away party. Chandra and Tanirika cooked the girls' favorite foods and Sanjay and Sandip played on their sitars until late into the night. There was dancing and speeches and gifts.

"For you, special present." Sanjay presented Leela with an old wooden relief. "Saraswati," he said with pride. "Goddess of knowledge. Of wisdom. Specially for you. You all the time with your head in your book." He laughed.

She was brightly colored, about thirty centimeters high, sitting cross-legged on a lotus flower, her raised hands pointing in opposite directions. Leela packed her carefully into her rucksack, along with her old photographs and notebooks and some pieces of clothing. Jonathan liked her too, although he had trouble pronouncing her name.

"Sara sweety?" he'd tease Leela. "Sweet Sara?"

"HAVE YOU FOUND what you were looking for?" he asked Leela when they settled for the night.

"Yes and no." Leela sighed. "I've learned a lot and found so much peace. Still, in many ways, I'm even more confused than before. I guess I can't find what I'm looking for," she chuckled sadly, "when I still have no idea what it is."

JONATHAN HATED MUMBAI and couldn't wait to get out. The monsoon rains had just ended and the streets were overflowing with people. Everything bothered him. The crowds. The noise. Even the air.

"I can't breathe," he kept complaining.

"There's a smell." He'd walk around sniffling. "Something faint, that seems to be following me around. A little sweet and a little sour, I can't really explain it, but it just makes me feel sick."

Leela was also somewhat overwhelmed. She had only passed through Mumbai, and although she had been living in India for so long, she had lived a very sheltered life, never venturing beyond the confines of Koregaon Park and Earthly Enterprises. Everything was new to her. The traffic and the tall buildings. The noise. The dirt. The sheer volume of people passing by. They lined up in front of India Gate for over an hour, and hardly had a moment to admire it, before they were pushed forward toward the sea. People were constantly coming up to them, touching them, holding up their palms, and begging. Jonathan gave a little girl a few rupees.

"Remember me!" She tied a yellow threaded bracelet around his wrist.

Soon the little girl and a whole group of other girls, not much older were following them everywhere. It took a good deal of negotiating and quite a few more rupees to get rid of them, but the moment they hit the Colaba Causeway they were harassed again, wheedled and cajoled by countless other peddlers and beggars.

"Let's go down some side streets," Leela suggested, heading away from the main road.

A few blocks away, they found themselves in a little fruit and vegetable market. There were no stalls, the women sat on the ground, their wares spread around them, children and goats and chickens running around squawking happily. At the end of the lane stood two heavily decorated canvas-covered shrines.

Jonathan was invited into the men's while Leela was given fruit to place on the women's. They both came out reeking of incense and with a bright red tikka on their foreheads. As they carried on walking, following the market road, they found themselves deep in a slum. At first it reminded Leela of the squatter's settlement, the same tiny cement boxes, only here they were all joined to each other, creating an enormous grey labyrinth, made up of tiny filthy passages and cubicles, into which hundreds of people were crammed. They sat in the doorways or lay listlessly on the floors, some sharing mattresses, others piled one atop the other on rusty iron bunk beds. Men, women, children, and animals rushed up and down the crowded alleyways, bustling about like ants in an anthill.

"So let's go somewhere else." Jonathan couldn't take it anymore, but it was easier said than done. Most people didn't speak any English, and by the time they found their way out, it was already getting dark.

"It's a bit too much for me." Jonathan felt totally overwhelmed. "I don't think I can take it."

"Don't worry, you'll get used to it." Leela tried to placate him. "And anyway, it's not like this everywhere. Pune's very different. There was a lot of poverty there too, but nothing like this."

"Well, then, let's get out of here," he decided, refusing to spend even one more day in Mumbai.

"SOMEWHERE NEXT TO sea." The travel agent rubbed her forehead, frowning. "It's strongest time of season. Many, many tourists. Everything chocka block."

They had made no plans, the only thing they knew for sure, was that it had to be by the sea. The pink balloon had been clear about that, taking Leela to the waterfront every night for weeks. And besides, she missed the ocean, not having seen it for so long.

The night before they had flown together, trying to decide where they should go. The pink balloon was overjoyed, carrying them high up above the enormous city, bouncing them about and frolicking merrily. Jonathan had missed it too, but he was so excited, he kept losing his control. He hadn't flown for years, and now with all the sudden colors, he was getting more and more confused. Up and down they went, sometimes speeding, often slow.

"To the ocean," he decided when they finally landed, clapping his hands dramatically and adding, "wherever the pink balloon decrees."

"These only flights I can get you today. Goa, two-thirty and Chennai, four." The clerk at the travel agency turned her computer around to face them. "Otherwise you wait two, three days. Or you want fly Delhi, get plane there."

"Goa," Leela cried eagerly. She'd heard so much about it and she'd never even heard of Chennai.

"Madras." The agent tried to help. "Before it called Madras."

But Leela had never heard of Madras either.

"But look, Goa's too near." She was so disappointed when the agent showed them the places on the map. "The pink balloon keeps flying and flying, I think it means to take us further."

"I don't think we should start there, anyway," Jonathan agreed. "I'd like to travel, see India first. Maybe we could go there later. Look." He pointed at the map. "Chennai's right on the other side."

"Chennai very good place to start trip. Very excellent place." The agent nodded enthusiastically. "You start Chennai, go all way round. Later you go Goa. Better also make reservation for hotel. Like I tell you before, everything chocka block."

GETTING USED TO India took Jonathan some time, but India was crazy about him from the moment he arrived. It was probably his fair skin and hair that drew everyone to him, but wherever he went, there was always someone following him. Children and adults stopped him on every corner. Young girls would beg to have their picture taken with him, while old men asked to shake his hand. No one approached Leela, unless as a means to capture Jonathan's attention.

"If no your eyes, I think you Indian," an old woman told her, snickering as she brushed her aside, eager to grab a place by his side where she smiled widely, posing for the camera.

CHENNAI WAS ALSO immense, but it was more laid back, with much less traffic and long endless beaches and promenades. The agent booked a hotel right on the waterfront, in one of the oldest areas of the city. Marina beach went on for miles, its wide promenade covered with little souvenir shops and food stalls. Although swimming was strictly prohibited, the shallow waters were always full of waders and the sands packed with people lazing about, jogging, cycling, or playing volleyball. Some came to watch the sun rise, others to watch it set. For the first few days Leela and Jonathan just walked or cycled along the beach, practicing yoga in the morning and meditating together at night.

"I can't really concentrate," Jonathan groaned.

"Just close your eyes and follow your breath," Leela instructed him. "Whatever you do is fine."

Sometimes they'd choose something from the list of "attractions" the hotel proprietor had eagerly written down for them when they first arrived, flag a rickshaw, and set off for a few hours of exploration. The city center was full of well kept, handsome government buildings, surrounded by colorful handicraft stores. They bought a few trinkets at Burma Bazaar and gorged themselves on freshly fried snapper and trout at the fish market. Fresh coconuts were sold on every corner and cost less than thirty rupees. The first day they ate so many, Jonathan had such a stomach ache, he thought he was going to die. Everything was new and exciting. And big. So, so big! Endless markets and churches and forts. And the temples. They couldn't get enough of the immense, spectacular, structures, so different from anything they had ever seen before.

In the evenings, the promenade erupted in a cacophony of sound, as fireworks exploded above the cheering crowd.

"Must go see." The proprietor ushered them out of the hotel, the first evening. "Dussehra," he shouted excitedly hurrying along with them. "Special celebration. Only in Chennai."

Down on the beach men were lighting torches, preparing to set fire to enormous effigies that grew so high, they loomed over the crowd like tall buildings.

"Ravan and his two brothers," the proprietor informed them. "In The Ramaya, one of our most important tales, Lord Rama destroy Ravan."

Before he could say anything else, the effigies suddenly came alive, moving and jumping about, crackling and popping noisily, as the hundreds of fire crackers stuffed inside them went off.

"Tak, tak, tak." The effigies exploded, sounding like machine guns, celebrating the victory of good over evil. The crowd went wild.

After dark, the promenade seemed to become one big, long restaurant, as stall touched stall and the smell of frying and fish spread out, covering everything, like a cloud.

"Can we eat from the stalls?" Leela had asked the proprietor, remembering Helmut's warning.

"Never in street." He shook his finger. "But the stalls on promenade and in big markets, they clean, no problem."

"I'm in love." Jonathan gulped huge mouthfuls of the piping hot dosa Leela bought for him, splatters of potato mash spurting out of the corners of his mouth.

"They're different here." Leela liked them much more than the ones in Pune. They were much thinner and crispier and the potato stuffing was mixed with tons of deeply fried onion.

For breakfast, the proprietor prepared piles of "idli," soft, spongy rice cakes that looked like white puffy pancakes and melted like clouds in their mouth.

"They didn't have this in Pune," Leela told Jonathan, trying to decide which bowl to dunk it in. The idli itself was almost tasteless and got its flavor from the accompanying foods. There proprietor placed two types of chutney in front of them and a little plate of "sambar," a yellow dahl, which, he warned, was always made hot and savory, even in the early morning hours.

AT FIRST JONATHAN was jittery, distant and anxious, but after a few days, he relaxed, becoming more the calm and sturdy person she remembered. Soon they were flying regularly again. For a while the pink balloon was content to remain near, hovering lightly over the beach and promenade, but soon it became demanding again, pushing them to get going, to start on their way.

"Where shall we go?" they kept asking it, unclear about its answer.

On the day they went to Mylapore to visit the Kapaleeswarar temple, they finally understood.

"Wow." Jonathan stared incredulously at the steep pyramid awaiting them at the entrance. It was intricately carved with layer upon layer of sculptures each painted a different color, the details so vivid, they looked almost alive. It was the most spectacular thing they had ever seen.

"That's what I came to India for." He clapped his hands.

They stayed there the entire day, walking the grounds, watching the priests and the worshippers, mesmerized by the music and strange prayers and rituals.

"That's what the pink balloon's been trying to tell us," Jonathan told Leela before they left. "We have to get going. There's so much more for us to discover."

THE SIGNS ON the front of the busses were never in English, and since they didn't seem to run according to any schedule, they were never sure where they were going. It didn't really matter, wherever it was they came too, there were always tourists bearing maps, more than happy to lend a hand. They would tell them what they should see and where to stay and they knew the best places to go and where you should never step foot. Strangely enough, everywhere they went, there were Israelis, and they spotted each other from afar, immediately becoming the best of friends and hanging around together in clusters. They shared stories and gang'a and Leela and Jonathan were often happy to drift along, constantly accompanied by a changing friend or two.

The busses were packed and the roads bumpy and dusty, but the trains were even worse, overcrowded and foul smelling. Whenever they could, they travelled by rickshaw, moving across short distances, trying to see as much as they could. The pink balloon took them to the most exotic places. They climbed two thousand stairs to pay tribute to Lord Vishnu and worshiped Shiva and Shakti in cave temples, deep under the ground. They walked through golden domed temples carved out of stone and marched with elaborately decorated elephants, burning lanterns to help Lord Ramana find his way home.

As they traversed through ancient temples and palaces, some thousands of years old, Leela began to feel a change. At first it was very subtle, but gradually it became clearer, as if her small, sheltered world, had suddenly become immense, opening up in time, as well as space. Walking these roads, past and present intermingled, and time became slow and elongated. She felt she could go on forever and prayed the road would never end.

They stayed at little hotels and ashrams, but never for more than a day or two. Jonathan was much calmer and relaxed, but after so many years in the army, he still felt mission oriented, as if someone was constantly on his tail.

"Slow down," she kept telling him, running to keep up with his marching gait. "We have all the time in the world. No matter how fast you go, this is India. It has a pace of its own."

It took him some time to get it, but early one morning, as they waited for the bus, he suddenly howled and roared, bouncing about vivaciously.

"What the hell?" Leela had no idea what was going on, but Jonathan just picked her up, his arms squeezing her tightly.

"We did it!" He whooped gleefully, as if it had just sunk in. "We left. We got away. We're free. Free to go wherever we want and be whatever we want to be."

"There's no one to tell us what to do." He shook Leela's shoulders, yelling joyfully. "We're free. We're free!"

"I know." Leela laughed with him. "Pull yourself together," she said a moment later. "The bus's here."

WHENEVER THEY MADE a detour, the pink balloon kept them on track, sending them back, to follow the coast. The bus dropped them off at a pretty, beach town, with a very un-Indian sounding name.

"Pondicherry?" Leela raised her eyebrow at the driver.

"We call it Pondi." He winked and drove off.

The French colonial quarter, called "white town," lay along the seaside. They walked along the pretty streets, with their pretty French names and pretty French churches and villas. Contrary to its name, the town wasn't white at all, its low colonial buildings were flamboyantly colored in yellow and orange hues. High above the colorful streets towered a beautiful pink church. They walked along the wide tree-lined boulevards.

"It doesn't even look like India." Jonathan rolled his eyes.

"I guess that's what a French town looks like," Leela agreed.

Since there were no vacancies in "white town," they crossed the "grand canal" to "black town," the old Tamil quarter.

"This is where I want to stay." Jonathan preferred the louder, more worn part of town, even though it was farther away from the sea.

"It's so full of character," Leela agreed.

"Black town" was even more colorful than "white town," the houses built so closely together the entrance verandas were often attached to each other. Most houses were simple one-story structures, but many of the larger buildings and older Tamil mansions had been restored, returned to their former beauty. Large wooden doors were elaborately carved, and round shiny pillars held up sloping terracotta roofs. They found a room in a restored two-story building, in a quiet alley, just outside of the main bazaar.

This time they took it easy, exploring the town's back streets and heritage buildings. The beach was rocky and the waters too rough to swim, but the promenade was covered with cafes and restaurants and at dusk the streets leading up to the ocean were closed to traffic, the entire area covered with food vendors and little stalls. They discovered little ashrams and temples, churches and even mosques. At Gouver market they met a group of Israelis on their way to "Auroville." They couldn't believe Leela and Jonathan hadn't heard of it.

"The City of Dawn" was the vision of "the mother," a French lady who was trying to create a new way of life. A life of utter freedom. No nation. No religion. It was only about an hour away, and Leela couldn't wait to get there. Everyone on the bus was excited, talking and gesticulating loudly, but as they grew nearer, she felt more and more disappointed. The "mother ashram" was immense, built in a circle, with circular streets surrounding a massive ball-like structure, still under construction. Everyone referred to it reverently as "matrimandir," "temple of the mother," but it gave Leela the creeps. For some reason, the whole place gave her the creeps. She was a very orderly person, but too much order, she knew, was always a sign of disorder. They joined everyone for a communal meditation in the great hall, but when they were invited to stay Leela refused.

"I just don't feel comfortable here. Too much structure," she tried to explain to her newfound friends, what she herself didn't really understand. "It feels as if they know everything here, as if they already have all the answers. But I don't even know the questions yet. I guess I have to figure things out for myself."

Some of the group shared her sentiment.

"I've heard of a festival not too far away," one of them suggested. "But it's already the last days. We have to hurry, if we want to make it."

THE BUS LET them off quite a distance away, at the edge of a makeshift encampment that had popped up just a few days before. It had only been a three-hour ride, but it was as if they had stepped into a different world, a world in which time had stopped or simply didn't exist. The holy town sat perched above the Malai Hill and the way to the temple was replete with half naked, hideously painted sadus flaying their long black whips on the ground and white clad holy men, their faces striped yellow and red. It seemed they had arrived on the final day, so although the festivities were only to begin in the evening, the temple and surrounding area were already overcrowded and they had to wait in line for hours just to get in. They had never seen so many people. Above their head, thousands more were climbing the worn paths of Arunachala, the mountain overlooking the town, the abode of Lord Shiva, who was believed to reside there as the mountain itself.

When she finally entered the temple, it was like entering an immense calm. Away from the chaotic ruckus of the outside world, people walked slowly among the many towers and courtyards, speaking in hushed tones, while priests blessed devotees, circling their foreheads with burning lamps. The energy was infectious and Leela felt as though there really was some kind of presence.

"Starting to believe in God?" Jonathan kidded, although he knew exactly what she was talking about. He too felt oddly tranquil and at peace, a little lightheaded even, as if he were floating.

AT NIGHTFALL A holy fire was lit in a huge lamp at the top of the mountain. Its flame could be seen for miles around, signaling the start of the celebrations. Brightly painted idols were brought out, carried around in golden canopies, followed by endless processions of ecstatic dancing and singing. The peak of the celebration began when the full moon reached its zenith, aligning itself with the six holy stars and a procession of tens of thousands of believers lit their torches and made their way around the holy mountain, helping Shiva restore light to the world. Leela and Jonathan walked through the night, completing the circle a long time after daybreak.

"Shiva accept your offering." A temple priest placed a garland of flowers around Leela's neck. "You are transformed." He dipped his fingers in the holy ash and painted two black lines across her forehead.

WHEN THE CEREMONY ended, the Israelis grouped together outside the temple, still exhilarated from the night. No one was in a hurry to leave. A teacher from a nearby ashram approached them.

"Soon Sri Ramana's birthday. We have our own festival. Many, many people come to celebrate," he informed them, eagerly inviting them to join in.

"We have to go," Leela decided, the moment she heard whose ashram it was. Sri Ramana Maharishi, although long gone, had been much admired in Pune, his sayings and teachings endlessly quoted. Many of the others had heard of him too.

"Will you have place for all of us?" Jonathan looked worriedly at the large group.

"We got lotsa space." The teacher turned and led the way.

LIFE IN THE ashram was simple and the rules clear and strict. It was nothing like Pune. Here their days began before sunrise and ended with lights out at ten. The dorm-like living quarters were small, but the rent was low and food abundant and cheap. They each had to practice karma yoga, volunteering for an hour or two a day, but the ashram was immense, and the possibilities endless. Leela usually volunteered in the kitchen or nirvana room, while Jonathan spent his time working with the animals or overseeing the ashram store. Cows and peacocks roamed the grounds peacefully, disturbed only by the awful monkeys, whose bickering shrieks could be heard throughout the day and night.

Satsung, or sitting with truth, was held early in the morning, before breakfast and then at night, just before bedtime. It consisted of inspirational talks, chanting, and meditation. There were two daily yoga sessions and the rest of the day was spent in silent reflection. Self-inquiry was the main tool of practice, but the more Leela inquired, the more confused she became.

"Everyone seems so happy, so at peace with themselves," she wrote in her journal, "as if they finally got it. But me? Still nothing."

Try as she might to figure out who she was, all that grew stronger was the recognition of who she wasn't.

EVERY NIGHT, JUST before she fell asleep, the pink balloon would come for her.

"Go away," she'd tell it in frustration. "Leave me alone." Or: "Not tonight. I'm too tired."

But it kept insisting, nudging her gently, keeping her up. Once she'd give in, it would always take her to exactly the same place, rising just high enough to carry her down the street and back to the festival, where it would set her down right in the midst of the ecstatic crowd.

"What are you trying to show me?" she'd ask, getting more and more desperate, but the balloon wouldn't answer.

The night before they left, she gave up and stopped trying to understand. Instead of just looking down from above, she decided to leave the balloon and join the crowd.

"Dancing and prancing about wildly, I totally forgot myself," she wrote in her journal the next morning. "And as I lost myself, for an instant I felt found. In the midst of all those people, in that brief moment of clarity, I knew it didn't matter who I was. It didn't matter who anyone was. There were no differences between us. Life was a constant dance, and we were merely puppets, whirling to its beat."

WHEN THEIR FRIENDS left, making their way back to the coast, the pink balloon had other plans for them. Now it took them inland, away from the sea and the big cities, traversing through long forgotten towns and distant villages. Setting off in the morning with no compass or map and only the pink balloon to guide them, they often got lost, but wherever they found themselves, even in the remotest hamlets, they were greeted with warmth and offered food and shelter. They took busses or rickshaws whenever they could, but often walked for days, catching random rides and sleeping in obscure guesthouses and ashrams, often even in people's houses or barns.

Many of the villages were ancient, the dwellings small and simple and the lives no different than those thousands of years ago. Most had electricity, at least for some part of the day, and some form of running water, though it didn't necessarily run through the houses, which meant that most of the homes still had an outhouse and a long pipe for a shower. Donkeys, cows, and chickens filled the narrow paths between the houses and it wasn't uncommon to find themselves face to face with an enormous buffalo, with absolutely no place to go. Nearly everyone worked in agriculture, carrying warm smelly compost out to the fields in long wicker baskets, returning with aching backs, their baskets filled with freshly picked fruit and vegetables or bundles of hay.

They travelled slowly, staying a day or two, at every place, sometimes even longer. Leela wasn't sure what they were looking for, but she loved the change of pace, for now she travelled differently, trying to stay aware, to pay attention to every detail, to every sight and sound and smell. She no longer had to sit still for a set time to meditate. Everything was a form of meditation. And every day, her world seemed to grow bigger and wider, as she realized she was learning more and more with every step. Everything and everyone interested her. What they thought or believed, how they lived. For the first time she wasn't standing outside, looking in, and no one she met was really a stranger. She no longer felt uncomfortable entering women's homes, talking to them about their lives and playing with their children.

"There's something different about you." Jonathan couldn't quite put his finger on it. "You're a lot quieter than usual, but you seem happier too."

"Yes. I feel so tranquil, more peaceful than I've ever been. But it's more than that," she hesitated, almost embarrassed to finish her thought. "I feel a closeness to people I've never even met. A kind of love, even."

"Seriously?' Jonathan raised an eyebrow, then engulfed her in a bear hug. "Hope it rubs off on me."

THE VILLAGERS WORKED hard and had few belongings, but they seemed content, most even happy. Their quiet, simple lives were replete with holidays and celebrations. Wherever Leela and Jonathan went, there was a procession of sorts. Shorter ones were usually just a local wedding or funeral, but the longer ones, often weaving through several villages and small towns, were always a celebration of the Gods.

Shiva and Vishnu, the forbidding forces of destruction and salvation, were reverently worshipped by all, but each village also had its own, private deity, living in its own little shrine. Sometimes it was a small brick house, but often it was simply a rough platform under a tree, with a pile of stones or some spearheads sticking out of it. They worshipped the spirits of the hills and the mountains, the rivers and the streams. They prayed to the forests and the trees and even the stones on the sides of the pathways. One village worshipped Gangama, the water Goddess, another had the shrine of Mutyalamma, the pearl Goddess. Pedamma was the great Goddess, Chibbanna, the little. Haliama was the tiger Goddess, and Mamillama the Goddess who sits under a mango tree. There were so many gods and goddesses, Leela very quickly lost count. There were gods to ward off evil spirits, and others to bring fortune and good luck and each and every one of the gods was alive to them, playing an intricate part in their world. Much, she realized after a while, like Taata Maryam with her God, David and Esther with theirs.

"They all believe just as strongly," she told Jonathan, "no matter their God. And this is the land of a thousand gods. Ten thousand." She laughed. "Maybe more."

Larger villages had shrines on their boundaries, often flaunting a statue of a god riding a horse, waving a sword or whip. Sometimes it was Ranganatha, a form of Lord Vishnu, resting on a huge serpent, other times it was the colorful statues of Ayyanar, the guardian, and his companions riding high above giant elephants.

IN THE SMALLER festivals, the local effigy was removed from the shrine, washed carefully, its face smeared with oil and turmeric. The villagers burned incense and offered flowers and coconuts and rice. Special torch lit pujas were held, and the sound of the tom toms, little barrel-like drums, beaten on both sides by hands and fingers, went on till late at night.

The larger celebrations went on for days. To gain Mariyamman, the main mother deity's protection, floats of Goddesses on lotus buds flowed through the streets, while women in yellow sarees danced in the street for hours, starting slowly, then gradually increasing in speed, their feet going faster and faster, beating the ground in a frenzy. Many would enter a trance-like state, when, it was believed, they could see the future. When they reached the shrine there was fire walking and nose piercing, but as Leela and Jonathan got closer to the effigy, they had to avert their eyes. As a sign of devotion, a group of devotees were inserting little spears and daggers into their tongues and cheeks, blood flowing everywhere.

"Not doing that," Jonathan whispered in her ear.

Leela didn't answer. She was too busy trying not to throw up.

Draupadi, the heroic princess, was carried through the streets on men's shoulders in her golden palanquin and Shakti, the great divine mother, was celebrated with processions of ecstatic singing and dancing. No matter who or what was celebrated, there were always torch-lit parades, singing and dancing, tom toms and fireworks. The devotees walked over hot embers, to the deafening din of trumpets and cymbals, impaled themselves onto sticks and poles, or placated an elephant or tiger, their faces tinged dark grey or a luminous burnished yellow with black and white stripes.

Foreigners were rare in those parts and the locals eagerly invited them to join in. Jonathan walked in processions with half naked men banging drums, while Leela danced with the women. They carried clay pots filled with water and leaves, circled little temples, and took part in all the special pujas, burning incense and making offerings. Once, Jonathan even did mokku, cutting off a piece of his hair and offering it to Vishnu. They wrestled against each other in a massive tug of war and fed pongal, a mixture of rice and milk, to decorated cows at the end of harvest. They flew kites on Sankrati, marking the sun's passage into Capricorn and threw the few useless items they had collected on their travels into a huge bonfire. When Vasant Panchami came around, they made their own little shrine, placing Sweet Sara on a pedestal in front of the house. The entire family and all the neighbors came by to pay their respects, placing books and musical instruments at her feet, hoping to get her blessing.

The only festivals they wouldn't go near were the ones in which animals were sacrificed. In the beginning, before they knew better, they'd accidentally seen a buffalo's head chopped off. The blood was collected in a shiny brass bowl while the crowd shrieked ecstatically.

"If I wasn't a vegetarian already," Leela thought, as she tried not to faint, "I'd definitely be one now."

THE BIGGEST FESTIVAL of all, the Mahamahum, was held every twelve years, in the temple town of Kumbakonum, some fifty miles from Wellington Lake, where they had been spending some time. It was the main topic of conversation wherever they went and whoever could get away was planning to attend.

"It's too dangerous." The proprietor of Shakti shook his head sideways and then up and down nervously. It was a small ashram in the sleepy village of Korakkai, nestled on the western, quieter bank of the enormous lake. "Last time big stampede. Many, many people die." He tried to dissuade them from going.

"What do you think?" Leela asked Jonathan. She wanted to go, but knew that he was hesitant.

"What the hell," Jonathan finally decided. "Everyone says it's once in a lifetime."

THEY HAD NEVER seen so many people. Later they heard that there were over a million and that was a lot, even for India. This time the government wasn't taking any chances. They brought the police and the military and everyone had to queue in long roped lines, which moved agonizingly slowly.

"Don't let go of my hand," Leela whispered to Jonathan.

They had been waiting for hours, but all she could see were the swarms of people surrounding them. When they finally reached the entrance, she gasped out loud, her breath catching in her throat. They were standing above an enormous square pool of brackish brown water, surrounded by small shrines and towering Gopurams, pyramid like structures, laden with vividly colored, intricately sculptured figures. Just beneath them were Ghat-like steps, five or six wide cement stairs that led straight into the water. Leela stood on the top stair and stared. Policemen holding ropes regulated the amount of people allowed in, still there were so many, she could barely see the water. Old and young men and women, together with children of all ages were bobbing up and down, splashing wildly and shrieking with laughter as police men in uniform stood at the sidelines, with long rubber hoses, shooting torrents of water over their heads.

THE SUN WAS high in the sky, its rays almost blinding. Leela placed her hand above her forehead, narrowing her eyes to ward off the glare. The more she narrowed her eyes the smaller the people in the tank became, until they didn't even look like coconuts anymore, just a million tiny specks, that seemed to move together like the waves in the ocean, forming momentary patterns and then breaking them up. Leela watched as a wave emerged, following it as it grew and grew. A sudden movement sent a ripple through the ocean, breaking it up, and another pattern began to emerge.

"Please, mam." Leela jerked her eyes open. The police man holding the rope was pulling at her arm. "You must to go down."

"Can't we just sit on the side of the pool?" Jonathan asked him. There were so many people in the water, he was afraid to go in.

"No, no." The policeman wiped the sweat off his brow. "Go in water, out other side. No sit."

"But we don't want to go in the water." Leela would have liked to go in, but Jonathan wouldn't let her.

"It's not just the crowd." He pulled her away. "The water's so filthy, just touching it will kill us."

"Please, sir," she begged. "We just want to watch for a while."

"But you must go in, you must." The policeman tried to persuade her, his face lighting up with excitement. "Today all rivers come together, here, in tank. All holy rivers. You go in water today, special good luck. No more better luck." He waved his arms enthusiastically, almost pushing her into the water.

"OK, OK," he finally gave in, raising the side rope and letting them duck underneath.

"But you sit there, eh." He pointed to a raised platform besides the nearest tower. "No walk around, make trouble for me."

They had barely settled themselves, half hidden beside the gopurum, when trumpets sounded, followed by loud chanting. The people in the pool clapped and cheered as a procession of beautifully adorned elephants marched around the temple to the beat of a drum that could barely be heard through the deafening din. A long row of elaborately carved wooden chariots followed, each baring a festive deity, freshly washed and painted and decorated with flower garlands and exotic silks. The crowd watched in hushed tones as the procession slowly made its way around the temple tank, but when the first chariot entered the water, allowing the God to bathe with his devotees, the crowd went ballistic, pushing and shoving to get as close as they could. Those who touched the idols were especially blessed.

Leela watched as the deities were pushed and pulled through the water. After a while, the sea of humanity disappeared and she no longer saw the babies held high in the air to touch the idols, or the shining, enlightened faces of the devotees as they went by. All she saw was one giant picture as the mass of heaving, moving humanity seemed to become one living, breathing entity.

And as she watched what seemed at first to be just random movements, patterns emerged, momentary designs carved through the water in the effigies wake.

"Like swallows, creating shapes and patterns in the sky," Leela thought lazily, and then she sat up gasping, as fireworks seemed to go off in her mind and everything she had learned in the last years suddenly came together, gaining another, deeper meaning. As her mind followed the patterns, it also noticed the connections, seeing that everything was connected, the tiniest movement changing the balance, starting a chain reaction that affected the entire dynamic of the pool.

As Leela sat there, watching the dance of the patterns, a deep peace engulfed her. For a moment it felt as if she had disappeared, as if she was no longer in her body, but a part of something bigger, something invisible that connected her to everything else. Looking at herself from the outside, she could see that she, too, was just a speck, a tiny dot in the pattern, a part of a much bigger picture. That was the moment she realized, that nothing she had ever thought about herself was true, and even more importantly, that it had never really mattered. In the midst of all the chaos, her mind was crystal clear. She had been asking herself the wrong questions. Looking out at the web of dots bobbing in the water, she saw it more and more.

"Muslim? Jew? American? Israeli? Palestinian?" she wrote in her notebook later that night. "They're not what's important. They're just names, labels. They don't define me and they certainly aren't who I am."

LEELA GROPED AROUND in the dark for her pen and notebook before silently making her way outside. The sun had just begun to rise and the first rays painted the horizon a grayish pink. This was the only time she had for herself, half an hour before the wake-up call. She wrote every morning now, jotting down everything she could think of, knowing it would help her make sense of things, or at least give her some sense of order. Since the sudden realization that she wasn't who she thought she was, she felt as though she were freefalling, as if the ground had been swept away beneath her feet. Throughout her life, whenever she had felt lost, writing had been her anchor.

But today she was too excited to write. She couldn't wait for everyone to get up, for the day to begin. Today was a special day, marking the middle of their three month stay at "Amita" and since it coincided with "Holi," straight after morning satsung, they would be given a pass to leave the ashram and return the next day. Leela was comfortable in the ashram, feeling that the sparse, rigid life was exactly what she needed to hold her together, but she couldn't wait for some free time with Jonathan, they'd hardly been able to exchange a word for weeks.

The ashram was nestled within thick forest land, beneath the towering Western Ghat mountain range. The long, sparse dormitory buildings were built on harsh dry land surrounding a central red tent, where all the group meetings and meditations took place. A path carved through waist-high vegetation led to a hidden pond and it was all very simple and orderly, yet also somewhat beautiful in its pristineness. "Amita's" had only been working for a few years, but was already well known, its teacher certification internationally accepted. Jonathan had fallen in love with yoga, quickly surpassing Leela and although they practiced every day and took classes and workshops whenever they could, he had decided he wanted to take it further. "Amita's Yoga Ashram" they had been told time and time again and the pink balloon didn't seem to mind. It, too, needed a break. It had become so hot and stifling, it could barely take off.

The moment the bell ending the morning session sounded, they were out the door.

"Three hundred rupees, no discount." The rickshaw driver wouldn't even haggle. "Madurai far, far."

Forty minutes later, the quiet peacefulness of the ashram was replaced by total mayhem. As they stepped out of the rickshaw, they were bombarded with powdered colors and water bombs. It was too hot for tourists, but it seemed as if the entire local population was out in the streets, making merry and looking as though they had fallen into a barrel of paint. They escaped into the colorful, quieter back streets, finding refuge in the enclosed banana market. Toward evening they made their way to the giant temple, perhaps the biggest they had come across, wandering through its immense pillared halls, examining them from all sides. Certain parts of the temple were off limits, still they walked around for hours admiring the twelve tall gompas, each one covered with the most elaborate life-like effigies. Standing in line before the entrance, they were called out by the attendants, who made Leela pull her hair away from her face and tie it in a knot above her head and only let them in after they had checked their attire and made sure their legs and shoulders were fully covered.

"No Hindu." An attendant pointed the way, explaining more in pantomime than words that they couldn't enter the central temple, but were welcome to watch the ceremony from the sidelines.

The temple was crowded and it was difficult for them to understand exactly what was going on, but they watched as Lord Shiva was taken to Goddess Meenakshi's room late in the evening, and only returned to the ashram after seeing him safely returned to his room in the early morning.

"I like ashram life," Jonathan told Leela on the way back, "but I can't wait for the course to be over. Madurai reminded me how much there still is for us to see."

"Another month and a half," Leela reminded him. She couldn't wait to get back.

"Madurai reminded me of all the noise and chaos outside." She crinkled her nose. "I'm actually looking forward to a little more peace and quiet."

THE PINK BALLOON must have agreed with Jonathan, for as their studies drew to an end, it bugged them again, soaring higher and higher up into the sky, telling them it was time to carry on. The monsoon was late again, and the air still hot and sticky, so they took a bus down to the coast and lazily travelled from beach to beach. They bathed with pilgrims, purifying themselves before entering Lord Shiva's temple, on the tiny, beautiful island created by Lord Rama as a bridge between India and Sri Lanka and even continued all the way down to Kanyakumari, the southernmost tip of the great half continent where Pavarati, the great mother, wife of Lord Shiva and mother of Ganesh resided among lush green patches and coconut trees, together with Laksmi, goddess of wealth and their own beloved friend and guardian, Saraswatti.

When the first rains came and the heat subsided, the pink balloon took them inland again, this time high up into the hilly ranges of the Western Ghats, to remote hill stations and forts. They trekked through dense forests and tall mountains, visiting forgotten temples and waterfalls, walking the path Ayyapan himself had taken, climbing thousands of stairs to his hidden temple. They travelled through lush rain forests and wild animal sanctuaries, riding elephants and searching for tigers.

"I think it's time to leave," Jonathan suggested, when the rain began in earnest, pouring down in sheets for hours every day, and the roads that were never very good to begin with, washed away and disappeared.

"Where shall we go now?" Leela had heard that the north was the best place to go at that time of year.

"Too far." Jonathan thought they should stop for a while. "I think I need a break."

The pink balloon had also started to slow down, often just hovering or flying in circles.

"Where do you think it wants us to go?" Jonathan wasn't sure what it was telling them.

"Look." Leela pointed to a dot on the map, right by the shore, only a few hours away from them. "Amritapuri. That's Amma's ashram. I've heard so much about her. Let's go there."

"Hugging Amma?" Jonathan couldn't stop laughing. "Seriously?"

"It's not just the hug," Leela tried to explain, although she, herself, wasn't sure why she wanted to go. "I've never met a real, living guru. They say you can feel her energy, the unconditional love that radiates from her."

"I don't even know what that means." Jonathan shook his head.

"Well I don't either." Leela shrugged. "They say it's so strong it's enough to be around her to feel it, that it'll change you forever. But it's more than that," she added after a short pause. "I feel a little lost, like I don't know what I should be doing next. Maybe she can help."

"I'm not sure what you expect from her." Jonathan wasn't crazy about the idea. "And anyway, there'll be a million people. You won't be able to get anywhere near her."

AS IT TURNED out, hugging Amma didn't quite give Leela the answers she was looking for, but the visit to Amritapuri changed their lives, or at least moved them in a certain direction.

The tall pink buildings of the seaside ashram towered above the surrounding fishing village. They walked over a pink bridge and through a large pink gate.

"No audience today." The white robed attendee waved them away. "Next darshan, day after tomorrow."

As they moved aside, trying to decide what to do, a tall young man with long, light hair caught in a tail at the back of his neck, came up to them.

"You came on the wrong day, too, uh?" he said in Hebrew, offering his hand. "Ronen." It was love at first sight. Ronen and Jonathan couldn't take their eyes off each other.

Ronen had been a high school sports teacher for a few years, before turning to yoga. He himself practiced hatha yoga, daily pushing himself beyond his limits, but he mainly taught breathing techniques.

"Everything," he told them proudly, "from healing chakras to rebirthing."

He had been living in India for quite a few years, the last two in Goa and had come to Amma with two of his friends. They were doing the rounds of all the famous ashrams in the area. At the end of the monsoon season they would be opening a little ashram of their own. They were a little older than Leela and Jonathan, but they all took to each other right away. Adi had started as a psychology major, fast graduating to Eastern psychology and she and her partner, Ori, were practicing Buddhists. They taught meditation and gave dharma talks. The three had taken a little apartment in the village and they invited Leela and Jonathan to join them.

BY THE TIME the darshan with Amma arrived, they were all fast friends. After waiting in line for over four hours, it was finally their turn. Leela watched as Adi was engulfed in Amma's arms and then Ori and Ronen.

"Go, go," She pushed Jonathan ahead of her. She saw the white robed attendee help Jonathan to kneel and then before she understood what was happening, she too was on her knees, her face pushed into Amma's chest, her arms wrapped tightly around her. She smelled of lavender and sandalwood.

"Sorry," she heard Jonathan say. He was standing right beside her, yet his voice seemed to come from far away, faint and muffled, like under water.

"I waited so long . . ."

Lia could barely make out what he was saying.

"I forgot my question." Jonathan chuckled, embarrassed.

"So maybe I'll ask you a question." Leela felt Amma's chest wheeze as she answered him.

She asked Jonathan why he had come to her, what he expected to find. Jonathan told her he didn't really know. He started talking about the army and his parents, but Leela couldn't hear him, she was sweating so profusely, her head still stuck in Amma's bosom. For as long as they spoke, Amma hugged her tightly and she hugged Amma back. The hug went on and on forever. When Amma finally released her, Leela found herself at a loss for words. There was so much she wanted to say, but nothing would come out.

"Yes." Amma smiled at her gently.

"Where should I go from here?" she managed to blurt out, just as Amma was about to turn to the next in line.

Amma laughed loudly, her face a beaming moon. She wiped her forehead with the back of her hand and pushed back her spectacles.

"Nowhere left to go," she whispered in her ear. "The answers are all inside."

"DID YOU FEEL the energy?" Ronen asked excitedly, when the white robed attendee led them out of the immense auditorium. Amma told him he would be a great healer. "I felt like I was floating the whole time."

Leela also felt rather light-headed, although she wasn't sure what Amma's answer meant.

"We've actually been discussing it." Adi surprised them. "Ronen suggested it." She smiled. "But the more we got to know the two of you, the better we liked the idea. We decided to ask you to join us."

"In Goa?" Leela wasn't sure what they were suggesting. She and Jonathan had often discussed going there for a visit, but they'd never actually thought of settling down.

"We want to create something different," Ori tried to explain. "Unlike the big ashrams, we want something small and intimate, a place where we can devote ourselves to studying and teaching whatever interests us."

He told them that Rani, their fourth partner, had stayed behind, while they visited as many Ashrams as possible. "I spoke to him just before darshan. He said he found a great place, but we have to hurry back if we want to get it ready for the season. There's a ton of work."

"I told him all about the two of you," Ori added. "He can't wait to meet you."

"Well, what do you say, pardner." Jonathan drooled. He didn't need any convincing.

"You know what they say." Leela winked at him. "When the student is ready, the teacher appears. And anyway," she clapped her hands together decisively, "we've heard so much about Goa. Everyone says it's so beautiful there. Even during the monsoon."

"THE PINK BALLOON gently starts to rise, carrying you higher and higher. It rises above the treetops . . . above the buildings . . ."

"This time," Leela thought, 'I'm going to let them fly on their own. I'll take them up high in the sky and then send them on their way."

She had been teaching for a few weeks now, guiding them, taking them to secluded beaches and dense forests, telling them where to land and what to do.

"Time to let them go." She smiled to herself.

Leela looked around the silent room. Everyone was sitting up straight on their cushions, eyes closed, pen and notebook beside them. She couldn't believe how much the circle had grown since she had first started. The ashram was doing so well, she seldom now went down to the beach to hand out flyers. Their rooms were always full and their classes and workshops well attended. There were even guests during most of the monsoon season, when many of the other local establishments closed shop, their owners moving north for the duration.

"Are you crazy?" Adi screamed at Rani, when they had first arrived. "The place is falling apart. We'll never be able to fix it up."

"It looks much worse than it is." Rani pushed aside the debris on the worn path leading up to the house. "A good clean and some paint and it'll be good as new."

He wasn't very tall, but he was well-built and muscular and Leela liked the way his long curly black hair fell across his face when he moved his head. But she, too, thought he was being far too optimistic.

The house stood on a large plot of land that jutted out like an island, right at the bend of the river. It was an ancient Portuguese mansion, converted into a guest house in the sixties, but left abandoned years before. A columned balcony, many of the pillars broken off or damaged, ran around the entire second floor, the only remnant of the house's rich history. The ground was covered with weeds and tall wild bushes and the outer walls, once painted a bright sky blue were mostly grey and peeling. The rains had just begun to ease off, but the hot, moist air enveloped Leela like a steam bath, making her feel droopy and languid. She climbed gingerly up the broken front stairs and through the front door, but once inside, she felt oddly excited.

"The structure's strong and well built." Rani walked confidently around the large hall knocking on the walls.

"It's a great room," Ori agreed, starting to see the potential. "How many people do you think it will hold? Twenty? Twenty five?"

"At least." Ronen waved his arms about eagerly. "We can do yoga and meditation, there's place for everything here."

"And it's mostly water damage," Rani continued. "Some glass in the windows and a few tiles in the roof and we're set to go."

"We'd better get moving, if we want to do it." Adi still wasn't entirely convinced. "We have less than a month till the beginning of the season."

They all worked hard, scrubbing and painting and polishing and by the end of that month, the garden was weeded, flowers planted, and a huge wooden deck stood between the house and the river. The house dazzled from afar once again, sparkling in its original sky blue. The big hall was freshly painted, its floor covered with soft straw woven matting and piles of different colored meditation cushions while the second, slightly smaller hall had been converted into a comfortable kitchen and dining room. Upstairs, the nine existing bedrooms were covered with rugs and mattresses and the adjoining verandas with little straw tables and chairs. Ronen and Jonathan shared one of the larger rooms, as did Adi and Ori and the tiny room, right in the corner, that had previously been a closet or storage room had also been transformed and was now Leela's. It was the smallest room in the house, but it overlooked the river and had a double sized veranda.

"You take the bigger room," she had insisted when Rani offered it to her.

She didn't care what size her room was. All she wanted was a room of her own. Jonathan put up some shelves and built a small cupboard. She placed sweet Sara on the wall above her head and scoured the flea markets, finally buying a brightly colored camel hair rug and some cushions, a little bronze Buddha head and a few other small items and trinkets.

The spare rooms were taken right away. Most of their guests were Israeli, which wasn't surprising, since the entire beach, a few minutes' walk away, seemed to have been taken over by them as well as many of the village houses and enterprises. Most of the signs were in Hebrew and coffee shops and restaurants offered hummus and shakshuka. Since theirs was the only Israeli ashram and their activities offered for free, word spread quickly and many came to visit, to take in a class or listen for a while. When they left, a box by the door allowed the participants to practice dana, giving whatever they felt like giving. And people gave. Generously. By the end of the day the box was always full, stuffed to the brim with rupee bills, dollars, and euros.

AT FIRST THEY gave daily yoga and meditation classes, but as the number of participants grew, they offered workshops and silent retreats. Sometimes there were so many attending, they had to sleep three even four people in a room, but no one complained.

The month before they had held a special seven-day retreat. So many had arrived on the first morning, they had to be put up in the big hall. Leela had never worked as hard in her life. She was responsible for the ashram kitchen and although she had more volunteers to help her than she needed, she worked from early morning till late at night.

"Never again," she announced when the week was finely over.

"Overly ambitious?" Adi asked no one in particular.

"Way beyond our capabilities," Rani agreed, mockingly mopping his brow. He was in charge of the guest house, but the entire building had suddenly become a guesthouse and even the yoga mats had to be used for sleeping.

LEELA SOUNDED THE bell at seven o'clock every morning although she was up even earlier, collecting the warm bread and freshly made dairy products left by the door. She'd cut up a pile of vegetables into tiny, even pieces, for the "Arab salad," prepare a big bowl of tahini and a giant shakshuka base, pull off her apron, and rush off to yoga. Whenever it was dry, Ronen and Jonathan taught outside. "The boys" alternated, switching classes and often even teaching together, but early morning yoga was usually Jonathan's domain and Leela never missed it. Since they didn't serve lunch, after breakfast was cleared away, she had loads of free time, all day almost, until she had to start preparing for dinner. In between, she did the shopping, walking all the way to the market at the far end of the village and then stopping at all the little stores on her way back. Much of her time was spent cooking up special dishes and treats, but as she considered these to be "her choice," she made sure to prepare them with as much love and joy as she could muster.

She learned to cook with coconuts, mixing coconut milk into all her stews and curries, scattering tons of the grated white flakes over every dish and frying almost everything in coconut oil. Everything in Goa seemed to be cooked with coconuts. And bananas. Lots and lots of bananas. She cooked special rice dishes and made different colored dahl. There were always a few vegetable dishes and a yogurt raitha.

The evenings were devoted to study. After an early dinner, Adi and Ori would lead a group meditation and then give a short dharma talk. For Leela it was another déjà vu, sending her back in time, to the pink house in Venice, watching herself from above, sitting in the circle beside her parents, a voice droning on and on in the background. Like them, they would study a Buddhist sutra, reading the text out loud and then discussing it until everyone felt it was clear. As a child she had been bored out of her skull, quickly escaping in the pink balloon, but now she was fascinated.

"Could this be what I've been searching for all this time?" she asked herself.

Leela always brought along her notebook. She liked to choose a passage or a sentence from a text they were working on, sometimes just a word or two, meditate on it, and then write down everything that came to her mind. Writing had always given her a sense of order, but now it was more than that. Now she found that just putting the words down haphazardly on the page, without even thinking about them, was enough. The words she had battled with all her life, suddenly flowed freely, but they seemed to be taking her in another direction, moving beyond logical, linear thought to make new connections and create different understandings and ideas. If before she had felt she had been writing to save herself, now she felt she was writing to set herself free.

At first it drove them all crazy, the incessant scratching of her pen as they were trying to meditate.

"Maybe you could move a little," Ori pointed to the back of the room. Leela moved to the far corner, but it still didn't help.

"Maybe you should try it?" she suggested, promising to bring a supply of pen and papers to their next meeting.

"Only if you show us how," Adi insisted.

In the beginning, Adi and Ori made the selections, giving her a little time once or twice a week, but as her confidence grew, Leela decided for herself, adding little writing assignments or exercises she made up. She loved her work in the kitchen, but for the first time she felt she was really one of them, a part of the group, not just an onlooker, staring in from the outside.

Whatever they studied, Leela attempted to practice, memorizing entire passages of the Buddha and chanting them softly to herself. She gave herself tasks and assignments, beginning each week with a clear intention.

"If you have nothing good to say, keep your mouth shut," she wrote in her notebook, when they were discussing right speech.

That week she paid particular attention to what she said, trying not to swear or criticize, or even say anything that could be interpreted as negative in any way. When they talked about Kusala, wholesome, harmonious thoughts, she practiced not even thinking anything negative, jotting down all her slips, observing how they became more and more infrequent as the days moved on. When they learned "metta," she practiced loving kindness, trying to be as compassionate as she could to herself as well as to any living creature that happened to cross her path, and when it was "kaiya," she spent as much time as she could outside, thanking the sun and the wind and the trees.

Outside the ashram, everywhere she looked, "wrong view" ran rampant, people fighting and screaming and cheating each other. Street brawls often broke out late at night and as the beaches filled up, even the days became increasingly violent.

"It's just ignorance," she'd tell herself whenever something bad happened, beginning to see everything as "misinterpretation," as "a distorted view of reality." She, herself, was intent on practicing "right view," not only becoming aware of her thoughts, but also understanding why she thought what she thought.

The only thing she couldn't get her head around was the Buddhist concept of "annata." The more texts they read and the more they discussed it, the more frustrated she'd become.

"No me," she'd write in her notebook, or "no self," filling page after page with all her thoughts and reflections. But whenever she went back to read what she had written, all she could see was still only what she wasn't.

"Why can't I get it," she'd moan. "I try and I try, but whatever I do, I still don't seem to be any closer to figuring out who I am."

She never gave up though, practicing diligently day after day, completing every task and duty. Some mornings she'd begin her meditation by sweeping through her mind and body, checking even the slightest sensation. She'd go over every part, even her skin and hair and nails, seeing how they were always changing, getting sick and old. Other times she'd sit with a half-smile, inclining her mind to be light and full of joy.

"Today you will be happy," she'd tell herself, or "today you will be compassionate."

"Ohm mah nee pahd may hum," behold the jewel in the lotus, she'd chant, imagining herself to be a Buddha.

LEELA LOOKED AROUND the room. Everyone seemed completely relaxed and flying peacefully.

"The pink balloon starts gliding down slowly, gently setting you on the ground. Climb out of the balloon. Look around you. Where are you? Where has the pink balloon taken you?"

Setting out in her balloon, Leela flew lightly above her students' heads. She flew differently now, the pink balloon no longer taking her far away to exotic imaginary places, preferring instead to stay nearby, hovering gently, forcing her to look at things more closely, to examine them, to see them the way they really were. She flew mostly during the day now, letting herself drift lightly, airily, paying attention to every sight, every sound, every smell.

"Just like a magical broomstick, taking me everywhere undetected," she said to herself, as she playfully studied her students' heads.

Everything was so clear from within the pink balloon. She could immediately see that Matty, a young guy, who had been living at the ashram for quite some time, was distressed, moving his neck up and down and sniffing in irritation.

"Down," she told the balloon.

"What's happening?" she asked, sitting down on the floor beside him.

"I don't like where it's taking me," Matty whispered agitatedly.

"Then don't go." Leela hugged him and handed him his notebook. "Start writing. Write as freely as you can, without stopping. Don't go back to read what you've written. Don't worry about the way it's written. Just let everything out."

She hovered for a moment over Rani's shoulder. He must have felt her, because he opened his eyes for a brief second and sent her a huge smile, his eyes crinkling into slits. Leela could feel the warmth emanating from him, wrapping around her like a blanket. He was the one who had encouraged her to teach, although he didn't call it that. For him it was all "sharing."

"This is your chance to give back." He tried to persuade her. "You keep saying that you want to do more, that the kitchen isn't enough."

Leela floated in place, suspended above him, dreamily thinking back. She had liked him the moment they had met. She smiled to herself, remembering how he had pulled them excitedly from room to room, enthusiastically leaping over the piles of filth and damage, ignoring all their dirty looks.

"Just a good scrub and some paint." She laughed to herself, remembering how hard they had all worked. She and Rani had often found themselves working side by side, but there was little time for anything else. Still, from time to time toward evening, when their day was finally over, he would walk down to the beach with her, to watch the sunset. The beach was beginning to be flooded with tourists, but they always found a quiet spot to meditate, sitting silently together, watching as the sky turned a glorious spectrum of colors, high above the glimmering Arabian sea.

When the heat became too intense for travel, the number of visitors dwindled and, though the rooms were usually full, they had more time for themselves. Rani bought a small beaten-up scooter, taking it upon himself to show her around. He had already been in Goa for two years, so he knew all the best places. Usually they travelled up and down the coast, visiting the colorful fishing villages or walking along the sun-drenched beaches, buying each other beaded bracelets and necklaces from the peddlers they passed by. They navigated the dreamy backwaters, visiting bird sanctuaries and turtle enclaves, stopping at every temple and church they came across along the way. Leela loved ambling through the flea markets, admiring the old Portuguese architecture and beautifully preserved houses and churches, eating on the beach or in the small organic cafés that had begun to pop up everywhere.

Sometimes they travelled further inland, past the lush coast through jungles and coconut palm forests, to old crumbling forts and fragrant spice plantations. They walked through rice paddies, plucked tea leaves, and harvested coffee beans or hiked to hidden waterfalls, carefully avoiding the enormous wasp nests that could be heard buzzing from afar or the spider webs hanging from the branches, gigantic hairy black spiders still wrapped up inside them. Somewhere along the line, they even became lovers for a while.

"Come with me," Rani suggested before he left for Sri Lanka. "I'll be back just before the start of the season. There's nothing to do here anyway. It'll be a long time before the rains stop."

It was the peak of the monsoon and there were very few visitors. The rain thundered down incessantly, often for entire days. Leela would wait for a lull in the rain to run to the village for provisions, but more often than not she'd come back soaking wet. The grass outside had turned into mush and the path to the village had almost disappeared.

"I think I'd rather stay." She turned down his offer. "There's so much I still want to do."

She knew the area well, thanks to him, and there were many beautiful places she'd marked in her head, meaning to return to one day on her own.

"Don't worry." She grinned, spotting the look on his face. "All I'm going to do is write and meditate. Maybe I'll fly off somewhere, too," she added in afterthought.

"Fly?' Rani jumped up. Now he was really worried.

"In the pink balloon, silly."

WHEN THE RAINS stopped, Rani returned, but he was different, quieter, and somewhat withdrawn. Living with the monks had changed him. He kept to himself and was much more restrained and introverted. They never picked up their relationship, but they remained good friends. Leela thought how much she'd miss him. Come the next monsoon, she and "the boys" would be leaving.

LEELA PICKED UP the wooden striker and gently hit the singing bowl with a slight circular movement, sending light musical notes around the room. As the sound stopped reverberating, she hit it again, this time a little louder and everyone opened their eyes.

"Welcome back." Leela looked around the room. "Hope you had a good flight. Now pick up your notebooks and start to write. Don't overthink. Actually," she added, laughing, "try not to think at all. Write as freely as you can."

Leela glanced at the clock. She wanted to leave extra time for "sharing." It had become her favorite part. Everyone participated, even those who usually kept to themselves, some just speaking briefly, others reading entire sections out loud. It was clear how much they loved it. It wasn't just what they said, she thought, it was the way they sounded. The way they looked. So different from when they had walked into the room a short time before. They spoke in low, tranquil voices, their bodies moving freely, smoothly, so much more relaxed on the one hand, while at the same time also alive and invigorated. Like it had done for her, the pink balloon was opening their lives and taking them away from themselves, from the life they were living and everything they knew. Flying away in the pink balloon they could see themselves differently, sometimes in totally unfamiliar ways. It showed them other options, other possibilities.

Leela thought how much the pink balloon had already given her and where it would take her next. It was with her almost all the time now, taking her on short quiet trips, leading her into deep, quiet meditation. It taught her to sit still, her mind quiet and aware. To look. To listen. To be present, moment by moment. Sometimes it took her so far into herself, the entire world would disappear, and she became the cooking or the writing, the sun or the sea, the cows and dogs playing peacefully on the beach. On those rare moments the feeling of battle disappeared and she felt whole again.

Often, she'd just sit quietly, watching her mind, observing her thoughts as they came and went. She learned to still her thoughts and contain her emotions, finally beginning to feel that she was controlling her mind and not it her. Still, it remained powerful, flaring up at the slightest irritation, beginning its cycle, unrelentingly telling her the same story again and again, working on its own, as if it had a life of its own.

"Ok mind," she'd tell it, "I got it, we've been over it a hundred times, let it go."

"Learn to make friends with your mind, not battle with it," Rani would tell her. "It will keep throwing things at you. That's its job. To guard you. To protect. You have to accept it, to observe it and let it go."

She felt as though the pink balloon had taken her far away, but was now bringing her back. To herself. To the world. She felt attached again, alive, taking part, as if the entire world was within her, just as she was the entire world. As she looked around the room she was aware of herself and her own private world, but at the same time, she felt irrevocably connected to everyone else.

"Coconuts." she smiled to herself. "Just coconuts."

"O.K." LEELA CLAPPED her hands. "That's it for today. But remember," she paused, looking around the room, "till now we've been asking ourselves the wrong question. Instead of asking yourself: Where will I go on my journey today, I want you to get up in the morning, meditate, and ask yourself: Where will my journey take me today?"

"GLIIING, GLIIING, GLIIING . . ." The densho tolled, its beat gradually becoming louder and faster. The monk waved the long wooden mallet and hit the large brass bell standing at the entrance to the main hall one more time, sending an eerie, elongated, and slightly jarring sound reverberating across the room.

She was still in her room when the first round of tolling started to sound faintly in the background.

"C'mon," Jonathan called from the doorway. He and Ronen were already ready and impatiently waiting for her.

"Go ahead," Leela shouted out to them, as the ringing faded.

"Keep a place for me." She pulled on her sweater, grabbed a warm shawl, and rushed out after them.

The bell tolled again. Leela stood aside as a long line of monks slowly entered the hall. It was barely dawn, the first rays only beginning to light the sky and the great hall was freezing.

"Here." Jonathan waved to her from the far side of the room. They had kept a place for her in the second row, right behind the monks. Leela pushed her way through the crowded room, and sunk into the meditation cushion, wrapping herself in her shawl.

"OOOooo." A deep, haunting wail began to resonate through the hall.

"Dungchen," Leela said to herself, looking up.

Two monks stood facing the assembly, blowing into slim long brass and copper trumpets.

"Like elephants singing," Ronen joked, the first time they heard it.

"ooooo . . ." the trumpets began again, their wail so low, it seemed to be rising from the bowels of the earth.

"OOOOooooo . . ." The lament rose higher and higher, lingering about the great hall, before disappearing into the sky.

Someone beat a large flat drum. Hand bells were pulled out and cymbals clashed. When the monks started to chant monotonously, Leela leaned back and shut her eyes.

"WE'VE DECIDED TO become Buddhists," Jonathan told Leela a few weeks earlier. The group had always been interested in Buddhism, but during the last months they had begun to study and practice every day, all intent on taking the vow.

"We want to go somewhere where we can learn more and really practice. Maybe to Ladak. We don't know too much about it, but everyone says it's the best place to go."

Leela wasn't sure. She studied with them and practiced diligently, but had become wary of any dogma or "ism" and wasn't sure she wanted to commit to anything. They had to wait for the monsoon, though.

"The roads are only open for three, maybe four months," Rani told them. He had been there a few years before. He knew many of the lamas and sent them off with a list of names and addresses. They promised to be back before the start of the season.

"I CAN BARELY see." Jonathan strained his neck, squinting at the windshield as he drove. It was pitch black. They had been told they had to leave before daybreak if they wanted to make it through the first mountain pass.

"Drive slowly," Leela kept muttering from the back. They had only just set out and the road was already bumpy and uneven.

"It's the wildest, most beautiful road in the world," Rani told them.

"Also the most dangerous," Adi warned.

Just before the first pass, they saw little puddles of snow and slush and as they climbed, the landscape became whiter and whiter. A sign covered with a million colored flags told them they were 3978 meters high. Leela pulled on her gloves and jumped out of the car. As they were taking each other's picture, it began to snow, at first just lightly, then turning into a storm. Leela raised her arms, watching her green sweater turn white. She was so excited. She had never seen so much snow. It had snowed from time to time in the settlement, but it rarely piled up. Once she remembered waking up early in the morning to find everything covered with a soft white carpet. Roads were closed, schools cancelled, and everyone stayed home. They spent the morning building snowmen and pelting each other with balls, but toward the afternoon it had all begun to melt and by evening, all that remained were a few shallow puddles of squirming mud and slush.

Beyond the pass the road became narrower and more and more treacherous as it wound its way through the snow covered mountains. Ronen and Jonathan drove carefully, dividing the driving between them, but Leela couldn't relax. She sat on the edge of her seat, her nose stuck to the window, constantly begging them to drive even slower. From time to time a car would appear from the opposite direction and they would have to find a way to maneuver past. As they inched toward the rim, Leela held her breath, staring down at the terrifying plunge below her. Hanging there, on the rim of the world, she felt she could see all the way down to its bowels.

The view changed drastically from moment to moment, as did the weather. One minute it was sunny and warm, the next the road turned icy, covered with sleet. The road itself often disappeared, becoming a slush-filled path or stream.

The pink balloon did cartwheels, somersaulting in glee, as it guided them through the enormous expanses. It took them through sleepy valleys and serene mountain passes, over pristine rivers and sparkling lakes, gliding like a flying carpet over surreal glaciers and gushing waterfalls. They drove for three days, stopping at tiny hamlets and remote monasteries, sleeping in tents with groups of bikers, who like them, were making their way to the top of the world.

The terrain on the third day had become somewhat monotonous, nothing but rough reddish cliffs on both sides of the road. Leela was staring out of the window, half asleep, when the car took a sharp bend, and then came to an abrupt halt. She sat up with a start, hearing herself gasp. The road before them had suddenly leveled out and opened up to reveal a long hidden valley, which seemed to stretch on forever. Snow-capped mountains enclosed the valley from either side, and a long, clear river ran all the way through it. The land leading up to the mountains was red arid desert soil, but besides the river the terrain was green and lush with vegetation. Little white stupas and prayer bells dotted the landscape, like mushrooms in a fairyland.

"It's totally surreal," Ronen looked about in disbelief, "like stepping into a painting."

"I think we've died and gone to heaven." Jonathan lifted his arms in awe.

"The entrance to the promised land." Leela smiled, feeling a little lightheaded. She wasn't sure if it was the altitude or the view, which had changed so abruptly, almost as if they had been hurled into another dimension. Beyond the bend a magical world had opened up, revealing an enchanted kingdom, hidden on the top of the world.

"Aladdin." Leela broke the silence, as they drove through the dreamy valley. "That's what I keep thinking of. Aladdin's enchanted kingdom."

"High up in the sky." Jonathan finished her thought.

The roads were almost deserted and even Leh, the only real city, while vibrant and mulling with people, remained un-crowded, different from any other city they had been to in India. The people didn't even look Indian, with their large heads and wide, square faces and even the food was different, the strange exotic smells seeping out of the little Tibetan stalls that were scattered all over, serving a variety of dumplings and thick wheat noodles in a rich aromatic vegetable broth.

"This is definitely Aladdin's city," she decided when they arrived.

It was straight out of *A Thousand and one Nights*, suspended in time and totally out of context, complete with a castle on the top of the hill. They spent the first few days wandering about the winding streets, visiting the little colorful markets, getting used to the altitude. The air was bright, crisp, and clear, and Leela's mind felt light and empty.

"Ooooo," the horns wailed again, bringing Leela back to the room. A young boy was walking around handing out books. His head was shaven and he was dressed in monk's clothes. When he came up to Leela she could see that he was no more than seven or eight.

"No thanks." She waved him away.

"The boys" opened their books diligently, doing their best to follow along. Leela had tried throughout their first puja but had since given up. The texts had been especially written in English letters, but since they were in Pali, she didn't understand a word. Instead, she leaned back again into her cushion and closed her eyes, letting herself be lulled by the voice reading monotonously in the background.

The last few weeks had gone past like a dream, travelling from monastery to monastery, often coming back to spend a few days in Aladdin's city. Time was different in the enchanted kingdom, slow and magical, and moving through the huge almost deserted expanses, Leela felt a freedom even bigger and wider than ever before. It was a freedom beyond place and time, a spiritual almost holy feeling that engulfed her, bringing with it a great joy.

Although the distances weren't great, the roads were bad and the terrain so uneven, the smallest trip took hours. Still, it was never boring. Leela would sit on the edge of her seat, straining to see what appeared at the other side of each bend. The monasteries were hidden away, tucked into the folds of the mountains, far from the main roads, sending them over tall snow covered ridges and through hidden valleys, sprawling deserts and immense salt lakes. Leela would hold her breath, waiting for that first glance, that moment when a magnificent forgotten gompa suddenly appeared as if from nowhere, standing straight in front of her in all its glory.

The structures were unlike anything she had seen before, ancient and eerily beautiful, but even more importantly, they were live, working monasteries, where Buddhism was a way of life. Leela had studied Buddhism for so many years, but had never really seen it in practice. They stayed in little hotels and guesthouses, rising early to attend "puja" and then spending as much time as they could with the monks. Leela had never felt such peace.

The gompa they were visiting was one of the farthest, almost six hours drive from Leh and they had had to go through the highest ridden pass in the world to get to it. Beyond the pass, the landscape changed dramatically.

"Feels like going to a different planet," Jonathan joked.

"Like going to the moon," Ronen agreed.

It really did look like the moon, Leela thought, gazing out at the endless expanse of reddish yellow pockmarked terrain. The rugged desert-like soil was almost barren, with very little vegetation and a few oddly shaped trees and dunes. Here too, the landscape was crisscrossed with tranquil white stupas. At first Leela thought that the small mound-like structures were graves, but although she still didn't understand exactly what they stood for, she could feel their magic.

The road leading up to the monastery was lined with enormous magnificently carved and brightly painted prayer wheels. Every now and then Ronen stopped the car and one of them would run out and push the wheel around. For luck.

"Clockwise," Ronen called out. "Clockwise."

"And count the number of circles out loud."

On the hill besides the gompa, an immense golden statue stared down at them. After climbing a thousand steps, they discovered it was the "Maitreya," the future Buddha. Leela was intrigued. She'd never heard of him before.

"Clockwise," she heard Ronen whisper as she began to circle the enormous platform.

"Yes, yes." Leela waved him away. "I remember. And always an even number."

A CACOPHONY OF blowing horns and trumpets, clashing cymbals, drums, and bells signaled the end of the puja.

"C'mon." Jonathan pulled her up. "We've got a long drive."

Rani's friend, Adam, had arranged for the boys to stay inside a gompa. It was rare for the lamas to accept outsiders, but he had been volunteering there for years and had provided them with a personal letter of recommendation.

"What about me?" Leela was disappointed to learn that Buddhism in practice didn't necessarily include women. She had seen nuns on the way, but now that she thought about it, there had been none in the monasteries and the only women she had seen attending the puja, were westerners like herself.

Adam found her a place in one of the nunneries. "The hostel's about a mile or two from the monastery," he told her. "Very simple and basic, but clean and well-run."

Leela didn't mind. She couldn't wait to live with the nuns and learn their way of life.

"Finally," she told the boys excitedly, "I'll have a chance to really live a Buddhist life."

"MAYBE WE SHOULD walk up with you?" Jonathan was hesitant about leaving Leela on her own.

The road had come to an abrupt end right at the edge of the mountain and only a narrow trail led the way to a number of small buildings, nestled about half way up.

"Don't worry, I'll be fine." She grabbed her bag and started up the path. "See you in two weeks."

As Leela came nearer, she could hear women calling out to each other and loud hammering sounds. These she soon saw, were coming from a group of nuns doing construction work on one of the little square houses, scattered behind the larger central building. The long two story building was freshly renovated, sparking in its crisp white coat, a thick maroon stripe below its flat roof the only decoration. A few more of the small structures were also newly restored, but most of the little buildings were in a terrible state, run down and falling apart. One of the nuns climbed up onto a small wooden scaffold. When she saw Leela, she waved, and the entire group stopped working and came toward her. There were a few elderly nuns and a group of young girls, most in their early teens. Their heads were shaven and they were dressed in maroon robes.

"Cho-mo Tsetan." An elderly nun introduced herself, bowing her head. "But you can call me Ani."

Later she explained that they were supposed to call themselves "Cho-mo," which simply meant "female religious practitioner," but no one really used that name, preferring the traditional "auntie."

Unfortunately Ani Tsetan was the only one who spoke any English, but the other girls slowly surrounded her, chattering and giggling abashedly behind their hands. A few pointed to her eyes and an argument broke out.

"Some of my girls never see blue eyes." Ani laughed.

"Do they like them?" Leela asked jokingly.

"Depends." Ani's eyes twinkled. She told her the girls were mostly illiterate and deeply superstitious.

"Some say you have wise man eyes, eyes that know. But the others? They say you demon eyes."

"C'mon." She dismissed the girls, sending them back to work. "I show you around."

The old Buddhist nunnery had just been renovated, after standing in ruins for many years. There was a prayer hall and a classroom on the first floor, along with a large kitchen. The second floor consisted of eight cell-like bedrooms, four of which had been converted into a hostel. The rooms were not completely ready, but Adam had done a lot of work at the nunnery and Ani felt she couldn't refuse him.

Only a few of the nuns lived in the nunnery. All the others lived with their families and spent most of their day away doing hard manual labor. Ani told her that her family had chosen her to be a nun when she was a small child and that she had spent most of her life at their service. She was one of the lucky ones, though, having attended school until the fifth grade. Most of the nuns had had no schooling at all.

"Before few years they make change. They say now nuns important again," Ani told her as she showed her around.

The women had been given the old monastery, but very little else and with the help of family and volunteers had been building ever since.

"Not good." Ani shook her head when Leela asked for the corner room. "Leaky roof."

But Leela insisted. It wasn't any bigger than the others, but it was the only one with an extra window. Other than the straw mat and orange mattress, the room was bare, but Leela felt it was exactly what she needed. She leaned Saraswetti on the wall behind her head and lay down, sighing contentedly.

She made a point of getting up early, together with the other nuns, joining them first to chant sutras in the prayer hall and then for an early breakfast, but by seven-thirty in the morning they had all disappeared or were busy working at their chores, and she had no idea what to do with herself. She helped in the kitchen for a while and then volunteered to help carry cement for construction. Three times a week, Geshe La came to teach and all the nuns tried to attend. The first time he arrived, Leela was waiting for him impatiently by the door.

"Sorry." Geshe La waved his hands in the air. "I can't help you. I don't have time to teach dharma."

He explained that since that was the only schooling these girls were ever going to get, he wanted to make sure they could at least read and write.

"I teach basic skills. I want these girls to have a better future. But for you," he shook his head sadly, "there's nothing for you here. Unfortunately, I think there's no place in Ladak for a female, specially a foreigner."

Leela was taken aback by his candor, but although she was disappointed, she had been beginning to see it for herself. "Wrong view" was everywhere. The pink balloon had stopped flitting jovially from place to place and had now started brooding, flying moodily over short distances and then refusing to continue. That evening, as she was chanting with the nuns, it took her for a surprise ride, flying her up to the ceiling and then gently hovering there, inviting her to look down. Leela smiled to herself for a moment, thinking what a beautiful picture they made, all the women working tranquilly together, in such perfect harmony.

Just then, the balloon tilted, moving slowly, changing her point of view. Leela squeezed her eyes into a tight squint, but all she saw now was a blue and green coconut in a sea of maroon. All night the Pink balloon flew, taking her back to all the gompas and shrines they had visited, but from whichever angle she now looked, the view below her was always the same. Except sometimes, among all the maroon coconuts, there were a few bright orange ones too.

"WHAT ARE YOU talking about?" Jonathan couldn't believe his ears.

He and Ronen had had a profound experience and felt even more committed than ever. They had spent the entire two weeks within the confines of the monastery, studying and teaching and debating with the monks.

"I've never felt so much at peace," Ronen told her. "I feel like I've finally come home."

"I felt it too," Leela nodded, "when we first arrived. I was sure I had finally found what I was looking for. But it's just another illusion, no more real than anything else. They've created a world within a world, out of time and context, but with its own strict rules and regulations. This isn't the Buddhism the Buddha envisioned. It's just like any other religion, just without a God. Where's the freedom?" She stared first into Jonathan's eyes, then into Ronen's. "Where's the freedom we've always been talking about?"

"Don't misunderstand," Leela continued, noticing the distressed looks passing between the boys. "Buddhism changed my life. I love what we learned and the work we did together. I just don't think you have to leave the world and become a monk."

"Actually, that's kind of what we wanted to talk to you about," Jonathan cut her off. "We've been asked to stay on at the monastery, to teach at the school."

"It's just for a few months," Ronen intervened. "You could stay here, or maybe teach. There're loads of volunteering opportunities. We can check out the bulletin board at the youth center."

LEELA PLACED A cushion on the grass, right at the edge of the rim, sat down, crossed her legs, and straightened her back. This was her favorite spot. She could sit here for hours silently meditating or just watching the world go by. Behind her there was nothing but forest, while in front an entire world opened up, like a scene in a play. From where she was sitting, she could follow the narrow road as it twisted and turned, making its way down the mountain, winding through the little village and past the school, all the way down to the river.

She looked around her. Everything was in full bloom, the grass long and green and the flowers large and succulent, their loud, vibrant colors shimmering, still wet from the morning rain. Tall green stems of monshood densely covered with brilliant violet flowers shot up from the ground, competing with orange petaled pheasants eye that grew even taller. Enormous pink and yellow daisies pushed their way through clusters of marigold and delicate white thimbleweed. Behind them, right along the ledge, wild roses bloomed, their half open flowers revealing long, fleshy pink and white petals. Just yesterday they had still been enclosed in a tight ball.

Leela stretched out her hand and carefully grabbed a stem, trying to avoid its little thorns. She bent her head, bringing the flower to her nose. A strong musky fragrance filled her nostrils. She rubbed the petals between her fingers. They were soft and silky, still covered in tiny drops of moisture. She sat silently watching as a tiny drop made its way slowly down the side of the petal, before taking its final dive and disappearing into the wet ground beneath it. Soon the flowers would be gone, leaving a hard red fruit in their wake. The locals would extract the juice to make soap and perfume. They had taught Leela to brew fragrant teas and had shown her how to grind it up to use as a poultice. Once, when she was sick, she had been given a special concoction of lime, musk rose juice, and honey. It tasted so good as it made its way smoothly down her throat, instantly calming the burning sensation and stifling the coughs.

The sun popped out from behind a cloud, sending its brilliant rays out toward the ground, covering everything with a light shiny gleam. The flowers raised their heads jovially and the grass seemed to come alive. She watched a bee alight on a pink daisy. Some flies buzzed by. A cricket chirped from somewhere in the shrubs by her side. She sat there every day, watching the sun as it rose and then when it set. She watched as the seasons changed, the leaves changing color and falling and the flowers withering. She watched when they grew again many long months later, almost the same but also slightly different. The picture she saw in front of her changed daily. She watched as it transformed from hour to hour, and from minute to minute.

"Nothing," she told herself as she watched, "ever stays the same."

The warming sun sent down slivers of light yellow heat and she felt her body relax, becoming lighter and lighter, till it was ephemeral and she was no longer. Only light and warmth remained. There was no world, no Leela, only a sense, a presence, an awareness watching as life unfolded from moment to moment.

It didn't last though. A loud clang in the distance made her jump, and the world came rushing back. She moved her head from side to side, feeling her body still light and vibrating. Normally she wouldn't have even noticed the noise, but today she was distracted, every little sound or smell pulling her out of herself. She heard a door opening behind her and turned to look back.

"Anything?" she asked Giri.

"Nothing yet." He shook his head. "They'll be here, don't worry."

"Not even a call?" She couldn't help herself, even though she knew the answer. They were already a little late and she was starting to drive herself crazy. Leela hadn't seen "the boys" for over three years, and now that they were finally coming, she realized how much she missed them. After six months in Ladak, Jonathan and Ronen had returned to Goa, but when the landlord refused to renew the lease, the ashram was closed. They had moved around, studying and teaching at different ashrams before settling down in Pune, where they had been for almost a year.

"No jaanu," Giri laughed, "I'll let you know the second I hear anything."

Leela smiled back at him. She loved it when he called her "jaanu," my life. In bed it was "priya," my darling, and she would answer with "aashiq," "lover." He came up to her and planted a kiss on the top of her head, his freshly shaved cheeks smelling of sandalwood and rosewater. She couldn't wait for them to meet him.

She had liked him the moment they met, maybe even before. They hadn't said much that first phone call, but it was more the way he spoke. Slowly. Precisely. Every word clear and well thought out. His voice was strong and at the same time soft and although his English was perfect, he had a strange accent.

"Well," he laughed when she asked, "it's complicated. I was born in England, but lived in Australia since I was ten. I've been in India most of my life, though, so I guess I'm more Indian than anything else."

"I don't even know what I am anymore," Leela joked, telling him about herself.

The flyer had caught her eye almost immediately. She had just begun browsing through the bulletin board when she noticed it, slightly smaller than the rest and standing a little separately. It was the only one that didn't have "Ladak" underlined on top. Instead it said, "Green Himalayas" and seemed to be exactly what she was looking for, a small, secluded meditation resort, high up in the mountains. She needed a time-out, a quiet time to contemplate, to peacefully reflect, perhaps even put order into everything she had learned. And she wanted to get as far away as she could get from everyone and everything she knew.

"Nowhere left to go." Amma's voice still whispered loudly in her ear.

She even liked the name, "Maya in the Mountains," and the warning at the bottom made her chuckle: "Not for the fainthearted."

"It can be very lonely," Giri warned her. "Especially in the winter."

"I think it will be perfect," she answered. Winter was still a long time away and since it was only a three month commitment, she wasn't really worried.

"When do you want me to come?" Leela asked him.

"Tomorrow?" Giri joked. He told her the last volunteer had left two weeks before and he was on his own, the resort swamped with visitors. "There's quite a large group coming next week. It's usually very quiet, with only one or two cabins taken, but when we have a group it gets really busy."

GIRI TOLD HER to hire a private driver, promising to pay the cost, still it took almost three days to get there. The last few hours were the worst, the road becoming a worn narrow path, large sections of which had turned into slush or were simply washed away by the rain. At the last moment they missed the turn to the resort and only discovered it after wandering about for a couple of hours. When they finally made it back, a man wearing a white Indian kurta, his long cotton shirt reaching just below his knees, was standing in the middle of the path, just before the turn, waving for them to stop. He was quite tall and very slim, seemingly in his early forties.

"Leela?" he stuck his hand through the window and grabbed hold of hers. "Giri."

He had short greying blond hair, light blue eyes, and a pale round face. When he smiled his cheeks crinkled into the kindest, deepest dimples she'd ever seen.

"You can pull up over here," he told the driver, grabbed Leela's bag, and started walking. "C'mon," he called behind him. "It's just up the road."

Leela followed him up the steep incline, till the ground suddenly leveled out and she found herself standing on a flat basin, almost a platform, the edge of which jutted out of the mountain, like a natural terrace. A long narrow building stood in back, tucked into the harsh stone cliff, a few wooden bungalows scattered around it. The basin edges were teeming with low shrubs and flowers and tall apple and apricot trees surrounded the borders. The sight was so jarringly beautiful she stopped in her tracks, catching her breath.

"Nice view eh." Giri smiled, giving her a moment. "We have five bungalows and only four are taken. I'll set you up in the fifth."

He showed her around the main building. There was a large hall, a kitchen, and dining room. "We have enough space for yoga inside, when we have to, but whenever we can, we work outside. We put our mats right at the end of the cliff. It's absolutely magnificent."

His room was on the upper floor. He had been living there for over twenty years. He and his wife Maya had built the place from scratch.

"The land belonged to her family. She was born and raised in the little village, just below us."

He had run away from home when he was eighteen and had travelled all over eastern Asia, quickly discovering yoga and meditation. They had met in a Buddhist temple in Sri Lanka.

"My name was Allen, but when we came here she started to call me Giri. She said I was her mountain. When she died, five years ago, her family asked me to remain. They said the place was mine for as long as I wanted it."

The cabin he showed her to was surprisingly big, with a large double bed, and two more mattresses on a wooden gallery above. The furniture was minimalistic, but it had everything she could possibly need. There was a small fridge and a kettle and an enormous veranda overlooking the view. It was really lovely, but Leela didn't quite manage to enjoy it. Five days after her arrival, she had moved in with Giri.

As the images of their first night filled her mind, Leela felt her belly stirring gently and then becoming warmer and warmer, as hot pulsating little tremors of love and desire spread throughout her body.

"I haven't had a meaningful relationship since my wife died," Giri had warned her, right at the start. "And I'm not looking for one."

Then he had taken her hand and led her up the stairs to his room. He lit candles and incense. She could still feel his fingers on her body the first time he touched her, caressing the outlines of her face before going down to her shoulders and then her arms. His touch was soft and delicate yet also firm and decisive, his experienced fingers bringing alive parts of her she hadn't even known existed. He was well-built and muscular, his body still slim and youthful. They made love all that night and when she awoke in the morning, cradled in his arms, it felt so familiar, as though she had been there all her life.

"Where did that come from?" Leela asked herself, trying to shake away her thoughts, but they kept bouncing about in her mind, the cacophony refusing to change into music.

"Watch your thoughts, your feelings, like a movie," Giri would always tell his students. "Watch them as they arise and disappear."

But nothing Leela did stopped the incessant stream for more than a few short moments. She cleared her mind, took a few deep breaths, letting the air out slowly and followed her breath as it entered her nostrils and filled her lungs. She noticed her tummy first blowing up and getting rounder and then as it deflated. She thought she heard a car coming up the road and jumped up excitedly, but it was just a motorcycle in the distance.

Leela sat down again, right on the edge this time, her legs hanging over the abyss, chanting softly to herself.

"A hum brah mass me," she repeated under her breath. "I am the universe. I am the totality."

It was how Giri had taught her to let go when she got too attached to her thoughts or her feelings. He kept telling her to take things less seriously, especially herself.

"You have to try to move yourself away from the equation," he'd remind her calmly whenever she got upset or angry. "Take a step back. Don't let yourself get so totally involved in everything that happens. It's not against you. Be an island in the storm, not pulled and pushed by everything impersonal that comes your way."

Like her father, he always taught her to look for other angles, to see things from other people's eyes. He had taught her so much. He was the kindest, most patient man she'd ever met. Sometimes she felt he was totally selfless, always putting the guests' wellbeing as well as hers ahead of his own. As if he could read her thoughts, Giri appeared and sat down beside her. He placed his hand above hers and began to recite:

"I am a mountain, erect tall and stable, nothing can move me."

"The wind comes and goes," Leela joined him.

"But the mountain stays," they both recited together.

"The rain comes and goes," Giri chanted.

"But the mountain stays," Leela called out into the abyss in front of them.

"The snow comes and goes," Giri called out, but just as Leela was about to finish the sentence, they heard the distinctive whirring of a car climbing up the road. This time Leela stayed seated, holding her breath. The car slowed down and turned into the driveway.

"They're here," she shrieked, jumping up and running toward them.

"YOU'VE CHANGED," JONATHAN told her between hugs.

"You too." Leela laughed, pulling at his beard.

For as long as she had known him, he had always kept his hair short, but now it hung loosely about his face, reaching beyond his shoulders. "Never thought you'd go for the Jesus look."

Ronen, on the other hand, had lost his tail, and she almost didn't recognize his clean-shaven face. It made him look so much older and more serious than she remembered. He was slimmer than before and for the first moment, seemed to have grown even taller.

"Our little girl's all grown up." Ronen smiled, looking her up and down. "I remember the first time we met."

"When I first met Leela, she was eleven." Jonathan shook his head in disbelief.

"Just before my Bat Mitzva." Leela grimaced. Images of her childhood rushed into her mind. She thought of her house and David and Esther and all her little brothers and sisters.

"The brain's a graveyard," Giri always said. "You have to let the past go."

And she had tried, shutting the memories out as much as she could, consciously choosing to stay in the present, living each moment as fully as she could. But now that her friends were finally here, all her memories burst out like a flood, images of the three of them in Goa and Ladak, even Amnipuri, bombarding her, vying for her attention.

"WOW, WHAT A view!" Jonathan threw himself down on the bed, his eyes glued to the window.

"It's our best room," Leela told him proudly.

All the cabins were exactly the same but this one was built so close to the edge, it seemed suspended above the valley. "Luckily we don't have guests the whole week, so we have the entire place to ourselves."

"Don't you get lonely?" Ronen asked.

"Not at all." Leela shook her head. "I love it here. It's not really as isolated as it looks. There are a few houses just over the bend and the village's right below. And anyway, there are nearly always people here. It's rare not to have guests at all. Except in winter, brrr . . ." She shivered. "Then weeks can pass without a visitor. Not that I mind, actually, sometimes I even prefer it."

Leela rarely left the resort, spending her free time meditating or walking in the surrounding woods. She knew them like the locals, often taking groups and visitors for long hikes to hidden shrines and temples. She told them about the nearby villages and life on the river.

"We're right at the end of the season, so everything's quietened down, but you can't believe what goes on here. There's an onslaught of tourists and activities. Snappling and kayaking, markets and fairs. Everything comes alive. If we're lucky, some things will still be open."

For dinner she prepared their favorite foods, sending Giri off to a faraway town for chickpeas and sesame paste. She usually made light breakfasts and lunch and mainly Indian food for dinner and hadn't used any of Tata Maryam's old recipes for a long time, but they were always fresh in her mind, waiting for an opportunity. Early that the morning she had walked all the way down to the edge of the village to pick up fresh fruit and vegetables. The stall owner had kept his word and brought her two long purple eggplants and a handful of shiny green zucchini. She had soaked the chickpeas overnight, cooked, and ground them. Now all she had to do was turn half into humus and the rest into her famous falafel balls. She made some tahini for the baba ganoush, cut the vegetables for the salad into tiny teeny pieces, just like they liked them and even baked her own pita bread.

"Kussa mahchi." Jonathan poured more of the mint yogurt on top of the stuffed zucchini and shoved a huge bite into his mouth.

"Mm . . ." he murmured, chewing happily. "God, how I missed this. No one can cook like you."

"Nothing's like Leela's shakshuka." Ronen spooned more of the red mixture onto his plate.

"She's the shakshuka queen," he boasted to Giri.

"We had the best food in Goa. It wasn't the same after you left." He smiled at Leela.

"Nothing was really the same without you." Jonathan hugged her.

"AAA UUU MMM . . ."

"aaa uuu mmmmmm . . ."

The sound reverberated through the silence, becoming lower and lower as it made its way down the mountain. Leela breathed in the cool morning air, following it as it filled her lungs and belly, travelling down her arms and legs until even the tips of her fingers and toes were tingling and her entire body felt refreshed and invigorated.

They had been practicing Sudarshan Kriya with "the boys" since their arrival. After Goa, Ronen and Jonathan had travelled far and wide, visiting holy men and ashrams, deepening their knowledge and practice of yoga. They spent several months studying on the outskirts of Bangalore and Ronen had fallen in love with the "kriya." He had heard of the breathing technique before and thought it would be a good addition it to his repertoire, but now it had become his main work.

"It's a fantastic method." Ronen considered himself quite a guru, after having been invited to teach in Pune. "It reduces stress and makes you more focused and relaxed. By harmonizing the rhythms of the body, you can learn to control your emotions and change the way you feel."

"I've been dying to learn how to do it," Giri told him enthusiastically, asking him to teach them. "I've heard so much about it."

"aaaaa . . ." The start of the third "om" broke the silence.

"aaa . . . uuu . . . mmmmmm." Leela joined the chant.

"We've reached the final kriya. Let's start with slow cycles and then move to medium and faster ones. Remember, breaths cyclical and rhythmic, your inhalations twice the length of your exhalations."

"Eeeeeeeee, hhhhh." Ronen breathed loudly.

When he taught, Leela could see how far he had come. His voice was soft but distinct and firm, full of confidence and it was clear to her that he had found what he was looking for.

"No lazing around today," she told them after it ended. "We have a long hike ahead of us."

She was so relaxed and tranquil she didn't feel like doing anything, but she had promised. "Leave in half an hour?"

Leela filled a basket with freshly baked naan, paneer, and two different kinds of chutney. She added a few apples and a small jar of apricot jam.

"Paper and pens," she reminded herself. "Just in case."

"The boys" were bringing the mats and bottled water. It was almost a half day's walk, but she knew the route by heart. At first she and Giri would take their visitors together, but once she knew the way she preferred to take them on her own, sometimes only going as far as the hidden shrine and waterfall. Today she would take them all the way to the iron temple, right at the peak of the mountain.

They followed the path from the resort through the forest to the ancient village, a few miles away. It was hidden in a little opening in the woods, almost overcome with wild grass and vegetation. The old wooden houses were badly damaged, some almost slipping off their old stone foundation. As they walked around a loud clanging coming from above caught their attention. A tiny, wizened old lady smiled down at them from a second story window, vigorously waving her arms.

"Namaste," they called up to her, bowing their heads and waving back.

"I was sure the place was deserted." Ronen couldn't believe anyone still lived there.

"Only a few of the old timers remain," Leela explained. "But it's all going to change. They say someone bought a few of the old houses and plans to renovate. I've heard that several of the young people are thinking of returning too. Makes sense. The whole area's changing."

Some monkeys followed them back into the forest, chattering maliciously. Leela covered her basket and held it close to her chest.

"Anything to worry about?" Jonathan asked.

"Just ignore them," she answered, waving her hand dismissively. "They'll lose interest in us soon enough."

Although the grey long tailed macaques were larger and more intimidating than the monkeys they were used to, Leela knew they weren't vicious. She met them often in the woods and although inquisitive, they were always friendly enough.

"You come here on your own?" Ronen thought it was far too dangerous.

"Always," Leela told him.

"It's the best place to think and meditate. Don't worry, Grandma." She laughed at his horrified expression. "I'm careful not to go too far and I'm always back before dark."

"And what about strangers?" Ronen picked up her game.

"Not many strangers around here." She laughed, motioning them to the left at the fork in the path, and beginning to lead them up the steep incline. At the top of the ridge the land leveled out and the trees seemed to have retreated, revealing a large, grass covered clearing in their midst. Right in the center stood a wooden structure, with a large pyramid like roof. As they got nearer, they made out snakes, carved so intricately into the woodwork, they seemed almost alive. Immense fat pythons slithered along the beams, while long, thin vipers wrapped themselves around the columns.

"Serpent worship." Ronen couldn't take his eyes off the brass-relief in the center. Two majestic intertwined king cobras stared right back at him. "I've heard about it, but I've never actually seen it before."

"They look so life-like, they send chills down my back every time I come here." Leela shivered.

A group of people came up the incline. As they came nearer, Leela recognized them from the village. They brought their hands to their chests, bowed, and exchanged namastes with them before continuing on their way.

"You seem to know everyone." Jonathan smiled at her. "Do you have a lot of friends?"

"Not really." Leela shook her head. "Most people around here don't speak any English. But it doesn't bother me," she added quickly, when she saw his look. I have perfectly enough people coming and going. And I'm not really interested in making friends right now. I need all the time I can to be by myself. Anyway," she smiled, "Giri's all the company I need."

"He didn't strike me as over talkative," Ronen teased.

They all got on well together and enjoyed each other's company, but Giri often excused himself and left them on their own.

"Oh, he's a great talker," Leela corrected him. "But even more importantly, he knows how to keep quiet."

That was one of the things she liked best about him, his ability to keep to himself, never allowing himself to be intimidated by silence.

When they finally reached the mountain peak, the families they'd met on the way were already there, grouped in front of the temple, together with many others who had arrived before them. A priest stood facing them, waving a copper incense lamp and praying loudly.

"Where the hell did all these people come from?" Jonathan looked about him. "No one else passed us on the way."

"They must have come from the other direction." Leela pointed to another path leading up to the clearing. "The road over there almost reaches the temple."

As they drew nearer, the devotees lit incense sticks and the air, intermingling with the fragrant smoke, became heavy, sweet, and intoxicating. Several people prostrated themselves, touching the bottom of the platform with their foreheads before throwing themselves to the ground.

"What's going on?" Ronen looked bewildered.

The entire temple was made up of a giant, open wooden platform, covered with hundreds, maybe thousands of iron rods, bars, spears, and tridents of all shapes and sizes.

"Make a wish. But when it comes true you have to come back here and give an iron offering. Or suffer the wrath of the gods," she threatened, wagging her finger at their faces.

Little kids came up to them, offering tiny white sugar sweets. Leela put some on her tongue, savoring the sweet warmth that spread through her mouth as they melted.

"C'mon." She took them to the far side of the clearing and told them to take out their mats. "It's the perfect place to meditate or do some yoga. I always come here with my groups for a little rest before heading back."

"I know exactly what I want to do," Jonathan told her and Ronen immediately nodded in agreement. Clearly it was something they had discussed.

"Well?" Leela looked from one to the other.

"We want to fly," both said together.

"In the pink balloon?"

"Of course." They nodded eagerly.

It had been such a long time.

"Where shall I take them?" Leela pondered, all the exercises and meditations she had ever thought up running through her mind. Then she had an idea.

"We're going to do something simple." She gave them each a pen and some paper.

"You too," Ronen insisted. "We all fly together."

"Well," Leela began, "usually I do it differently, but I think the pink balloon can give us new insights, take us where we normally wouldn't go. We'll start with a short flight, so don't get mad."

"Sit comfortably." She crossed her legs and lengthened her back.

"Close your eyes. Take a deep breath." Leela counted to five slowly. "And now exhale, one . . . The pink balloon begins to rise, shuddering slightly as it leaves the ground. It rises slowly, smoothly, taking you higher and higher. You've reached the tree tops, and you're rising even higher. The pink balloon stops rising and remains hovering in place. Look down. What do you see? Look at the forest just under you. The trees are dense and green. Do you see the clearing? Look at the temple. Is there anyone there? What are they doing? Look around. Do you see yourself? The pink balloon starts to go down. It stops just above your left shoulder. What do you see? Who do you see sitting there? Take a few minutes. When you're ready, write anything that comes to your mind."

Usually she had to give much more instruction, but they had flown with her so many times, they knew exactly what to do. She closed her eyes and rose up in the pink balloon, until she was hovering just above them. She looked down at her friends and smiled to herself. They were so beautiful, sitting tranquilly on their mats on the mountain peak. During the last few years they had both matured, becoming confident of their way and of each other. She could see it all so clearly from the pink balloon. Now she turned around and looked at herself, seeing how much she too had changed. No longer a girl, the woman she saw before her sat upright, shoulders square, and chin straight, her long brown hair flowing smoothly down her back.

Leela thought she was quite pretty, her light olive cheeks slightly flushed, her face relaxed and peaceful.

She started to think about her life and the woman she had become. She loved the resort and Giri was a wonderful partner, never demanding and always careful to give her the space that she needed. She thought of his kind smile and quiet strength. There was a solidness about him, a strong silent presence she could feel whenever he was around. He didn't say much, mostly keeping to himself, but that suited her fine. Except for the rare occasion when they were booked solid and worked round the clock, she had plenty of time for herself. She loved the quiet solitude, especially in the winter months and was able to work and write almost every day. Her mind was tranquil, mostly quiet and on the rare occasion a nagging thought or emotion appeared, she knew how to control it.

Here in the Himalayas the pink balloon never flew very high, content to hover in place, watching the world as it slowly flitted by. It was with her all the time now, helping her to see, to be aware, but it also stopped now and then to let her out, making sure she talked to others, felt or touched them in some way.

Sometimes, as she flew, she'd forget herself completely, becoming everything she saw or felt or heard. For long moments she was the wind or the earth, the asphalt or a soaring bird. Writing in the pink balloon, she became the writing, disappearing into her notebook sometimes for hours at a time. When the link was finally broken and she came back to herself, all she remembered was that feeling of wholeness that had engulfed her. The sense of fullness. Of harmony. A perfection in which she no longer thought or analyzed, but just lived, danced, or wrote her life.

Leela heard a movement and opened her eyes. Jonathan was reaching for his notebook. He looked up at her and they exchanged a smile.

"Still time," she thought, closing her eyes again and inhaling deeply.

She took a few more breaths, watching the air fill her body and then empty it out. As her breath became quieter, a warm, pleasant sensation rose at the pit of her belly, wrapping around her body like a protective sheath. She felt peaceful and happy, her mind clear and empty. She moved her attention to the pleasant sensation, feeling it grow and grow, until she was surrounded by an open, infinite space. A silence permeated her, bigger than anything she had ever experienced before. At first she felt she was in it, but then she began to expand and expand, finally realizing it was all in her. For a moment she was nothing but an infinite expanse of time and space.

She heard papers rustling and then the sound of someone clearing his throat. Leela kept her eyes tightly shut, trying to hold on to the experience, but the moment she became aware of it, it was gone. Opening her eyes, she still felt a sensation of deep peace and unity, a feeling of oneness, as if she and the world around her had melded into each other.

"Ready for the next flight?" she asked, stretching her arms and legs, trying to pull herself out of herself.

"Sure." Ronen nodded.

"Make it a long one." Jonathan waved his finger at her. "You gypped us last time."

"Don't worry," Leela reassured him, chuckling to herself. In her workshops, she would now take her students to a secluded beach, allowing them to see themselves not as they were, but as they wanted to be.

"What's stopping you?" she would ask, halting them in their tracks.

But this time she decided, she'd move them in time, not only in space.

"LEAN BACK COMFORTABLY, it's gonna be a long ride."

Leela's voice was soft and confident and Ronen and Jonathan felt their bodies become more and more relaxed as they sunk into the balloon.

"The balloon's rising higher and higher. It's just under the tree tops. Everywhere you look, there's only green. The balloon continues to rise. It rises above the trees, above the dense forest. It begins to circle the mountain, taking you forward in time. Every circle takes you forward a year ..."

"The balloon finishes its fifth and last cycle. Five years have passed. The balloon starts to go down. Watch where you land. Look around you. Where are you? Look at yourself. What do you see?"

Leela closed her eyes and leaned back into the balloon. She had circled the mountain with them, now all that was left was to see where it would take her. She didn't think it would be very far, though and she was right. The pink balloon rose slowly, stopping just above her head. Leela looked down and sighed contently. Ronen and Jonathan were sitting in front of her, still in deep contemplation and she was doing exactly what she wanted to do. Writing and teaching the pink balloon. Leela laughed softly to herself. She couldn't tell them apart anymore.

"They're my vehicle," she told Giri. "My special gift."

And people had begun to notice, coming not only for him, but now also for her. She taught at every retreat and even offered one to three day workshops of her own. The resort was becoming more and more known and the next season was already almost fully booked.

As she lost herself in thought, the balloon suddenly shook and swayed, as if it had changed its mind. Leela held herself tightly in place as the balloon jerked violently and soared up into the sky. The pink balloon flew faster than ever before, crossing low above the high mountains, gliding over lakes and deserts and immense metropolises before finally letting her down before a vast tempestuous ocean.

"This could be anywhere,'" she thought as she looked around the secluded beach.

"Pink balloon, where have you taken me?" she began to ask, but before she had time to contemplate, she heard Jonathan and Ronen moving about. They had both finished writing and were waiting impatiently for her to begin. She could see they had a lot to say.

"Both flights were almost exactly the same," Ronen reported. "Only right at the end, I suddenly realized there was a difference."

"Mine were totally different," Jonathan interrupted. "Just as I expected."

"What about you?" he asked Leela.

They both looked at her questioning.

"Let's start with you guys." She looked from one to the other. "I haven't had time to work out what happened in mine."

"The first flight didn't show me anything new. I saw myself, a little older than I expected," Ronen chuckled, "but I really liked what I saw. I think it was in one of the halls in the great pyramid in Pune. I was standing in front of rows of mats, demonstrating slow ujjai breathing. It felt so comfortable, so right. Jonathan was in the first row, just in front of me." He paused for a moment. "The second flight seemed to have taken me to the same place, but at a different time. Now it was the end of the class and everyone was leaving. When I stepped outside I noticed there was an ocean gleaming in the background. I looked around me. A short distance away I saw Jonathan, walking toward me, pushing a baby chariot."

"Baby?" Leela stared at them wide eyed. They told her they had decided to commit to each other.

"We want to get married," Jonathan announced smiling happily. "Maybe have a child."

"What about you?" Ronen asked her. "Don't you want children?"

"Giri doesn't," Leela shrugged, "so I guess I never really thought about it."

She couldn't have been happier for her friends though.

"What do you think the pink balloon's trying to tell you?" she asked when they were through hugging.

"First of all, I think it's showing me that I've found my calling, that I'm doing exactly what I should be doing. But at the end of the ride the balloon took me somewhere else, so I'm not sure really sure what it meant."

"Well I'm certainly not in the right place," Jonathan said. "The second flight took me to a large Western city. I think it was in the US somewhere. I was sitting in a classroom listening to a lecture. I don't know what I was studying, but I was already in my final year."

"College? Going to the US?" Leela was hearing things she'd never heard before. He told her he'd been considering it for quite some time.

"Don't misunderstand," he tried to explain. "I love yoga and practice every day, but unlike Ronen, it's just not enough for me. I don't feel I've found myself. I need something else. I'm just not sure what that is."

"The boys" told her they argued about it all the time. Jonathan wanted to leave, but Ronen was happy where he was.

"Maybe that's what it was telling me." Ronen finally thought he understood. "I've definitely found myself, but not necessarily the place. I think that's why it only showed it to me in the end. I think it's telling me to move, but maybe not right now. Perhaps it means I still have things to do before I go."

"Finally!" Jonathan whistled in relief. "But how long do you think it will be before you're ready?"

"Who knows." Ronen shrugged. "Another year, maybe."

"One more year and we leave." Jonathan waved his finger in Ronen's direction, catching him at his word.

"One more year and we'll see." Ronen laughed, before turning to Leela. "You look a little shaken up. What happened?"

"The weirdest thing." Leela told them about her flight.

"Where did it take you?" Ronen asked.

"I couldn't tell." She wrinkled her nose, trying to figure it out. "But it certainly wasn't the Himalayas. In fact, the balloon flew so far, I don't think it could have been India at all."

"Not India?" Jonathan raised an eyebrow. "Do you think it's telling you to leave, that you haven't reached the end of your journey?"

"I don't really know what to make of it." Leela frowned. "But then I've never asked the pink balloon to move forward in time before."

"You seem so happy here, so serene and at peace." Ronen looked at her questioningly. "I thought you had finally found what you were looking for."

"Well, I have," Leela started to say, and then hesitated. "Or at least that's what I've been telling myself. But I guess the pink balloon sees right through me."

"It's not that I'm not happy," she continued after a short pause. "I am. Almost. I have a good life here with Giri and like the woman I've become. I like being Leela but I still can't shake that sense of something missing, of still not seeing the whole picture. Wherever I go, whatever I do, I still feel a certain discomfort, a longing, that old familiar feeling of not quite being there. As if I'm constantly waiting for something, although I have no idea what it is. But it's more than that." She took a long breath, unsure how to continue.

"It's like being in the balloon watching the world go by," she tried to explain more to herself, than to them. "You feel a part of everything, but at the same time you're not. I feel as though I'm floating through life, looking at the world from the outside. Everything's happening around me, almost as if I don't even exist. Sometimes I feel like the bottom's fallen out of my world and I'm just hanging in space, neither in nor out, with nothing solid to hold on to."

"I'm not sure I'm making any sense." She looked from one to the other.

"Not totally following you," Jonathan admitted, smiling.

"I am." Ronen nodded. "I know exactly how you feel. I felt like that for years, like I'd found myself, but somehow still felt lost."

"Exactly." Leela nodded. She took Jonathan's hand. "It's not like I'm sad or unhappy, not at all. It's just the nagging feeling that I'm still missing something, that there's something else that I'm not seeing."

"So what happened to you?" She turned to Ronen. "What changed?"

"I don't really know," he answered after a long pause. "But sometime after the ashram in Bangalore I began to feel different. I guess everything just somehow came together and clicked. Maybe you just have to wait. Maybe it'll happen to you too."

"And maybe you should be thinking of making a change, the pink balloon's never been wrong before," Jonathan reminded her playfully.

"I don't even want to think about it now." Leela decided to stop the discussion. The pink balloon had made her look at what she didn't want to see.

"It's sometime in the future, anyway." Ronen folded his pages and put them away in his bag. "But, if you had to leave, where would you go?"

Leela shrugged. She had never even thought of leaving.

"You'll always be welcome in Pune." Ronen hugged her.

"At least for the next year," Jonathan added, winking.

"I DON'T WANT you to leave." Giri sighed, shaking his head sadly.

"But you don't want me to stay either." Leela stared straight into his eyes.

"Of course I want you to stay." Giri looked back at her for a moment, then closed his eyes, and rubbed his forehead dejectedly.

"But I'm too old, Leela, and I never wanted children anyway, even when I was younger. Maya and I decided that when we first got married and even after she died, I never felt differently. I love our life together, just the way it is." He extended his hand towards her. "I thought you did too."

"Of course I do." Leela took his hand. "But you're the first to say nothing ever stays the way it is."

"I know." Giri nodded. "But we never even talked about having children."

"It's not like I planned it," Leela tried to defend herself. "And you're right, I never really considered it before. But now that it's happened, I have to admit I've been feeling a need for a change for quite some time."

"But a baby?" Giri let go of her hand and shook his head miserably again. He had thought about it constantly since she told him, but he just couldn't bring himself to ask her to stay.

The monsoon rains were late that year and the mountain unusually hot and damp.

"It's just the heat," Leela told herself, noticing her period was also late, but when the rains fell and it still hadn't appeared, she began to worry. She only told Giri when she was absolutely sure and her belly had begun to swell.

"You don't have to leave yet." Giri tried to persuade her to stay longer, but Leela had already decided.

"I'll stay until the end of the monsoon," she promised. "But then I have to go."

A SOFT RAIN ACCOMPANIED them as they made their way slowly down the mountain, the silence between them heavy and stifling as a blanket. They'd barely exchanged a word in the days leading up to her departure.

"Even the skies are crying." Giri tried to contain his tears as he gently maneuvered the car around a sharp bend.

"Or smiling," Leela thought to herself as the sun suddenly peaked out behind a cloud, sending a brilliant arch of colors across the sky, stretching all the way across the immense open valley in front of her.

"YOU HAVE TO come stay with us," the boys insisted, delighted to hear her news. "We'll help with everything."

They moved to a new apartment, with two bedrooms and no stairs.

"Except the five at the entrance," Jonathan told her apologetically over the phone. "But those don't really count."

The building was on Lane five, a block away from North Main Road, right next to Malaka Spice. It had its own kitchen, a small living room, and a large enclosed patio where they generally chose to sit. Although it was a few minutes' walk from the area she had lived in before, Leela felt as though she had come back home. Ken's coffee shop, like most of the cafes and restaurants she had frequented, was gone, but several of her favorites were still around. Darios was as popular as ever, Yogi Tree had grown even bigger and ancient Ujjal still sat waiting for customers at the entrance to the Pizza Parlor. His mustache had grown so long, she could barely make out his smile, but when he waved at her, his eyes crinkled mischievously under his snow-white turban.

Mostly she cooked at home, carefully choosing the freshest spices and vegetables on display at the new organic store that had opened on the corner of their street. When she felt too lazy, they'd take a rickshaw to Adyata's, where they sat on cushions on the floor, stuffing themselves with rice and freshly baked rotti dipped in little fragrant tali bowls, filled with savory vegetables and sauces and a mouthwatering spicy yellow dahl. She still charged eighty rupees a person and her husband and children walked around filling Leela's plate until she felt she would explode.

"Enough, Adyata, tell them enough," Leela'd plead, placing her hands on her stomach, but Adyata would just tell them to fill her plate once again.

"You eat two now." She'd raise two fingers in the air and cluck her tongue. "Look you! You just skin and bones."

Raj still sat on the same corner besides the fruit stand. He had a new "Pepsi" umbrella, but other than that everything remained just as it had been, the pile of bamboo baskets stacked high as ever above the old grey kerosene stove. The first time she went by, he leaped out of his white plastic chair and rushed toward her, his legs shaking and wavering even worse than before.

"Baby?" He pointed at the little bulge in her tummy.

"No eat." He waved his finger at her. "You come tomorrow, wife make special momo, just for you."

Whenever she came by after that, he had a special parcel waiting for her. Her momos were stuffed with spinach and vegetables, cheese and pine nuts and were even more delicious than the regular.

"I've never tasted anything like this," she'd tell him.

"They for baby," he would say, beaming at her proudly. "Special momo from momo man."

"GOT TO RUN." Ronen gave her a hug and rushed into the ashram, late for his first class.

"Shall I wait with you?" Jonathan offered to stay with her at the admissions office. "I only start in an hour."

"Catch you later." Leela dismissed him.

It was still early, but the line in front of her was already long.

"Looks like it'll go on forever," she said to herself after a while, beginning to feel impatient. "I don't even know why I'm waiting here." She looked around. "I don't really want to go in."

She picked up a pamphlet, looked through it briefly, and then put it aside. "There's nothing for me here anymore," she decided, feeling she no longer belonged. "Perhaps I never did." She shook her head.

"I think I'm going to go for a walk and come back later," she told the woman standing in front of her.

She didn't return to the ashram that day. In fact, she never went inside again. She felt a great gratitude, but also that she had moved on. Instead, she started frequenting her old haunts. First, she went to visit her friends. Leah Neah's tombstone slanted crookedly, as if it were about to topple over and Master Sunny's was barely visible under the cover of weeds and small thorny shrubs that had grown all over it. The entire cemetery looked even more desolate and neglected than ever, the ancient graves now totally abandoned and forgotten. It was clear to Leela that no one had been there for quite a while, perhaps even since she had left. She worked for days, slowly clearing the path and then carefully weeding the area surrounding the caskets. She washed the aged stones, rubbing their surfaces with oil until the letters became legible again.

"Have you lost your mind?" Jonathan yelled, when he found out what she was doing. "In your condition?"

"Someone has to do it," was all Leela would say.

"You should come to the ashram." Ronen kept trying to persuade her. "There are loads of new things for you to do."

"I'll come," she kept promising, although she never did.

IN THE MORNINGS she practiced walking meditation, moving slowly and precisely, paying attention to every step, remaining aware of every breath. Keeping away from the boisterous north main road, she walked wherever her path took her, wandering through the small back paths, noticing new growths and little changes. She took every step intentionally, noticing how her foot raised and then arched as it moved forward. She felt her toes touch the ground and then the little cushion before the instep, followed by her heel. She noticed the flow of her arms and listened to the swish swash of her growing belly. She watched the patterns of the trees, their limbs intersecting above her head, and traced each falling leaf until it settled. Every day the path was different.

One day she lost herself entirely, walking on and on until she found herself in the squatters' encampment. It was even dirtier and more crowded than before, having grown so large the little ramshackle structures now crossed the railroad and billowed out as far as she could see. Groups of ill-clothed youngsters, mainly male, sat around talking idly, eyeing her curiously as she went by. When she saw the old tent, she began to get her bearings.

"Naaz's house is just up the road," she thought, deciding to pay her a visit.

"Hum?" A young woman opened the door slightly, pushing her face through the crack.

"I'm looking for Naaz." Leela smiled at her.

"Hum?" The woman repeated again, crinkling her nose. "Nahin, nahin." She shook her head vigorously and slammed the door in Leela's face.

After that, she'd walk in the opposite direction, stopping every now and then to make sure she hadn't wandered too far. Inevitably, she'd find herself at Osho Park, staying there until the guards gave their final warning. At first she'd go to her old spot, the raised grass platform in front of Osho's sitting statue, but there were always people there now, and besides, she soon discovered she could no longer sit comfortably on the floor for long periods of time. The baby had begun to kick furiously and after a while the muscles in her legs twitched and spasmed. The park had more visitors than before and few undiscovered hideouts and Leela tried several before finally discovering the secluded bench in the little cul-de-sac, slightly off the beaten track, just before the stream disappeared beneath the bridge, on its way to meet the river. Hardly anyone walked that far down, so that's where she'd go, nodding and smiling slightly to the people she passed by, but never stopping to talk to anyone or even look them in the eye. She didn't want to. Leela felt good about herself, happy and at peace and all she wanted was to sit quietly on her own, meditating or writing, often content to do nothing at all, but sit and watch the world go by.

"WHAT A LOVELY day," Leela thought, as she lowered herself, gently onto her bench, a few weeks after she had claimed it. She placed her hands behind her back to steady herself and then just sat there quietly, rubbing her belly. The little hideaway was empty, as usual, so she could simply relax and look around her. The days were growing gradually cooler and the light breeze caressed her face and body. Every now and then a soft shower of tiny feathery raindrops brushed her skin like snowflakes, cooling the air even more but not really wetting her. She listened to the gushing of the water as the stream flowed rapidly by, leaving tiny magical waterfalls in its wake as it gathered speed. Birds chirped in the trees and ducklings quacked, calling out to their mothers.

Leela leaned back and closed her eyes. She took a few long breaths to clear her mind and smiled softly to herself, allowing the gentle pleasant sensation that had begun in the tip of her tummy to grow and fill her body, until it flowed right out of her and wrapped itself around her. Within the sweet warmth, she felt utterly quiet and peaceful, an immense sense of joy and oneness pervading her every pore. Her mind remained clear and spacious as she sat there, shifting her attention to the nothingness in front of her. Veil like cloud strings played in the vast empty abyss and for a moment she felt as though she were hovering in space, no longer aware of herself as a separate entity. Leela opened her eyes, her warm, pulsating body now just part of the earth. She didn't see the clouds, anymore, she was the clouds. She didn't hear the river, she was the river. She was the wind and the rain, the trees, and the ducks.

A noise followed by a sudden movement brought her back. Someone was entering the clearing. Leela looked up and froze. The young woman walking toward her looked so much like her, for a moment it seemed as if she were staring into a huge, life sized mirror. Wearing a bright yellow printed Indian kurti, in place of Leela's light blue, she was about her height, her long, curly dark hair similarly caught behind her back in a loose plait. She was even pregnant, though obviously not as advanced as Leela, but it wasn't just the physical resemblance that took Leela's breath away. It was more the way she held herself, her head high, pointed straight ahead, her eyes blank and her lips curved into a little smile, as if she knew something more, as if she had all the answers. There was something almost smug about her, so knowing, as she floated above the grass.

"Just like a saint or an angel," Leela heard herself whisper as the woman moved closer, attentively paying attention to every step she took. Leela could see the way she consciously lifted each foot, moved it forward, and then set it slowly back down on the ground. She walked toward Leela, but didn't look at her or acknowledge her presence in any way, as if neither of them were actually there. When she was almost on top of her, she raised her eyes briefly, folded her hands below her chest, and nodded in Leela's direction before slowly continuing on her way. Leela stared, watching herself slowly recede from view, recognition growing even stronger.

Suddenly she heard Osho's voice, drumming in her head. "If you meet me on the way, kill me," it kept repeating.

She had heard that sentence so many times, but had never understood it before. She knew it had something to do with not being a follower, with finally saying goodbye to one's master, but since she had never really followed anyone, she'd failed to see the relevance. And then it came to her. She had been on her own for so long, she had become her own master. And now there was another Leela, standing right in front of her.

"She's always been a creation," she whispered to herself. "A creation of my mind, just like all the other people I've been."

Only this time, she realized, she'd fallen in love with her creation, actually believing she was her. Her mind lit up like a bulb, and four distinct images of herself appeared before her, floating above her head in little clouds, just like in a comic book. Lilly. Lila. Lia. Leela. She recognized them all right away.

"Are you me?" she asked each one of them. "Am I you?"

"They'd all been me for a while," she thought, 'or perhaps I'd been them."

But the more she looked at them, the more she saw. They were all just her coconut creations. None of them were real, and none of them were her. Yes, she was Lilly and Lila and she was Lia and Leela too. But she was also so much more.

For the first time in her life she realized she could be whoever and whatever she wanted to be, changing from moment to moment as she wished.

"Neither this nor that." She laughed out loud as the images in her mind broke down and disintegrated.

She saw that she had never been any of them, or anything else either. Like the growth and shedding of the leaves on the trees in the mighty Himalayas, everyone and everything was in constant movement, changing from moment to moment, becoming a form and losing it. No matter how far and hard she searched, she hadn't been able to find herself because there had never been anyone to be found.

She had tried so hard to become Leela, only to find she was an illusion too. That was what Osho had told her so many years ago. "Lilly is who you are, Leela is what you can be."

Throughout the years she had attributed his choice of words to his bad English, but now she finally understood what he meant. Leela was a game, a final understanding of the true nature of things. Finally she knew who she was. She wasn't Lilly or Lila or Lia or Leela or anyone else. She was the play of Leela, freedom itself.

"Finally," she said to herself. "I know what I've been looking for."

"It's been such a long quest," Leela smiled, "and the end so surprisingly ordinary."

She looked around her. Everything was perfectly in place. For the first in time in her life, she could see nothing wrong with the picture. The ground seemed to drop beneath her feet. She felt light as a feather, weightless and limitless, as if she had become unattached and was floating in the air, just like the pink balloon.

"I am the pink balloon," she realized, laughing out loud, "flitting through life, hovering, going wherever I want. Perhaps that's what it's always been trying to tell me."

She felt a shortness of breath, as if the whole world was closing in on her and then it was over, and only an immense quiet remained.

LILY

I RETURNED TO Venice with the boys a month before Zen was born. We all live together in a tiny cottage a short walk from the promenade, just a few blocks to the left of the canals. They were still filled in when I was a child, but now that they're flowing again, Zen thinks they're the most magical place in the world. We go there nearly every day, walking over the little bridges and throwing stale bread to the ducks. I go by Lily again, not because it has any particular meaning or reason, but just because I like it. It was, after all, my original coconut name.

We live a simple life, with few possessions or needs. Jonathan is finishing his studies to become a social worker and does a lot of work with the homeless on the beach. There are so many of them now, come nightfall the entire area is transformed, turning from a bright, sun drenched little strip of happiness to a dark, gloomy patchwork of makeshift huts and shelters. I often help him, collecting food and clothing from the stores along the boardwalk and handing it out to the needy. Every Sunday we prepare a special meal. All the cafes and restaurants in the area participate, storing their leftovers and sometimes even preparing a fresh little treat. Last week we fed over a hundred people. I'm often reminded of my mother. These are exactly the things she used to do.

Ronen has a large studio overlooking the boardwalk. He teaches an array of yoga and breathing techniques, but his expertise remains the sudarshan kriya. Being one of the few western practitioners qualified for teacher certification, his classes are packed and his workshops booked months in advance. Jonathan gives a few morning classes and I teach meditation and writing in the evenings. On Tuesdays and Fridays we offer free early morning yoga on the beach. It's become so popular, we often arrive to find dozens of mats coloring the sand, groups of smiling faces awaiting us.

My cousin Jasmine usually arrives before me. Friday is her day off, so after practice we have time for a long breakfast. She moved to Los Angeles when she got married and lives in the marina with her husband and kids, just a few minutes' drive away. She and Kevin are both civil rights attorneys and work in the city, but when they're not working they spend most of their time with us. Adam is already ten, tall and handsome. He has his father's pale skin and eyes and looks nothing like our side of the family. Sophia has just turned four, exactly the same age as Zen and the girls are inseparable. I would have recognized her anywhere, she looks so much like her mother did when she was a child, with her thick charcoal hair and huge, almond shaped eyes. The first time I met Jasmine after all the years of separation, I was so shocked I could hardly speak. She walked into the coffee shop and I just stood there frozen, gasping and stuttering, trying to get my bearings, she looked so much like my mother during the last years of her life.

We're fast approaching the age she died.

"You have to get tested." Nadia won't leave us alone.

"I'll make an appointment," Jasmine finally promised her mother, last time she visited. Genetic testing has become the rage and we know she has a point. Taata Maryam died shortly after I left, although everyone agreed it wasn't the cancer that killed her.

"Losing both her girls was too much for her," Ali always says.

Nadia and Ali visit often. They've fully adopted Zen and treat her as their own. She has loads of grandparents. Sami never misses a visit and although he's close to Adam, the two little girls have become the love of his life.

"My little princesses," he calls them, spoiling them with outings and presents.

I talk to Hanna all the time. She recently married a lovely widower with two grown daughters and has grandchildren of her own. Still, she and Zen have become close and she keeps promising her to visit.

"Pease, pease come," Zen persistently implores her.

"Maybe I'll come with Saba and Safta," Hanna told her last time they spoke.

David and Esther plan to visit next summer, during the school vacation. I can't wait to meet Naomi. I haven't seen her since she was a baby and she's already in high school. Her pictures portray a tall slim fair-haired girl, with a pretty, slightly too serious face. Hodi and Emmanuel won't be joining them. They're both in Yeshivot Hesder, intermittently praying or fighting for their country. Rachel came over last year, heavily pregnant with her second baby. To me she's still a child, but she seems perfectly happy, living in a little house adjacent to our parents, and helping Esther run the day center. It's grown so large, it now encompasses two buildings and has its own enclosed playground with slides and seesaws and swings. The settlement was legitimatized many years ago and has since swelled to over ten thousand people. A high wall separates it from neighboring Nabi Musa, whose houses it now almost touches. Every now and then violence erupts between them, as Allah and Hashem go at it once again. I don't think it will ever end.

I HEAR VOICES on the porch.

"Shoes!" Jonathan calls out to Zen, but she just ignores him, bursting through the door and rushing into my arms giggling happily. She has my dark hair and blue eyes, but she looks nothing like me, with her father's round face and the same endearing dimples when she smiles. And Zen always smiles. Sweet Sara looks down at us from her perch on the wall. I think she's smiling too.

"C'mon, Mummy, you promised." She throws her things down and grabs my pants, trying to pull me toward the door.

"Just a sec." I grab my bag and hurry out behind her. We stop for a moment on the sidewalk, just outside the gate, hold hands, and close our eyes.

"Pink balloon, where shall we go?" I ask in my most dramatic voice.

"To the walk, to the walk." Zen can't control herself.

"To the boardwalk?" I ask, as if I don't know.

Rami promised her an ice cream and she hasn't stopped nagging me since. Swissa, his old partner, left many years ago, but "Rami and Son's" now own half the beach. Rami doesn't have to work, but he likes to hang around their first store, bossing the workers and treating all his old friends to huge portions of ice cream.

The pink balloon gently lifts us up and we move slowly down the sidewalk. Zen chatters on happily, but although I hear her every word, I'm not really listening. Beyond her words, beyond the images that flicker momentarily before me, remains a great tranquility. That's where my journey's taken me, to a great silent emptiness that seems to underlie and overlie everything, overriding all the noise and chaos of the universe. For so many years I'd tried to quiet my mind, only to realize the silence was already there, beyond the words, beyond all thought. And once I recognized the silence, I realized that it had always been there, that I was the silence, the all and the nothing from which all arises, a sea of tranquility in an ever-tilting world.

"Look, Mommy." Zen pulls me out of myself.

A group of squirrels are playing on the grass by the roadside. We sit down on the curb and watch them. Zen giggles merrily as the largest does a set of backward flip flops, his long tail thumping loudly on the ground. A huge warmth spreads out from the bottom of my tummy, engulfing me as waves of joy and gratitude wash over me.

The true me had always been there, staring me in the face, so small, so ordinary, that I had missed it, always looking for more, for what was beyond. Instead of enjoying what is, I had blinded myself, chasing after rainbows, constantly trying to be something else. But that day in the park, in that split second I had finally seen myself, I also understood what I had always misunderstood. Trying so hard to totally erase myself, to become "no me," I had been trying the impossible. For the first time I realized that I would always be creating a "me," a "somebody" to appear whenever I was called.

"But never again," I vowed to myself, "would I think that somebody was true, or mistakenly believe it to be me."

It has taken time for all the old images of myself to disintegrate and disappear, and I still feel a constant unburdening as if the weight I've been carrying around all my life is finally slipping away and dropping off. I feel so light so free, and at the same time whole and full, as though I've finally come home. I try not to dwell on the past or the future, trying instead to be fully present, watching every moment of my life. My mind is mostly quiet and calm, though it is still often active, throwing its stories at me, trying to get me riled up, but I don't pay it much attention and certainly no longer try to shut it up.

Everyone's welcome to visit, I made friends with all my memories a long time ago. Knowing who I am and therefore who everyone else is, I know we are all the same and it is only the stories we tell ourselves that divide us. I've seen it so clearly throughout my life. Now, when the stories appear, I know I have a choice. I can let myself become attached or just rest in the quiet, letting the noise die down and the stories unravel. The world still tilts and slants and jolts, it always will, but I'm no longer at its mercy. I know that all I have to do is change my point of view, to simply see things differently.

"Ice cream." Zen suddenly remembers, jumping up and grabbing my hand. "Chocolate," she says more to herself than to me. "Chocolate 'n' nems."

"Zen, haim sheli, my life," Rami shouts out, the moment we reach the boardwalk, scooping her up in his arms and carrying her into the store. He's put on a lot of weight and has a heart condition and is constantly pressing his sons to give him grandchildren.

"So, princess, what do you feel like today?" He places her on the counter above the huge array of colors and tastes and they begin their usual ritual.

"What's that?" Zen points to one of the mounds and Rami fills a spoon and hands it too her.

"Strawberry sherbet."

"Yummy." Zen licks it all up.

"That . . ." She points to another flavor and Rami immediately fills another spoon for her.

"Chocolate 'n' nems," she finally decides, after trying a few more. Rami and I exchange amused looks, chortling noisily. No matter how many flavors she tries, it's always chocolate 'n' nems.

"Chocolate 'n' nems coming up." Rami fills a cone with a huge scoop of rich dark brown ice cream and then plunges it into a bowl of colored M&M's. I take a small portion of chocolate ice cream, minus the M&M's. As usual, Rami won't let me pay.

"Fishes," Zen announces, beginning to march down the promenade. I follow close behind her, running my tongue over the cool bitter sweetness. I know exactly where she's going. The old fishing pier was also my favorite place when I was a child.

We weave our way through the packed boardwalk. I can hardly hear myself think, everyone's talking so loudly, trying to be heard above the din. People walk past shouting and gesticulating, some joyful, others full of anger.

"Look where you're going." A young woman dragging a screaming child bumps into me, almost knocking me over.

"Sorry." I smile at her and hurry after Zen.

"La puta," I hear her swearing behind me, but I don't pay her any attention. I've learned to look behind the façade, beyond the hollow shell of beliefs and desires and stories, to see the patterns, the larger picture. Floating along in my pink balloon, I see so clearly what everyone I pass by is looking for. We're all searching for the same thing. Just to be happy. Everywhere I look, beneath the pain and suffering, Buddha nature is so strong, struggling to shine through.

"Everyone needs a pink balloon." I sigh beneath my breath.

The pink balloon saved my life, taking me away from myself to show me I wasn't who I thought I was and then bringing me back, to show me who I was. When I'm not with Zen I teach a few times a week, offering full day workshops one or twice a month, but more than anything I write. I've even started writing a book. It tells the story of a coconut girl and her coconut lives. And a pink balloon, of course.

I think about the book and laugh, not sure if I'm writing the book or the book is writing me. Finally moving out of my own way, I write so freely now, with such abandon, it feels as if my whole body is writing, the words pouring out almost effortlessly, as if on their own. I write until the world disappears and I am no longer there. Only the writing remains. Everything is writing. Writing writing itself.

"C,mon, Mommy." Zen yanks at my hand.

We walk all the way down to the end of the old pier and sit on the edge facing the beach, dangling our legs above the water. Dazzled by the rays, for a moment all I can see is a bright yellow ball embedded in a glittering turquoise blue sea. I take my time, allowing my eyes to slowly adjust. I no longer meditate, so I just sit quietly, marveling at life, as it slowly unfolds before me. I look at the opaque blue green waters and the silky caramel sands, listen to the grey gulls calling to each other frantically just above our heads. My eyes run along the yellow wizened cracks, enjoying the simple, utter beauty of the mundane, the frequently overlooked ordinariness of things. A wisp of hair falls across Zen's forehead as she looks down at the waves. She swings her legs backward and forward, playing with the sun's reflections. I feel her warm hand in mine and an immense love fills me. What more could I possibly want?

"Mommy, look," Zen shouts out excitedly, narrowing her eyes and pointing at a group of swimmers in the distance.

"One coconut." She chooses one and begins to count.

She's just learning and can go all the way to seven. I narrow my eyes into slits, changing their focus, and look out towards where Zen is pointing.

"Two coconuts." I point to the one swimming right beside it.

"Three." Zen points out another one.

"Four." My coconut is floating about in a puffed pink ring. Zen giggles.

"Five coconuts," she shouts, pointing to the green one right next to it, giggling even harder.

"Six coconuts." I choose the farthest one.

We look at each and point together at the coconut floating right in the middle of the bunch.

"Boom," we yell together at the top of our lungs.

Sample Pink Balloon Meditations

Sit comfortably in a quiet room. Close your eyes. Focus your attention on your breath. Breath in deeply, relaxing more and more as you exhale.

Imagine a pink balloon floating towards you. It stops right in front of you. A huge, round pink balloon. Step inside the balloon. Sit down and make yourself comfortable.

I

The pink balloon begins to rise slowly. It floats gently up and out of the window, rising higher and higher into the calm blue sky. You're rising above the cars and the houses and the trees. Look down at the tree tops. See how they move in the wind. Watch how the branches sway. You're so high above the ground, the people down below you look like tiny ants.

The balloon picks up speed, flying high above the city and then low again, swooping down over a serene little lake, skimming its surface. You begin to see the ocean in the distance, a vast sheet of tranquil blue.

The pink balloon begins to descend, coming to rest on a secluded beach. Step out of the balloon. Look around you. What do you see? Look at yourself. What do you see?

II

The pink balloon floats upwards slowly, gently. Watch as the trees grow smaller and smaller and the skies larger and larger. Lean back into the balloon, make yourself as comfortable as you can. Feel how safe you are inside the pink balloon. When you look down you feel light and completely calm. Look at the birds as they pass by.

You fly past your neighborhood and out of the city. The balloon takes you farther and farther, across rivers and oceans.

The pink balloon ſtarts to descend. Step out of the pink balloon. Look around you. Where are you? Where has it taken you? Look at yourself. Who are you?

Who would you like to be?

What's ſtopping you?

III

The balloon is rising higher and higher. It hovers just under the tree tops. Everywhere you look there's only green. The balloon continues to rise. It rises above the trees, above the houses, above the entire city.

You see a tall mountain in front of you. The pink balloon begins to circle the mountain, taking you forward (backward) in time. Every circle takes you forward a year.

The balloon finishes its fifth and last cycle. Five years have passed. The balloon starts to go down. Watch where you land. Look around you. Where are you now? Look at yourself. What do you see?

Orna Taub was born in Israel, but spent most of her childhood in South Africa. Starting out as a journalist and translator, she did her MA in TESOL in New York and then taught for almost twenty years at Tel Aviv University, before leaving to write full time. She has a PHD in Comparative Literature. Three former novels have been published in Israel in Hebrew. *The Pink Balloon* is the first book she's written in English and is the result of a lengthy spiritual journey. Orna lives in Jaffa with her partner and son in an ancient well-house they are still lovingly restoring.

www.ingramcontent.com/pod-product-compliance
Lightning Source LLC
Chambersburg PA
CBHW022003010726
47494CB00003B/860